3

JACOB Z. FLORES

Published by
Dreamspinner Press
5032 Capital Circle SW
Ste 2, PMB# 279
Tallahassee, FL 32305-7886
USA
http://www.dreamspinnerpress.com/

3

Cover Art by DWS Photography   cerberuspic@gmail.com
Cover Design by Paul Richmond

ISBN: 978-1-61372-773-7

Printed in the United States of America
First Edition
October 2012

eBook edition available
eBook ISBN: 978-1-61372-774-4

To Bruce

For being my anchor when I need to be grounded.
For being my wings when I need to soar.

CHAPTER 1

2010

"IS THIS Justin Jimenez?"

"Yes," Justin muttered into his hastily answered cell phone. When Katy Perry suddenly began singing "Firework" in the middle of the night, he had quickly picked up the annoyingly loud device without checking the caller ID. He had no idea who was speaking to him, even though the woman's voice sounded vaguely familiar. All he knew for sure was that he would change the ringtone to something less jarring after breakfast.

"Justin, did you hear what I said?" The woman's question was tinged with urgency and fear.

"No," he mumbled in response.

Sleep still clouded his vision, and despite the fact that a late-night call was rarely a good omen, his eyes fought against consciousness. Through sheer will, he forced his right eyelid open enough to note the time.

It was 3:17 in the morning. He had at most three hours of sleep before his blaring alarm sent him into another day as principal of Luther Burbank High.

"Who is this?" he asked, quietly. He didn't want to disturb Spencer's peaceful slumber, which appeared to be coming to an end anyway. His partner mumbled a complaint about the "damn phone" before promptly turning over and pulling the majority of the bedcovers over his head. Apparently, Spencer intended to burrow away from the noise.

"This is Heidi Armstrong," the voice on the other end told him. Her name struck a chord and made him uneasy. "Lukas's sister. But I think you called him 'Dutch' like most everyone else."

Justin sprang into a sitting position, as if the mere mention of Dutch's name released some secret, inner catch that spurred his body forward like an old-fashioned jack-in-the-box.

He was wide awake now. The warm folds of his sheets and his desire to return to his Ricky Martin sex dream disappeared. Hearing

Dutch's name over his cell phone was the equivalent of having a bucket of cold water thrown into his face.

He hopped out of bed, jamming his little toe into the sturdy oak bedside table. Cursing and hopping toward the wall, Justin feared his yelps would cause Spencer to dig himself out from underneath his den of warm blankets.

He steadied himself against the bedroom wall with his left hand while he cradled the cell phone in his right until the pain subsided to an angry throb. When he surveyed the bed, he found Spencer sitting up, freshly emerged from the tangle of sheets. He looked at Justin with narrowed green eyes, his blond eyebrows knitted together. It was Spencer's way of saying *what the fuck?*

"Sorry, love," he told Spencer. "You go back to sleep. I'll take this in the other room."

Before Spencer could reply, he limped in pain down the hallway toward the kitchen, hopefully far enough away not to be heard talking on the phone. This wasn't a conversation Spencer was meant to overhear. Dutch was a secret Justin intended to take to his grave.

Heidi's voice buzzed in the cell phone as he hobbled down the hallway, into the living room, and past pictures of him and Spencer through the years. Their smiling past selves mocked him, as if to say that those days were gone and never to return.

When he opened his mouth to finally reply, no sound would escape his constricted throat. His body, frozen in shock, had yet to recover from the suddenness of Dutch being catapulted back into his life.

It had been months since he last spoke with Dutch and at least a year since he ended their affair.

"Justin, are you there?" Heidi's voice lost its urgency. Annoyance took its place.

"I'm here," he replied. He turned his back on the pictures. There was no way he could talk to Dutch's sister *and* look at Spencer's happy face. "What's this all about?"

"I have some bad news. Dutch has been in a very bad accident."

"Is he going to be okay?"

Justin felt his head spinning. He felt trapped in a whirlpool of emotions, threatening to rip him asunder.

"The doctors don't know. His injuries are severe," she responded.

Justin held his breath. The whirlpool was winning, and he was going under.

Though they were no longer together, he would never wish any harm to come to Dutch. He was a wonderful man with a gentle soul and caring heart, at least he had been when they were together. Since their breakup, Dutch had become someone he didn't recognize, a fact he'd realized a few months ago when their paths accidentally crossed.

"I'm really sorry to hear about this," he told her, which was true. But Justin wondered why he was getting this call. *Why now?* It was a question he didn't want to voice for fear of dredging up a past better left buried. Still, the words escaped from his mouth before he could reel them back in.

"Why are you calling me? I haven't spoken to Dutch in quite some time."

At first, silence was his only answer. He was wondering if they had been disconnected when he heard the faint sound of Heidi's slow breathing. She was in deep concentration, as if part of her didn't want to reveal the reason for her call, her urgency replaced with hesitancy.

"He keeps calling for you," she said at last. "Will you come?"

His fear of Spencer learning the truth ebbed away. In its place, concern for Dutch flowed to the shore.

Kept buried deep within him, like a treasure his heart kept secret even from himself, his love for Dutch remained. It was sealed within a heavily chained chest, buried underneath millions of grains of sand, but it was there. Justin could feel it. Even worse, he felt unseen hands, urged on by the knowledge he just received about Dutch, begin to dig through the sand.

Justin closed his eyes and mentally erected a stone blockade around the chest. He'd buried those feelings for a reason, and he had no intention of exhuming them.

"I don't know if that's such a good idea," he said. "You see...."

"Sweetie, who is it?"

Justin swiveled around and saw Spencer standing at the entrance to the kitchen, naked. His sandy-blond hair was a disheveled mess, and Spencer moved his hands through his locks in vain attempts to tame them. The sight of his lover's smooth, naked alabaster flesh stirred both Justin's heart and his passion.

"Can you hold on a minute?" Justin asked Dutch's sister before covering the phone with his hand. "It's nothing, love. Why don't you go back to bed?" He knew the suggestion wouldn't work, but he figured it was worth a try.

Spencer moved his hands from his hair to his hips, his way of saying *bitch, please*. "When my man gets a call in the middle of the night, you can bet I'm not going back to bed."

"Fine," he told Spencer. Justin did his best to school his face and quell the upsurge of panic. "Just let me finish the call."

Spencer gestured for Justin to finish the conversation and then he sat at the kitchen table.

"I don't think I'll be able to make it," Justin said into the phone. Spencer's eyes narrowed again. He was wondering what Justin wasn't going to be able to make. Thankfully, though, his expression was merely curious, not accusatory.

"I understand," she told him with a sigh of disappointment. "I'm aware of your situation." She said *situation* as if he were an expectant teen hiding a pregnancy from her parents. He didn't know what the correct tone was for an affair, but he was certain the one she used wasn't it. Adultery and teenage sex were two different offenses. In the grand scheme of life's violations, his *situation* was a capital offense, not a misdemeanor. "I know I shouldn't have called, but I just didn't know what else to do. He keeps repeating your name over and over. I just thought—" She stopped, a rising sob interrupting her words. She breathed deeply and then continued. "If you change your mind, and I hope you do, Dutch is in ICU at Methodist Hospital."

"Thanks for letting me know," he said and then ended the call.

For a few moments, he stood silently in the kitchen, with his cell in hand. The normally cool rubber protective phone case was warm to the touch, heated by the phone during the conversation. Now, Justin waited for a different heat to descend upon him, the inevitable barrage of Spencer's questions.

"So," Spencer said, dragging out the "o" for at least five seconds. It was his typical verbal tick that corresponded with either a piqued or pissed Spencer. "Who was on the phone?"

Justin didn't know how to answer. In a split second, a dozen scenarios ran through his head of how best to avoid suspicion. He had been blessed with a mind capable of quick thinking. But his mind had slowed, either dulled by weariness, pain, or both. He decided to let the answers be honest. "There's been an accident."

Immediately, Spencer's attitude shifted down from pissy to concerned. He rushed from the table to Justin's side. "Who is it?" he asked in alarm. "Is it your mother? Your uncle? Your *grandparents*?"

As usual, Spencer worried more about Justin's family. If the late night call came through on the landline, the welfare of the Harrison's wouldn't elicit this much anxiety from Justin's lover. Spencer and his family had a distantly cordial relationship that stemmed from when he came out of the closet while in high school. Conservative military families didn't appreciate learning one of their own was a homosexual.

"My family is fine," he said.

Spencer exhaled in relief and a smile lighted on his lips. The smile, though, was quickly chased away by the winds of curiosity. "Who, then?"

Justin twisted away from Spencer's tender green eyes. Instead, he stared at the kitchen cabinets, recently painted wine purple instead of the plain white they had once been. Spencer had decided the house needed more color, and the kitchen was where he chose to start. While Justin didn't particularly like the look, he let Spencer have his way. After all, Spencer was more of a domestic than Justin. If he wanted purple cabinets, then purple cabinets he'd get.

Spencer rested his hands gently on Justin's bare shoulder. The touch of his dear, sweet man brought tears to his eyes, but Justin refused to let them fall. *How could I have been so stupid?* he thought. *This was never supposed to happen. How did I let this happen?*

"Sweetie, what's going on? You're scaring me."

Spencer turned him around and gingerly caressed his face. Always the caregiver, always putting others' needs before his own, Spencer was the epitome of giving and sacrifice. It always made Justin feel inferior and unworthy of such a man. "Who was on the phone? Who's been in an accident?"

More than anything else, Justin wanted to lie. A lie would deliver them from pain. A lie would allow them to return to bed and live in the dream of their happy life together. But if he lied, no, if he *continued* to lie, then their life would *only* be a dream.

He had no other option. He knew that now. If things were going to get better, if they were really going to mend what had once been broken, he needed to be completely honest at last. He had to tell Spencer. If he didn't come clean, then their relationship would be rebuilt upon a lie. He respected their love too much to continue on such a shaky foundation any longer.

"Dutch Keller," Justin finally said.

Spencer stared down at him, confused. "Dutch? The photography adjunct that I helped hire last year at St. Mary's?"

Justin nodded. As a member of the faculty at St. Mary's University in San Antonio, Texas, Spencer was often asked to be on various hiring committees within the School of Arts, Humanities, and Social Sciences. As fate would have it, the dean had solicited Spencer's help to fill some part-time teaching vacancies, which included photography, a job for which Dutch applied and got.

Having Spencer and Dutch in such close proximity to each other on the same campus had been the final nail in his relationship with Dutch. Their worlds were getting too close to colliding, and there was only one world he was committed to living in.

"I don't understand," Spencer said. "Why would anyone be calling you on your cell phone about Dutch Keller?"

Justin didn't respond. He simply stared at Spencer through watery eyes.

The welling tears melted his vision, obliterating Justin's stable reality. Spencer's form turned fluid and wavy; the vibrant yellow kitchen walls became drab. All around him, the familiar house distorted into a foreign landscape seen only in nightmares.

This was no bad dream he could easily wake up from. Justin's secure life teetered on the edge of disaster, a disaster he'd set into motion one year ago.

This had been the moment he dreaded for months, the moment when Spencer learned he had been unfaithful. He had thought he could hide the affair forever. He'd hoped he could keep it a secret for the rest of his life, but keeping the lie alive would be a disservice to their renewed commitment.

He should have been upfront when he and Spencer had started patching things back up, but he'd been too afraid the news would shatter any chance they had at reconciliation. All he could hope for now was that their relationship was strong enough to withstand one last explosion.

Slowly, as if the world were only advancing one frame at a time, Justin watched as understanding crashed upon the man he loved like a tidal wave. The weight rested heavily upon Spencer's shoulders, causing them to slouch under the burden.

The only reason Justin would receive such a personal phone call about Dutch was if Dutch and Justin shared a personal relationship.

Spencer's jade eyes drained of their vibrant green, turning pastel. He searched Justin's face for confirmation, and deep within the pool of regretful tears, Spencer found the answer neither of them wanted to be true.

Spencer inhaled sharply, as if he had been stabbed in the chest. He turned around and fled the kitchen.

When the bedroom door slammed shut, Justin's teary eyes dried in response to the numbness that quickly consumed him from within.

CHAPTER 2

1999

"THAT one," Xavier said, pointing at a crowd of people. Xavier wanted Justin to share in a lascivious leer over some brand-new hottie he'd spotted in the crowded bar, but a finger pointed at a crowd of homosexuals, dressed in the standard uniform of tight shirts and jeans, didn't exactly pinpoint Xavier's find. "The one walking through the door," Xavier elaborated, as if sensing Justin's inability to follow his pointing finger. "Doesn't he just make you want to be very, *very* naughty?"

Justin still had no idea who Xavier was pointing at. It was New Year's Eve at the Bonham Exchange, and there were people everywhere. The Bonham was typically crowded on most weekends. It was San Antonio's premier gay club, after all. Most gays would flock to the Bonham on weekends to party with friends or meet their next ex-boyfriend. It was a place where all were welcome, even the occasional straight people who accompanied their gay friends.

The straight women reveled in the adoration of their gay boys. They hooted and hollered on the dance floor, generally making nuisances of themselves to the dancers around them. They drank excessively and released all inhibitions. They were in the safest place for straight women—a gay bar. Where else could they totally cut loose and go buck wild without the fear of being taken advantage of by their date?

A straight woman's biggest problem was being abandoned by her gay who found a hot dick to play with for the evening. At the end of the night, a gaggle of hags could be found flocking together, offering each other a ride home and bemoaning their abandonment, often swearing to never go out with their gays again. The following weekend, they would all return, and the cycle would start all over again.

The straight men were a different story. A few had no problem knocking back a couple of drinks with their gay friends, but there weren't many straight men *that* comfortable in their own skin. The other "straight" men, most of whom meandered through the bar with a beer bottle in hand and a pissed-off look on their faces, were on the down low. If asked who they were here with, they were all invariably looking for a missing girlfriend who *dragged* them here.

Most everyone knew the truth. They were looking for some cock on the side and didn't have the balls to admit it. For all their bravado and strutting, they would be the first on their knees or on their backs. As Xavier often said, many of the supposed straight men made the best power bottoms.

Tonight, the Bonham was even more packed than usual with gay men, straight women, and other men who fell somewhere in between. It was a special night, dubbed as the "Party to End All Parties," and with three levels and three dance floors, the Bonham was a place where the new year could be properly rung in.

It was the end of the millennium, according to most people, who were wrong. Every time Justin corrected someone by saying the year 2000 was actually the last year of the twentieth century, they typically stared at him as if *he* were stupid. Eventually, Justin had given up and gone with the flow. It was easier. Aggravating, but easier.

"Don't tell me you don't see him." Xavier's voice pulled Justin back to the situation at hand. His friend took a swig of his Dos Equis and leaned against the bar, a smirk dangling from his lips.

Justin knew what the smirk meant. The games were about to begin.

Whenever they went out, they would survey the crowd and select who they wanted the other to try and pick up. If they both took someone home, then they both won, as the ultimate goal was to fuck or be fucked. If one of them didn't pick up a trick, the loser had to not only face a week's long torment over his failure but also had to buy the first three rounds of drinks the following weekend.

The rules of the game were simple: the person they picked out had to be a guy at least somewhat hot; they weren't supposed to pick someone excessively ugly or fat. Doing so was a violation and cause for swift justice—four shots of Jose Cuervo, purchased at the offender's expense.

The game was meant to test their pickup skills, of which Xavier was always the undisputed king. Since the game's inception, by Xavier, of course, Xavier had never bought Justin drinks the following weekend. The Dos Equis his friend was currently downing was the third and last of which Justin had to pay from the previous weekend.

Truthfully, Justin hated playing the game. He was no good at picking up men. More accurately, he was awful at it. He was too painfully shy to open himself up to such bald-faced rejection. Xavier had tried to teach him some moves, but whenever Justin tried one, he either came off as a pervert or an idiot, neither of which got him laid.

Xavier claimed Justin had the goods required to make a sale but hadn't learned how to properly package the merchandise. Whatever the hell *that* meant.

Xavier had no trouble with rejection. He always said it was their loss, even though rejection rarely happened for Xavier.

Xavier wasn't exactly the hottest ticket in the bar. His nose was excessively large, as were his ears. They made him look more like a caricature than a real person, but his confidence more than made up for his physical flaws. Whenever he approached someone, he did it with the confidence of a perfect ten instead of the five or six he was.

Justin was always amazed at the guys Xavier could snag. Last week, it was a bodybuilding dentist with pecs of death. The week before that it was a corn-fed football player visiting San Antonio from Oklahoma. He'd bedded most of the Bonham's bar backs, bartenders, and even some of the go-go boys, and this club's reputation was built on hiring the hottest staff in town.

Despite the active bed acrobatics, none of Xavier's flings ever amounted to anything substantial. The one-night stands satisfied Xavier's sexual appetite, but for the most part, his friend was lonely.

Justin saw it in the corners of Xavier's eyes, hidden beneath the endless sexual craving. It was a spark that flickered, hoping *this* one, *this* trick would be the one to stay more than a couple of hours. None of them ever did.

His friend wanted a man to call his own, but his own player ways kept tripping him up.

He had been like that in college too. Only back then Xavier chased girls in order to appear straight to everyone on campus, including their fraternity brothers. Since Justin was trying to do the same thing in college, he latched onto Xavier and the two became fast friends. Naturally, Xavier was the first person he came out to after graduation, and Justin was surprised when Xavier admitted he was also gay.

At first, Justin toyed with the idea of potentially dating Xavier, a subject Xavier brought up first. He couldn't do it. They were too good as friends. It was best to leave the relationship as it was.

That turned out to be one of the best decisions Justin had made in the twenty plus years of his life. Xavier's sluttish ways would have eventually broken them up, effectively ending their friendship.

"I think someone's growing chicken wings," Xavier said, clucking like a chicken.

"What the hell are you talking about?" Justin asked as his mind once again returned to the present. The DJ was spinning the latest mix of "We Like to Party" by the Vengaboys, and the gays were tearing it up on the dance floor. "And I'm no chicken."

"Then go pick him up."

"Pick *who* up?" Justin asked, aggravated. "Are you blind to how many people are here?"

Xavier laughed and took another gulp of his beer. "I'll give you one minute to do it before I go get him and bring him to you. Which, as you know, is a penalty, punishable by—"

"Two tequila shots, I know," Justin said, cutting him off. "Will you just point him out to me? And be more specific than 'walking through the door'."

"He's the Mexican leaning against the wall on the right."

"Really?" Justin asked. "*Mexican* is being specific? We live in San An-fucking-tonio!"

Xavier laughed like a fifth grader at recess, something he did whenever he teased Justin, which meant he heard the snicker on a daily basis. "He's wearing a black muscle shirt and acid-wash jeans. Thick black hair. He's also wearing a puka shell necklace that all the fags are wearing these days."

Justin scanned the crowd and saw him, leaning against the far wall with a pink Cape Cod in his hand. He was muscular and rugged, and way out of Justin's league. Well-sculpted arms and shoulders framed the black shirt. Even at a relaxed stance, his biceps and triceps were clearly defined. Justin hated him for that. He had been working on his arms for months and had yet to develop such muscle tone.

The muscle shirt also clung to his body as if the fabric was wet, and it revealed an absence of love handles on his tightly packed form. Small, perky nipples poked out from the cloth, and the shirt's fabric ended about an inch before the jeans began. A treasure trail of hair started at his navel and disappeared beneath the waistband of the jeans. Just below the waistband was a package ready to be delivered.

"Do you see Puka Shell Boy?" Xavier asked.

"Yup," was all Justin could say.

"Then go get him."

Justin swallowed hard. This wasn't going to end well. The image of a B-52 going down in flames flashed before him.

Then he noticed Puka Shell Boy's friend.

His friend was a few inches taller than both Puka Shell Boy and Justin. If he had to guess, he would put him at almost six feet tall. Sandy-blond hair lay perfectly manicured and parted to the left. Longer strands of hair curled inward at his cheekbones and lightly kissed the most unbelievable alabaster skin Justin had ever seen. His skin looked smoother than silk, as if a sculptor had spent hours chiseling the precious stone into perfection. Draping his skin was a green short-sleeve button-down, neatly tucked into his dark-blue denim jeans. The shirt was fitted but not painted on him like Puka Shell Boy. His lean body resembled a dedicated runner and was neither waifish nor frail.

Then Justin noticed his eyes. Dark-green tinted eyes decorated his features, magically cutting through the dimly lit bar and outshining the sparkling disco ball. They weren't a green he had seen before. He had seen light green and even olive green eyes, but these eyes looked to be made of jade. They were a deeper, richer green hue than he had ever seen before in his life. They looked exotic and expensive, found only in jewelry from a faraway Asian country like China or Japan.

They were breathtaking. Justin didn't understand how people were walking by him and not staring into those eyes. He could stare at them for the rest of the night.

"What's the matter with you?" Xavier asked. "You're standing there with your mouth open like a fucking retard."

"He's so beautiful."

"No shit!" Xavier exclaimed. "Think of him as my New Year's present to you. You just have to close the deal." Xavier put his arm around Justin's neck, Xavier's sign of friendship and love. "By the end of the night, Puka Shell Boy will be on his back looking up at you, or you know, looking down at *you* on *your* back." Xavier then pushed Justin forward. "Now, hurry up. It's almost midnight."

Justin didn't know what came over him. All it took was a simple shove, and he was crossing the room toward the stranger with the perfect skin and the amazing green eyes. He felt drawn to him, as if he were caught in an unbreakable gravitational field.

Puka Shell Boy noticed Justin coming first. He elbowed his green-eyed friend and flashed a disinterested grin, most likely thinking Justin was coming to talk to him. He wasn't. Puka Shell Boy no longer existed in his world.

As he approached, the crowds around him got louder. Apparently, the stroke of midnight was approaching. Someone was speaking on a microphone, most likely the drag queen hostess for the night's festivities, but he couldn't make out what she was saying. All he could see were the green eyes and the white skin pulling at him like the moon pulls on the ocean.

"Ten, nine, eight…"

Closer still he drew, passing by couples with their arms around each other, preparing for their New Year's kiss.

"… seven, six, five, four…"

Six feet from the most beautiful man he had ever seen, Justin found he was holding his breath. He had to remind himself to breathe for fear that he would pass out only a few feet away from his intended. Up close, his eyes were more radiant than from across the room. Flecks of gold glinted within the green irises.

"… three, two…"

Then he was standing before him. Puka Shell Boy leaned next to his friend, amazed that he wasn't the object of Justin's attention. He whispered something in his friend's ear, but his friend wasn't paying attention. He, too, was staring straight at Justin.

"… one …."

Justin reached up and put his left hand around the green-eyed beauty's neck. Pulling his head toward him, Justin crossed the remainder of the distance.

Their lips met, and the world suddenly came crashing back to life. Noisemakers exploded throughout the club. People were yelling "Happy New Year," and confetti and glitter were tossed about. The DJ began playing "Auld Lang Syne."

Through the noise, the revelry, and the singing, the two never stopped kissing. Their tongues jostled in each other's mouths as they each inhaled the other's hot passionate breaths.

Never had Justin been more excited about a new year.

CHAPTER 3

2010

SPENCER HARRISON leaned against the bathroom door; the cold wood against his bare skin made him shiver. He pushed harder against the door, forcing his skin into the wooden fibers and rubbing his flesh up and down, hoping to bring forth pain, discomfort, or even a splinter, anything was better than the numbing stiffness currently creeping through his body.

He wondered if this was what a dead body succumbing to rigor mortis felt like as, one by one, each digit, and then each extremity turned lifeless and frozen. The flesh extending out from his limbs fell prey to the sedated state, as it grew first warm then coldly numb until the sensation at last captured his heart.

It throbbed in protest as the icy fingers squeezed the organ in a deathlike grip. The anger that previously had boiled his blood upon learning Justin had cheated, *with Dutch Keller, of all people,* cooled and iced over.

Looking down at his naked body, he expected to find himself encased in ice. Instead he saw the usual fare—white skin and body hair around his nipples and genitals, which drooped impotently toward the floor.

He ran his hand over his skin, and the sensation felt foreign, as if he were touching someone else's flesh instead of his own. Brushing over his chest hair or his pubic hair elicited no reaction from the follicles. Red marks appeared when his fingers pinched or clawed at his skin, but he felt no pain.

Even the body quakes, a term he had given to shivering in his childhood, went unnoticed by his mind. His limbs flinched and his muscles contracted, he could see it happening, but he felt nothing.

He was in shock.

"Spence, please come out and talk to me," Justin pleaded from outside the bathroom door.

Justin's voice shattered his emotional catatonia. He locked the bathroom door and backed away from it like he'd seen so many helpless victims do in the horror movies Justin loved and forced him to watch. He regarded the door with fear, as if at any moment the killer would burst through, ready to dismember him with a machete.

Except Spencer wasn't a helpless victim. A victim? Maybe. He had been mortally wounded by the man he loved, but that didn't make him helpless. A lesson taught to him by his father. He wasn't helpless when his parents practically disowned him for being gay, or when he was bullied in school, or even when he received that letter long ago from the life insurance company.

No, he faced every problem head-on. He might not have been the soldier his army father wanted, but his father had made sure he learned how to survive.

He closed his eyes as he always did when he needed to revisit a fatherly lesson from his past in order to overcome an obstacle of today. On command, from the depths of his subconscious, the father of his childhood materialized before him.

Ice-cold blue eyes stared down at him; the tendons in his father's neck spread out, and spittle flew from his enraged mouth.

"An enemy is only as big and bad as you make him out to be, boy!" His father's jaw muscles clenched like an African cat's hind legs before chasing its prey. It was standard protocol whenever his father was extremely angry and ready to rip into someone. "Don't go cryin' like some sissified pansy when a bully knocks you on your ass. Get off your ass, dust yourself off, and then crack open his skull." His father waved his massive fist before Spencer to demonstrate what righteous anger looked like.

"But, Daddy," he sobbed, nursing a swollen eye. "It was Brandon. He's the one who hit me!"

Upon the revelation, Spencer winced, expecting his father to go nuclear after learning his oldest son had treated his younger one so rudely. His father simply stared at him. He couldn't interpret what that meant. His father was rarely at a loss for words. In fact, he usually raised his voice to its loudest decibel until he was the only *one who could be heard.*

"Your brother did this?" his father asked. He ran his fingers across his buzzed head. Spencer heard his hair bristle against his calloused hand.

When his father spoke, his voice contained no anger, only pride. "Well, damn!"

Spencer was crushed. He didn't understand why his father wasn't angry.

"That don't change a fucking thing!" The rage in his father's eyes returned, the pride discarded in favor of his favorite emotion—resentment. Resentment at producing such a weakling boy, capable of only love not hate. Resentment from looking at Spencer and seeing nothing resembling himself. "He took you down. Now do something about it. Don't just sit there holding your face like a girl. Hurt him. Hurt him so he'll think twice before doing it again."

Spencer couldn't believe what his father had said. He expected his old man to be angry with Brandon, not with him. After all, he was the innocent victim. He was the one who was minding his own business, playing hopscotch outside. He didn't do anything to cause his big brother to walk up to him, push him down, call him awful names, and then hit him. Why couldn't his father see he was the innocent victim?

Now his father wanted him to hurt his brother? He couldn't do that.

"But he's my brother. I love him. I don't want to hurt him." Spencer couldn't stop the tears. He tried to hold them back, but they were too strong for him. Everything was too strong for him.

"It didn't stop him from hurting you, did it?" His father yanked him up from the ground by his shirt collar. Spencer's stomach dropped to his feet from the sheer force of his father's actions. "And you can stop the innocent-victim routine. You're big enough to know there are no innocent victims. There are only two types of people in this world—the strong and the weak. You better decide now which one you want to be." His father turned him around to face the street before him. "Only the strong survive. Now you go find that brother of yours and whoop his ass."

"He's bigger than me," he protested as his father pushed him toward the street. "He's in seventh grade!"

"Enemies will always be bigger than you, boy. You just have to learn how to cut them down to your size. No matter who they are."

Afterward, his father turned around, dismissing him. It was his father's way of telling those he commanded to follow his orders.

He found Brandon an hour later in an abandoned and secluded field five blocks from their neighborhood. His brother and a couple of his friends were riding their bikes along a dirt course carved out by years of use. The big hills and sharp turns called to the adventurous boys, and they jumped and turned at breakneck speeds, each one trying to outdo the others in an effort to be king of the course.

He made his way to a pile of rocks left by one of the city's construction crews after repaving a nearby street. He plucked a large rock from the pile and then proceeded through the tall grass along the course's perimeter. He waited among the tall reeds like a lion stalking a gazelle, crouching near Big Bertha, the biggest and scariest hill, and also the boys' favorite.

While Spencer didn't have his brother's strength, he did have accurate aim, the only physical trait his father appreciated.

When Brandon approached the hill, Spencer stood and revealed himself. His brother's eyes widened in surprise. Then he threw the big rock that waited anxiously in his small hand. The rock struck Brandon square in the chest. The force and surprise of the impact caused his brother to tumble off his bike and down the hill, ultimately dislocating his shoulder and breaking his right ulna.

Brandon was in a cast for six weeks. And he didn't bother Spencer again for a few months.

Spencer opened his eyes to a far clearer world. The fog of numbing pain lifted, giving him clarity of vision. His father was right. There were no innocent victims, only those who allowed themselves to be continually victimized.

When he retaliated against his brother, he'd found his voice, the strength he needed to meet any adversary eye to eye. It gave him direction and purpose. His fair and delicate skin transformed into armor, capable of deflecting any weapon hurled against him. It had served him well for years after that, keeping those who wished him harm—classmates, lovers, and family—at arm's length.

Until he met Justin.

Justin pierced the armor and shattered his defenses far too easily. With a single kiss, he'd disarmed Spencer, making him powerless and weak.

That was about to end.

Throwing open the linen closet, he retrieved his Louis Vuitton suitcase and slammed it against the tub. The explosive clang reverberated through the plumbing, causing the entire house to tremble. He could only imagine what kind of effect the sound had on Justin, whose shadow he could see crouching in front of the bathroom door.

"If you won't come out, can I come in there?" Justin asked.

Spencer scoffed in answer. The doorknob turned as Justin tested the lock.

Does he really think I'm that easy? Spencer thought as he threw clothes inside the suitcase. *Have I been* that *forgiving,* that *spineless for ten years?*

The fuse of Spencer's anger relit, threatening to blow the entire house skyward. Fire surged through his veins, melting the paralyzing ice that had threatened him previously. Warning bells and klaxons wailed inside his mind as his body prepared for war.

"How about this, then?" Justin asked, trying to break through his defenses once again. His tone was contrite and calm, but Spencer heard it for what it was. It was simply the silencer attached to the end of a pistol, cocked and ready to deliver another mortal blow. "How about I stay out here, but you open the door, so we can talk?"

"How about you go fuck yourself?" Spencer replied. His voice boomed like a thunderclap. At first, the intensity of his words frightened him, not because he regretted them or the tone, but because he sounded just like his father. He hoped Justin cowered on the other side of the door like he used to as a child whenever his father spoke to him like that.

"If it would make you feel better, why don't you come out and hit me? I won't put up a fight. You could hit me as hard as you want."

Spencer responded by violently slamming shut the closet door inside the bathroom. The pictures hanging on the opposite bedroom wall rattled. He resumed his packing, grabbing his black leather Dopp kit from under the sink and scooping his toiletries, lined neatly along his side of the bathroom counter, into its open mouth.

"I'll do anything you want, Spence. Anything at all. Just please open the door."

He hesitated. The self-hate and remorse he heard in Justin's voice tugged on his heart, reaching through the newly erected armor as if it were paper thin. For reasons beyond comprehension, his heart begged him to open the door, to let down his defenses and go out there and work this out.

You love him, his heart told him. *Even now, even after knowing he cheated, you love him. You can't deny that.*

"I can deny anything I want to," Spencer whispered quietly.

He caught a glimpse of himself in the bathroom mirror, and for the first time he noticed the body quakes had returned. He wrapped his arms around his body, hugging himself like he used to before he found his strength, before he knew he could stand on his own.

The sight of him trembling, still naked, in the mirror disgusted Spencer. He looked more akin to a terrified kitten than a man capable of standing on his own two feet and marching out of this house and out of Justin's life.

Open the door, his heart insisted. *Yell at him. Do what you must, but go to him. Remember, Justin's not the only one with secrets.*

"Fuck you," he told his reflection.

"I love you, Spencer," Justin said from outside the door. His words choked over a sob stuck in his throat. "I truly do."

He's crying, his heart told him. *Justin doesn't cry; you know that. Can't you see how much he loves you? How sorry he is for what he's done?*

Spencer's armor unfastened and dangled to one side. He could feel it slipping off, threatening to leave him vulnerable once again. Clawing after it, he tried to snap it back into place, but he felt it slip from his grasp.

His heart was right. Spencer guarded his own secrets. Could he punish Justin for his trespass when he had yet to pay for his own? Cautiously, he approached the door. Should he give Justin another chance?

You've done it before, his heart reminded him. *You can do it again.*

Are you fucking kidding me? This time it was his father's voice speaking to him, and his father wasn't pleased. *Are you really that much of a sissy that you would walk back into the arms of the person who has broken your heart not once, but twice? Do you lack that much self-respect? Did I teach you nothing?*

Spencer recoiled from the door.

Don't compare your sins to his, his father bellowed. *He cheated on you. You never cheated on him.*

His father was right. What he had done didn't come close to Justin's betrayal. He retreated into the walk-in closet and pulled on a pair of underwear lying on the floor.

That's my boy, his father said.

He shoved his head through a T-shirt and threw on a pair of jeans.

Put that armor back on.

He slid his feet into his white Puma sneakers, and picked up his suitcase and Dopp kit.

For good this time.

Spencer opened the bathroom door and found Justin on his knees in front of the door. At first, Justin smiled, relieved that he'd finally emerged from the bathroom. When he noticed the suitcase, the relief died in his eyes like a flickering candle in a hurricane.

"Spence, I...."

"I'm leaving," he told Justin and walked past him.

"Where are you going?"

The question stopped Spencer in his tracks. He had no clue where he was going. His life stretched before him like a darkened country road with no headlights to illuminate his path. "I don't know. Even if I did, I wouldn't tell you," he said at last. "You've lost the right to know where I go or what I do."

"Please don't leave me," Justin pleaded. "I can't live without you."

He turned his head slightly to the right, so he didn't have to look at Justin directly. "You'll be fine," he said. "You obviously were the *last* time I left you."

He walked out of the bedroom and out the front door. As he got in his car, his father's voice applauded him, telling him how proud he was. *Your parting words were like a grenade. A good way to finish off the enemy.*

When Spencer pulled out of the driveway, he listened intently for his heart, but he couldn't hear it over his father's congratulatory laughter.

CHAPTER 4

2000

SPENCER allowed Justin to lead him toward the patio behind the second level dance floor. When he agreed, he was surprised not only by his consent, since he rarely went off alone with a guy he just met at a bar, but that he tolerated Justin holding his hand as they wove through the many drunken revelers at the Bonham.

Public displays of affection bothered Spencer, but not because he was embarrassed about being affectionate with another man. He had gotten over that in college. He simply felt that broadcasting your affinity for another person revealed insecurity, as if your hand-holding or tonsil-hockey session needed to be seen by others in order to validate the relationship.

Yet, here he was, holding this guy's hand for *all* to see. That wasn't even the worst of it. He had actually kissed this guy for what seemed like an eternity in front of the entire bar. At *midnight*. On *New Year's Eve*. He certainly had never been *that* carefree before.

All of which begged the question: *Why had he allowed any of that to occur?*

Spencer had no answer, no matter how hard he racked his brain for one. He simply felt compelled, as if he had drunk some powerful drug that rendered his typically reserved nature powerless.

When he noticed Justin approaching, he at first assumed he was coming over to talk to Alex. *Everyone* came to talk to Alex. Alex claimed it was his puka shell necklace, which Spencer abhorred. The necklace was a good-luck charm, according to Alex. As if he needed one.

But Justin never once looked at Alex. His eyes had been fixed on him, as if the rest of the world spun away, leaving only the two of them standing. Typically, such an approach, with such singular and focused will, would have sent up warning flags. Yet Spencer felt nothing inherently predatory, a common sensation at a gay bar, where most guys scouted the crowd for the next score.

Then what did *it feel like?*

It just felt right.

Right? That's *your answer?* his rational mind told him. *Right is hardly an acceptably quantifiable evaluation of this incident.*

Yeah, well, I'm not a scientist, he argued with his inner voice.

You might as well be, his mind retorted. *You may be a man of language, but your heart is cold and logical. You know that better than anyone else.*

"Watch your step," Justin told him. His eyes were as refreshing as a coastal breeze on a scorching day, and their brown hue reminded him of the cool, packed sand that lay between the ocean's edge and the sandy beach. When his family went on a summer vacation that involved a beach, that is where he stayed—at the water's edge. While his brother and sister swam in the ocean and his parents lay out on their beach blankets, he sat in the cool, wet sand, thrusting his toes into the velvety folds.

He felt safe, as if by sinking his toes into the sand the earth had somehow claimed him as its own, grounding him and giving him the companionship he lacked in his family or at school.

When he gazed into Justin's eyes, as he looked back to make sure Spencer didn't trip over any one of the inebriated patrons in the small stairwell, he felt transported back to that beach, toes in the sand and connected to another life force much greater than his own.

Going past the small series of stairs that led to a walkway, they skirted the packed dance floor where the gays were getting down to Cher's "Believe."

Justin surprised Spencer by pulling him onto the dance floor, where they joined their gay brethren in their fevered adoration of the ultimate gay icon. Rarely, if ever, did Spencer dance at the clubs. He preferred observing the standard mating ritual as the dance partners gyrated on the floor with the express purpose of gauging each other's sexual prowess through thrusting hips to the syncopated beat.

He found the custom distasteful, yet here he was grinding in sync with Justin, whose hands rested on Spencer's hips and whose crotch was currently scraping against his ass.

What has gotten into you? his mind asked him. *Since when do you engage in such immature and improper activities? You're practically copulating on the dance floor?*

I know, Spencer returned. *It feels great!*

He turned around in Justin's embrace so that Justin's crotch now ground against his own. The friction stirred their passions to life as their growing erections rubbed against each other.

Spencer had never felt more alive in his life. He surrendered completely to the passion freely flowing between them. Screaming at him from the recesses of his brain, his rational side pleaded for him to stop, telling him he was making a spectacle of himself.

He found that he didn't care.

His life had been lived behind armor, watching the world go by while he stayed safe and secure within his own carefully constructed ramparts. He envied the romances and casual dalliances of his friends, secretly wishing he too could partake in the ecstasy of romantic love and casual sex. Endless hope and unfettered optimism reflected in their eyes, whether it was warranted or not.

For years, he'd thought them careless or just plain stupid for constantly blundering into the same trap time after time. Broken hearts and tear-stained faces often sought his solace, and he advised them all, trying to pass on the lessons he'd learned as a child. When they didn't listen, when they threw themselves into the next romance without thought, like a suicide jumper leaping off a building, he averted his eyes.

He had no intention of watching as they plummeted to the ground, victims of inevitable heartache, which was as definitive as gravity in Spencer's mind.

Living that way had been a necessity. It kept him safe from those who wanted to do him harm. Those enemies were everywhere in his life, in places both expected and unexpected. To keep himself safe, to be able to stand the strain without cracking under the pressure, he stayed safely within the armor that had protected him since his retaliatory strike against his own brother.

Now, the armor fell from his body, piece by piece, and each section shed from his body corresponded to where Justin's hands touched him.

The first to fall were the gauntlets. As they danced, Justin's fingers flitted gingerly across his hands and fingers, sending electrical impulses traveling through his arms, causing the vambrace to clang to the floor. His hands proceeded to Spencer's face, stroking his cheek then his chin and effectively knocking the helmet from his head, which elicited a wail of fear from his rational brain. Justin ran his hands down Spencer's back, releasing the cuirass with one sweep, and as his hands ran across Spencer's upper thighs, the greaves collapsed onto the dance floor.

When Justin's hands stroked his chest, the breastplate slipped and slid askew, refusing to be unceremoniously cast off the area in need of the most protection. But Justin's tender hands plucked this last section of defense from his body with little more than a flick of his index finger.

Unburdened for the first time in his life, Spencer wrapped his arms around Justin's neck and drew him into another kiss. His tongue found Justin's and greedily wrapped around it, sucking it into his mouth. His basest instincts, free from the constraints of his rational mind and his armor, wondered what other body part of Justin's might find its way into his mouth before the evening was over.

He moaned softly as Justin cupped his ass, passionately massaging it in wanton lust. In response, he forced his engorged erection against Justin's, savoring the feel of the hardness against his own. Their shafts pulsed in beat to the music as Cher's raspy voice continued to sing about love.

He ran his hands through the back of Justin's shaggy hair and over his firm chest. Justin's right hand rested at the nape of his neck, forcing their moist lips and hot tongues into a suction that could not be reversed. When Justin's left hand squeezed the swollen mound inside Spencer's jeans, Spencer's knees almost buckled.

His body could take no more, not without relieving his years of pent-up frustration in the middle of the dance floor.

Justin pulled away from their kiss, his hands coming to rest on Spencer's hips. "How about we go to the patio now?" Justin asked, straining to be heard over the music. "I could use some fresh air."

The blush in Justin's cheeks revealed that Justin was also much too close to losing control. It pleased Spencer to know the condition was mutual.

"Let's go," Spencer said, placing his hand in Justin's of his own free will.

Justin parted the dancers before them as they made their way to the patio door.

Cher's gravelly voice slowly gave way to Enrique Iglesias as he sang "Bailamos," to the delightful screech of young men who were in lust with the Latin heartthrob. As they exited the dance floor and then the building to the patio beyond, Spencer looked back at the ecstatic crowd. They resembled an ocean as they flowed forward and backward, the rainbow disco ball spinning over them and casting its light downward, revealing in their faces the full emotional spectrum of life that, until this moment, had been foreign to Spencer's soul.

"It was pretty hot in there," Justin said, leading Spencer to one of the benches on the far side of the patio. He sat on top of the table, his hand still holding Spencer's.

Spencer nodded in agreement, unable to speak for fear of igniting anew his now abating passion.

"And I was talking about you. Not the club." Justin pulled Spencer to him. Spencer rested his body between Justin's open legs, and the proximity of their bodies and the slight whiff of Justin's now musky body ignited another stirring in his pants.

He had to turn his thoughts to something else. "What happened to your friend?"

"Xavier?" Justin asked with a laugh. "The last time I saw him, he had his tongue down *your* friend's throat."

Spencer laughed as well. "Alex is such a slut."

"So's Xavier. They're perfect for each other."

Spencer stared into Justin's eyes, and he once again felt the comforting pull of his childhood beach tug at him the way the water pulled upon the sand, drawing grain upon grain within its aquatic arms. Their power over him was not only astonishing but unprecedented. Never before had simply staring into another pair of eyes caused him to feel as ensorcelled as he did now.

Spencer wondered why they had such power. Was it the slight almond shape of the eyes? Did the exotic feature, never before seen by him on a Latin male, somehow entrap him with its intoxicating blend?

"Just so you know, I'm *not* a slut."

Justin's voice brought Spencer back to the conversation. "Good to know," he said. "Neither am I, despite evidence to the contrary."

"I really don't know what came over me. One minute Xavier is talking to me about your friend Alex, and the next thing I know I'm walking over to you and pulling you into a kiss."

"Pretty smooth move," Spencer told him.

Justin laughed again. His laugh was hearty and lacked guile. It told Spencer Justin was not only sincere but confident in both the positive and negative aspects of himself. "I'm also *not* smooth, either. When it comes to meeting guys."

"Despite evidence to the contrary?" asked Spencer.

"Definitely," Justin replied. "I've *never* done something like that before." Justin looked into Spencer's eyes, apparently trying to gauge whether Spencer believed him or not. While Spencer's rational mind would have set up arguments disproving Justin's claim, Spencer's heart told him the revelation was accurate. As if sensing this, Justin let the matter drop without further comment.

"Will Alex get mad at you for spending this time with me?"

Spencer thought about it. While Alex never once gave a second thought to abandoning him at the club, he knew Alex wouldn't be amused to find himself abandoned. "He'll be pissed," he finally said.

"Should we go find him?"

"No," replied Spencer, more quickly than he intended. "Turn about is fair play. Besides, isn't he busy making out with *your* friend?"

"True," Justin said. "For all we know, they might've already abandoned us in favor of a more intimate location."

Spencer knitted his eyebrows. "Why do *we* always get abandoned?"

Justin grinned and stood up from the table. He pulled Spencer back toward the doors they'd previously exited. On the other side, he saw the sea of dancers still swaying to the music.

"Back to the dance floor?" Spencer asked.

"No," Justin replied. "How do you feel about abandoning Xavier and Alex in favor of a more intimate location?"

Before his rational mind had time to react, Spencer replied, "Let's do it."

Justin pulled Spencer through the doors and led him through the crowd. This time the beating of his heart overpowered the bass beat emanating from the speakers. He was anxious, but not out of fear or vulnerability. No, the armor had already been cast aside.

For the first time in years, he was anxious about the possibilities and never once thought about the consequences.

CHAPTER 5

2010

DUTCH KELLER drifted upon a dark ocean, the waves carrying him farther and farther from the shore. Craning his neck right and left, careful not to upset his tentative buoyancy, he searched for signs of life or land. Only darkness reached out in all directions. Inky waves of water lapped mercilessly against him; the sky, at least he thought it was the sky, seemed to have been thrust into an endless night absent of even the moon or the stars.

Ursa Major and her little sister appeared to have vacated the premises above, taking with them all their friends—Sagittarius, Orion, Perseus, and even his favorite, Pegasus.

When he was younger and still childishly afraid of the dark, his father had told him to look to the heavens, and there he would find a friend to stay with him all through the night. According to his father, the constellations were guardians of little children, and all a child had to do was pick one. Once chosen, that constellation would forever look over the child, long after the child had drifted asleep.

"Do you have a guardian, Poppa?" he asked, quite certain that his big, strong father needed no protection. After all, his father was over six feet tall, with muscles to rival Superman. What could he possibly need protection from?

"Yes, little man, I do." In response, Dutch gasped. He'd had no idea that daddies needed protection too! Was the world so scary a place that even grown-ups like his dad needed someone to watch out for them? If it was, then Dutch never wanted to leave his parents, not for anything!

His father rose from his bed and walked over to the window with the drawn curtains. Crawling out of bed and joining his father at his side, Dutch looked out his bedroom window into the heavens above.

For a few minutes, they stared skyward in silence. Dutch didn't care. He loved spending whatever time he could with his father. Whether they were throwing around a football, completing household chores assigned to them by Momma, or just sitting quietly next to each other, he inhaled every moment, gobbling it up as if it were his last breath of air.

They could sit there all night, and he would have been perfectly happy.

At last, his father pointed southward, toward the horizon. The only reason he knew they were looking south was because his father spoke of places around town in compass directions as they related to where they lived. His school was to the west of his house, and their church and the grocery store were to the north. The awful dentist, whom he hated, could be found by going east, as well as the places where his mom and dad worked. To the south of their house was his favorite place—the ocean.

"You see that group of stars just above the southern horizon?"

"There's a lot of stars that way. Is your guardian all those stars?"

His father laughed. Normally, whenever anyone laughed at something he said, he thought they were making fun of him. That was what happened when he'd said eight divided by four was three in class yesterday and stupid Nancy Rosenberg had laughed so hard she fell out of her seat.

With his dad, though, he never thought he was being mocked, not even if he might have deserved it. No, his father laughed only when his son actually said something he found funny.

"No, silly boy," his father said, his chuckle causing his eyes to water. He ran his fingers through his son's hair, making it a tangled mess. "Not even your old man needs that much protection."

"Then which one is yours?"

"You see that star almost touching the horizon? The one right above Bobby Hill's house?"

Dutch squinted. He found it difficult to focus on one star out of so many in the sky. It was like trying to spot one blinking firefly amidst a swarm. The lights from the neighborhood made the task even more difficult, but at last he found it. "The one twinkling just to the left of their chimney?"

"That's the one," his father said, placing his hand on Dutch's shoulder. "Now follow that star up and you'll see another one right above it. That star forms a diamond with three others on the left." He looked down at his son, who was peering through squinty eyes.

"I see it!" he exclaimed joyfully. He wondered why he had never seen it before. Sometimes late at night, before his parents called him in for bath time, he looked up into the stars, searching for familiar patterns. He'd located spoons, arrows, circles, and squares, but he'd never before seen that diamond. Now that he did, he thought it was the most precious sight in the sky.

"Across from that diamond, to the right and going up a bit, is another star. It connects to two other stars that sort of make a tail." Dutch followed his father's pointing finger, connecting the dots in the night sky.

"Wow," was all he could say. "Is that your guardian?"

"Yes," replied his father. "It's called Phoenix."

"Felix is a stupid name," he told his father. He had no idea why anyone in their right mind would name such a beautiful cluster of stars "Felix."

"Not Felix." His father again chuckled. "Phoenix. P-H-O-E-N-I-X. Phoenix."

"Oh, Phoenix," Dutch repeated, turning over the weird-sounding word in his mouth. "That's a better name but the spelling is awful!"

A broad smile stretched across his father's lips. "Do you know what a phoenix is?"

Dutch shook his head, still gazing at the special stars that protected his dad. He wondered what the phoenix had protected him from, and if the phoenix could protect him too.

"It's a great big bird made of fire."

Dutch's eyes grew wide with excitement. "Fire? Really?" He just couldn't believe it. He wanted a bird made of fire.

"The special thing about the phoenix is that it lives for five hundred years, and when it dies, it's reborn from its own ashes." Dutch's already wide eyes and mouth broadened. It was a magical bird, and he loved anything that dealt with magic. He just had to have a phoenix now. "A phoenix is all about hope and love. It's the hope that keeps its fire burning, and the love that causes it to be reborn." His father looked down at him, while Dutch's narrowed eyes communicated he was trying to put all the information together. "Do you understand?"

"I think so," he finally said after a few moments of thought. "With hope and love, nothing can ever die, right?"

His father smiled and kissed him on the cheek. "Right."

"I want the phoenix to be my guardian too!"

"He can be," his father said. "But your guardian should be something special to you. If the phoenix is special, he'll be yours, but if there's something else that's even more special, then you should choose that one."

"Like what?" Dutch asked. He didn't understand. It sounded like his father didn't want to share the phoenix with him, and that wasn't like his dad at all. They shared everything—ice cream, soda, cake, and even Momma's yucky broccoli.

"Well, let's see," his father said. "Ever since you saw that movie Clash of the Titans, you've been talking about a particular animal nonstop."

"The Pegasus!" Dutch replied, remembering the white winged horse sent to Perseus by his father Zeus. From the moment Dutch first saw the horse fly onto the screen, he had been hooked. He wanted a Pegasus even more than a phoenix, which he thought was still pretty darn cool.

His father nodded. "Don't you remember from the movie? Pegasus is a constellation."

"Oh, yeah!" he exclaimed, remembering how Pegasus's image transformed into the stars at the movie's end. "I want Pegasus to be my guardian," he told his father. "But the Phoenix is all hope and love. If I choose Pegasus, am I choosing not to hope and love?"

"Not at all," replied his father. "Hope and love are what the Phoenix means to me. What does Pegasus mean to you?"

He wrinkled his forehead in deep thought. He had no idea what Pegasus meant to him. The horse was a gift from Perseus's father, to aid in his quests, and Pegasus fought by Perseus's side no matter what, even when the gigantic Kraken was trying to kill everyone in that town.

"Loyalty and bravery," he blurted. "That's what Pegasus means to me."

"Then there you go. Now, when you look into the sky at night, you'll see brave and loyal Pegasus protecting you, and you'll also know that your dad's love for you and the hope he has for you will always be there."

"Always?" he asked.

"Always," his father assured.

Without another word, he ran back to bed and got under the covers. He laid his head on his pillow and imagined Pegasus swooping over his house, keeping away the monsters that lived in the shadows, like Calibos from Clash of the Titans.

He pictured Pegasus standing vigil in the distance, perched on a nearby tree. While his father kissed him good night and as he drifted off to sleep, secure in the bravery of Pegasus and his father's love, he knew he would never be afraid of the dark again.

Except now he was.

The darkness all around him terrified him. Pegasus and Phoenix were missing in action, stolen by whatever power could rob the sky of its celestial bodies. Did that mean his father's hope and love were gone too?

The prospect frightened him even more than the engulfing darkness. Had he disappointed his father so much that the living beacon of his love and hope was snuffed out? Did the fiery bird take flight away from the tragedy of a man lost in a sea of hate and despair?

When he closed his eyes and relived the past few months of his life—the binge drinking, casual sex, and cavalier attitude about life, he saw no other option. He *was* a disappointment. He'd lost his way, and as a result wound up adrift in this dark sea of nightmares.

He had forgotten his father's lessons about love, hope, loyalty, and bravery, the characteristics he once followed like a compass through the sea of life. Now, the compass was broken, and its arrow no longer pointed to a true north. It whirled wildly in all directions, unsure where to point, unsure what direction to follow.

Love turned to hate, hope became despair, loyalty morphed into infidelity, and bravery changed to cowardice. His aimless wandering upon this sea mirrored his unsure trajectory in life.

If he wanted to drift upon the shores of home, he needed to change. The man he once was needed to rise out of these waters, and the man he had become needed to stay lost at sea forever. It was the only way to survive. If his true self didn't triumph, then he would be lost in this darkness for eternity.

He just didn't know what to do, how to change direction and get home to himself.

All he knew was that he *wanted* to change. He *wanted* to go home.

That was when the words floated up from the deepest core of his being. "I forgive you, Justin." The words reverberated through the nothingness all around him.

Like a spell, his words calmed the churning sea; peace descended onto his soul.

A pinprick of light flashed above him. Its warmth invigorated him, spreading across his flesh.

Forgiveness became mercy, and a ribbon of light shot across the sky. It then widened to an arc and didn't disappear. The light was fuzzy and faraway, but it remained.

His soul felt lighter, less encumbered. The shackles were released as he willingly cast off the darkness that had constricted his soul.

When mercy changed into absolution, the heavens opened. Rays of light descended upon his world, and his father flew into view on the back of the Phoenix, and beside them trotted his guardian, Pegasus.

CHAPTER 6

2000

JUSTIN fumbled with his keys, which were caught on the inside of his jean pocket, tangled onto a thread that appeared to be made more out of iron than denim. His clunky fingers, numb from the cold and wet weather, only aggravated the situation.

"It's not supposed to get this cold in San Antonio," Spencer said, his teeth chattering together uncontrollably. He rubbed his hands up and down his exposed arms in an effort to warm himself up. "And *why* did I fall victim to the homosexual fashion code that mandates appearance over comfort? What was I thinking wearing short sleeves in January?"

"Well, it *was* December when you decided on your ensemble."

"Spoken like a true smartass," Spencer responded, mimicking Olympia Dukakis's line from *Steel Magnolias*, one of Justin's favorite movies. The fact that Spencer obviously loved the movie as well made Justin want him even more.

"Don't worry, Clairee," he told Spencer, calling him by the character Olympia Dukakis played. "It's almost loose." Finally, Justin pulled the keys free from the viselike grip of the unusually resilient string. "Got it!" he said, holding his keys up for Spencer to see.

"Now do you know what to do with it?"

Justin raised an eyebrow at Spencer's suggestive comment. He thrust the key into the lock and quickly turned it before swinging open the door to his apartment.

Spencer flew past him toward the warm interior, and Justin followed him inside. When he shut the door to the cold outside, Justin immediately regretted asking Spencer back to his place, not because he doubted the decision but because he was embarrassed about the poor condition of his living space.

"It's very *nice*," Spencer said upon looking around. His eyes swept past the stacks of papers on the kitchen table, the pile of textbooks next to the bookshelf, and the computer desk overfull with the odds and ends of his job as a high school teacher.

"Sorry about the mess," Justin said, deeply mortified that he had failed to clean up before going out. He rarely, if ever, brought someone home from the club, so he never gave the mess a second thought.

"Don't worry about it," Spencer said. He stepped over Justin's briefcase to get to the couch. "I'm just glad to be inside."

Justin sighed. His place was a dump and didn't look like a gay man inhabited it. Not only were his belongings strewn about, but the décor was pathetic, something Xavier commented on at length whenever he visited. Justin always ignored Xavier's complaints, chalking them up to the ramblings of a prissy queen, but now that he surveyed his surroundings through Spencer's eyes, he wished he had listened to Xavier.

His green floral couch was dated by at least two decades. Brown, splotchy carpet met cracked linoleum kitchen tile at the boundary between the living room and the kitchen. Justin told his guests the stains on the carpet were from a previous resident's toddler, but Justin wasn't so sure that was the truth. He'd be happy to never know what the stains were and gave them a wide berth whenever he crossed the room.

An old wooden entertainment center sat askew in the living room; it had been in his bedroom at home since he was ten, and his mother gave it to him when he moved out of the house. Next to the entertainment center leaned a dusty plastic ficus tree. No pictures adorned the walls, which were hospital white, and a secondhand pine coffee table squatted on wobbly legs in the center of the room. On the coffee table were various gay publications like *Out* and a couple of skin magazines with bare-assed models adorning the covers.

Justin instantly ran to the coffee table to hide the porn underneath the other papers and bills littered across it. "Sorry," he apologized again. "I wasn't expecting company."

"Obviously," Spencer said, laughing. When he laughed, his eyes sparkled a vibrant green. Justin had to fight the urge to take Spencer in his arms right there. "Like I said, don't worry about it. I have my messy moments in life."

Justin didn't believe Spencer for one second. Just by looking at his well-groomed hair and perfectly manicured fingernails, he seriously doubted Spencer lived in anything less than a spectacularly spotless residence. The realization only furthered his embarrassment.

"I have the same magazines at my place too," Spencer said, nodding to the now hidden porn. "I just keep them in my bedroom closet."

Justin blushed even though he had nothing to be embarrassed about. Porn was commonplace for men, especially gay men, but he wanted to make a good impression on Spencer. He didn't want Spencer to think he spent his evenings masturbating on the couch, even though he sometimes did.

From the corners of his eyes, Justin spotted a tissue box and a bottle of lotion lying on the carpet opposite from where Spencer was sitting. He quickly rushed to sit down while carefully moving the tissue and lotion out of sight.

There's no way he saw that, Justin thought. *He* can't *have seen that. Please, God, don't let him have seen that.*

"I keep *those* things in my nightstand," Spencer said.

"What?" Justin asked, hoping against hope Spencer wasn't referring to his jack-off paraphernalia.

Spencer nodded toward the opposite side of the couch, where Justin had hidden his supplies. "The lotion and the Kleenex," he said matter-of-factly. "Although I prefer using a towel for cleanup. Tissues stick to your junk and then you have to pick it off. I'm not a fan of that."

"I'm so embarrassed," Justin admitted. In shame, he hid his face in his hands. All he wanted now was to slink off and die in a corner. Although in his messy apartment, there might not *be* a corner to slink into. Due to his lack of tidiness, he had no other option but to sit there and accept Spencer's ridicule. "This isn't a great first impression. I'm sorry."

Spencer laughed again. Justin looked up from his hands to see his eyes once again flash a deep green. "Why are you apologizing?" Spencer asked. "Jacking off is a way of life. Plus, it's fun. It's nothing to be embarrassed about. I do it at *least* once a day."

Now, it was Spencer's turn to blush. His white skin flushed, as if two cherries were suddenly suspended from his cheekbones. To combat the reddening of his cheeks, he changed the subject. "Besides, this apartment wasn't the first impression."

"It wasn't?" Justin asked. He was curious as to how this apartment could be anything *less* than a mood killer.

"Nope," Spencer answered, scooting closer to Justin on the couch. "The midnight kiss was the first impression. *That* one was a doozy. Best first impression ever."

"You really think so?" Justin asked, closing the gap on the couch between them.

"Yes," Spencer whispered. "In fact, I think it's time for a second impression." He then leaned in for a kiss.

If possible, this kiss was even better than the first. The one a couple of hours ago, at midnight on New Year's Eve, had been magical. Fanfare and confetti followed it; it was a herald of more to come. More intimate, more personal, and more seductive, this kiss held more than passion, which was overflowing—it also contained a hope for something more. It burned as an all-consuming flame, threatening to reduce their clothes to cinder if they didn't discard them immediately.

He had no choice but to pull away from their kiss, and as Spencer's sweet-tasting lips still lingered on his tongue, his fingertips blazed a trail down the soft fabric of Spencer's shirt. In response, Spencer's breathing quickened and he shivered. When Justin arrived at Spencer's waist, he untucked the green polo from Spencer's jeans and yanked the shirt free of his creamy skin.

While Justin's right hand caressed the lines of Spencer's face, from his cheeks to his clean-shaven chin, Justin's left hand traveled along his smooth chest. He traced a path across Spencer's lean but toned pecs, running his fingertips over the sensitive nipples. He rolled one between his index and forefinger, urging the flesh to harden.

Spencer bit his lip and his breathing became labored, so Justin increased the pressure, tweaking the nipple roughly, which caused Spencer to squirm and whimper. When Spencer started thrusting his pelvis against his leg, Justin knew it was time.

He pounced on top of Spencer, and they fell backward onto the couch. Their tongues resumed their incessant wrestling match, slipping and sliding within the hot confines of the other's wet lips. Justin then worked his way from Spencer's mouth to his neck, where he lapped at the salty skin, teasing Spencer with quick flicks of his tongue that caused him to moan and buck his pelvis harder against Justin's raging hardness.

"You're driving me crazy," Spencer whispered, his voice thick with passion.

"I'm just getting started."

He lifted Spencer's right arm, exposing the light blond bush of armpit hair for the first time. The sight of the soft coating of fur sent Justin's passion into overdrive. He dove right into the musky pit and inhaled deeply, savoring the heady aroma of man scent that had accumulated over hours of bar hopping and dancing. For him, man smell was the most powerful aphrodisiac in the world, and he liked nothing better than burying his face in it and savoring it all. His tongue instinctively darted outward, twirling through the hair and savoring the intoxicating blend of sweat and musk.

"Fuck!" Spencer shouted, mad with desire. He sat upright, tugging Justin's shirt from his body and then jerking his jeans downward in two quick motions.

"Fuck is right," Justin responded as he speedily unfastened Spencer's belt and tossed it into the ficus. Spencer's jeans soon joined the belt, dangling precariously from a branch of the fake tree. Bare-chested and only in their underwear, their hands developed minds of their own, pinching nipples, running through hair, and venturing down to the straining fabric of their briefs.

They forced their erections together, dueling their swords in the most primal of conflicts. Even through the fabric, he felt waves of heat emanating from Spencer's groin, and the weight of his engorged rod against his own threatened to drive him mad.

Spencer freed Justin from his Unicos first, taking his cock in his warm hands while slowly jacking him to a hardness his body had previously only reached at the dawn of puberty. Justin slid Spencer's briefs down his lean thighs, and Spencer's thick manhood bobbed before him. He longed to take Spencer into his mouth, to feel the thick head of his cock nudge the back of his throat, but he had yet to have his fill of Spencer's bare body against his.

Justin pushed Spencer back onto the couch, where he once again fell on top of him, grinding their pelvises together and forcing their stiff pricks to slide in the sweat that coated their bodies. Looking down at Spencer, he realized he couldn't get enough of him, something that hadn't happened to him in years. Spencer's white skin radiated like heavenly light against his dark flesh. Once again, like a kitten at a milk bowl, Justin drank covetously, as if Spencer's naked flesh quenched a raging thirst never before satiated. It was creamy smooth, and a meal he could feast on for hours.

He dove into Spencer's neck again, which drove Spencer wild, eliciting countless groans. His body shuddered with pleasure as Justin nibbled at the delicate flesh just under the right ear lobe. His hair smelled of pomegranate and mango. While Justin feasted on Spencer's neck, inhaling the intoxicating scent, Justin's left hand caressed Spencer's smooth face then ran through his sandy locks while his right hand kneaded a handful of Spencer's well-toned butt.

Spencer went just as wild. He rubbed up and down Justin's back and then clawed down to his ass. His touch set Justin's passions roaring. When Spencer slapped his ass, the sting stoked the flames higher, but when his finger ran down Justin's crack until finally arriving at the warm center, his fervor reached temperatures far hotter than the sun.

Justin left Spencer's neck and returned to ardently kissing his lips. Their tongues played in each other's mouths, probing farther than either had ever gone before.

"We need to stop before we go any further," Spencer said breathlessly, hesitantly pulling away from their eager kisses. "I have to tell you something first."

"Stop?" Justin asked, not believing what he was hearing. "I don't think I could if I tried." He left Spencer's lips and proceeded to his nipples. "We can talk later," he said while he licked the small, delicate pink areola of the right nipple, which slowly hardened as he brought the sensitive skin to life. Spencer moaned and his hips bucked upward. The firmness that rested against Justin's stomach turned steel hard.

"Please, we need to talk," Spencer begged as Justin kissed his way down from Spencer's chest to his smooth stomach.

Justin darted his tongue inside Spencer's hairless navel, causing more body tremors and words of protest. Spencer kept asking him to stop but his body told Justin to continue. Something he planned on doing.

After teasing Spencer's belly button, Justin trailed his tongue down to Spencer's neatly trimmed crotch. Again, the musky aroma invigorated him. Justin shoved his nose into Spencer's bush and inhaled deeply, taking in the smell of the night's sweat and the cologne modestly sprayed in the area before going out. The spit from his insistent tongue matted hair against bare flesh.

Finally, he moved down enough to once again see Spencer's manhood. At an impressive eight inches, it throbbed in his hand, which strained to encircle its girth. Justin's salivating mouth told him he had to taste it immediately.

But before he had a chance to sample it, Spencer yelled for him to stop and pushed Justin away.

"I'm positive!" Spencer exclaimed.

Justin sat on his haunches on the sofa cushion while Spencer rose from the couch.

"What are you positive about?" Justin asked, very confused and extremely frustrated.

"You're not listening to me," Spencer told him. "I'm *positive*."

Justin still had no idea what Spencer was referring to. *Was he positive about wanting to stop? Or talk?*

When he looked into Spencer's panicked, wide eyes, realization slowly dawned.

Spencer's positivity wasn't an emotional state; it was a medical condition.

CHAPTER 7

2010

JUSTIN lost track of time. He had no idea how long he knelt on the floor inside the house he'd owned with Spencer for the past seven years. When Spencer walked out the front door, leaving it standing open, as he often did when he took out the trash or checked the mailbox, Justin found his body incapable of movement.

He simply waited for Spencer to reenter the house, and his life, like a loyal canine anticipating the return of its master. Staring at the door for long intervals, he dared not even blink for fear of missing the exact moment when Spencer once again crossed the threshold.

Sitting there, his mind flew back to the first time he saw Spencer at the Bonham. He relived each moment as if New Year's Eve 1999 were only yesterday. Instead, ten years had passed, and those years had brought changes Justin never imagined when he and Spencer took the first steps down the path of their life together.

He expected disagreements and upheavals, common events in a committed life between two people. Not once did he anticipate adultery and estrangement.

How did we get here? he wondered. To Justin, their relationship had changed too swiftly for a reason to be easily found. One minute they were immensely happy, fawning over each other incessantly. The next moment, a chasm opened between them, and they were clueless how to bridge it.

No, you *were clueless,* he reminded himself. Spencer was guiltless of all crimes. This was *his* doing. No one else's. The blame was his burden alone. Accepting that might be the first step to getting Spencer back.

"I'm to blame," he announced to the house, as if speaking the words out loud to the furniture and their possessions somehow equated with confessing to a priest. "I messed up, and I'll do whatever it takes to get him back."

Looking around the room, Justin hoped for some sign of absolution, willing the twin reclining leather back chairs, or the television armoire, or even the PS3 to suddenly come to life and accept his act of contrition.

They didn't move. They simply sat in quiet condemnation.

What now? he asked himself.

How about getting off your ass and finding him? a voice from deep within answered. He wasn't sure, but it sounded like his mother, chiding him. The only problem was his mother never cursed.

Oh, I curse all right, his mother's voice said. *I just never have in front of you, but since you're approaching forty, I figure you're old enough to hear it. Now move!*

Justin rose from his kneeling position quickly. A command from his mother was always to be obeyed. *But I don't know what to do,* he told his mother. *Spencer left me.*

Not yet, he hasn't. He's just left. If you don't do something about it soon, then he'll really be gone. Is that what you want?

He shook his head.

Then find him.

Where do I look?

You know him better than anybody. Where would he go?

His mother was right. He *did* know Spencer better than anyone else, and there was one person whom they would both go to in a time like this.

Justin ran to the kitchen, where he'd left his cell phone. He brought the phone to life by hitting the home button and dialed the number on his contact list. When a groggy voice answered after the fourth ring, he asked, "Is Spencer there?"

Tyler Scott was Justin and Spencer's best friend. He had been their best friend for five years, after wresting the title from both Xavier and Alex, whom they rarely spoke to anymore. Like most of their single friends, Xavier and Alex only hung out with *other* single gays. To them, *partnered* gays were too reminiscent of the heterosexual establishment that wanted to oppress the freedom of being gay.

In reality, jealousy over their relationship was the most likely cause of their now distant friendships.

Tyler was different than most gay men. He despised the club life and preferred quiet nights at home, watching movies and playing games. He and Justin had met through a mutual fag hag at least a year before Justin and Spencer met. He and Tyler had even hooked up on and off before

Spencer's entrance into his life. There was even a time when Justin thought he might have been in love with Tyler.

That was then. Tyler was now the closest thing to a brother Justin had and even better than the brother Spencer *actually* had. If there were anyone Spencer would have gone to, it was Tyler.

"Spencer?" Tyler asked, his voice heavy with sleep. It was still very early in the morning. "No, he's not here. Did y'all get into a fight?" As always, Tyler's thick Texan accent made Justin smile, even when he didn't feel like smiling.

"Yeah," he told Tyler. He had no intention of divulging the full details at the moment. At some point, he would tell Tyler everything, but now wasn't the time. He needed to find Spencer, to convince him to come home. "You sure he's not there? You're not lying for him, are you?"

"I don't lie," Tyler told him, which was true. Not only did Tyler not lie, he was awful at it when he tried. That was why no one ever told him what presents were purchased for Christmas or birthdays. If he knew, he would tell. He just couldn't help himself.

"I've got to find him." Justin couldn't believe he was wrong. Tyler was the obvious person Spencer would seek out.

"Wait," Tyler said. "What's going on?"

The concern in his friend's voice was apparent, and Justin desperately wanted to talk, to find some solace within another person, and in that solace feel less alone, less frightened. But he didn't have the time for such luxuries. This wasn't about what Justin needed. This was about what he *and* Spencer needed to salvage their relationship. "I can't talk about it right now. I need to find him."

"I can go looking if you want. I'll drive around town and see if I can spot his car."

Tyler's offer made Justin love him even more. He was lucky to have such a good friend in Tyler. Tyler would offer the shirt off his back, even if he had no other shirts to wear. Tyler rarely thought of himself and was the first to arrive whenever a crisis occurred in someone's life. He was a friend to all, even when they didn't deserve him or his friendship.

"Thanks, but I need to do this," Justin said. "It's my mess. I have to clean it up."

"Okay, babe," Tyler told him. "Babe" was Tyler's term of endearment for those he loved. It applied to boyfriends *and* best friends. "I'm here if y'all need to talk, or I can come to you. Okay?"

Justin thanked Tyler for the offer and promised to call him later.

When he hung up the phone, Justin was at a loss. If Spencer wasn't at Tyler's, where would he be? Spencer's parents lived in Universal City, which was on the outskirts of San Antonio, but there was no way Spencer would go there.

Are you sure? his mother's voice asked.

Yes, he answered unequivocally. Spencer's parents weren't exactly welcoming of the gay lifestyle. They were cordial to Justin, but definitely not warm. Whenever Justin and Spencer visited them or his parents came over to their house, their attitude was frigid at best. They were uncomfortable with anything not Republican, military, or white. To have a gay son who was a Democrat and living with a Latin male was more than they could handle.

Spencer's brother Brandon wasn't stationed in San Antonio at the moment, but even if he were, Spencer wouldn't go there. Brandon and Spencer had a general loathing for each other born from a childhood disagreement that had ended in Brandon's broken bone.

Where else, then? his mother asked.

Carolyn, he answered. Spencer's younger sister Carolyn lived in Alamo Heights, a more affluent neighborhood within the city. Spencer and Carolyn weren't super close, but she was the person in his family whom he was the closest to. It was possible he might be at her house.

Anything's possible, his mother said doubtfully.

Justin decided he had to call Carolyn and find out, even though it was approaching five in the morning.

She answered on the second ring.

"Carolyn, it's Justin," he said into the phone.

"Justin?" she asked, as if she had no clue who he was. Her voice wasn't sleepy like Tyler's. Obviously, Carolyn had been awake. Spencer might just be there after all.

"Spencer's partner," he told her in slight aggravation.

"Ah, yes, Spencer's *friend*," she said with a hint of venom. She wasn't accepting of their relationship either, but she was the only one in the Harrison clan to make an iota of an effort to get along. Although at this moment, she wasn't making much of an effort at all. For Justin, that meant Spencer was indeed there.

"Is Spencer there?"

"Why in the world would he be here?" she asked him. "It's five in the morning, and no time for social calls or *any* calls, for that matter."

Justin didn't believe her. She typically had an abrasive personality but right now she was coarser than fresh sandpaper. "I don't believe you."

Carolyn cackled into the phone. "Well, I don't give a good hot damn what you believe."

This was getting him nowhere. Continuing to verbally spar with Carolyn wasn't getting him closer to finding Spencer. He needed to change tactics, appeal to her emotional side, if she had one. "We had a fight," he told her. "He was really upset. I just want to make sure he's okay. If I could just speak with him—"

"I already told you," she interrupted him. "He's. Not. Here."

Justin's anger got the better of him. "I know he's there because you're being even bitchier than usual. Which means you know what's going on. Now stop being such a fucking cunt and put him on the phone."

"Awwww," she said, mocking him. "You've finally grown a pair. You're usually so *damn* nice, going out of your way to impress me or Mom and Dad. It never works, you know. Mom and Dad hate you. And me? I've only been nice to you for Spencer. When he kicks you to the curb, and it sounds like this one might finally do it, I'll be happy to never have to see you again." Over the phone, he heard the flick of Carolyn's lighter as she lit herself a cigarette. "How's *that* for being a fucking cunt?"

Justin definitely didn't have time for this. "Thanks for being *so* helpful."

"I would say anytime," she replied, "but I wouldn't mean it."

Justin ended the call without further response.

That could've gone better, his mother said.

Ignoring his mother's assessment of the phone call, Justin thought through the situation.

Carolyn was a dead end after all. Spencer wasn't there, he could feel it, but she definitely knew more than she was letting on. Spencer might have called her, but she most likely pissed him off with her judgmental and holier-than-thou attitude.

Where would you *go?* his mother asked.

Justin was at a loss. Having already tried the two obvious answers and failed, he had no clue where Spencer might have gone.

Listen to my words, she said. *Where would* you *go?*

He thought about her words. If the situation was reversed and Spencer had an affair with someone *he* knew, the first place he'd go would be to confront the *other* man.

"Methodist Hospital," Justin mumbled to the quiet house. "He went to see Dutch."

Immediately, he dashed into the hallway, found his keys, and headed for the garage. Although he didn't know what he would say when he found Spencer, he knew finding him was the only hope they had to repair what he had destroyed.

CHAPTER 8

2000

FOR a few minutes after Spencer's revelation of his HIV-positive status, Justin sat in stunned silence, uncertain what to say or do. He needed to say something; anything was better than the awkward quiet that slowly consumed their previous passion.

"When did you find out you were HIV positive?" Justin asked Spencer. He aimed for a casual tone. He wanted it to sound as if he had no problem with learning Spencer had a dangerous virus coursing through his bloodstream. From the blank look on Spencer's face, he wasn't successful.

Spencer stood up from the couch and reached for his underwear. He pulled them on and then sat back on the couch, sighing heavily. "I don't do pity," he announced while he snatched his jeans and belt from the ficus.

"I'm sorry," Justin told him. Pity definitely was a far cry from his casual intentions, and he never intended to offend Spencer. Surprise merely got the better of him, strangling and twisting his words.

No, he knew that was wrong. Surprise merely revealed his genuine emotion, and it *was* pity. Being HIV positive wasn't exactly something people hoped for. It was a potentially dangerous virus, and the stigma it carried in society was quite the burden on the individual.

Justin had only met one other person who was HIV positive, at least that he knew. His name was Ritchie. They'd met at The Bonham about four years ago. They went out on a date a week after they met, and Ritchie told him about his HIV status over dinner. The rest of the night was uncomfortable, to say the least. Justin tried to be nonchalant about it, but the news had bothered him a great deal.

The only thing he'd thought about during dinner was Ritchie's condition. It lingered over the evening like a nuclear cloud just after detonation. It reduced the conversation to mindless chitchat, and after dinner, Justin lied that he had an early morning class. He and Ritchie went their separate ways, and he never spoke to him again.

He saw Ritchie every now and then at the club, but they never acknowledged each other.

It must have been hard on Ritchie to be so quickly rejected because of his status. Justin had felt ashamed about his treatment of Ritchie *before* meeting Spencer. Now, it made him feel even worse.

"Don't worry about it. It happens all the time," Spencer said while pulling his shirt down over his body. The quick, jerky motions revealed Spencer's anger and disappointment. He was almost completely dressed while Justin still squatted, naked, on the couch. He wanted to put clothes on too, but his muscles remained paralyzed.

"Are you leaving?" he asked Spencer.

"Well, yeah," he answered. "Nothing ruins the mood like learning your trick could kill you if you had sex with him."

"There are such things as condoms," Justin responded.

Spencer stopped dressing with only one sock left to put back on. "True," he said. "So," he began, drawing out the "o" for longer than was needed, "why don't you go get one of those bad boys and slap it on? Or better yet, let *me* slap it on. I *am* versatile. I'm not some Nelly bottom."

Though Justin understood the resentment, he didn't appreciate it. He'd never meant to be rude or insensitive. He was simply shocked. It wasn't every day someone admitted they were HIV positive. "Why are you mad at me?" Justin asked.

Spencer exhaled, his anger slowly vacating with the air in his lungs. "I'm not," he admitted. "And I apologize for taking it out on you." He pulled on his last sock and then slid his feet into his black tennis shoes. "I'm just tired of being rejected. It's not your problem, really, and I hold no grudge against you."

Spencer's jade eyes lost their sparkle, as if Justin had somehow removed the light from within that set them ablaze. It made him feel awful. "I wasn't rejecting you," Justin replied.

Spencer's face showed complete surprise. His eyes widened and his eyebrows arched like a McDonald's sign.

Justin meant what he said. He wasn't rejecting Spencer, not the way he did Ritchie. But he wasn't rejecting him out of pity or out of some misplaced notion to right the wrongs inflicted upon Spencer. His reasons transcended such courtesy and were quite simple.

When he saw Spencer at the club, there was something about him that drew Justin to him. It was a force he was powerless against. That meant something, and he knew it. It was the universe's way of telling him Spencer was meant to be in his life.

Justin never went against such signs.

"So," Spencer said, again drawing out the "o," which Justin found quite charming, "what does that mean?" He sat back on the couch, arms crossed, the universal sign of a defensive posture.

Justin thought carefully about his words and his tone. He likely only had one chance to get this right. "Well, you mentioned your status," Justin said. "In the middle of what was going to be a pretty hot experience. I figured we better talk about it, since, you know, you *did* bring it up."

Spencer's face no longer betrayed his emotions. His anger, along with all the emotions previously displayed, appeared to have been sucked back inside and replaced with indifference. "I had to," Spencer said. "I couldn't in good conscience sleep with you without you knowing."

Justin somehow knew this was only a partial truth. There was more behind Spencer's revelation than he seemed willing to admit. But calling him on it wouldn't pull Spencer out from behind his walls. He needed a gentle approach.

"You could have," Justin pointed out. "We would've eventually gotten to the condoms. I don't bareback, just so you know." Justin expected some acknowledgment of his safe-sex practices, but got none. Spencer's fortified walls allowed no emotions to proceed beyond the constructed barriers. "We could've had sex, and you could've left guilt-free."

"Is that the way you prefer it?" Anger fired from within the barricade in an unanticipated salvo. Justin saw it for what it was, though. Spencer was merely defending himself from further hurt. "Do you prefer your tricks to just cum and go?"

Justin laughed, and the laughter seemed to take Spencer by surprise. He watched as Spencer visibly wrestled with securing the emotion back behind his confines. "I'm not a prude," he told Spencer. "I've had tricks that have left immediately after, and I was happy for them to just go. Sometimes, all you want is to get off and then get out."

Spencer grunted in response, as if Justin had just admitted to being a man slut looking only for no-strings-attached sex.

"I was kinda hoping this might not be one of those times, though."

"Why not?" Spencer asked. His eyes sparkled once before he blinked them back into submission.

Justin wanted to tell him about the feeling at the club. How he felt magically drawn to him, as if someone had cast a spell that suddenly removed everyone else from the room except the two of them. He wanted to explain that he'd felt an immediate connection to him, a connection he had never felt before, not even with someone he had dated for months.

But that would be too weird.

There was only one answer Justin could give that was both honest and not creepy. "It was the kiss."

Spencer nodded. He obviously felt it too.

"It was an amazing kiss, the best one I've ever experienced. You don't just let an awesome kisser get away that easily," Justin admitted.

Slowly, the Spencer he had previously met drifted back to the surface. "I do like a good kisser," he admitted. "There's nothing worse than a fish mouth or a snake tongue."

Justin laughed. "I know exactly what you mean. Those fish-mouth kissers are the worst! Laying there with their mouths open like a fish out of water. It's pretty gross."

"Snake tongues are the ones I can't stand," Spencer said, a twinkle returning to his eyes. "Give me a fish mouth any day. Why those guys think darting their tongues in and out of anyone's mouth like that is sexy is beyond me!"

Their shared laughter felt good. The previous tension evaporated, and Spencer's walls crumbled.

When their laughter finally subsided, Justin felt uncomfortable. He was completely naked while Spencer was completely dressed.

"I guess I should put some clothes on," he said while finally standing up.

"I would rather you didn't," Spencer said.

Justin looked down at Spencer, confused. "Why not?"

"Do you still want to discuss *it*?"

There was no need for Spencer to clarify the pronoun.

"Only if you do," Justin said.

"Sure," he said. Spencer's unease returned, but the walls weren't resurrected. "But talking about it always makes me feel pretty vulnerable. If, you know, we discuss it while you're naked, you'd be just as vulnerable as me. At least to my insane mind."

Spencer attempted a laugh, but his laughter only showed how uncomfortable he now was at the prospect of discussing such a personal topic. Justin sympathized. He hated to be vulnerable. He preferred the upper hand. But this wasn't about him. This was about Spencer.

"Naked it is, then," Justin said while sitting back down on the couch.

Spencer smiled at Justin. His smile communicated gratitude as well as relief that Justin hadn't made fun of his request.

"So," Spencer began, yet again drawing out the vowel sound, "where do we begin?" He looked nervously around the room.

"Why don't we start with my initial question?" Justin asked. "When did you find out you were positive?"

"Four years ago," Spencer answered after a moment's hesitation. "Ironically enough, I was trying to get additional life insurance coverage. My father had been on my back to get more than what I had through work. I hadn't really thought about life insurance much. You know, I was young, dumb, and full of cum, as they say."

Spencer's nerves rattled him. His speech patterns quickened and his hands moved about wildly, unsure of where they should settle.

Justin reached out with his right hand and lightly rested it on top of Spencer's left hand, which had been nervously grasping at the couch fabric. Spencer immediately calmed at his touch.

"Well, my dad was in the army," Spencer continued. He held onto Justin's pinkie finger for the support he needed to get through the story. "A lieutenant colonel. USAA is a good insurance company, according to him. I already had them for auto insurance, so I figured I'd just bite the bullet and get life insurance through them too. I called and set up a time for their nurse or whatever to come over. They had to ask me questions, run some tests, and draw blood."

"That's how you found out?" Justin asked. "Through the insurance company?"

Spencer nodded. Sadness reflected in his green eyes. "I got a letter from them, telling me they were denying me life insurance and for me to go see my doctor. I called them to ask why, but they wouldn't tell me. They said it was really important for me to go see my doctor and for him to run blood work. Once they told me that, I knew what it was."

For a few minutes, they sat in silence. Spencer needed time to recover, as evidenced by his sweaty brow. Justin also needed time to process. Justin imagined how lonely Spencer must have felt at that moment, not only learning he was sick but finding out without anyone there to comfort him. He must have felt lost in the deepest recesses of space.

"What happened then?" Justin asked after an appropriate interval of quiet.

Spencer exhaled, mustering his reserves to proceed with his story. "I went online and found a county-run STD clinic that offered free and anonymous tests. I took the test the next day and the following week I learned I was positive. They sent me to an HIV specialist in the area. He ran some blood work and told me my white blood cell count was one hundred and that my viral load was pretty high."

Justin wasn't an expert on HIV, but as a gay man, he felt it was his duty to have some basic knowledge. With such a low white blood cell count, Spencer was pretty sick at that time. The average person typically had a count of five hundred or more. At the time he found out he was positive, Spencer's immune system was failing. This meant he was open to opportunistic infections that were life-threatening. He was lucky to still be alive.

"Is that usual?" Justin wondered. "For someone's white blood cells to be so low when they first find out?"

"I don't know," Spencer answered. "I guess so, but I'd apparently been sick for about three years."

"Three years?" Justin said, unable to believe someone could be sick that long without knowing it.

"I know. It was hard for me to believe too," Spencer added. "My previous sexual partners had to be contacted and tested. I was mortified, but the county promised that my information would never be given out. Anyone who was contacted would only be told that they had been intimate with someone who tested HIV positive, and that it would be imperative for them to get tested too."

"Did they?"

"I assume so," Spencer said. "I never checked on them. I guess that was pretty chickenshit of me, huh?" With his eyes cast downward, Spencer resembled a child seeking forgiveness.

Justin squeezed Spencer's hand reassuringly. "You were going through a lot at that time. You needed to take care of yourself," he said. "Besides, it's not like you *willingly* set out to infect anyone. Someone had infected *you*, and *you* had no idea. It was only right for them to know *they* needed to get checked."

Justin's pardon caused a smile to form on Spencer's lips in obvious appreciation. He then wondered if Spencer had ever shared this much of his story with anybody else prior to this evening. That, however, was a conversation for another day.

"Did you ever find out who infected you?"

Spencer's cheeks immediately flushed red, as if he were an angry chameleon displaying his fury for all to see. "Yes," he said. "I did the math. It was my college boyfriend at Rice. Mike Lane. We were together for two years in college. We were pretty serious, at least *I* thought we were." His eyes, though aflame with resentment, also looked to be tinted with a grave sadness. "He apparently cheated on me throughout our last year together. Spent a lot of time at the bathhouses from what I've heard too. He most likely picked it up there. He loved getting fucked, so I imagine he was offering up his ass to any guy who was walking around in a towel and with a hard-on."

"Did you confront him?" Justin asked, his own anger swelling at Spencer's ex-boyfriend. He found Mike Lane's actions inexcusable and wanted to seriously hurt the man for wounding Spencer.

"I went looking for him to do just that," he told Justin. "But when I called his house, I found out he had died the previous year. His mother didn't tell me from what, but I think it was pretty obvious."

Justin nodded in agreement. He didn't know what else to do. He couldn't even imagine the depths of Spencer's hurt and betrayal. He had spent the majority of his twenties dealing with issues most people went their whole lives without experiencing. For Spencer to still be so full of life, as he'd seen reflected in those beautiful green eyes when they first kissed, drew Justin even closer to him.

"What about now? How are you doing healthwise?"

"Pretty good," Spencer answered. "It was rough for a while. I was pretty sick and it took my system some time to adjust to the medicines, but it did. Obviously, I'll always be HIV positive, at least till they find a cure." His voice contained such hope that Justin couldn't help but wish one would be found soon. "But my regimen has been good. My viral load is undetectable, and my white blood cell count is almost four hundred."

"That's pretty close to normal," Justin said.

Spencer nodded. "My doctor says that as long as I keep taking my medicines and practice safe sex I have virtually no chance of infecting any sexual partners, since my viral load is undetectable."

For a few moments, they once again sat in silence. Spencer had opened up to him in a way that no one had ever done before, and Justin had a feeling doing so was unusual for him. Justin had never felt closer to another individual than he did to Spencer at that moment in time.

Like a balloon filled with helium, Justin released any previous fear he'd held onto about HIV. The virus was simply a virus. It wasn't who Spencer was; it was something he had. Being positive didn't make him a pariah or any less deserving of love or human contact. In fact, it made him more deserving.

More than ever, Justin wanted to once again relish in the feel of Spencer's skin against his body. His flesh yearned for it, and it called out to Spencer.

Spencer turned to him in response to Justin's unspoken desire.

Still naked and vulnerable, Justin moved over to sit closer to Spencer and reached out to caress his cheek. Once again, Spencer's body shuddered. Justin drew closer and kissed his cheek, then his chin, and finally his lips.

They both knew instinctively what the contact meant. This was no longer about sex. This was an offer. More than a simple fuck, their caresses acknowledged that something real existed between them. Somewhere between the midnight kiss at the Bonham and this moment, their souls had become intertwined.

"I've never wanted anyone more than I want you right now."

Spencer ran his fingers through the back of Justin's hair. "I've never wanted to give myself to anyone more than I do right now."

Without another word, Justin removed Spencer's clothes, piece by piece, and though he had already seen him naked, the sight of his smooth, white flesh and erect cock excited him as if this were his first time. Once undressed, he led Spencer to the bedroom, where he crawled onto the bed.

Justin maneuvered on top, hovering above Spencer but not yet touching his body. Even though he longed to feel Spencer against him again, he couldn't stop looking at the gorgeous man beneath him. A lustful fire blazed brightly behind Spencer's eyes. His blond hair, disheveled from their almost-sex on the couch, spread about his head in a ring of angelic light. And his skin, pure white and fragile, shook with anticipation, begging to be touched.

When Justin finally lowered himself onto Spencer, the breath left his body. Spencer immediately kissed him, breathing life back into him with his hot passionate exhales, and their tongues resumed their dance as if there had been no lapse to the music that brought them together.

Their rigid shafts slid between them, thrusting against the smooth flesh of the other and leaving trails of sticky juice across their stomachs. Spencer wrapped his legs around Justin's waist, grinding their pelvises more roughly together.

When Justin chewed on Spencer's neck, Spencer whimpered in delight. His hands immediately sought out Justin's ass and squeezed them tightly.

"You feel so good," Spencer told him.

"Not better than you," he replied breathlessly before gliding his tongue down from Spencer's neck past his nipples to the engorged piece of meat lying across his stomach. The last time he tried this, Spencer had stopped him. He knew there would be no stopping now.

He took Spencer's stiffness in his hand, gently moving the flesh up and down while teasing more liquid from the purple knob. Lightly, Justin flicked his tongue across the swollen glans, and even though no condom separated his lips from Spencer's leaking shaft, he savored the fluid before swallowing him whole. It wasn't the safest practice, but right now he needed to taste Spencer unencumbered, with nothing in between them.

Their souls had been laid bare, and for the moment so must their contact.

"Oh, God, yes!" Spencer exclaimed while clawing at the bedsheets. "Your mouth is so hot."

Justin nuzzled Spencer's cock all the way down to his pubic hair. When he inhaled, the musk of Spencer's sex filled his nostrils. Intoxicated by the scent, he slowly began to bob up and down on Spencer's manhood, using his tongue and throat to tickle and massage the throbbing member.

"Just like that," Spencer cooed. "You're so amazing."

While he worked Spencer in and out of his mouth, Spencer turned him around so he could sample Justin's cock. He massaged Justin's balls in one hand while the other rubbed his groin and inner thighs. The combination sent shockwaves throughout Justin's body. His cock became so hard it hurt, and sweat began to pour down his body.

When Spencer's hot mouth finally wrapped around him, he almost fainted. Spencer's tongue swirled around the head as he increased both suction and friction at the same time. He took the length of Justin down his throat, working his throat muscles in a sensual massage before pulling off and starting again, which was a dangerous combination.

"You're gonna make me come," Justin warned.

Spencer allowed Justin's dick to fall from his mouth and wiped the spit from his chin. "Not yet," he said. "You have to fuck me first."

Justin reached for the bedside table while Spencer positioned himself on his back. While he pulled out the condom and lube and made the necessary preparations, Spencer spread his legs and revealed his pink center. "This is where you belong," he whispered. "Inside me."

Unable to speak, Justin nodded in response before climbing between Spencer's legs. He held onto his sheathed cock, aiming it directly at the core of Spencer's being. He drew closer, then hesitated at the threshold, wanting to prolong the moment forever.

"Please," Spencer pleaded in a husky voice, and that was all Justin needed to hear. He pressed into him, parting his flesh and losing himself in the tight grip. Spencer whimpered, begging him to go deeper.

Within moments, Justin was firmly buried inside. They were now one.

He stared into Spencer's eyes as he slowly worked himself in and out of Spencer's hole. When he pulled outward, leaving only the head of his cock inside, Spencer's ass muscles tightened, drawing him back to the silky interior. When he was all the way in, when his balls rested against Spencer's crack, their bodies trembled.

They both teetered on the edge of climax.

"Do it," Spencer commanded. "Make us come."

Justin rose up, holding Spencer's legs in front of him by grasping him behind the knees. With Spencer's legs as his anchor, he began slowly thrusting in and out of Spencer before picking up the pace.

As he hammered away inside, Spencer jacked his hard cock, furiously matching his strokes to Justin's thrusts. Faster and harder he fucked. His lungs begged for air. His muscles ached from the strain of his animalistic pace, but he had no intention of stopping.

Whimpering beneath him, Spencer writhed in pleasure as Justin's every thrust obviously stimulated his pleasure button, bringing him ever closer to blowing his load.

Spencer grunted as his cock exploded thick ropes of cream, coating both their stomachs. As he climaxed, Spencer's ass contracted around Justin's dick, bringing him over the edge. With a final hard thrust, Justin groaned as he climaxed deep within Spencer.

Spent and exhausted, he collapsed. Spencer wrapped his arms around his chest and his legs around his waist. They held each other tightly, refusing to let the other go, as their rapidly beating hearts slowed to a joint rhythm.

CHAPTER 9

2010

PEERING through the men's room door, just outside the ICU of Methodist Hospital, Spencer's heart raced like Secretariat's during the last leg of the Kentucky Derby. All he could do now was wait for the night nurse to abandon her post, so he could sneak into Dutch's room.

What he would do once he actually made it in there hadn't been formulated yet. After he left home—no, he couldn't think of the house as home. Not any longer, not if he wished to maintain his strength *and* his sanity.

After he left *Justin's* house, he drove without purpose, without direction. He entertained the idea of heading to Tyler's, but that would not only be an imposition but also unfair. Tyler didn't deserve to be thrust in the middle of their dissolving union. Besides, that would likely be the first place Justin would look, and he had no intention of running into him today, tomorrow, or the foreseeable future.

He dismissed the idea of heading to his parents' house as quickly as it entered his mind. Carolyn was the next logical choice, and when he called her and woke her up, his sister had sounded too pleased to hear the distress Justin caused him. He had enough to deal with than to add her gloating to the mix.

That was when the idea hit him like a Mack truck doing ninety on the interstate. He needed to see Dutch, to confront him, to ask him *why,* after....

But he was getting ahead of himself. He needed to bide his time and wait for the right moment to strike.

I love it when you use my words, son, his father said, appearing like a wraith at his side. *Makes me damn proud.*

Ignoring his father, who never once had admitted in real life how proud he was of him, Spencer turned his attention back to the nurse. She busily typed away at the computer. The light from the screen cast dark shadows upon her thin, angular face. It twisted her features, making her look sadistic and cruel. More of a modern Nurse Ratched than Florence

Nightingale. All she needed was the white nurse's cap and the out of style page-boy cut. Instead, her hair was tightly pulled back into an even tighter bun.

What is it with you gays? Are you all experts on classic movies and hair? his father asked, completely disgusted. *You've lived a good ten years on the Hershey highway. Look where that's gotten you. A good wet pussy will cure what ails you. It always worked for me.*

Spencer's body shuddered at the thought of female genitalia and his father's obvious relish for the lady parts, a fact he'd never hidden from them as children, as adults, or in front of others. He found the entire topic disgusting and inappropriate for *any* situation. As he'd done on those occasions, he tuned out his father, focusing on the nurse instead.

You can pretend to ignore me all you want, son. You and I both know that at times like this, mine's the only voice you ever *listen to. Whether I'm talking about pussy or not. Hell, I'm the one who gave you your damned armor you always wore like a fucking Knight of the Round Table.*

The nurse rose from the computer and looked at her watch. Spencer hoped it was time for her rounds. Picking up a stack of metal charts, she rounded the desk and started in his direction. Spencer froze. With the men's room door ajar, she appeared to be looking at him. His mind spun stories about getting lost or looking for some made-up person, but when she turned around and went the opposite direction, he exhaled in relief.

She disappeared into one of the rooms on the far left side. When the door closed behind her, he cautiously stepped out of the men's room and into the dimly lit hallway. No one rushed at him, questioning his presence on the floor. He took that as a good sign and hurried past the nurse's station to read the name on the first patient's door on the right side of the hall.

R. Gonzales occupied this one, according to the handwritten label adhered underneath the room number. A quick run down the hall revealed rooms with L. Jefferson, C. Goldman, and P. Hunter within them.

Spencer worried he would be unable to find the room before the nurse reentered the hall to find him scurrying from door to door, or that Dutch's room was the one the nurse had entered. Finally, at the end of the hall, he located a room with L. Keller as its occupant.

He paused, his hand upon the door, wanting to open it but also wanting to vomit. His desire to see Dutch vanished. Seeing him would make everything more concrete, turn it into something that could obliterate the armor he once again wore.

Don't be a fucking sissy, his father said. *You came here with a purpose. Now see that purpose through. Just like you did when you broke your brother's arm.*

Spencer shoved the door open and entered the room.

Before him, Dutch lay on the hospital bed. Numerous tubes and lines extended from his sleeping body to the panel behind the bed and to the machines to the left and right. Spencer recognized the heart rate monitor and the IV drip, but the others were foreign to him, as if he were looking at equipment more extraterrestrial than man-made.

Dutch's lips were swollen and bloodied. Angry, red scabs spotted his face and blood-soaked gauze bandages clung to his chest, face, and arms, which disappeared beneath the cream-colored blanket.

The hospital gown was decorated with what appeared to be blue flowers of some unrecognizable variety, and the gown lay open and pulled down, revealing his broad shoulders and fur-matted chest. No tubes disappeared down his throat, and his chest rose and fell on its own, which meant that Dutch was breathing without assistance. Spencer took that as a good sign.

A good sign? His father balked. *This faggot fucked Justin. Or Justin fucked him. I never know how it works with you people.*

Shut up! he told his father. *Now's not the time.*

Now's the perfect time. He's asleep and defenseless. It's time for you to pay him back for what he did to you.

I have no idea what you're talking about. I'm not here to....

Don't pretend you're not here for payback. That's the only reason you're here. Hell, it's the only reason I'm here. You want this motherfucker to suffer for the pain he's caused you. I couldn't agree more. Find something to bash him over the head with. Or break one of those vases filled with flowers and plunge the glass into his stomach.

Spencer approached the bed and looked into Dutch's defenseless face. He couldn't lie. He wanted to hurt Dutch. He wanted to make him suffer and feel the devastation that he himself felt.

I told you, his father said, egging him on. *Now, do it before it's too late.*

He shook his head. It was already too late. Seeing Dutch like this, bruised and broken, seemed repayment enough.

Oh, for Christ's sake! his father bitched behind him.

Spencer didn't listen. His father's protests and curses drifted away, drowned out by the roar of time, which washed over him like a wave, dragging him back to the moment a little over a year ago, when he'd first met Dutch.

"Dr. Harrison, I'd like to introduce you to Dutch Keller."

Spencer looked up from the application he was reading, and when he saw Dutch, his breath caught in his throat. Dark-black hair cut short, most likely by a number four clipper blade, surrounded a ruggedly handsome face lined with a short boxed beard.

He mumbled his usual greeting, saved only for applicants being interviewed for a position on campus. Dutch responded, but Spencer never heard the words. Crystal blue eyes gazed from behind dark-rimmed glasses, and the hand that shook his was warm and strong. All he could think about were Dutch's eyes and hands.

"Please take a seat, Mr. Keller," someone to his left said. Spencer shook his head, trying to regain his composure. He realized Dr. Darcy was the one who spoke as she waved Dutch into the seat next to Spencer.

Dutch took his seat, opposite the department chair, Dr. Peggy Cutting, and to the left of Dr. Jeanette Darcy, Dean of Arts, Humanities, and Social Sciences.

Dr. Darcy, as always, kicked off the interview. She asked Dutch why he was interested in teaching as a photography adjunct for St. Mary's University, her standard first question.

Spencer never heard Dutch's reply or even most of the other answers during the interview. He participated when it was his turn to ask a question, as indicated when everyone was suddenly looking at him, but during the thirty-minute interview, Spencer couldn't halt the inappropriate thoughts playing in his mind.

He tried to force the images out by imagining a white board that, when erased, wiped his mind free of Dutch naked in bed.

When the enticing images faded, Justin came into the picture, smiling at him with that warm smile of his that always made Spencer's toes tingle. Picturing Justin made him feel guilty. He had been back only a few weeks, and they were in the process of rebuilding their relationship from the disastrous state they'd left it in before his departure for Europe.

His mind should only be imagining Justin, not some random man he'd just met. After all, they had both committed themselves to ironing out the problems that had driven them apart. That was why he couldn't understand what was happening to him.

For reasons incomprehensible to his rational mind, his primordial side burned his logic to the ground, and images of Dutch's bare flesh once again emblazoned themselves into his mind.

He felt dirty, as if the images somehow equated with being unfaithful to a relationship he'd recently rededicated himself to. Were these thoughts portents of the unavoidable demise of his relationship with Justin? Was this his subconscious mind's way of telling him the life he lived with Justin had effectively ended when he boarded that plane? Were the two of them simply delaying the inevitable?

"Thank you for your time," Dutch said, rising from his seated position. He shook everyone's hand, and when Dutch once again took Spencer's hand in his, the touch felt more like a convergence than a farewell.

"I must have somehow known," Spencer whispered to Dutch's unconscious form. "All this time, I thought I was to blame for those thoughts, for what happened later. But it wasn't me at all. I just somehow *knew* upon meeting you that you would lead to the end of me and Justin."

"Excuse me?" a voice from behind him said, filled with irritation. "Visiting hours don't begin until 9:00 a.m."

Spencer turned to face Nurse Ratched, whose face was still twisted into a sadistic snarl. "My apologies," he muttered and rushed out of Dutch's room.

In a matter of minutes, Spencer found himself standing next to his car. The warm August sun broke across the sky, but its presence didn't fill him with hope or joy. It served merely to remind him how dark his present had become.

He unlocked his car door and prepared to enter his vehicle, but as he stood there with the car door open, he saw Justin sprinting through the parking lot, barreling toward the hospital doors, no doubt anxious to reach Dutch's bedside.

You should've killed him when you had the chance, his father's voice said.

"A dead man can't kill," he told his father as his cold, lifeless hand turned the key in the ignition.

CHAPTER 10

2002

SPENCER had never been happier, more full of life than in the past two years with Justin. Their relationship grew serious rather quickly, which at first frightened the still tentative side of his personality. He preferred going slow, getting to know someone before deciding that love might be in the future. It was the way he'd handled all his previous relationships, dissecting every conversation or date in search of the character flaw that would ultimately cause the relationship to fail.

With Justin, none of that happened.

Justin wasn't perfect; he was quick-tempered, stubborn, and probably the messiest man he'd ever met. He was obsessed with childish items like comics, cartoons, and video games, but those traits never once caused Spencer to question his decision to shed his protective armor and welcome this man with open arms.

Instead, Justin was a gift he cherished daily.

A few months after meeting at the Bonham, Justin asked Spencer to move in with him. Spencer said yes, without ever once weighing the pros and cons of such a move. Not only was he surprised by his speedy consent, but so was Alex, who was vocal in his disapproval.

Since they had been roommates and best friends for the past two years, Alex believed he had some say in the decision. He appealed to Spencer's rational side, citing one reason after another for why the move was hasty or ill-conceived—they had only known each other a few months, a serious relationship might deter his dissertation progress, and, the point Alex believed to be the most persuasive, they were gay men, *not* lesbians.

Spencer couldn't refute his first two arguments. He simply ignored the last one, which was a stereotypical observation of lesbian relationships. Without a successful rebuttal, Alex claimed the argument won and therefore believed the matter closed.

When Spencer packed up his things and moved out the following week, Alex watched in disbelief.

Based on his time with Justin, Spencer learned love wasn't a logical argument that could be refuted or needed support by verifiable evidence. It simply existed, and one either chose to accept it or not.

Since accepting it, he'd never once regretted his decision to leap into the open air of a new relationship and leave the safety and security of his previous plane of existence.

Their love grew and adjusted, as all living organisms do, and their love *was* alive. They nurtured it together, adding or subtracting what it needed to maintain its health. And in their tender care, it grew to contain more than just them.

Justin's family became a welcomed part of their life. Spencer had never known a family so loving and so accepting of each other's faults. With them, he belonged in a way he never had in his own family, the people he actually shared a bloodline with. He finally understood the elation in other people's voices when they talked about their families with such unwavering love. That was the way he felt about Justin's family.

Their circle of friends also widened beyond Alex and Xavier, who started to feel left out and slowly withdrew from the overall picture. Tyler, a good friend of Justin's, was fast becoming an indispensable part of their lives. Tyler's partner Rene seemed like a good enough guy, but he remained aloof, like a German Shepherd trotting around the perimeter of the friendship, uncertain whether he wanted to join or attack.

They had other friends too, both gay and straight, Chris and Jill, Heather and Pat, Chuck and Don, and Teresa and Sam.

Overall, life was great socially as well as professionally.

Justin had been promoted to assistant principal, an accomplishment for a man in his late twenties, at one of the high schools within the San Antonio Independent School District. The district finally stood up and took notice of the great things Justin had accomplished not only in the classroom but also with the parents and the community.

After completing his dissertation and working as an adjunct instructor both online and at various local campuses, Spencer had been recently hired as an assistant professor of Spanish and French at St. Mary's University.

With stable jobs, they had a bright future ahead of them. A future that now included being homeowners.

When they first saw the house in the Monte Vista area of San Antonio, which was a mile from downtown and in the heart of one of the largest historical districts in the city, they didn't think they could afford it.

The asking price was quite steep, especially for two young men early in their careers.

The house wasn't much, but it had a lot of potential. Two bedrooms and one bath, a living room that was longer than it was wide, and a nice-sized dining room.

The kitchen excited Spencer the most and was the primary reason he fell in love with the house. As the cook in the relationship, a role he gladly assumed when he realized Justin's culinary talents included throwing ground meat and a can of beans into a pot, he demanded a house with a kitchen large enough to make nice meals. Abundant cabinet space and an open concept were required.

This kitchen met his needs. It even had a sliding glass door out to the small, bricked patio in the backyard.

The master bedroom had enough space for the king-sized bed they wanted but didn't have. Right now, Justin's old full-sized bed from their apartment was where they slept. They were in no hurry to buy the bigger bed; they enjoyed being close enough to cuddle.

The master bedroom even had a sitting room off to the right separated by two pocket doors. Spencer envisioned changing the pocket doors to paneled French doors, but they would have to wait a few years to afford that renovation.

An enormous old-fashioned claw-foot tub took up the majority of the space in the bathroom. Justin hated it since he preferred to shower. Spencer convinced him that taking baths together would be romantic. With so much room to move around, there would be no limit to their bath-time fun. Justin quickly conceded, but only after getting him to promise a bathroom renovation with a shower as an add-on to their master suite.

The second bedroom was down the hall from the bathroom and the master bedroom. It was cozy, with a good-sized window looking out into the backyard.

The lawn was adequate, neither too big nor too small.

For the two of them, it was perfect.

They crunched the numbers and decided if they scrimped and saved, they could afford a good down payment to help lower the monthly mortgage.

A few months after finding the house, they had purchased it and were moving in.

And, today, family and friends were helping them settle in.

"Where do y'all want this?" Tyler asked, carrying a box with KITCHEN written along the side.

"How about the kitchen?" Spencer responded. When Tyler disappeared into the kitchen, he chuckled silently to himself. While Tyler was a sweet man, he had a penchant for overlooking the obvious.

"Can we start unpacking stuff?" Jill asked, sitting on the living room floor with four boxes surrounding her. Teresa and Heather each held a box, awaiting his approval before tearing open their contents.

"That would be great," he told them while noticing two boxes in the living room with BATHROOM clearly marked on the side. He didn't need to ask who'd placed the boxes there. In his haste to unload the U-Haul, Justin simply deposited boxes helter-skelter instead of following the detailed plan Spencer had designed.

"I hope we find some good stuff in here," Heather snickered to Teresa and Jill.

"Oh, yeah," Teresa replied. "Like when we found Tyler's naughty drawer."

The three laughed in unison.

"All *our* naughty things are safely tucked in our suitcases," Spencer told them while picking up the boxes clearly marked for the bathroom. "I know how nosy you three get."

Teresa called him a spoilsport while Heather and Jill booed.

"Why are we booing?" Justin asked carrying a box labeled MASTER into the house.

"The girls are looking for our toys," replied Spencer. He watched as Justin set the box down in the living room.

"Not in the boxes," Justin told the girls, tapping his right index finger to the side of his head. "We're far too clever for your shenanigans."

"Justin Jimenez, I am just about at the end of my rope with you!" Spencer said, quoting Shirley MacLaine's Ouiser Bourdreaux from *Steel Magnolias*.

"Well, then, why don't you tie a noose and slip it 'round your head?" Justin replied, doing his best Tom Skerritt impersonation.

"Oh, God!" Chris said to Pat after walking into the house with two small boxes in his arms. "They're doing *Steel Magnolias* again!"

"What bothers me more is that we *know* it's from that damned movie!" replied Pat. "We need to do something manly to balance things out."

Chris nodded in agreement. Boxes still in hand, both of them scrunched up their faces and farted. The girls screamed in disgust while Justin laughed.

Spencer waved their toxic gases away from him as best he could. "Justin, *please* do what *everybody* else is doing and place the boxes you bring inside the house into the appropriate *designated* room."

"Yes, Dr. Harrison," replied Justin.

Spencer swatted him on his ass in response.

"Do it again," Justin said, sticking his behind out farther.

"Just go!" Spencer said, placing the two other misplaced boxes on top of the one Justin carried. Justin mumbled a complaint but then carted them to their appropriate locations.

A quick inspection of work detail told Spencer the move was progressing nicely. Justin, Tyler, Chris, and Pat were unloading the U-Haul, the girls were unpacking the living room, Chuck and Don were picking up lunch and beer, and Sam was in the backyard, keeping children entertained.

"Such a beautiful house," a voice said from behind him brimmed with pride. Without looking, Spencer knew who had arrived.

"Elena!" he exclaimed, rushing over to give Justin's mother a hug.

She returned the hug and kissed Spencer on the cheek. "I know you'll both be happy here for many years."

"Hello, Mrs. Jimenez," each of their friends said, greeting her with a hug and a smile.

"A house full of good friends too," she marveled. "My boys are *truly* blessed."

Whenever Elena said *my boys*, Spencer beamed. Those two words meant the world to him. He not only felt loved and accepted but claimed as one of her children. It was an honor he always hoped he lived up to.

"*Mama!*" Justin exclaimed upon reentering the living room. They exchanged hugs and kisses. "Thanks for coming to help."

"Where else would I be?" she asked, shrugging her shoulders and turning her palms up, something she did every time she asked a rhetorical question. The gesture always made him grin. "Now, put me to work. What do you want me to do?"

"Careful, Mom," Justin said, putting his arm around Spencer. "Spence is quite the taskmaster. He's been cracking the whip."

"What you boys do when you're alone is none of my business," his mother deadpanned. Her comment caused the house to explode in laughter.

"Mother!" Justin exclaimed. His cheeks turned several shades of red. Justin was the only Latino Spencer knew who blushed like a white boy.

"Is Olga coming?" Spencer asked, swooping in and changing the conversation.

"Yes," Elena responded, apparently annoyed. "That woman could drive the pope to murder with all her chatter. We better get lots accomplished before she gets here."

Everyone laughed since they had all experienced Justin's Aunt Olga. She was a very sweet woman, who loved to talk and who talked nonstop from the moment of arrival to the last second of departure. Even as she drove away, her lips moved. The conversation, which was really always more of a monologue, continued whether anyone was there to hear her or not.

To Olga, no subject was off-limits. Her hemorrhoids. Her husband's missing testicle, removed due to cancer. Her irritable bowel, a family trait Justin had unfortunately inherited, and one she constantly discussed at every shared meal.

"Is Uncle Ricky coming?" Justin asked while helping Jill open a box marked VIDEOS.

Justin's Uncle Ricky was a truck driver for H-E-B, the popular Texas grocery store chain. Often out of town making deliveries, he missed many family gatherings.

"No," she answered. She now sat on a chair, brought to her by Chris, and worked on opening one of the boxes in the living room. "He's driving to Corpus, Beeville, and Goliad today."

"That's too bad," Spencer said. He picked up packing popcorn and started shoving the numerous pieces into a trash bag he'd left in the room for that specific purpose.

"Eh," Justin's mother responded with a shrug. "He needs the money. Plus, he's lazy. He'd be more trouble here than anything else."

"What about Gran and Gramp?" Justin asked. His grandparents typically didn't miss a single event involving the family. While unpacking was a mundane task for most families, for Justin's, it was a chance to get together.

"Your grandparents are coming," Elena replied. "They're picking up Snookums at the vet."

"They're bringing Snookums?" Justin exclaimed. "Why?"

"You know how much your grandfather loves that dog."

Snookums was an overweight Chihuahua who weighed at least thirty pounds. Never before had Spencer seen such a typically lightweight dog grow to such massive proportions.

Justin's grandfather fed the dog Church's Fried Chicken on almost a daily basis, so Snookums rarely ate anything else. If presented with dog food, she turned her head and snuffed in disgust.

"He's going to kill that dog," Justin remarked.

"Don't get me started," Elena answered. "Let me tell you all about the time…."

The voices and the laughter faded as Spencer looked around the room. Every single face he saw loved him and accepted him for who he was, and the realization filled him with so much happiness it eclipsed the sadness lurking deep within.

He had invited his parents and his sister to the house, to help them unpack and to meet all his friends.

They weren't coming. His parents had a previous engagement, and his sister was driving to Austin with her latest boyfriend. As always, his family's lives rarely included him.

At first, the news saddened him. He'd felt shunned and abandoned. But now, sitting here with a house full of love from friends and his new family, Spencer could only smile. His life felt complete.

He'd never thought a life without his armor was possible. Justin's love had shown him how wrong he was. It turned out love was sturdier than *any* armor he could fashion alone.

CHAPTER 11

2010

PEGASUS and his father, riding on the phoenix's back, led Dutch back to the light, and when he awoke, someone was standing in the room with him and the nurse. The daze of pain and drugs prevented him from recognizing his visitor, who left the room far too quickly.

The man looked familiar, though, his identity kept clouded under the numbing fog of morphine. His right hand, though heavy, lifted off the hospital bed, reaching for the visitor who was no longer there.

"Welcome back to the land of the living, Mr. Keller." The nurse's voice sounded more disappointed than relieved at his conscious state. "But you must remain still. Your body needs all the rest it can get."

Dutch opened his mouth, but no sound escaped. Scratchy and sore, his throat felt like he had gargled sand. Still, he willed himself to speak. When he once again tried, a coughing fit wracked his body, sending spasms of pain throughout his injured muscles and bones.

"I told you to relax," the nurse scolded. She poured a glass of water from the container at his bedside. She placed a straw within the cup and held the cup under his chin so he could drink.

As he took in the water, his throat instantly felt refreshed. The grains of sand stuck within were washed away. "You were intubated," she said, as if it was something he should have known.

"Thank you," he told her in a gravelly voice. "It feels better already."

"I can't tell you how happy that makes me," she replied with no hint of kindness to her voice.

Dutch wondered if the pain medication was dulling his perception. The nurse couldn't be *that* much of an uncaring bitch. He'd fought his way back from an endless black ocean that threatened to drown him. He deserved a better welcome than the one Nurse Ratched provided.

Maybe she's having a bad day, he thought.

"Who was just here?" he asked, suddenly remembering his mysterious visitor.

"I don't know *who* it was," she replied. Her arched eyebrow let Dutch know she didn't appreciate the after-hour's visitor. She looked at his chart and then took his vital signs. "He didn't tell me and I didn't ask. I'm sure he'll be back *during* visiting hours."

Dutch didn't like her tone or her bedside manner. Not only was her personality gruff, but she was now needlessly rough when checking his wounds. Gauze with adhesive tape should be gently removed from a hairy body, not violently tugged free, taking with it skin and hair.

"Damn, that hurt," he complained as she yanked yet another gauze bandage free. She looked at him with mild disgust, as if he were the problem. "I'm sure there are gentler ways to remove the tape."

"Perhaps," she said. After her cursory examination of the wound, she reapplied a fresh bandage.

"Are you this mean to *every* patient?"

"Not at all," replied Nurse Ratched. As she wrote in the chart, she looked crossways at him. Dutch got the sinking feeling she was estimating how long it would take to kill him with a hypodermic filled with oxygen. "I just have no sympathy for patients brought in because of a DWI."

Did she just say DWI? he thought.

Images splashed up from his subconscious. He was at a club, drinking. A lot. He was angry, but he didn't remember why. There was a hot, dark-haired, dark-skinned Latino. They made out and practically had sex on the dance floor. Afterward, they stumbled out of the club, and he got into his car.

His memory ended there. The next thing he knew, he was adrift in the ocean, alone. At least until his father showed up with their trusted guardians at his side.

"Oh my God," he whispered.

"God?" she asked. Her eyes blazed with ire, as if Dutch's comment stoked the simmering embers just beneath her surface. "You think God is going to answer *you* when he did nothing for my sister?" Putting the metal chart on the rollaway table, the nurse crossed over to him. She leaned very close, her breath hot against Dutch's face. He immediately felt vulnerable. Under normal circumstances, defending himself wouldn't be a problem. He'd inherited his father's strength. But doped up on morphine and God knew what else, merely talking drained his meager reserves. If she wanted to do him harm, there was little he could do about it.

"Where was God when my sister was killed by a drunk driving the wrong way?" The anger in her eyes spread to her mouth. She sneered like an attack dog. "She was only thirty-five. She had two kids who will never know how great their mother was all because some dumb fuck got drunk and got behind the wheel of a car." She paused, putting pressure on his chest, which was bruised. Flares of hot pain surged through his body. "You want to know what happened to him?"

The pain she caused prevented Dutch from responding. Not that he would have if he could. Since her eyes resembled a rabid dog's, he decided silence was the best response.

"*Nothing* happened to him," she finally answered. "Not a *fucking* scratch. Sure, he did some time and probation, but he's walking around this earth while my sister is buried beneath it." Her anger gave way to unfathomable grief as her voice caught in her throat.

He sensed she wanted him to say something, and that his words would determine what further punishment he would receive on her shift. "I'm sorry," he finally told her. "Nothing I can say will absolve me of my actions."

"Damn straight!" she replied.

"What's going on here?" a voice from the door asked. It was his sister.

Backing up, Nurse Ratched stood rigid before him, made of steel instead of flesh and bone. The disgust in her eyes was still palpable. "Your brother has finally awoken," she informed Heidi. "Isn't it a joyous event?"

"Lukas!" she screeched. She was the only one in the family to call him by his first name. Everyone else addressed him as Dutch, the nickname his father gave him. "Thank God, you're awake," Heidi said before rushing over to his side, oblivious to the previously tense situation.

His sister hugged him gently. Her love and her tears eased his nerves and abated his pain. Still, he eyed the nurse warily as she stepped back into the shadows of the room.

"I've been worried sick," Heidi said, rising up enough to look into his face. "I've been here for the past two days, and you wait till I go back to your house for a few hours' rest to wake up?"

"Sorry," was all he could manage, still not taking his eyes off Nurse Ratched.

"I'll inform Dr. Gupta that your brother is awake," she said.

Heidi nodded her head in reply. Judging from the tears and the wide grin, she was too choked up to speak.

Nurse Ratched turned to leave, picking up the metal chart on the way out. Before exiting, she looked back over her shoulder. "I hope you learn from this situation, Mr. Keller."

She then opened the door, the light from the hallway momentarily blinding him, before she disappeared into the glow beyond.

"What was *that* about?" Heidi asked, nodding her head to the closed hospital room door. As always, curiosity got the better of her.

"Don't worry about it," he told her. "We were just getting acquainted."

His sister responded, but he didn't hear what she said. Instead, Nurse Ratched's final words echoed inside him. *"I hope you learn from this, Mr. Keller."*

The words reverberated inside him, setting off a soul quake that decimated everything he was before this moment.

Although the details were still fuzzy, Dutch vowed to learn from his mistakes. After all, Nurse Ratched was right. No matter how awful she was or how potentially dangerous she might be, the major threat to his continued well-being wasn't some vengeful nurse. It was him.

That was going to change, starting now.

CHAPTER 12

2005

JUSTIN brushed his teeth, listening to the cold November rain rattling against the bathroom window. As always, rain patter made him horny. Spencer had thought the idea bizarre when he first shared the fact a couple of months into their relationship. He proceeded to ask questions like some grand inquisitor, trying to find Justin's link between sex and rain.

For Justin, there was no rhyme or reason. All he knew was during a rainstorm, just like during sex, everything changed. Electrical impulses traveled up and down his flesh like an insistent lover's fingertips, gently tantalizing his skin into sexual awakening. Heavy and moist, the air pressed upon him, trapping him underneath its weight. Waves of sexual frenzy rippled through his body, building up pressure like a thundercloud about to burst.

When the rain finally fell, when the heavens suddenly released the contents of its pendulous, dark clouds, the forceful collisions of one wet substance against another sparked his desire like a flash of lightning. The splatter of water, the rivulets of rain, traveling down drenched bodies like sweat, urged him to seek the flesh of another, to find similar release within the warm folds of another's body.

He longed to build up his own sexual storm, to churn up the atmosphere with the heat of his desire. He sought to pound his sweaty flesh against the dripping flesh of another, to mimic the fall of the rain with his own rhythmic thrusts until the storm he created reached its own climax and he could relish in the culmination of his own deluge.

Whenever it rained, he and Spencer had some of the best sex of their lives. The first time was shortly after they moved in together, and a huge storm system rolled into San Antonio one Sunday afternoon. Spencer was busy working on his dissertation, but Justin convinced him to give it a rest for a few hours. Justin topped him against the sliding patio door, blinds open for all to see. Sliding in and out of Spencer's ass as he watched the rain fall outside brought him to climax quickly. Which meant they did it again. This time Justin bottomed for Spencer in the study, where the wind was slamming the rain hard against the window. Spencer's frenzied thrusts timed perfectly with the onslaught of rain and wind against the window.

There were other times. The time they did it in the car on the way home from a Houston trip. The heavens opened up on I-10, and Justin just had to have some. They pulled off into a hotel parking lot, parked toward the back, and crawled into the backseat. They traded fucking each other during the entire storm. When they were done, their bodies were as wet as if they had been running around in the deluge.

In New York, they had a quickie in a restaurant bathroom. There was the hot tub in Cape Cod, the balcony of their hotel room in Hawaii, and the rainforest in Costa Rica with the rumbling Arenal volcano as a backdrop.

Those were *extremely* hot times.

These days, though, they rarely had the energy for such impromptu sexcapades. *Although, I could be persuaded into a good fuck right about now*, he thought. He squeezed his cock, which pulsated at his touch.

"We going to sleep or having sex?" Justin asked Spencer who entered the bathroom. He cocked his head to the window, where the rain clicked against the glass.

Spencer looked at him and laughed. "You and the rain," he said, feigning exasperation. "What am I going to do with you?"

"I can think of a few things," replied Justin. Standing behind Spencer, he rubbed his hard cock against Spencer's ass.

Spencer leaned back and kissed him. "For now, your fetish will have to wait," he told Justin. "I have a routine to perform."

Justin sighed. Knowing the routine all too well, he backed up and perched at the end of the claw-foot tub. Spencer had already brushed his teeth. Now it was time for the applying of his nightly lotions to keep his skin vibrant and taut. Vanity and Spencer were best friends, and together they kept a strict, nightly beauty regimen. Nothing interfered with that. Not even ball-busting rain sex.

First, Spencer applied the body lotion to keep his skin from getting ashy. Then he went to work on the eye cream to stave off crow's feet and prevent bags from forming under his eyes. There was an assortment of other products in blue, white, or cream-colored tubes and containers, all designed to battle saggy skin and unsightly wrinkles.

Spencer was only in his early thirties, but he feared looking old before his time. He was intent on doing anything he could to keep his age from marching across his face, something Dolly Parton's Truvy declared to her friends in *Steel Magnolias*.

"Would you be terribly angry if we went to bed?" Spencer asked while putting his eye cream away. He then picked up another container, this one blue, and proceeded to rub its contents across his cheeks and forehead. Justin had no idea what that one was for, but he caught a whiff of mint. "I'm beat."

"I understand," Justin replied. He did his best to hide the disappointment. "It's been hectic for both of us."

They were both tired from a long week of work and had an even longer week of household renovations ahead of them.

They were currently in the process of remodeling their master suite, a project they had put off for a few years but were now tackling. Spencer was finally getting the French doors he wanted. They were replacing the pocket doors that used to lead to the sitting room just off their bedroom. For the past year, Spencer had complained how much of an eyesore they were, whether open or closed. They were outdated and unworthy of a gay couple such as themselves.

Justin didn't really care about them, but Spencer did. New doors were therefore picked out, and plans were made to install them. Since they were tackling the doors, though, Justin felt it was time to add on a master bath to their bedroom.

He wanted a shower very badly. He had lived without one for five years. And while the baths he and Spencer shared were romantic, they weren't commonplace.

Their lives were busy, and bathing together started becoming an inefficient use of their time, especially since they both primarily bathed in the morning before work. For the first few years, they bathed together twice a week and were often late to work as a result. Sudsy, naked flesh was simply a temptation they couldn't avoid during the first couple of years in the house. They didn't care, though. At least not then.

Now that they were more firmly entrenched in their professions, being late was not the wisest career move. Justin was in the middle of his first year as a high school principal, and not just the principal of any high school, but of his own alma mater. Some of the teachers who taught him were still working there, and regrettably the students were the children of some of his old high school classmates.

Those two things combined with his relatively young age prompted him to be extra cognizant of his professionalism. A principal in his early thirties was just not usual, but Justin had worked hard in his previous assistant principal position. The school district had taken notice of that.

Many of the ideas that turned his previous school around were his. He'd started a community mentor project that paired at-risk youth with a successful alum. The mentor and mentees all developed strong bonds that not only increased academic performance but decreased truancy and a relatively high dropout rate for an inner city school.

Their scores on the mandatory statewide test increased, largely due to his curriculum-enrichment plan that set aside school time for students to seek extra assistance in subjects they were struggling in. Teachers were no longer teaching to the standardized test but were focusing on teaching students skills to master concepts that had previously eluded them. As a result, the students naturally scored better on the standardized tests.

Parents also became more involved when they saw how much their children were learning. The Parent Teacher Association for his former high school raised $100,000 to outfit the new school with updated technology and a secured Wi-Fi system.

Now, Justin had been charged by the district to recreate his magic on the Luther Burbank High School campus. The district had been considering closing the school based on its declining enrollment and plummeting test scores. Upper administration had given Justin four years to turn the school around. Justin hoped to accomplish the task in half the time.

Doing so meant less time at home recently. Most nights were filled with committee meetings, and Justin often didn't get home until after 8:00 p.m., which was about the time Spencer was getting home these days.

Spencer had recently received tenure at St. Mary's University. As a result, the expectations placed upon him by his department chair and dean had increased threefold.

He was chair of the university reaccreditation committee, which was a huge sign of respect and an even greater burden. Spencer's success meant the university would maintain its accreditation status and continue to be a degree-granting institution.

Spencer was also Director of Graduate Studies in the Foreign Language Department, where he taught two undergraduate classes and one graduate class each semester. He had six students in the graduate program who had requested him to chair their master's thesis. Naturally, he accepted all six requests.

He was secretary of the faculty senate and served on at least four other university committees. Spencer was a bright, shining star on campus, beloved by students, faculty, and administration.

Being so beloved took a lot of time.

Finally finished with his lotions and potions, Spencer joined Justin in the guest bedroom, where they had both slept since the renovations on the master suite began.

"I'm so tired," Spencer told Justin while resting his head on the pillow. He stared at Justin from his side of the bed. "I'm really sorry about not taking you up on the sex. It would have been hot."

"It always is," Justin told him. Spencer's green eyes still captivated him, holding him in their power and causing blood to once again engorge his cock. Then he yawned, and like an outtake valve, the blood rushed out of his manhood, leaving it flaccid once again. "Don't worry about it, though. I'm tired too."

For a few moments, they stared into each other's eyes, wanting to get closer, needing to feel each other's flesh, but their weary bodies prevented them from movement.

"Dinner was good tonight."

"Yeah," Spencer laughed. "Sonic is *awesome*."

Justin laughed too. Spencer used to make gourmet meals every night. Recently, takeout had become their shared meal. It wasn't fair for Justin to expect a home-cooked meal when Spencer was working as many long hours as Justin was. And since Spencer insisted he not cook, since he was so bad at it, something had to give.

Now they took turns picking up dinner. Tomorrow night was Spencer's choice. It was likely to be something Italian.

"I miss you," Justin said. He reached over, bridging the chasm between them, and stroked Spencer's face. His snow-white skin and his haunting green eyes still seemed like magical forces to Justin.

"I miss you too," Spencer replied. He smiled as Justin rubbed his smooth chin. "How about we plan on some hot sex this weekend?"

"It's a date," Justin said. He leaned over and kissed Spencer good night. The kiss was warm and comfortable.

"Sleep tight," Spencer said while switching off the bedside lamp. He then rolled over and faced the opposite wall.

In the darkness, Justin watched Spencer sleep. He wanted to scoot over and lie behind him, to feel his naked body against his own, but he was so tired. He lacked the strength to move one inch. Instead, he listened to Spencer's breathing. Outside, the rain continued to pelt the windows. Eventually, he closed his eyes and fell asleep to the soothing sounds of the man he loved and the hypnotic drum of the rain.

CHAPTER 13

2010

RAIN fell in slow, sad drops from the sky as Justin sat in his car outside of his mother's house, his car's engine still running. The water ran like tears down the windshield, snaking lazy, cheerless paths across the glass. A few years ago, such a rainstorm would have sent him into a sexual frenzy. Now, he felt lost and alone.

Outside, parked in the driveway in front of him, sat Spencer's black Ford Explorer. He had found him at last.

After the hospital and his encounter with that damn Nurse Ratched, he didn't know what else to do, where else to look. After exhausting all the likely destinations Spencer might have fled to—Tyler's, Carolyn's, and the hospital—he was clueless about where to go next.

The answer arrived to the tune of "Stop! In the Name of Love" by Diana Ross and The Supremes, his mother's favorite group and her assigned ringtone on his cell phone. When she told him Spencer was with her, relief descended upon his body, relaxing his tense muscles and almost releasing a flood of tears.

Within minutes, he was pulling into the driveway of his childhood home, anxious to see Spencer. Now that he was actually here, he was too scared to venture inside.

When he was younger, 210 Francis Street had been a haven, a place he escaped to when life turned too difficult. Safe behind walls reinforced by his mother's love, he'd been shielded from bullies and bad grades. He was free to create his own worlds that didn't contain an absent father or the longings of a boy struggling with his sexuality.

It was his refuge. Nothing bad could touch him inside his mother's house.

Until now.

Inside his mother's house was the man he loved *and* had hurt. Once he crossed the threshold, the haven would turn into a battle zone, where he would have to fight his way through Spencer's barricades and release the hurt little boy Justin turned Spencer back into.

A knock at the driver's side window caught his attention. He turned to see his mother standing in the rain underneath her navy blue umbrella. Quickly, he pushed the button that automatically lowered his window.

"Why are you sitting out here when he's in there?" she asked.

"I'm too terrified to move," he told his mother. Her eyes were red and puffy. Her attempts to comfort Spencer had obviously caused her to weep as well, not for herself but for the pain her boys were enduring.

"Fear will only push you further apart," she said.

Justin nodded. He couldn't argue with her, not that he could if he wanted to. His mother was the only person in the world capable of refuting any argument or claim he made. He found her logic uncanny.

"I've made a mess of things, Mom," he managed to choke out. A sob was stuck in righteous retribution in his throat, unwilling to move up or down. Unable to either repress or express his misery, he felt trapped in its web of torment.

"I know," said his mother. "Spencer told me what happened."

Justin figured as much. Although he'd wanted to be the one to confide in his mother, she was Spencer's mother now too. Spencer couldn't be faulted for turning to the most caring and loving woman on the planet in this time of distress.

"I'm sorry," he told her. "For what I've done. For letting you down."

"Letting *me* down?" she asked, incredulously. "I'm your mother. I love you no matter what you do." She opened the car door and pulled him out. As always, he marveled at how her strength was superior to a man half her age. "You can *never* let *me* down. But I'm afraid you *have* let down not only Spencer but *yourself.*"

Again, his mother's words were as accurate as a beesting.

"Now, the man you love is inside. Go to him. Do what needs to be done. Scream. Throw things. It doesn't matter. All that matters is that the two of you work through the bad to find the good hidden beneath."

"Does he know I'm here?"

"Yes," replied his mother, her eyes full of regret. "He didn't want me to call you, and I told him I wouldn't. But I lied. He should've known better than to ask that of me. What choice did I have but to lie?" Even with her umbrella in her hand, she held her palms up and shrugged. Spencer always loved when she did that.

Justin nodded and walked toward the house. After a few steps, he noticed his mother wasn't following him. Instead, she was walking toward her car, which was parked on the street. "Where are you going?" he called to her.

She didn't answer. She only waved good-bye, got inside the car, and drove off into the early morning light.

When her car had disappeared from view, he turned tentatively toward the house and went inside.

From the kitchen off to the right of the living room, he heard dishes clanging together. He walked past his mother's Audubon clock, which chirped away the hour. It was seven in the morning. It had only been about four hours since the phone call that shattered their lives. It felt more like four years.

The unmistakable *poof* of flame from the gas stove told him Spencer was cooking, a task he often turned to when upset. Suddenly, Justin realized how ravenous he was, as if his hunger were somehow tied to the swoosh of flame. His stomach complained loudly. Still, he didn't expect Spencer to be cooking *anything* for him.

Sopping wet from the rain, he headed for the bathroom first and retrieved a towel. He disrobed and then patted himself mostly dry. He then wrapped the towel around his waist and pointed himself toward the kitchen.

Crossing through the living room, he noted how different this walk felt from the first time he'd traversed a room to get to Spencer. The first time magic drew Justin to him. Now, he felt the polarity had shifted.

It worked against him as if he were walking into a strong wind. It pushed him away, telling him to go back, to leave Spencer alone. He had done enough damage and had lost whatever chance he had of living a long, happy life with Spencer.

Justin foraged ahead. He didn't care what the magic thought. He didn't care what *anyone* thought. Magic might have brought them together, but it wasn't needed to *keep* them together.

Relationships weren't sustained by magic; they thrived on hard work and persistence. He had enough of both for the two of them.

When Justin finally turned the corner into the kitchen, he saw Spencer scrambling eggs in a pan while drinking a cup of coffee. There was also another cup of coffee sitting on the breakfast table. The light brown liquid within the cup told him that Spencer already added cream, which probably also meant that the sugar he craved with his coffee had already been stirred into the beverage, just the way he liked it.

So far, Spencer hadn't acknowledged his presence. Staring intently at the eggs as he stirred them, he ran his fingers through his sandy hair, trying to convince the pesky strands to lie down instead of stand up. Then he adjusted the belt of Justin's mother's pink terrycloth robe, which Spencer had taken the liberty of wearing. He must have recently taken a shower.

Justin had never seen a sight more beautiful in his life.

"Breakfast is almost ready," Spencer said. "Grab some plates."

Justin wanted to apologize; he wanted to spout out a litany of promises and regrets. He did none of those things. Instead, he crossed the kitchen and retrieved two plates from his mother's yellow cabinets.

He placed them on the kitchen table. Then, he went to the utensil drawer and got out two forks, which he placed next to the plates.

He then sat down and waited for Spencer to portion out the eggs.

"Your mother didn't have any green onion or cream cheese," Spencer said as he scooped some eggs onto Justin's plate. "So it's just eggs and cheddar cheese."

"It looks great," Justin said. "Thanks."

Spencer didn't reply. He slid the remaining eggs in the pan onto his plate and then placed the pan in the kitchen sink before he returned to the table and sat down.

They ate in silence. In spite of his desire to speak, Justin knew he had to follow Spencer's lead. Rushing things wouldn't help. He was at Spencer's mercy, and if he truly wanted to make things right, he had to wait until Spencer was ready.

When their plates were empty and his stomach no longer grumbled, Justin rose from the table. He placed Spencer's dirty dish on top of his and took them both to the sink. He ran water over them and then filled the sink with warm water and soap.

As Justin washed the breakfast dishes, he looked out the small kitchen window over the sink. Outside, he saw the kids across the street, running away from parents already late for their early morning work shifts and who were trying to corral their children for school. The unmindful children dodged in and out of flowerbeds, which were bursting with red and pink blooms of late summer.

A dog barked at them from the neighbor's yard. It was tied to a tree and apparently unappreciative of all the noise the kids were making. Two cardinals sang to each other in his mother's magnolia tree, and he also heard a lawnmower engine running from somewhere down the street.

The world outside was somehow oblivious to the pain he and Spencer were feeling. Since they had been brought together by what could only be described as magic, he expected the world to feel the pain as well.

He anticipated the light would be less radiant, the flowers not so full of bloom, and the people not so full of life. Instead the world was marching along as always. As if something beautiful wasn't in danger of dying.

"I guess I should've known better," Spencer said, still sitting at the kitchen table.

"What do you mean?" Justin asked while shutting off the water. He didn't want to give the impression he wasn't paying attention.

"I made Elena promise not to tell you where I was," he said. "I guess breaking promises is standard operating procedure for the Jimenez clan."

Justin winced. He'd expected for several grenades to be thrown at him, but he never expected one to be volleyed at his mother. He let it slide. Justin suspected Spencer was immediately regretting including his mother in the jab at him.

"You know how she is," Justin said. "Whenever her boys are hurting, she does whatever's possible to stop the pain."

Spencer said nothing further.

Justin went back to washing dishes. He scrubbed the egg particles off the pan rather easily. He wished all messes were so easily cleaned, but he and Spencer weren't Teflon-coated pans. They were flesh and blood, and real wounds required time and care to heal.

When the dishes were done, Justin began wiping down the countertop and the oven, two chores he typically didn't do at home. Spencer never approved of how Justin cleaned up after he cooked. Truthfully, Justin never thought to clean the countertop and oven. He was responsible for dishes, so dishes were what he washed. The stove and counter weren't dishes.

They used to bicker over it at the beginning of their relationship, but Spencer had let that one go years ago. Spencer obviously felt battling over a clean countertop and oven wasn't worth it, when he could do it himself.

"*Now* you clean the countertop and oven?"

Justin nodded. Words weren't wise. Spencer was trying to pick a fight, and he wasn't going to help.

"I guess you're doing a lot of things you haven't done before these days," Spencer said. "Cleaning *and* cheating. What else is there in your repertoire that I don't know about?"

"I guess that's about it," Justin said while tossing the sponge into the soapy water.

"Just the cleaning and the cheating?"

"Yes."

"I approve of the cleaning."

"I know."

Justin stood at the sink, staring into Spencer's green eyes. They were still pastel green, the color they turned when Spencer learned of the affair. They had yet to return to the rich, jade hue that so captivated him ten years ago.

In their dulled reflection, he saw his broken promise. The one Spencer made him agree to a few months into their relationship. Justin swore he wouldn't cheat. The last time someone cheated on Spencer, he had been infected with HIV.

Justin made the promise easily. Then he broke it just as easily several years later.

"How did we get here?" Spencer asked; his question was filled with sadness deeper than the Pacific Ocean was wide.

"I don't know how to answer that," Justin replied.

"Why don't we try with honesty?" Spencer asked. "It's what we used to do so well."

Justin exhaled. Honesty was where the deepest hurt would reside, but it was also the only place where renewal would spring.

"I think we started taking each other for granted," Justin finally said. "We stopped putting in as much time on us as we were putting into our careers."

Spencer nodded. "I agree."

Justin was pleased that even in the heart of an emotional storm, their communication could be logical and mature.

"We lost sight of what was *truly* important," Justin continued. "I know I did. I hate that I can see it so clearly now, Spence, but I can."

He walked over to Spencer and sat down next to him, twisting the towel so it wouldn't slide to the floor. In his nakedness, he felt vulnerable, exposed. But he knew that in that defenselessness lay the potential for rebirth.

Spencer sat back in his chair and placed his hands in his lap. It was his way of telling Justin not to touch him. Justin didn't dare dismiss that warning.

"We let the everyday minutiae of our lives interfere with the magic that brought us together," he told Spencer. "But that magic's still there. I can feel it. Whenever I see you, whenever I hear your voice, whenever I touch your skin, I feel that spark. That *force* that brought us together. All we have to do is close ourselves to the rest of the crap. Let that force back into us."

"I don't know if I believe in that force anymore," Spencer admitted after a moment's silence. "I did at one time, but I don't think I do anymore." He swallowed hard. It was obviously as difficult for him to admit as it was for Justin to hear.

"If that force was so powerful, then it should've kept us safe," Spencer said. "We should've never gone through what we have. There should never have been any problems. Not what we went through last year. Certainly not what we're going through right now." He wrung his hands together, something Spencer did whenever he was about to say something really unpleasant. "Maybe we were never meant to last this long. Maybe we were never meant to be together forever."

"Don't say that," Justin shouted. "We *were* meant to be together for the rest of our lives. I can feel that inside every cell in my body."

"That makes one of us."

"You're only saying that because you're hurting," Justin said. "And you have every reason to be hurt. I betrayed you, your trust, our relationship, and the magic that brought us together. I'm the one who's thrown us out of whack."

"It takes two people to make a relationship," Spencer told him. "It also takes two people to destroy one."

"I don't believe that," Justin said. "I'm the fuckup here. You've done nothing wrong."

"I wish I could believe that, but I can't." Spencer reached out and patted Justin's hand. He then quickly withdrew it when he realized they were touching. For a moment, the walls fell, but they went back up just as quickly. "I'm not the wide-eyed twentysomething anymore, who believed that cheating was always the fault of the cheater. I'm in no way saying I'm equally culpable for it. You share a major part of *that* blame, but I've played a part too."

Justin was confused. "What do you mean?"

"When your mother and I were talking, I was saying the most awful things about you. I was surprised she didn't throw me out of her house for talking about you that way. When I asked her why she wasn't angry with me for what I was saying about you, do you know what she said?"

Justin shook his head.

"She told me that I was just as angry at myself as I was with you. At first, I thought your mother was going senile. But then she told me about your father, and the affairs he had while they were married. The first time he cheated was shortly after you were born. She was no longer interested in sex as she had you to take care of. Since his needs weren't being met at home, he went elsewhere."

"She never told me that," Justin said. "She's never talked about the affairs."

"She blames herself more than your father for them," Spencer told Justin. "She was angry at him, but she never said anything about it. Her silence gave him permission to continue. Her lack of self-respect. Her lack of respect for their marriage helped the affairs to continue."

Justin was dumbfounded. He never knew his mother blamed herself for her marriage falling apart.

"Afterward, I kept asking myself what I did to start us down this path."

"What do you possibly think you did?"

"I'm the one who came on to Tyler," Spencer answered.

CHAPTER 14

2005

"I FEAR Tyler's drunk," Spencer told Justin. "Again."

"You think?" Justin asked.

Tyler stumbled from the kitchen into the dining room carrying a freshly poured martini. His black hair looked disheveled, a result of stumbling into the couch on his previous martini run. His hazel eyes were vacant and rolled around in his head like gumballs in a gumball machine.

"Don't talk about me like I'm not here," Tyler said, doing his best Julia Roberts impersonation from *Steel Magnolias*. Recently, all their friends, when they had time in their busy lives to get together, had begun quoting the movie as much as they did. Spencer enjoyed the mimicry. It proved that despite their now hectic lives, filled with children and new jobs, their friendship still played like background music in their lives.

Tyler was the only one from the group who they saw on any regular basis. And at this moment, he was quite a sight to behold. He staggered around the coffee table, telling it not to move, and then plopped down on the couch adjacent to where Spencer and Justin sat.

"You okay, Shelby?" Justin asked.

They laughed, but Tyler guffawed as if he had just heard the funniest comment in the world. His hysteria resulted in a spill, which Tyler dutifully lapped up.

It wasn't unusual for Tyler to get drunk on their weekly night together. They spent every Saturday night hanging out, watching movies or playing games. The others were invited, but Chris and Jill and Teresa and Sam were busy with their clutches of children, Heather and Pat had moved up to New Braunfels and rarely came to San Antonio, and Chuck and Don worked night shifts.

Still, Saturday night was the one night of the week Justin and Spencer didn't do anything work-related. They cut loose and had fun.

It was also the best way for them to keep track of their best friend's progress. Tyler's partner of five years, Rene, had left him six months ago.

Tyler came home to find all of Rene's possessions gone and a note taped to the kitchen refrigerator. The note said, "I'm sorry. Love, Rene."

The hurtful way Rene abandoned Tyler had infuriated Justin. Spencer, however, had seen it coming. Never a part of the group in the three years they had all been friends, Rene had skirted its periphery. At first, Spencer had thought Rene to be painfully shy. He finally realized a few months ago what the problem was: Rene was unhappy and most likely having an affair.

The never-ending texts during dinners coupled with the late-night shifts at Red Lobster, no less, raised Spencer's suspicions. He never voiced them for fear of a false accusation, but he recognized the signs. His father, a self-professed womanizer, had introduced him to them all.

Like his mother, Tyler and Justin refused to see the signs. Spencer wore no such blinders. His world had been rife with deception and hidden agendas, from his parents to the friends and lovers he had before Justin and his current group of friends.

His past gave him clarity of vision others didn't possess. He could spot a cheater and a poser at ten spaces.

Tyler, however, couldn't.

He tried countless times to contact Rene, to find out what happened, to get some closure. Tyler hounded mutual friends and even stalked the Red Lobster where Rene worked. He never found him. After a few weeks, he learned Rene moved to Houston, but that was the only fact anyone ever heard of his whereabouts.

Tyler didn't take the breakup well. He fell into a deep depression and was drunk most nights of the week. Justin and Spencer called him every day to check up on him. Typically maudlin on the phone, Tyler bemoaned his life and his situation. While they both understood his depression, they longed for Tyler to return to the man he'd been prior to Rene skipping out on him.

He refused to get back on the dating wagon and hadn't had sex since before Rene left. Tyler was a mess of pent-up tension that screamed for release. They tried setting him up, but he refused. He told them he was destined to be alone, and he was okay with it.

For the first few weeks, even the first few months, they let his attitude slide. Lately, though, they'd both decided it was time for some tough love. Tyler needed to snap out of his funk before he sank too deeply into depression he couldn't climb out of.

That was what this night was supposed to be about, a sort of intervention for their friend. They wanted him to see that he wasn't meant to be alone. That what had happened between him and Rene wasn't his fault.

The night hadn't gone as planned.

Tyler was already tipsy by the time they arrived. Starting a serious conversation proved impossible since he kept changing the subject. He preferred to discuss *Days of Our Lives,* more concerned with Bo and Hope's lives than his own.

It was Tyler's way of escaping. Spencer knew that. But he was still frustrated. He wanted to make things better for his friend, but there was nothing he could do for someone who needed help but didn't realize that he did.

"Y'all need another drink?" Tyler asked. His inebriated state always deepened his South Texas drawl. He sounded more like a cowboy from east Texas than a gay man born and bred in San Antonio.

Tyler took another sip of his ghastly martini. Spencer wondered why someone with such a thick Texas accent didn't drink beer. Instead, his poison was straight vodka, some olive juice, and a splash of vermouth. It was the Tyler special no one but Tyler drank.

"I'll take another," Justin said. "It's been a long week."

"Okay, I'll get it," Tyler said while attempting to get up from the couch. The top half of Tyler's body moved. His legs refused to cooperate. He looked like a newly born fawn trying to take its first steps.

"Don't hurt yourself," Spencer said. "I'll make the drinks."

"You sure?" Tyler asked. He was already comfortably settling back into the couch with a huge grin on his face.

"Positive," Spencer said while rising from the couch. "Another vodka and Sprite, sweetie?"

"Yes, please," Justin said. "And while you do that, I'm going to pee."

Spencer took Justin's glass and Justin trotted down the hall to relieve his insanely small bladder. Spencer headed to the kitchen where the alcohol awaited, all lined up on the island like soldiers ready to be called into service.

As he walked into the kitchen, he thought about how this night was supposed to turn out. They'd intended on helping Tyler climb out of his depression, but instead, they were using his method to escape their own problems.

Alcohol was a great anesthetic, after all.

He and Justin were trudging through a low point in their relationship. Every relationship went through peaks and valleys, he knew that, but they had been in this valley for about three months, with no end in sight. It was starting to feel more like Death Valley than anything else.

They needed to address the problems, change aspects of their lives, but it was easier to focus on fixing Tyler than themselves.

They would climb out of the valley eventually. They were Justin and Spencer, after all; they were meant to be together. Of that much, he was sure. They were just insanely busy. Their jobs consumed more and more of their time.

The lack of quality time together was taking its toll. Typical lively conversations at dinner had been replaced by a question and answer session about their days. Instead of planning a trip for the summer or a party the following weekend, they watched numerous television shows on opposite sides of the couch.

They hadn't been on a couple date in a few months, and they hadn't had sex in about two weeks. Once a nightly occurrence, sex had been reduced to a rare event. Logically, Spencer knew the frequency of their sexual encounters would decrease. No relationship could continue the sexual pace they'd once kept. He just wasn't prepared for sex to become routine.

On the rare occasion when they had sex now, he could predict with precise accuracy the order of events and how long each event would last. They would start by kissing, not as passionately as before, but with still *some* fervor. After a couple of minutes of kissing, one of them would get on top of the other. Frottage ensued for about five minutes, which typically ended when whoever was on top turned over, so they could sixty-nine. An orgasm followed about three minutes later, which led to cleanup, a kiss, and then sleep.

It wasn't exactly the wild, scorching, ass-numbing sex they'd had for the first few years of their relationship, but the passion was there. It bubbled beneath the surface, suffocated by hours of exhaustion and endless responsibilities.

They were both overworking themselves, and they knew it.

They'd discussed the problem over dinner a few nights before, and they were both extremely honest about their feelings. It was one of the aspects of their relationship Spencer was most proud of. The two of them talked about anything, and they kept nothing from each other. Every fear, every concern, every lustful thought was shared.

It made Spencer feel secure. Their honesty was his new armor, the only thing he needed to remain safe. It was also the only reason they both opened up about the sexual fantasies they were each having.

Spencer had revealed his attraction to the new gardener, Alejandro, who often worked shirtless in the flowerbeds. He watched him work on the weekends while Justin slept late. His hands caked with dirt. Sweat running down his bare chest. Muscles straining as he rooted around in the hard-packed ground. Alejandro starred in a number of his masturbatory sessions.

The news didn't surprise Justin. He thought Alejandro was hot too, but paled in comparison to Oscar Herrera, a parent of one of the sophomores at his school. Oscar was a firefighter and often picked up his son while still wearing his uniform. Rain wasn't Justin's only fetish. He had an obsession for uniforms as well.

Their fantasies told them their sexual drives hadn't shut off; they were simply on pause. As a remedy, they promised to cut back at work. Instead of coming home at eight, they planned to shoot for six thirty. Instead of routine sex, they intended on spicing it up. The bedroom was going to be off-limits for a while. They would try sex in other rooms of the house, like they used to.

His last suggestion, though, threw Justin for a loop.

Since they were fantasizing about other men, he wanted to know how Justin felt about inviting a third man into their bed.

When the idea first entered Spencer's mind, he quickly dismissed it. A three-way seemed too much like cheating, no matter how much the idea uncharacteristically intrigued him. His logical side pointed out that if they were having sex with a third person *together*, it wouldn't be cheating. Cheating meant sneaking around and lying. There would be none of that. They would be enjoying the third person at the same time.

No lies. No deceptions. No sneaking.

The third person would be more of a marital aid than anything else.

Intellectually, the idea made sense, but he worried what the heart would think if they ever decided to cross that line.

They made no definite decisions one way or another about loosening the monogamous constraints of their relationship. They agreed to stay open to the possibility without actively searching for a third, especially since they were clueless as to how one went about finding that elusive third person.

"What's taking you so long?" Tyler asked. He entered the kitchen on unsteady legs, his martini glass empty. "I've already finished my drink an' I need another."

Could Tyler be the answer? he thought. Tyler was someone they both loved, but he was also someone who shared a sexual past with Justin. *Was a ménage a trois with Tyler opening a can of worms better left untouched? Besides, he was drunk. That would be taking advantage of him. Wouldn't it?*

"Why are you staring at me like that?" Tyler asked, stirring his freshly poured drink. His eyes were glazy from the alcohol but still surprisingly perceptive.

It's now or never, Spencer thought. *This is something Justin and I need, and who else but our dear friend to help us out of this dry spell?*

Spencer took the martini glass from Tyler's hand. He complained and tried to take it back, but Spencer easily blocked his attempt and set the glass on the counter next to his and Justin's drinks.

Swiftly, he pulled Tyler into a kiss, and his friend's rigid, panicked body communicated that Tyler seemed uncertain how to respond to Spencer's sexual advance. Spencer's hot tongue and insistent kisses told Tyler it was okay, and soon, Tyler's tongue was just as wild as his. At first Tyler tasted like his nail-polish-remover martinis. But after a few seconds, the tangy twist of lust filled their hungry mouths.

Justin turned the corner, finally done in the bathroom. His jaw dropped at the sight of his partner and his best friend feverishly tonguing each other. Spencer could tell Justin didn't know whether to break it up and kick the shit out of Tyler or join the fun.

"Why don't you come join us?" he asked, hoping his invitation would settle Justin's internal conflict.

Noticing Justin at the doorway, Tyler turned around and pulled Justin to him. He drew Justin into a kiss that was first tentative but then quickly grew in passion as each sought to devour the other.

In their kisses, Spencer saw pure lust, something he hadn't seen in Justin in months. He held Tyler's throat with his right hand, pushing him against the refrigerator, while he thrust his left hand beneath the waistband of Tyler's jeans, vigorously massaging its contents. The stubble on their cheeks scraped together like sandpaper.

Spencer joined them against the refrigerator, and their arms opened to include him in the embrace. He kissed Tyler, then Justin. Then the three of them kissed as one, their tongues and lips freely mingling, sliding back and forth from one greedy mouth to another.

Saliva dribbled down his chin, and Justin licked it up and gnawed at his cleft. Tyler dove into his mouth again, the taste of their communal kiss still on their lips like fresh cinnamon.

As Tyler's hot breath panted in his ear and Justin's strong fingers tweaked his right nipple erect, Spencer felt liberated from his stresses and responsibilities. The yoke, which had choked him for months, fell from his neck. He was free.

"I've wanted to have sex with the two of y'all for so long," Tyler said. "I'm so happy we're doing this."

"Me too," he and Justin said in unison.

With consent given, the three of them slowly shed their clothes, delighting in the revelation of their raging masculinity. Tyler's plump cock stood out amidst a shock of black hair that fanned upward from his groin to a light coating of fur on his chest and stomach. Justin's stiffness throbbed angrily from his trimmed crotch, and a thread of precum dangled from its head. As Spencer drew them both into another kiss, his normally pink prick turned a deep red and stood at such attention that it brushed against his hairless stomach.

Together, they inched back to the living room, continuing their shared kiss, not wanting to break their circle of passion for fear that its raging fires might subside.

When they reached the couch, Tyler lay down. "Fuck my face," he told Justin.

Justin mounted the couch and slid his hard cock inside Tyler's wet mouth. Spencer watched as someone other than him gave his man a blowjob. The jealousy he expected to crash down on him never fell. Instead, his own cock turned rock hard at the sight of Justin receiving pleasure from another man's mouth, his pulsating dick slick with the spit of their best friend.

Justin peered over his shoulder to look at him, his brown eyes burning red with lust. "Suck that cock," he commanded Spencer. "I want to see you swallow him whole."

He did as commanded and slowly lowered his mouth onto Tyler's cock. As the engorged purple head drew closer to his mouth, Spencer flicked out his tongue. Immediately, the sweetness of Tyler's juices coated his taste buds with their slickness. Spencer could wait no longer. He slid the shaft between his lips and savored the sweaty meat and the waves of musk emanating from Tyler's dark, thick bush.

"Oh, fuck yeah," Tyler muttered, his mouth still full of Justin's cock.

"You like that?" Justin asked as he slammed his rod in and out of Tyler's throat. "You like my man's mouth on your cock?"

Tyler could only grunt yes. Justin's unrelenting assault inside his mouth prevented any words from escaping.

Spencer watched as Justin pumped in and out of Tyler's chops, his trimmed balls smacking loudly against Tyler's chin. His frenzied movements caused Tyler to slurp and gag as Justin worked himself ever deeper inside Tyler's throat.

The sight of his man losing himself in his pleasure and the taste of Tyler's fleshy hardness caused his own cock to leak uncontrollably. He feared if he touched himself he would shoot his spunk all over Tyler's leather couch.

As if sensing a load was about to be released without his personal assistance, Tyler crawled out from under Justin's legs and came over to Spencer. His needy eyes and open mouth indicated he now wanted to return the pleasure Spencer had so freely given.

After sliding a condom over Spencer's shaft, Tyler wrapped his warm hand around Spencer's girth and guided the throbbing pole inside his waiting mouth, which stretched wide to accommodate his size. Tyler's wide eyes, no longer vacant from his alcoholic buzz, indicated how much he wanted this to happen. His tongue immediately danced all around Spencer's shaft until Tyler began to bob up and down on him, his velvety lips inching him dangerously close to climax. To prolong the occasion, Tyler pulled on his balls, adding a hint of pain that caused the escalating churn of release to subside.

On the other end, Justin buried his face inside Tyler's hairy crack. His tongue rolled around and lapped at Tyler's furry opening, causing Justin's eyes to roll inside his head. Justin enjoyed few things more than eating a hot ass, and the wet smacks of his hungry mouth indicated he had moved far beyond the throes of passion. In response to Justin's magical tongue, Tyler grunted and reached back with his free hand, shoving Justin's face farther up his butt.

"Eat it," Spencer commanded Justin. "Get his hole ready for you."

"Yeah," Tyler agreed. "Lube my ass real good. Open me up for you."

Urged on by their commands, Justin feasted more eagerly while Tyler increased his suction on Spencer's cock, which was slick with saliva. The excess spit coated his brown bush and ran in a steady stream down his balls before falling onto the couch. Determined to swallow his girth, Tyler relaxed his throat and took Spencer's thick rod all the way to its hilt. Tears streamed down his face, which was red from the strain, but still he managed to use his throat muscles to massage Spencer's tool.

"Your throat feels fucking great!" he told Tyler, who looked up at him appreciatively. He grabbed Tyler by his head and pushed himself even farther down Tyler's gullet.

"I'm gonna fuck that ass now," Justin announced from the other end. Spencer looked up and observed as Justin rolled a condom onto his cock before spitting four times into his palm. He then used it to further coat the rim of Tyler's already dripping backdoor. He teased Tyler's hole, rubbing his stiff member up and down his crack.

"Fuck me," Tyler moaned. He took Spencer's cock out of his mouth and looked back at Justin with pleading, wild eyes. "Fuck me hard!"

"Beg for it," Justin demanded. "Beg for me to fuck your man pussy."

"Fuck me," Tyler begged. "Fuck my pussy like the whore I am."

With no further urging required, Justin plunged into Tyler's waiting ass in one swift motion. Tyler shouted; a mixture of pleasure and pain colored his voice. Still, his dreamy eyes told the truth. He was delighted to be filled at both ends.

Justin relentlessly hammered away in Tyler's chute, gripping his ass and slamming him backward against him. Their bodies loudly slapped together as Tyler cried out in pleasure.

"Clench that ass," Justin told him. "Grip my cock. Make your ass nice and tight."

Tyler complied, bearing down as hard as he could while Spencer continued pumping in and out of Tyler's mouth. Sweat now poured down his and Justin's chest, snaking down their bodies to drench Tyler's face and ass. Rivers of perspiration also ran between Tyler's shoulder blades and the small of his back. In a frenzy, he worked both hard cocks in and out of his body, rocking back and forth like a ship in turbulent waters.

Spencer felt his balls churning. He was close. When he looked into Justin's eyes, he saw in their faraway reflection Justin's own impending release.

"I'm getting close," he told Justin.

"Me too," Justin grunted. "I'm gonna cream."

"Do it!" Tyler ordered. "Give it to me!"

Justin withdrew quickly from Tyler's ass and ripped off the condom. In a few short strokes, his load erupted from his cock, sending milky threads flying across Tyler's back.

"Fuck!" Spencer yelled as he pulled Tyler's hungry lips from his tool and exploded across his friend's cheek. Gooey streams of come splattered across his skin before sliding down his face.

Moaning, Tyler frantically yanked on himself until he emptied a large pool of spunk inside his palm.

When Spencer and Justin looked into each other's eyes, Tyler's moans of pleasure drifted away, and they, instead of him, took center stage. Having been plugged into the same body, their connection sparked to life once again. The chasm separating them ceased to be.

CHAPTER 15

2010

SPENCER saw the confusion in Justin's eyes. He fiddled with the towel that had fallen open and no longer covered his nakedness.

Whenever Justin was confused or in deep thought, he played with the nearest object. For months, it was a pen. He tossed it into the air, until he found a resolution. After the pen was lost, then came the remote control, which he broke after a particularly hard day. Since then, Spencer had banned him from picking up delicate objects, so Justin had resorted to snatching up unbreakable items around the house in times of distress—a pillow or an empty water bottle he hadn't thrown away.

Today, it was the towel. He wrapped and unwrapped the edge around his index finger, trying to understand how having sex with Tyler had led them here.

"I still don't see it," he finally said. His hands started twisting the towel instead of wrapping it around his finger.

Spencer sighed. He felt Justin was being intentionally dense, a tactic he often resorted to in order to avoid uncomfortable subjects. "Our three-ways with Tyler started because of me," he reminded Justin. "*I'm* the one who started us down this path. I not only introduced the idea of a third, but I was the one who got the ball rolling."

"Maybe," Justin admitted. He was now rolling the end of the towel up like a tamale. "But I was a willing participant. It's not like you forced me to have sex with Tyler the first time or *any* time after that."

"I know that," replied Spencer. Justin's slow acceptance of a perfectly logical fact irritated him.

He wasn't talking about being forced. Nobody forced either of them into doing *anything*. Being two uncompromising men was one of the first hurdles they'd learned to jump shortly after moving in together.

"Then what does Tyler have to do with anything?"

Spencer rolled his eyes. It was an automatic response brought on by his complete exasperation. Justin hated having someone roll their eyes at him, and when he learned that fact, he'd done his best to check that behavior. At this point, however, he felt it appropriate to let his rolling eyes express his frustration.

"If we never started having the three-ways with Tyler, we never would've had *any* of the hookups that followed. Tyler was a slippery slope that brought us to this point," he said plainly. "Since they started because of me, I'm just as culpable as you are in all this."

"I still don't see it," Justin told him. Justin stared at him crossways, apparently trying to gauge the level of aggravation before continuing. "Neither of you played a part in my relationship with…." He averted his eyes and stopped speaking, unwilling to say the name, as if doing so would summon a demon.

And in a way it did. While they hadn't brought Dutch up, his presence filled the room like a poltergeist. Instead of the magic that had brought them together and kept their souls tethered, Dutch became a negating force to the magic, nullifying, if not completely severing, their link.

After all, Justin *did* go to Dutch first. Spencer had seen him running madly toward the hospital, as if his most precious possession in the world lay within. The image might have hurt, but it was something he needed to see. It brought him closer to closure, which was what he desperately needed.

Then why am I doing this? he wondered. If Dutch was his first consideration, was there any need to continue this conversation? Didn't that prove Justin's heart was no longer his?

That's why you should've killed the faggot when you had the chance, his father's voice scolded from deep within.

"Where'd you go?" Justin asked. His face creased with concern. "I lost you there for a moment."

"Don't worry about it," he told Justin. Shoving his father's angry voice deep into his subconscious, he sat up straight. His armor refortified itself for the next devastating blow that was most certainly on its way.

"I just don't agree with what you're saying," said Justin, continuing their conversation. "I can't let anyone else take blame that is mine."

"It doesn't matter what you can or can't do," Spencer told him. His previous calm vanished. The almost utterance of Dutch's name riled him and his anger. "The truth is the truth. Sex with Tyler opened a door we previously kept shut on purpose." Spencer got up from the kitchen table and paced back and forth from the kitchen sink to the table. Pacing was something he often did when he was about to lose control emotionally.

"Our hookups with Tyler led to more hookups with Tyler." He stopped before the kitchen window before asking his question. "How many do you think we had with him?"

"I never counted," Justin told him. "We were having sex with him every week for a while there, but it tapered off when he stopped trying to meet other guys and was completely fixating on us instead."

While their three-ways with Tyler had been a good marital aid for them, it hadn't been so beneficial for Tyler. Tyler loved the two of them immensely. Bringing sex into the relationship had confused him. He saw himself as a *part* of the relationship instead of merely a part of a sex act. When he and Justin realized the disservice they were committing against their friend, they ended the sexual part of their relationship with him.

Deeply hurt at first, Tyler's depression returned. This time, it didn't last. He reevaluated his life and took stock of his situation. A few weeks later, he began dating. At first, the dates were disasters, but Tyler eventually met Jerry, who had moved in last month.

"You see," Spencer said, realizing the troubles they unexpectedly caused Tyler served as an indictment against them. "That should've been our clue to stop. Instead of working on our relationship, we brought Tyler into it. He wasn't helping us. He was something else we were using to not deal with our own problems, our own inability to connect with each other."

Justin's silence told Spencer he couldn't argue against that point. While their three-ways with Tyler had jumpstarted their sex life at home, their relationship sputtered shortly after their sexual relations with Tyler ended.

Before they knew it, they were right back where they started.

Spencer hated himself right now. Though he was loath to accept part of the burden, he had no other choice. Their relationship had been floundering the whole time, and neither of them had done anything to rescue it. Instead of tossing a life preserver, they'd added more water, cubic metric tons of water, into the already deeply churning sea.

"And what did we do?" Spencer asked, more to himself than Justin. "We turned to Cyber."

Cyber was a social app for the iPhone Spencer discovered. It allowed them to create individual profiles where they could search San Antonio or other cities for guys looking for hookups.

Shortly after he told Justin about it, the two of them downloaded the app on their respective iPhones. At the beginning, they'd spent a great deal of time on Cyber, chatting with guys from San Antonio and the surrounding areas. They'd developed online personalities that were separate from who they were as a couple.

Now that Spencer thought about it, that was when their lack of a connection had turned into a rift. They sat together on the couch, chatting with other guys and trying to lure them into a hookup. It was time they should have spent together as a couple.

Cyber became an obsession for both of them. They often tried to see who could catch the hottest trick, which wasn't too different from what Justin and Xavier used to do at the club in their single days.

Instead of being a couple embracing their love, they split into individuals on the hunt for sex.

They enjoyed some hot encounters with some very sexy men. Every now and then, though, they came across a dud. Someone who was a fish mouth or a snake tongue. Someone who didn't know what he was doing in bed or someone who turned out to be a little too crazy.

After those tricks left, they reevaluated the app and talked about deleting Cyber from their phones. They didn't. The high they each received from the chase was too satisfying to abandon.

"That's when our fights got worse," Spencer said. "Especially after I deleted Cyber and you didn't."

Justin's nod told Spencer he was right. Their fights did get worse because of Cyber. At first, Spencer was just as intrigued with the hookups as Justin was. But while his interest waned, Justin's only increased.

At last, Spencer saw what was happening to them. The disconnect widened from a rift to a yawning chasm, but Justin was too blinded by the hot profile pictures. The cruising and the promise of sex enraptured Justin. He had finally found a platform where he was good at flirting.

Online, he was better at snagging men than he had ever been in person. Justin had scores of men interested in him, simply based on his profile picture. That alone was an ego boost. More confident online, Justin felt powerful, magnetic, and unstoppable.

Justin became a man he didn't recognize. Drunk with the power of seduction, he spent more and more of his day on Cyber, chatting with guys he would never dream of approaching in person. When they agreed to come over, he was ecstatic, as if he had just completed some impossible task. In a frenzy, he rushed around the house, unmaking their bed, turning on the bedside lights and turning off the brighter overhead lights, opening a bottle of wine, and then retiring to the bathroom to make sure all his manly parts were clean for up-close inspection.

Spencer didn't always feel up for a three-way, and when he said no, Justin became sulky. He complained about how his hard work was for nothing and then retreated to the bedroom like a sullen child.

"You're right," Justin finally said. "The three-ways led to Cyber."

"Which led you to Dutch?" Spencer asked, invoking the name for the first time. In response, his already weary heart thudded sluggishly.

Justin nodded. His hands immediately returned to the towel, this time picking away at the fibers and pulling them one strand at a time.

Spencer had suspected Cyber was to blame for Dutch and Justin's relationship.

Still, the admission troubled his mind and soul, for he had yet to admit his own secrets. Justin still had no knowledge about the completely different set of circumstances that had set him on *his* path with Dutch. Even more, he feared his righteous anger was nothing more than guilt that, once acknowledged, would render his armor completely useless and result in his ruination.

CHAPTER 16

2008

FED up, Spencer marched from the bedroom to the living room in search of Justin. The proof he needed was in his hand. From Justin's cell phone, which he'd commandeered while Justin took out the trash, he had learned exactly how much time Justin spent on Cyber and exactly what he was doing on the app.

Simply chatting had become passé. Sexting and trading X-rated pics were apparently all the rage. As far as he was concerned, cheating was only a stone's throw away. That wasn't going to happen to him again.

Fear settled into his soul at the thought of losing Justin, and for the briefest of moments he felt the first piece of his armor strap to his body.

No, he thought to himself. *Not again. I let you go years ago. I don't need you anymore.*

I wouldn't be so sure of that, his father's voice echoed. *What have I always told you? When you prepare for battle, you don't leave your body armor behind. It saves lives. It's saved* your *life for years.*

Shut the fuck *up!* he railed at his father, whose voice immediately went mute.

It had been years since his father's voice rose from his subconscious, offering unsolicited advice on how to take care of himself. Justin's love had silenced him almost from their first kiss. To have his voice return now terrified him. *Does this mean we are in* that *much trouble? Have I let the situation deteriorate that far?*

Spencer feared he had.

When he deleted the app a few months ago, he'd banked on Justin doing the same within a few weeks, if not days. It didn't happen. Justin's time on Cyber increased exponentially. Spencer felt Justin slipping away from him, so he had to do something, anything, to refocus Justin on him and not the damn phone app.

Getting Justin's attention was easy. A kiss or a flash of skin revved him up. For the past few months, they had been enjoying a sexual renaissance. Their appetites for each other's bodies were insatiable, so he felt confident Justin still found him sexually desirable. After all, they had sex at least four times a week, which was a lot better than where they were before they started having occasional three-ways.

Recently, though, Spencer felt more like a live-in trick than a partner. While the sex might have been great, the intimacy had all but vanished. Every now and then, he caught a glimpse of it in Justin's eyes, the way Justin looked at him or kissed his flesh. His arms still held him tenderly when they were physically joined, but once orgasm was achieved, the connection severed with the spilling of fluids.

After cleanup, Justin returned to the couch or to his work, his phone ever at his side. Every few minutes, he logged onto Cyber, checked his messages, and chatted. Spencer felt as if he was no longer enough, no longer what Justin ultimately desired.

Still, he did nothing. He sat back and watched Justin move further and further away until he was but a speck on the horizon. His culpability kept him from trying harder to bring Justin back. The changes in Justin and their relationship were partly his fault. He had to reap what he had sown. At least that was what he told himself.

Not anymore. Justin's obsession with Cyber needed to come to an end.

In the living room, Justin sat amidst a pile of Christmas ornaments, untangling the hooks they used to hang them on the tree. He resembled the little boy from his mother's yellowed photographs, anxiously preparing the house for Santa Claus's arrival.

The innocence of the scene stopped Spencer in his tracks; his anger caught in his throat, unwilling to shatter such a pure moment in time. He wanted to forget about the phone and place it on the bathroom counter, so Justin would think he forgot it there. Then they could decorate the tree together, without dredging up bitterness or hostility.

That idea seemed more in keeping with the holiday spirit.

It also means you've lost your balls entirely and become his bitch, you pussy!

The surprise return of his father's voice caught him off guard. He dropped Justin's phone, and it crashed upon the ceramic tile in the foyer.

Justin turned, a string of tangled Christmas lights in his hand. His eyes were wide with horror at the sight of his phone on the floor.

"My phone!" he yelled, struggling to disentangle himself from the Christmas lights. In his haste to reach his precious phone, he stepped on the first Christmas ornament they'd purchased for the house.

When they first saw it at an art gallery in Austin, the spyrograph pattern on the handblown glass caught his eye. The spiraling yellow lines along the dark-green disk reminded him of a sun, shining its light above a richly green pasture.

Justin fell in love with it too. Not as much of an art aficionado as Spencer was, Justin said the ornament resembled Spencer's eyes. Justin plucked it from the display and purchased it without once looking at the price.

Now the ornament lay in pieces, shattered underneath Justin's hasty stampede. The broken shards of green and gold enraged Spencer, especially as Justin gently scooped his phone off the floor, examining it to make sure it still worked. Not once did he notice that he had broken something so precious to both of them.

I'm not one for symbols, his father's voice said. *But even I get that one. It's kinda like a kick to the nuts, isn't it?*

Fury swelling within, Spencer snatched the phone from Justin's grasp.

"Hey!" Justin called out. "I want to make sure it still works."

"I'm sure it works fine," replied Spencer. He walked over to the ornament and stood over its broken carcass. Tears wanted to fall, but the heat of his anger dried them instantly.

"Can I have it back?" Justin asked. He now stood beside Spencer, still oblivious to what lay broken before them.

"No, you cannot!" Spencer said. With rage he didn't know he possessed, he pushed Justin backward, causing him to stumble and fall into the tree. The tree rocked back and forth; most of the ornaments held their perch, but some fell to the hardwood floor and shattered, joining the original in death.

Justin caught himself on the wall, which prevented him from falling completely to the floor. When he recovered and was once again standing, his brown eyes, which used to remind Spencer of a beach, turned as dark and ominous as the coastal sky before an approaching storm. "What the fuck?"

"Do you even *know* what you've done?"

"What *I've* done?" Justin asked him. "*You* dropped my phone and then pushed me into the fucking tree!"

"I'm sick of this, Justin," he said. His voice wavered, not from a loss of will but merely from impending loss of something far dearer. "I can't take this anymore."

"Can't take *what* anymore?" Justin asked, looking at the shattered ornaments. "The mess *you've* made?"

"The mess *you've* made," Spencer retorted. "Why can't you ever see the consequences of your actions? Why is *everything* someone else's fault?"

Justin blankly stared at him, completely clueless, as always. "What the *hell* are you talking about?"

Spencer held up Justin's phone. "I'm talking about *this*. I'm talking about Cyber."

"Cyber?" he asked. "You pushed me into the tree because of Cyber?"

"You're on it all the time!"

"No, I'm not."

The bald-faced lie stunned Spencer. Never before had trust been an issue between them. Whether the truth was hurtful or not, they always spoke it. They came to that agreement early on in their relationship. It was the ballast that kept them afloat. Now, they were listing to one side.

"Since when did you start lying to me?" he asked. "Are we that far gone from where we once were?"

"I'm not lying," replied Justin. "I'm not on it *all* day. I open it up during the day to see if I have messages and then log off. It's not like I have time to chat on Cyber all day long. I'm busy too, you know?"

Spencer felt tongues of flame coil from his body, sparked and fanned by Justin's continuing lies. "Really?" He pushed the on button on the cell phone and opened it to the home screen. The Cyber icon, a pair of white briefs amidst a yellow box, rested on the main page. He tapped on the icon, and then began scrolling through the chat logs.

"Message sent to Cub4Love at eight thirty this morning. Then again at eight forty-five. Another at eight forty-seven. Nine o'clock. Nine fifteen. Ten thirty-six. Eleven twenty-three. That's *six* before lunch, and that's only to this one guy. Let's not forget the seven messages to ManEater12, where you both describe how you would suck each other off. There's also the cock shots you sent to Latino2000, and the ones you received of him spreading his ass for the camera." He looked squarely into Justin's eyes. "Should I continue?"

"There's no need," was all Justin replied.

"I disagree completely," Spencer shouted. He threw the phone at Justin, who caught it in midair. "But I'm not going to do that to myself."

"Why are we even doing this at all?" Justin asked. He placed the phone in the pocket of his jeans. "You're the one who told me about Cyber."

He expected Justin to lob that argument over the net. Sometimes he was too predictable. He wouldn't deny introducing Justin to Cyber. Spencer told him about all the apps currently installed on his phone. If it weren't for him, Justin wouldn't have a single app.

"So," he said, emphasizing the vowel as he typically did when upset. "It's my fault, then? That's bullshit and you know it!"

"I'm not saying that, but you were the one who told me about it. Hell, you used it too." Justin stood before him, hands on his hips, with a smug look on his face.

"I'm not denying *any* of those statements," he conceded. "But you've become obsessed with it." Spencer crossed his arms over his chest and stared at him, hard. Justin's smug stature collided with his *fuck you* look. "You're on Cyber at work. If you were to get caught taking dick pics there, you could be fired. Do you realize that? Not to mention that you're on Cyber at home all the damn time. When we're watching TV together, you're chatting on Cyber. When you go to the bathroom, you take the damn phone with you and chat while you shit. I mean, come on!"

"I see your point," Justin said, hands still on hips.

"No you don't," Spencer replied. "You're telling me what I want to hear. You don't get it at all." Completely exasperated, Spencer paced the living room, walking in circles around the coffee table and the leather sofa.

He really *doesn't get it. He thinks I'm the problem. That I'm crazy.*

He's a dipshit, his father told him. Most Mexicans are. They siesta all day and then wonder why they have no money for food. They never see that they're their own worst enemies. Except this one. He does *know how much he's screwed up. He gets it. But he's too chickenshit to admit it. He doesn't have the balls to accept responsibility. So like the rest of his kind, he's gonna let you think you're the problem. Until you give in. Until you find a way to fix it for him.*

Spencer stopped pacing. He stared at his reflection in the dark television screen. Distorted by shadows, he didn't even recognize himself. *Is that what's happening to me? Am I losing myself? Have I already lost myself?*

You're long gone, amigo, his father announced. *You disappeared once you lassoed yourself to this burro.*

To the left of his reflection, he saw Justin standing behind him, watching. His hands still on his hips, he looked impatient, as if he were willing this disagreement to end.

He doesn't care anymore, and you know it.

Yes, he does, Spencer told him. *He loves me.*

You think so? his father asked with a snicker. *He hasn't even noticed the ornament yet.*

He hasn't?

Nope, replied his father. *You're gonna have to do something big. Something so big that it gets his attention. That's the only way you'll know for sure how he feels.*

Like what?

Like London.

He had completely forgotten about the upcoming spring semester in London. As part of the university's curriculum, St. Mary's sent interested students and faculty to London for an entire semester, where students get to take college courses from St. Mary's faculty while also broadening students' awareness of cultural diversity. It was a once in a lifetime opportunity for students and faculty alike.

While it was a bit late to volunteer, he was certain he could call in a few favors with his dean and department chair, if he was really interested in going.

It's also perfect for your situation right now. If you tell him you're going, he should beg you to stay, right?

"Are we done?" Justin asked. "Because you haven't said anything for, like, five minutes."

Spencer laughed, not because he found Justin's statement funny. His father was right after all. "Yes," he replied. "We are." Justin turned to leave, most likely to disappear into the bathroom and check Cyber in peace and quiet. "We're so done that I'm planning on going to London for the spring semester."

Justin stopped. His back still turned to him, he asked, "You're going to London? For the *entire* semester?"

"I just may be," he replied. He was pleased the news got Justin's attention.

"And you didn't think to discuss this with me, your partner, first?"

He snorted. "It's not like you would've noticed. Your head's been stuck in Cyber for so long I could've been gone for the entire sixteen weeks before you were even aware of it."

"That's not fair or true!" Justin said, turning to face him.

For the first time, he saw fear behind the anger. His plan *might* work after all. "I'm not so sure."

"You accuse me of keeping secrets when you've been keeping *this* from me? You've been planning on leaving for four months without even *once* discussing it?" Justin's explosive rage caught him off guard.

"You're a piece of work, you know that?" Justin asked. "You act all high and mighty. Claiming that honesty is the foundation of our relationship, and you pull this crap?" Justin walked over to him and got in his face. "What happened to being partners? What happened to talking *every single fucking thing through*? Where was all that crap you've been dishing out to me when you made this decision?"

Spencer felt Justin's anger boiling over. For the first time in his life, he was afraid of Justin. Justin always flew off the handle when he was this mad. He inherited it from his grandfather and his Latin blood. Anger was the one emotion Justin did the best, better than sadness, concern, or grief.

But he had never been scared of Justin like he was right now. Justin's anger swirled around him like a tornado, ready to rip apart whatever, or whoever, was in his path.

"You're just as guilty as I am about keeping secrets, of telling lies. Hell, you're better at it than I am. At least you knew about Cyber. I had no clue about London." Justin turned away and roared in fury. He punched the living room wall, leaving a fist-sized hole in the plaster. The outburst did nothing to quell his rage.

"Have I been chatting with guys on Cyber? Yes. Have I been spending too much time on Cyber? Yes. Am I guilty of all the things you've accused me of? *Yes!*" Justin turned to face him, a mad snarl on his lips. "Have I made plans to abandon my partner for another country? No."

Spencer swallowed back his tears. He knew what was coming, the final devastating blow, the one thing he *never* wanted Justin to say or feel.

"If you're looking for an excuse to leave, you don't need one. Just go. I won't stop you."

Without a word, Spencer walked past Justin and out of the living room, trying to put as much distance between him and the natural disaster that had just ripped through his house and his heart.

CHAPTER 17

2010

JUSTIN sat in silence, listening to Spencer breathe. Since admitting to meeting Dutch on Cyber, he expected an eruption of cataclysmic proportions. After all, his obsession with Cyber was what had sent Spencer packing for London. Had he deleted the app like Spencer wanted, had he focused on Spencer instead of being entranced by the pursuit of other men, they wouldn't be sitting in his mother's kitchen trying to piece together what they'd rebuilt a few months ago.

The dead calm, which hung about the air, worried him. Was it a calm before the storm or did it mean Spencer was now indifferent? Had Spencer given up on them?

Or was there something else?

Spencer's pastel eyes reflected more than sadness, which went deep. Underneath the sadness lurked regret or something closely related to it. Justin could tell by how his eyes not only drooped but by how they peered out of this world and at something far away but not forgotten.

He had seen that regret the night Spencer told him about being HIV positive. While he spoke, Spencer's body was present but his mind relived the relationship with Mike Lane. When he asked Spencer about what he was feeling, Spencer told him he regretted ever getting involved with Mike and not heeding the concerns of his friends, who had all hated him.

Justin had seen that regret before through the years, but not to the extent he was seeing it now. It was somehow stronger, more powerful than that first night. It swirled like a vortex amidst the sadness.

What did Spencer regret? he wondered. *Is he regretting meeting me like he regretted Mike?*

Justin didn't think so. He knew Spencer better than anyone. He regretted not listening to well-meaning friends, not using a condom, not standing up to his father, not granting a colleague tenure, or not telling the truth to a friend who needed to hear it.

His regrets weren't tied to other people's actions. His regrets tied to his own.

Then what was he regretting? Was there something Spencer wasn't telling him?

He couldn't entertain the idea. Spencer never lied. Although he'd kept the semester in London a secret, he'd ultimately owned up to it. If there was something Spencer was keeping guarded, Spencer would tell him when it was time.

"Why did this have to happen to us?" Spencer asked, his voice calm and distant.

The deadened emotional state frightened Justin. It gnawed away at his insides like an intestinal parasite, working its way through his gut until it hollowed him out completely. If only Spencer would yell or cry, then Justin would know there might still be a chance. That glimmer of hope would be enough to halt the hungry parasite's progress.

Anger and sadness meant feelings still remained. He could combat anger with love and sadness with even more love. The freeze of indifference was virtually impossible to thaw.

"I don't know," he finally said. "If I did, I'd fix it with a wave of my hand."

"You don't have super powers," Spencer replied. "Not even after reading comic books for as long as you have."

"If that's all it took, I'd be as strong as Superman, as smart as Batman, and as kick-ass as Wonder Woman by now."

They both smiled at the attempt to be humorous, but the weight of uncertainty quickly crushed it, leaving their world hushed and still. Becoming stronger, the silence engulfed not only the air around them, threatening to suffocate them, but it seized their hearts, clenching them in its massive fists.

Justin needed to speak, needed to drain the silence from the room and their hearts before the quiet killed any chance of reconciliation. "Is there a chance for us?" Justin asked, fearful of the answer. He played with the edges of the towel, a nervous habit Spencer hated, but he couldn't help himself. It was the only thing keeping him from completely losing control of his emotions. "Could you perhaps one day forgive me?"

Spencer didn't answer right away. Most people would take that as a bad sign. Justin knew better. Serious questions required serious thought, according to Spencer's philosophy. A hasty answer meant he didn't care. A carefully thought out response meant he did. That offered Justin a small measure of hope.

Still, the sadness weighed heavily in Spencer's eyes, beating out the swirling pool of regret. They were still pastel green, as if the jade spark within had been siphoned out. His eyes and his appearance, slouched and exhausted, proved he was currently only a pale version of himself.

"I don't know if I can answer that right now," Spencer finally said. "I need to process some more. I also have questions I need to ask."

"If you're ready to ask, I'm ready to answer," Justin told him. He sounded more confident than he felt.

"Are you?" Spencer asked. His eyes furrowed.

Justin saw anger rise to the surface, forcing the sadness and regret to the depths below. *That* was a good sign. It meant he still cared.

Justin nodded.

"You already told me you met Dutch on Cyber, but when did you meet in person?"

This was it. The dreaded questions he'd feared Spencer would ask had begun. If he hoped for a potential future with Spencer, he had no choice but to answer any question asked.

"We met shortly after you left for London."

Spencer nodded, as if he was expecting that answer.

"How long did the affair last?"

This answer wasn't going to go over well. If Justin lied now, though, Spencer would sense it. "Till the end of May."

Spencer didn't speak for a few minutes. He was having visible difficulty dealing with the answer. Eyes closed in pain, he wrung his hands in his lap. His feet tapped in quick beats on the floor.

His answer meant the affair continued even after Spencer's return from London. While Spencer was home or at work, he slinked off to meet Dutch for a secret rendezvous, adding lies and deception to the heaping mound of betrayal.

The answer might be more than Spencer could handle, considering his past with Mike and the promise Justin had made not to cheat.

The overwhelming silence in his mother's house opened its mouth to swallow them whole.

"Did you ever *fuck* in our house?" Spencer asked, driving away the engulfing silence with his embittered tone of disgust.

"Never," Justin said quickly. It was the truth. He hoped Spencer could sense that.

Spencer studied Justin, looking for some sign that the answer was a lie. Justin never faltered in his composure or his stare. He met Spencer's gaze with confidence. Lying now would accomplish nothing.

"I believe you," he told Justin.

"Good," Justin said. "Because it's the truth."

"Where, then?"

"Dutch's place."

"Did it happen often?"

Justin exhaled. Nervousness gripped him tightly. He wanted to be honest, but honesty would not only further hurt Spencer but might also destroy any chance of reconciliation. Still, he had no other choice but to continue down the path they started.

"For the first few months, yes," Justin said reluctantly. "When you came back, it wasn't as frequent."

"What does that mean?" Spencer asked. His fists were now clenching. "'As frequent'?"

"I don't know what to say," Justin said. "I didn't keep a tally."

"Then guess, *goddamnit*!" Spencer yelled. The suddenness of Spencer's fury startled Justin and caused him to jump in his seat. The desire for Spencer to express anger, to show there was still hope for them, fled in the face of Spencer's rage. Looking into Spencer's eyes, overcome with such powerful wrath, hope seemed lost forever. "How many *fucking* times do you think the two of you *fucked* around when I got the *fuck* back from *fucking* London?"

Tears welled up in Justin's eyes. The immense hatred he felt coming from Spencer was unbearable yet justified, so he sucked the tears back into his body. "Maybe once every week," Justin said; his voice crackled with suppressed sobs.

"So," Spencer said, drawing out the vowel, "that means you two were humping like rabbits while I was gone. I guess you couldn't get enough of each other."

Justin didn't reply.

"You must've spent a lot of time with each other while I was gone," Spencer said. His tone turned more caustic than battery acid. "Did you even stay in our house while I was gone?"

"Of course I did," Justin replied. He dreaded the question he knew was next.

"How often did you spend the night at Dutch's place?"

"I didn't, at first."

"That wasn't my *fucking* question!" Spencer bellowed, slamming his fist on the kitchen table. His mother's teddy bear cookie jar rattled in place, and one of her canisters fell over on its side.

"I guess it was a couple of nights a week," Justin replied. He averted his eyes, using his periphery vision to see Spencer. He couldn't stand gazing straight into the look of disgust staring back at him.

"Sometimes more?" Spencer asked, leaning forward like a prosecuting attorney going in for the kill.

"Sometimes less," Justin answered.

"Clever," Spencer scoffed, but he didn't back away. Instead, he closed the gap, getting so close Justin could feel the heat of Spencer's resentment. "But it answers my question anyway."

"It's been over for about a year," Justin told him. In a daring move, he stared into Spencer's eyes again. The fury still raged within. "My heart *always* belonged to you."

"Too bad the rest of you didn't *always* belong to me." Spencer rose from the table with such force that the kitchen chair slammed into the refrigerator behind him. He stormed out of the kitchen and into the living room.

Justin immediately followed him. "Please don't go," he pleaded. "We need to talk. We need to work this out."

Spencer stopped with his back toward Justin. He was facing the front door, obviously ready to leave the house for good. He couldn't let Spencer leave. If he walked out the door, he might never see him again.

"I'll do whatever you want," Justin said. He crossed the divide between them, standing close enough for Spencer to feel his presence but far enough away not to draw further anger by making contact. "I'll endure whatever punishments are necessary. Just *please* don't leave."

"That's funny," Spencer told him, still refusing to look at him.

"Why?"

"If only you would've said those words to me when I told you about London, I wouldn't have left." Spencer turned around to face Justin. His cheeks were on fire. "If you would've simply asked me to stay, I would've stayed. I *wanted* you to *want* me to stay. I kept waiting for you to ask me to stay. Even when we said good-bye at the airport, I waited for you to ask me to stay. You *never* did. Instead, you told me to go. And you never *once* took that back."

Justin's heart dropped. He'd never even thought to ask Spencer to stay. When Spencer told him he wanted to go, he figured there was no point in asking. Once Spencer's mind was made up, little could be done to change it. If he had tried, though, they might not be where they were today.

Once again stupidity and shortsightedness had gotten the better of him.

"I'm asking you now," Justin said. "I *want* you to stay. I *need* you to stay."

A stray tear, too strong to be held back, rolled down Spencer's cheek. "And I *need* to go," Spencer told him. "This isn't about you anymore, Justin. It's about me. I need to do what's right for me now. I can't worry about your needs or your wants. Not now. Maybe not ever again."

Justin's world crumbled. The glimmer of hope he clutched fell from his grasp.

"I've been honest with you," Justin told him. He heard the desperation in his voice, but he didn't care. At all costs, he had to keep Spencer from leaving. "I could've lied, but I didn't. I've been honest with you about everything."

Spencer stood there, staring at him as if all he felt was pity. Then he looked around at the living room. On the walls were family pictures Justin's mother proudly displayed. There was a picture of Justin and Spencer when they moved into their house. There were other pictures of them at various stages of their relationship. Scattered among those were pictures of Justin's family—his aunt, uncle, grandparents, and his mother.

All eyes were watching, waiting in anticipation for how the scene would play out.

"Okay," Spencer said. "Then one more question. I want you to be honest. I *need* you to be honest."

Justin nodded, pleased that Spencer had not yet fled his mother's house but fearful of what the question might be.

Spencer inhaled sharply, as if this question had been hanging on his tongue just waiting to be asked. It was a question Spencer was obviously afraid to voice, but Justin had no idea what it could be. What could be worse than what had been asked so far?

"Did you fall in love with Dutch?"

The question hit him like a jab to the gut. It was the worst question of them all, ripe with danger and ready to blow everything to smithereens.

"Be honest," Spencer said. He walked over to Justin, closing the gulf that separated them to mere inches. "It's what we used to do best. Don't tarnish that now."

"Yes," Justin finally said. "I did."

He flinched, waiting for the detonation. Instead, Spencer smiled. It wasn't a joyful smile. The smile told him the answer was what Spencer expected, no matter how much it devastated him.

"I suspected as much," Spencer finally said. "When I saw your face while you were on the phone. When you told me someone was in an accident. You looked so worried. As if someone very close to you was in danger of dying. That's why I thought it was someone in your family."

Tears freely flowed down Spencer's cheeks, the dam keeping them back unable to withstand the pressure any longer. "I know the kind of man you are, Justin Jimenez. You don't have sex with someone for that length of time and not develop feelings. You're not that kind of man." He wiped the tears from his eyes and pulled them back in until his eyes were bone dry. The dam had been restored. "How I wish you were! But you're not."

"But I love *you*," Justin said. "I chose *you*!"

"A choice shouldn't be necessary," Spencer told him. "When we were brought together by that magical force, as you like to call it, there wasn't a choice. It just *was*."

"What are you telling me?" Justin asked. "Are you telling me we're over? For good?" He took Spencer's hands in his own, hoping his touch would bring the walls back down and weaken Spencer's resolve to go.

"I'm telling you the two of us were *never* meant to be a choice. Choosing cheapens what we were, what we had."

Spencer withdrew his hands from Justin's grasp.

"I don't understand," Justin said, his body trembling. He was losing Spencer; he could feel him pulling away, scampering behind the walls, which were numerous and constantly refortifying. In a few moments, Spencer would be impenetrable.

"That's the saddest part of it all," Spencer said. He kissed Justin on the cheek and turned around, then walked out the front door without glancing back even once.

CHAPTER 18

2009

JUSTIN threw his car keys against the living room wall, below the hole he punched before Christmas. When Spencer revealed he was going to London for four months, he was furious, and the wall took the brunt of his anger. Since then, the hole served as a daily reminder of the cavernous void in his heart.

He'd contemplated fixing it, or asking Tyler to help him fix it, but he let it remain. No matter how much of an asshole it made him, he wanted them both to see that hole every day until he left, to remind them how broken their relationship was.

Whether it worked or not, he didn't know. They rarely spoke after the incident. Christmas was torturous, pretending to be the happy couple for his family and their friends, but they muddled through it without anyone being the wiser.

Everyone except his mother. Her ability to spot unhappiness despite evidence to the contrary was creepy and bordered on supernatural. She asked him many questions, and he lied through his teeth.

Nothing's wrong, he told her. *We're fine*, he reassured her.

Her skeptical eyes revealed she knew better. Still, she let the matter go. He hated lying to her, but he didn't want to talk about it. Not only was he ashamed about their problems but he feared discussing them with *anyone* else would make the problems stronger, give them more power than they already possessed.

If he ignored them long enough, they might improve on their own like magic.

That never happened.

New Year's, which was a special holiday in the Harrison-Jimenez house, came and went without the typical pomp and circumstance. They didn't spend it with friends or recreate the night at home, like they had done in the past. He watched the ball drop in Times Square on the bedroom television while Spencer read in the guest room, where he now slept.

Their lives rarely intersected and when they did, they fought. They argued about cold dinners, unwashed dishes, full trash cans, dirty toilets, or an assortment of household complaints. Not once did they broach the true reason for their anger—Spencer's pending departure. Sure, he'd messed up. He didn't deny that, but he wasn't the one who was running away.

At the heart of every disagreement, at the root of every shouting match, Spencer's upcoming trip lay between them, unmentioned and leaking poison that polluted every single day and every single moment until they said their good-byes a few hours ago at the airport.

"I guess this is it," Spencer said, holding his plane ticket in one hand and his Louis Vuitton carry-on in the other. His hand fidgeted with the leather strap, as if he were waiting for Justin to speak some magical incantation.

Justin had no idea what words he could possibly say now that would make any difference. He didn't want Spencer to go, but he wasn't going to beg him to stay. He didn't beg. Pride meant too much to him. If Spencer wanted to stay, he needed to admit it. After all, Spencer was the one who wanted to leave.

They stood silently near the airport security area, where Justin couldn't pass and where Spencer would spend the next few minutes being scrutinized. Countless travelers hurried past them, some running to make flights already boarding and others calmly strolling since they'd arrived with more than enough time to make their connections.

"I hope you have a safe flight," Justin said at last, feeling the need to say something.

Spencer looked down at his feet. "Thanks."

"Will you call when you arrive?" he asked. "If that's not too much trouble." He immediately regretted the last comment. His anger had gotten the better of him.

Spencer's eyes met his and turned cold. "Of course," he said. "Will you be able to answer the call while you're on Cyber?"

"I can always log back on afterward," he told Spencer. His hands chilled from the coolness of his response. If he exhaled, he was certain his breath would plume outward.

He didn't want their last in-person conversation to end this way. Spencer deserved a proper send-off. The man he loved more than anyone else in the world was leaving him for four *months. There would be no good-night kisses, no good mornings, and no tender touches to make it through a tough day.*

While they hadn't done such things for a few weeks, they could have if they wanted. They were only a room away. Now, thousands of miles would separate them.

To commemorate his departure, Spencer deserved a huge banner with I'LL MISS YOU written across it. There should be hugs and kisses and tears. There should be tender caresses and promises of seeing each other soon.

There shouldn't be cruelty and pissiness.

The resentment in his heart about being abandoned kept what should have been from occurring. While Spencer withdrew from the world for protection, Justin lashed out in order to make everyone feel as crappy as he did. That was his *defense mechanism. That was what he used to survive. Why suffer alone was his motto.*

"I'm just going to go now," Spencer said, finally breaking the silence.

"Okay."

Spencer hugged him quickly and then turned around, heading toward the security area. A few steps away from the line, he stopped but didn't turn around. He waited a few minutes then joined the other travelers in the line.

Justin watched Spencer make his way through security, waiting for him to get out of line and run back to him, telling him he wasn't going to go. He willed Spencer to change his mind, trying to find the magic that once brought them together and use it to bring Spencer back to him again.

When Spencer cleared security and disappeared into the hallways beyond, Justin turned around, got into his car, and came home.

Now, he was alone. The hole in the wall echoed the hole in his soul. For nine years, he and Spencer had spent every day together. Now, he had to suffer through sixteen weeks without the sound of his presence in the house.

He wished he had stopped him when he had the chance. Now, in the quiet of solitude, his pride seemed less important. The central heat hummed, and the outside wind chimes made eerie music as the cold January air moved about outside.

Needing someone, *anyone*, he retrieved his car keys from the floor. His mother seemed the most logical answer. Her shoulder was always a comfort in times like this. But going to his mother meant addressing the problems he had yet to share. He wasn't ready for that.

Tyler was always a source of comfort, as were all their other friends, but like his mother, they were in the dark about the true status of his relationship with Spencer. As far as anyone was concerned, Spencer's decision to go to London was strictly professional, a feather in his professional bonnet.

He never felt more cut off from his family and loved ones than he did right now. Cast adrift in this sea of misery, he longed for one person, one shining beacon to rescue him before the waters dragged him to the rocky bottom.

What about Dutch? he thought.

For the past few weeks, he and Dutch had chatted on Cyber. When their chats first started, he assumed Dutch was only looking for play. Had his and Spencer's sex life not stopped entirely, he would have brought Dutch's profile pic to Spencer as an opportunity.

Dutch's profile picture, at least before he changed it to Yosemite Sam, was hot. He sat shirtless before a mirror. Dark-black hair matted his chest and framed his face. His broad shoulders looked capable of supporting the world. But his eyes, a crystal blue, entranced Justin the most.

It wasn't merely the uniqueness of the color; it was the sincerity and rugged beauty it reflected, outshining the headless torsos and other smiling, horny men on the prowl.

Held helpless in their power, he sent Dutch a message on Cyber. Since that first message and over the past few weeks, they'd cultivated a strange online relationship, with honesty at its very core. While they kept private certain aspects of their lives, such as their identities, they told each other everything else—their fears, their hopes, and their longings.

Dutch knew he and Spencer, who he referred to as only "S" on Cyber, were in a rough patch. Telling a stranger, someone not invested in their relationship's success, helped him deal with the pain without feeling the need to censor himself. A mutual friend or his mother would have taken on the role of devil's advocate. Dutch didn't. He was simply there, and that was what he needed the most.

That was what he needed now.

Within moments, his phone was on and Cyber was loading. The number one blinked next to Dutch's profile picture, which meant Dutch sent him a message. The green light to the left of his profile name indicated Dutch was also online. Immediately, Justin felt connected, not just by the app, but by some unseen USB cord that electronically tethered them to each other whenever they were both logged on at the same time.

Having this connection made him feel less alone in a world without Spencer. Someone, beyond his family, was in his corner. For reasons he couldn't explain, the connection mattered for Justin. It gave him weight and substance at a time he felt cut free and adrift.

Justin tapped on the display, which maximized Dutch's profile picture on his small iPhone screen. The picture was no longer Yosemite Sam, the face that had graced his profile for weeks. In its place, Dutch now lay crossways on his bed. A white muscle shirt covered his expansive chest but couldn't contain the abundant chest hair, which peeked over the fabric's edges. Lifted slightly, the shirt revealed the coat of hair across his stomach and the waistband of his Unico underwear. Dutch's right hand rested behind his head, revealing tufts of armpit hair.

The image entranced him. Dutch's smile, seductive yet rugged, was also straightforward and genuine. It marked him as one of the good guys.

He tapped on the screen again, causing Dutch's profile picture to disappear. In its place appeared his message from Dutch.

DUTCH: How r u? Did S leave after all?

Tears flooded his eyes, but he wiped them away. He promised himself he wouldn't cry.

J-SQUARED: Yeah, but I don't want to talk about it right now, okay?

DUTCH: Sure.

J-SQUARED: How r u?

DUTCH: U not tired of my drama yet?

J-SQUARED: Better yours than mine.

DUTCH: LOL. OK. Got turned down for another job today.

J-SQUARED: Damn. I'm sorry.

Dutch had recently transplanted to San Antonio from Boston. He left his mother, sister, and home behind for a better paying job as IT Director at the main San Antonio Bank of America office. A recent breakup of his three-year relationship prompted the move more than the salary increase.

He settled into his new job and bought a house on the northwest side of San Antonio. Dutch even jumpstarted his graduate degree in photography online after contacting his old advisor at the Center for Digital Imagery at Boston University.

More than halfway to a graduate degree in something he loved and making a good chunk of change at his new job, his world bottomed out.

The banking crisis followed him from Boston. Layoffs at many Bank of America branches were necessary. As one of the most recent hires and one of the most expensive employees, Dutch was released from his job.

Now he was saddled with a mortgage he could no longer afford and had been unsuccessful in getting a job in an economy that wouldn't hire someone of his age and experience.

DUTCH: Me too. To make matters worse, I received a check in the mail today from my mother. I love her to death, but taking her charity makes it worse.

Justin understood. A proud man himself, he preferred to stand on his own two feet, which was one of the reasons no one knew about his problems with Spencer.

J-SQUARED: What about the photography gigs?

He hated asking Dutch about them because Dutch felt as if he was whoring out his artistic talents to make a few bucks. But in this economic climate, he had no other choice.

DUTCH: I have a wedding this weekend. It should help some.

J-SQUARED: Wish there was something I could do.

DUTCH: Wish there was something I could do for you too.

J-SQUARED: Thx, but I'll be fine.

DUTCH: Like I told you last time, businessmen sometimes have to go on extended business trips. Just because the trip came at a really low point doesn't mean anything.

Justin rolled his eyes. Dutch didn't understand Justin's reaction to Spencer's trip. When Justin told him about London, Dutch had assumed Spencer was a businessman. He never corrected him since their lives outside Cyber were to remain private.

J-SQUARED: It doesn't matter. Maybe the separation will be good.

He lied. The separation wasn't good. Dutch even told him to ask S not to go, but he told Dutch he shouldn't have had to.

DUTCH: Do you really think so?

J-SQUARED: No. But it wasn't my decision to make.

Dutch didn't agree with that statement, a fact he voiced the last time they'd chatted. He'd called Justin out on the real reason he didn't ask Spencer to stay: he was simply too proud to beg.

J-SQUARED: Let's talk about something else. I really can't talk about it anymore.

DUTCH: Okay. You pick the topic.

J-SQUARED: Let's talk about your new profile pic. WOOF!

DUTCH: What? You didn't like Yosemite Sam?

Justin laughed out loud. He knew Dutch's reason for swapping his previous profile pic with Yosemite Sam. Dutch had grown tired of the many messages he received on Cyber. Most were looking for a hookup, or they sent him a cock shot. Dutch wasn't a prude, but to arbitrarily receive someone's genitals as an initial message wasn't a good first impression, according to him, no matter how spectacular the package might have been.

So he changed his profile picture to his favorite cartoon character from childhood. Dutch related to Yosemite Sam. No matter what obstacles Bugs Bunny placed in front of Yosemite Sam, he did his best to overcome them. It was how Dutch approached life—with both barrels cocked and ready to fire.

Once Yosemite Sam's bright red hair and angry eyes took up residence on Dutch's Cyber profile, the shameless messages, along with pictures of erect cocks and bare asses, all but stopped.

J-SQUARED: You're MUCH hotter!

DUTCH: LOL! And not quite as hairy. ☺

The overwhelming sense of isolation he'd felt prior to logging onto Cyber slowly wafted away on the refreshing breeze of his electronic chat with Dutch.

It was bizarre, when he thought about it. They had never met. They never spoke on the phone, and they didn't have a way to contact each other besides on Cyber. They didn't even know each other's real names. He was "J-squared," and he assumed the screen name "Dutch" pointed to his Germanic lineage instead of his real name.

Their anonymity fostered a level of honesty he hadn't known existed in the digital world. Stripped of all the encumbrances of the real world, he found something surprisingly real in an environment with a reputation for being superficial and fraudulent.

J-SQUARED: Take the pic with your new camera?

DUTCH: Yup. Was playing around with lighting and angles. Went for something artsy yet provocative.

J-SQUARED: I don't know about artsy, but it sure made me want to crawl into that bed with you.

After he hit the send button, he regretted the message. While they had been flirtatious over the past few weeks, there had been a line they hadn't crossed. A line he had *just* crossed.

He was in a committed long-term relationship, even if it was on tenuous ground. He had no right to be so provocative and inappropriate with another man, especially since Spencer had just left.

Now he might have just alienated the one confidant he had been relying on.

DUTCH: You're always welcome in my bed.

Justin held his breath after reading Dutch's reply. He logged off Cyber and turned off his phone. They had both crossed the line now, and Justin was nervous about what it meant.

CHAPTER 19

2010

DUTCH breathed easy. Nurse Ratched's shift had ended and her replacement, Nurse Stacy, had a cheerful bedside manner. She tenderly removed the bandages that Nurse Ratched would have simply ripped off and even shaved the areas around the bandages to prevent any further hair from being unceremoniously yanked free.

Her relaxed demeanor made him feel safe, and he thanked her for her efforts before she departed.

Now he was alone in his new room having been transferred out of ICU a few hours ago. Nurse Stacy wouldn't return for a while, and he'd finally gotten his sister to agree to leave his side to get something to eat. All he had to occupy him were the television, which he wasn't really interested in, and his thoughts.

Even though Nurse Ratched scared him, her parting words still haunted him. *I hope you learn from this, Mr. Keller.*

It was past time for learning to begin.

As a result of his destructive streak, he was paralyzed from the waist down. Still, he remained positive. Outside the hospital window, the clear azure of the sky filled him with renewal; life was limitless now that he had faced death and survived. Even though he didn't deserve it, he'd received a second chance to make a better life, to make better decisions, and to forge something out of the ashes of his old life like his father's Phoenix.

The car crash was his wake-up call. It was fate telling him his previous life needed to perish. He needed to be born anew, into something better than he was before. As tough as it was for Dutch to admit, the car crash might have saved his life.

He had been on a path of self-destruction for the past year. He'd cared little about others and even less about himself. Late-night binge drinking at the clubs had led to anonymous, unsafe sex with countless partners. Even though he knew he should get himself tested, he didn't. Instead, he jumped in bed with the next piggy bottom he found.

While he fucked those guys, he hated himself. He despised what he had become, what he had let himself turn into.

But he couldn't stop.

The pain he felt when he wasn't drinking or hooking up was excruciating. The alcohol and the sex forced the pain into the pit of his stomach. When he drank, he became numb. When he came inside one of the slutty bottom boys, he felt alive again. At least until the pain reared its ugly head one more time.

When it did, it was time to go back to drinking. After that, it was time to fuck.

It had become an endless cycle.

His work at St. Mary's suffered as a result, and his chances of full-time employment were most likely destroyed. His department chair had called him in last week about his spotty attendance and his declining student evaluations. His part-time job was in jeopardy, so naturally, he drank and fucked the rest of the week away.

To make matters worse, a few months after Justin left him he went to the Bonham, the place where Justin and Spencer fell in love. He thought if he faced their love on its home turf, he could overcome it, get past the darkness that devoured him from within. Originally, he'd planned to return to where he and Justin first met, their special place on the River Walk, but he couldn't. Those weren't the memories he needed to defeat. It was the loss of Justin to Spencer he had to combat.

When he entered the doors and first stepped upon the wooden floors of the Bonham's entrance, he realized going there was a mistake. Justin and Spencer were there, laughing with friends at the bar to the entrance's left. Justin had his arm around Spencer, and they looked happy.

He wanted to run, to escape this torture. He meant to face the ghost of their love, not the actual physical manifestation of it. Instead of leaving, he hurried down the hallway and proceeded to the back bar, where he started to drink heavily.

After that, the events remained fuzzy. He remembered getting upset at someone, but he couldn't remember who. Then there was a dark-skinned twink, who was ready to party. They drank together, excessively, and made out on the dance floor before making plans to head back to the twink's apartment.

He vaguely remembered leaving the Bonham, shitfaced and in no shape to drive. Still, he got in his car and followed his latest conquest to his place.

He never made it.

He plowed through a stoplight a few intersections away from the club and crashed into a Cadillac. He'd failed to fasten his seatbelt when he entered the car, so the force of the collision ejected him from his vehicle and onto the pavement.

After that, he couldn't recall.

From what his sister told him, he fell into a coma a few days after the accident and was still in it when she arrived from Boston. The doctors were unsure if he would wake up, which had terrified Heidi.

He had no memory of a coma, but he did recall a black sea. Adrift, he felt lost and helpless, ready to drown, when his father descended from the heavens to save him.

Now that he had been rescued, he needed to prove worthy of being saved.

The previous year of his life had been a disaster, which he blamed on Justin. But while Justin was an easy scapegoat, his broken heart wasn't Justin's fault. Dutch entered into doomed relationships far too easily—Trevor, Manny, Carlo, Todd, and Justin. In his four decades on this planet, he'd managed to make more disastrous decisions in his romantic life than most people, including Britney Spears and Liza Minnelli combined.

That was going to end. His heart would still be his sail but his mind would take over the wheel. Working together, they would charter a safer path for his life.

His positive attitude and outlook made him feel like a new person, like someone he hadn't been in a long time.

According to the doctors, it also contributed to his remarkable recovery. He had many internal injuries and a busted spleen, but his body was healing itself, as if it had found a new energy source to spur it toward recovery. This morning he sat up and ate breakfast, and he could even wheel himself to the bathroom instead of relieving himself in a bedpan, which pleased both him and the nurses.

What he needed to work on now was walking. With a compression fracture of the vertebrae, lengthy bed rest, when he wasn't in physical therapy, was required, especially if he wished to walk again.

Apparently, when he was ejected from the car, his ass hit the asphalt first, causing some of the vertebra to break. Once the swelling subsided, which would only happen with bed rest and no physical exertion, the swelling would decrease and the pressure against the spinal cord would lessen. With strengthening and stretching exercises and some physical therapy, Dutch could walk again.

No, he *would* walk again.

This was a new beginning after all. The old Dutch had died in the car accident. When he took his first steps, it would be as a new man, a different Dutch Keller, who had never walked this planet before.

"I've seen you look better."

Startled, Dutch turned toward the open door to his hospital room. There stood Justin Jimenez, a man he never expected to see again and the man who indirectly led him down the path of destruction.

The refreshing breeze of his new beginning died. In its place, the familiar darkness reformed. The sight of Justin paralyzed his entire body, until he felt just as heavy and useless as his legs.

Justin walked into his hospital room and crossed to the chair under the television, across from his bed. Dutch hadn't seen Justin in a year, but that didn't *feel* right. It seemed like only yesterday when he last gazed upon his face, which had changed a bit since they were together.

Justin's hair was now shorter. When they first met, his hair came to just below his ears, and long strands constantly fell in front of his eyes. Now, cut clean, not clipped, the style better suited a high school principal.

The soul patch he'd once sported under his lower lip had grown into a Van Dyke.

If it was possible, Dutch found him even more attractive now.

You've got to be kidding me, he thought. *After everything that's happened, after everything you've been through, you* still *want to take him in your arms? He stopped talking to you. He cut all ties with you! He told you he loved you and then cut you off like an infected limb.*

The darkness within him hissed.

Justin's callous abandonment had caused him to spiral out of control. The cavalier way Dutch led his life afterward was a testament to his dreadful mistreatment. He no longer felt worthy of being loved, of being happy. He felt tainted, as if the love they'd shared was an aberration, something that never should have been born into the world.

As such, he'd lived his life like a ticking time bomb, slowly counting down to his inevitable death.

He refused to remain in that place any longer. The accident propelled the negativity out of his body the moment he slammed into the asphalt. He was paralyzed but stronger than he had been in a year.

Justin would not reignite the self-destructive spark.

"What the *hell* are you doing here?" he asked.

Justin's eyes widened in surprise to his acerbic tone. He, too, was shocked at the anger, but he didn't let the surprise show. His anger not only felt good, it was healing.

Justin rose from the chair in front of the bed. He looked uncertain, but even more than that, he looked shattered, as if someone had broken him to pieces and then hastily adhered all the pieces back together.

At first, Dutch hadn't noticed how awful Justin looked. His sudden entrance had caught him off guard. Now, though, Justin's distress was impossible to miss. His hair was disheveled, his clothes were wrinkled, and his eyes were swollen. Something bad had recently happened.

"I apologize," Justin finally stammered. "I thought you wanted me to come."

Justin's comment infuriated him. His concern for Justin's appearance washed away in a tsunami of resentment. "You *thought* I wanted you to come?" he asked, his anger swelling to violent proportions. "A *year* ago I wanted you to come. *Six months* ago, I wanted you to come. Hell, even *last week* I wanted you to come." He closed his eyes, willing Justin out of his room. "*Today*, I want you to get the *fuck* out of here."

"I'm sorry," Justin said while tripping over the leg of the hospital chair. "I'll just leave."

He exhaled sharply. "Good."

"You made it!" Dutch heard his sister exclaim. "I'm so glad you came."

When he opened his eyes, his sister was hugging Justin as if he were a long-lost relative. She looked at Dutch, and her eyes sparkled with the satisfaction of a job well done.

"You did this?" he asked her. "You asked him to come?"

"Of course not," she responded. "I was only the messenger."

He had no clue what was happening. He didn't understand why his sister was happy to see Justin, when she knew everything about their relationship and their breakup. She was the one who had wanted Dutch to end things with Justin. Now she was standing with her arm around Justin and kissing his cheek as if they were the best of friends. As if Justin wasn't the reason her brother had self-destructed.

She was also not sensing Justin's discomfort. His sister obviously hadn't overheard her brother's angry words toward Justin, and she couldn't see that Justin looked like a cornered squirrel, unsure whether to dash out the door or jump out the window.

As usual, his sister was more clueless than Alicia Silverstone. He thought she would grow out of it when she turned forty. Apparently, he was wrong.

"Heidi, what message are you talking about?"

"You know the message," she told him. Heidi finally untangled herself from Justin and plopped herself at the foot of his bed. She absently rubbed his leg. "Please, Justin, sit down. After all, you've come all this way."

"He lives in San Antonio," he practically yelled at her. "You make it sound like he just flew in from Tokyo."

"Lukas, what's the matter with you?" she asked him. "Why are you so sour?"

"It's me," Justin finally said. "I'm sorry for upsetting you," he told Dutch. Justin walked over to Heidi and shook her hand. "It was nice seeing you again. I wish it was under better circumstances."

"You're leaving?" she asked, still completely oblivious to the tension quickly filling the room. "You just got here."

"I know," Justin said. "But I have things to take care of."

"Tell Spencer I said hi," he said.

Justin flinched as if he had been slapped.

"Lukas!" his sister scolded.

"Don't worry about it," Justin told Heidi. "I'm fine." His eyes once again met Dutch's. "I'm glad to see you're recuperating nicely. I wish you nothing but a full recovery."

He stared blankly at Justin. He had no idea why Justin was here, but he wanted Justin to go. Justin's presence wasn't helping. It only depressed him, reminded him of what he lost and how he'd been treated. He didn't need that reminder. The memories he carried with him like an albatross were reminder enough.

Besides, Justin had made his choice, and it was Spencer. He didn't need Justin to check up on him, to see if he was okay. Doing so was like teasing an alcoholic with a shot of whisky. Justin didn't care, and his reentrance was merely a prelude to his imminent exit. It was time for him to walk out the door and stay gone for good.

On cue, Justin turned around and walked toward the open hospital door.

"Oh my *fucking* God!" Heidi shouted. "You gay guys are worse than straight men, if that's even possible!"

Justin stopped in his tracks. He turned around to face Heidi. "Excuse me?"

"What *he* said," Dutch told his sister. Her outburst was both uncharacteristic and alarming. He rarely saw her this way. "What are you talking about?"

"The two of you obviously have more unresolved conflict than an obsessive compulsive woman with daddy issues, but instead of hashing it out, you're ignoring it. I thought gay men were supposed to be in touch with their feelings."

"I'm in perfect touch with my feelings," he told his sister. He could see Justin squirming uncomfortably through his peripheral vision. "I know down to the very last detail what happened to me after I was left on the side of the road like a piece of trash. Forgive me if I don't want to travel down *that* road again."

"You think so?" Heidi asked him. "You think you're ready to move on, ready to finally get Justin out of your system? Ready to make a new life for yourself?"

"I'm just going to go," Justin said, inching closer to the door.

"You stay right where you are!" Heidi yelled at him.

Justin froze like a soldier before a drill sergeant. Dutch was impressed.

"So, big brother," she said, turning once again to him. "You think you're ready for all that?"

"I know I am."

Heidi scoffed. "You don't even know what you want. You're not ready."

"What makes you the expert on what I want?" he asked. "I wasn't aware you got your degree in psychology." She was starting to piss him off. Not only did she think she knew his wishes better than he did, but she had prevented Justin from leaving, which was what he wanted all along.

"No degree," she said while shaking her head. "But I have qualifications no one else on this planet does."

"What would that be?"

"I'm your sister," Heidi replied. "I know you better than you know yourself. I *know* you want to be over Justin. I *know* you don't want to love him anymore. You have no idea how much I wish that for you, but wishing it doesn't make it come true."

She moved over to him. Her hand hovered over his head. "Your head knows what it should want," she told him. Her hand then moved over his chest. "But your heart tells you something else. Otherwise, you wouldn't have been calling for Justin when you started to come out of your coma. For three days, you called for him. I finally asked him to come this morning."

Dutch didn't remember calling for Justin, but his sister's face told him it was the truth. He *did* call for Justin.

Why did I do it? Why did I spend what little energy I had calling for someone who abandoned me and broke my heart? Am I a glutton for punishment, even in a coma?

All those questions troubled him, but the one he worried about the most was the final question that floated to the surface. *Why did Justin come?*

CHAPTER 20

2009

DUTCH had no idea what came over him. He should never have sent that message. *You're always welcome in my bed? Really? What the hell was I thinking?* It was too salacious and too forward and would most likely cost him a dear friend.

J-squared told him as much by logging off Cyber shortly after he sent it.

When he saw the green light next to J-squared's profile blink off, he knew he had screwed up.

J-squared wasn't at a point in his life where he could deal with such inane propositions. His partner had just left the country and him for sixteen weeks. He was hurting and in pain. And instead of being there for him, Dutch basically tried to seduce him while he was at his lowest.

He wouldn't blame J-squared for never sending him another message again.

Dutch stood in the dining room, staring at his phone resting on the kitchen table, where he left it shortly after logging off Cyber as well. While only a few feet away, it appeared to be miles from his grasp. He needed to reach the phone, to apologize or laugh off the comment as a joke, but his feet would not obey.

His body locked up as if he were asking it to cross a chasm on an unsteady rope bridge. He needed to move, though, to salvage what he could of their relationship. Their chats had become very important to him. J-squared was his lifeline in these turbulent waters of unemployment and financial crisis.

He took his first step toward the kitchen, and his body screamed for him to stop. Ignorance was better in this instance. If he didn't know how angry or how hurt J-squared was, he wouldn't have to deal with the ramifications.

He refused to allow that to stop him. He was a big boy; he could handle whatever came his way because of his foolish comment. Making amends would be top priority, and if he couldn't, well, he would deal with the loss.

What other choice do I have?

Before he knew it, he'd picked up his phone and turned it on. He logged back into Cyber. Next to J-squared's profile picture was the number three, indicating Dutch had three messages from him. The light next to J-squared's profile picture was green. J-squared was back online.

This is it, he thought. *This is where J-squared tells me our online friendship is over.*

Hovering his finger over the screen, he hesitated. He didn't want to hear the good-bye, but he had to accept it. His father taught him that a man accepted the lumps he was due. A quick double tap on the profile picture delivered the three messages onto Dutch's phone screen.

J-SQUARED: Sorry about logging off before, but you took me by surprise. Your offer is tempting, but dinner first would probably be more appropriate.

J-SQUARED: Knowing our real names might help too. I'm Justin.

J-SQUARED: You still there?

Disbelief coursed through Dutch's body. The received replies were unexpected. He'd prepared himself for anger or even silence. Never once did he entertain the idea that J-squared, no, *Justin*, would be interested in meeting and potentially taking him up on his offer.

All he could do was stare at the messages and contemplate the possibilities.

Justin's responses revealed a great deal. Early on during their initial chats on Cyber, they had both agreed to keep their identities secret, hoping to avoid any embarrassing situations should their online chats somehow go wrong. It was also why he only knew Justin's partner as S.

Anonymity freed them from worry as well as inhibitions. They could be who they truly were and express any thought, opinion, or desire without fear of consequence.

It was an agreement they'd both lived up to and supported fully. Until now.

Now, he knew J-squared's first name. To pursue this further meant he would soon know Justin's last name; he would then be expected to return the favor. The anonymity they'd enjoyed and the relationship it helped cultivate floated skyward like a kite caught in an updraft.

Even more than that, they were on the threshold of transporting their online relationship to the real world. That, more than the revelations of their names, was dangerous.

A precipice lay before them. Once they jumped, a return to their previous arrangement was impossible.

Still, the thought of what they might be jumping into excited Dutch. He typically leaped first and looked later, just like Yosemite Sam. That had always gotten him into trouble in the past. This time, he felt it would be different.

J-SQUARED: Sorry for breaking our rule. I obviously scared you off. You don't have to share your name or anything. You were probably joking and stupid me thought you were serious. I'm just really stupid right now.

Dutch smiled at the message. It was sincere and honest, characteristics he had come to depend on.

DUTCH: You're not stupid. I was pleasantly surprised by your response. So much so I couldn't believe it. BTW, my name is Lukas Keller, but most everyone calls me Dutch.

J-SQUARED: LOL! So it's been Dutch all along!

DUTCH: Afraid so. Nice to know your name, Justin.

J-SQUARED: Same here, Dutch. My last name is Jimenez, btw.

DUTCH: Ah, Justin Jimenez. J-squared makes sense now.

J-SQUARED: I thought it sounded cooler than J.J. ☺

Dutch chuckled. The humor made it easier to deal with the nerves they both undoubtedly felt. A boundary had been broken; their names were shared. Searches on Google or Facebook would deliver information about their lives and pasts. They could read where the other went to school and learn other information that was freely shared or public knowledge.

Their lives were now an open book lying on the table, just waiting to be read.

J-SQUARED: Have you Googled me yet?

He laughed out loud. The two of them were definitely on the same wavelength.

DUTCH: No. You Google me?

J-SQUARED: No, but I'm tempted.

DUTCH: How about we agree not to? Let's meet for dinner instead and share the info in person.

J-SQUARED: I would like that.

DUTCH: Me 2. When should we do dinner?

J-SQUARED: You have plans tonight?

Dutch liked Justin's style. He too was a rip-the-Band-Aid-off-the-hairy-leg kind of man. Since they had broken one boundary today, they might as well break some more.

DUTCH: Dinner with you, I'm hoping.

J-SQUARED: Great! You like seafood?

DUTCH: I do.

J-SQUARED: Ever been to Pesca on the River Walk?

DUTCH: Never.

J-SQUARED: It's good. How about we meet there at 8:00? I'll make reservations.

DUTCH: It's a date.

Dutch grimaced at his sloppy word choice. He didn't mean to suggest anything more than a meeting of two friends.

J-SQUARED: A date it is. See you tonight.

The green light next to J-squared's profile picture disappeared. Justin had gone offline.

Dutch couldn't log off Cyber. He stared at the last message.

It *was* a date. Justin wasn't hiding behind pretense. They weren't two men meeting for a casual dinner; they were two men about to embark upon a risky romantic venture with potentially disastrous ramifications for them both.

Dutch had always fancied himself an adventurer, willing to try most anything once. This had the potential of being one of the greatest adventures he had ever plunged into. Despite the risk, it was a journey he was anxious to begin.

CHAPTER 21

2010

JUSTIN sat silently in the chair across from Dutch's hospital bed. After Heidi scolded the two of them for not talking about their problems, she ordered them to work things out, to find closure. She refused to leave until they complied.

He agreed to her request quickly. He had no other choice. The woman he'd met over a year ago wasn't the woman he'd faced a few minutes before. When they met in Boston, she made him feel welcome and comfortable, even though her mother had just died. She appreciated the fact that he accompanied Dutch to Boston to help him get through the funeral and his loss.

When he asked Dutch why his sister wasn't more grief-stricken, Dutch told him Heidi was rarely sad. She was the happiest, most optimistic person he knew. A trait she inherited from their mother. She almost never got angry and never had anything bad to say to anyone, even if they deserved it.

That wasn't the woman he'd just faced. This Heidi was fed up and angry. Her eyes were no longer welcoming; they were pissed off and irritated, not just at the two of them for leaving so many issues unresolved but at how those problems had led her brother to his current state. Her unfaltering gaze and unyielding posture told them it was time to put their lives in order.

He couldn't disagree with that. Their lives were a mess. He'd lost Spencer, and Dutch had almost died. Whatever needed fixing between them needed to be resolved if they had any hope of healing their bodies and their souls.

The problem was he didn't know where to start.

Dutch reluctantly gave in to his sister's demands, but once she left the room, he turned to look out the window, completely ignoring him. The only thing Dutch obviously wanted was for him to just leave and never return.

He couldn't leave now. Dutch was broken and in dire need of repair.

That realization hurt him because he knew he was partly, if not mostly, responsible. He needed to do something to make things right, not just with Spencer but with Dutch.

"Where should we begin?" he asked.

"I don't know," replied Dutch. He continued to stare out the window, preferring to occupy his mind with the outside world than deal with what was awaiting him in the room. It was something Dutch did when in turmoil. He shut down, cutting himself off from his feelings, until the hot sting became a dull ache.

"We should talk," he told Dutch. "I don't want your sister to get angry again."

"Okay," Dutch said, turning to face him. "Let's talk about you."

He was confused. "What do you mean?"

"You look like shit."

He attempted a smile, but it felt forced. His bone-crunching pain over losing Spencer floated on the surface of his emotions, no matter how hard he tried to cover it up. He didn't want Dutch to see it, but Dutch could always sense his pain. When they were together, Dutch had magically sensed when he was worried and pulled Justin into his arms to hold him. The beat of Dutch's heart and the soft cushion of chest hair comforted him and calmed his troubled waters.

He longed to once again be swallowed up in Dutch's embrace, to crawl up and lie beside a man whose touch had the power to dissipate the fog of distress. They weren't in that place anymore, though. His pain was his alone and no longer Dutch's concern.

"Look who's talking," he finally responded. "Swollen and scabby lips. A bruised face and lacerations everywhere. Pockets of shaved chest surrounded by a forest of dark hair. You're not the picture of perfection yourself."

"I still look better than you."

"You always did."

Dutch's eyes narrowed in anger. He'd meant for his compliment to ease the tension. Instead, he made it worse.

"Let's dispense with the pleasantries," Dutch said. His crystal blue eyes frosted over. "Closure is what my sister thinks I need. Closure is what I intend to get."

Dutch's bitter words hit hard. He shrunk into the seat, feeling like an abused pet awaiting the next blow from its vicious master. He wanted to scamper away and seek shelter, but this wasn't about him. This was for

Dutch. He needed to voice his anger, to set free the rage that blew within like a tempest.

Justin sat up, bracing himself for the storm. "I'm ready," he said. "Let me have it."

Dutch stared into his eyes. The frosty blue hue chilled even further, dropping to temperatures approaching absolute zero. The change told him there were things Dutch needed to say, things that had gone unsaid when their relationship ended.

"You're a bastard!" Dutch said. "You made me believe we had a future when you told me you loved me. And like a dumbass, I gave you my heart and let you inside." Dutch stared at him; the heat of his words couldn't melt his permafrost stare.

"I know," was all he mustered. "I'm sorry."

"Is *that* the best you can do?" Dutch asked. The temperature in the room dropped to match his chilling stare. "We practically lived together for sixteen weeks, and during that time I thought we built something that *meant* something. To both of us. I guess it was only important to *me*."

"That's not true," he responded. Anger overpowered the hurt in his voice. He couldn't believe what Dutch had said. "What we had was just as important to me. I never expected to fall in love with another man. I never expected to become *that* guy."

He had told Dutch that much when Justin admitted he had fallen in love with him. Neither of them thought it would happen, but it did. He expected the declaration to be taken at face value since Justin never fell in love easily, a fact Dutch knew.

Still, he didn't know what being in love with Dutch meant. *Would they be able to make it through Spencer's return from London? Was his relationship with Spencer really over?*

He didn't have the answers then. All he knew was how he felt, and he *loved* Dutch.

"I know you never expected it to happen, but it did," Dutch said. "When you say you love someone, though, you don't leave them like you left me."

His bitter, cold gaze slowly thawed, giving way to pain within. Seeing the pain made Justin wish for the chilly indifference to return. "What was I supposed to do?" Justin asked. "I hadn't stopped loving Spencer. He and I had history. We built a life together."

"What were *we* building? *A lie?*"

"Of course not," Justin said. His anger was on the rise. "What I felt was never a lie, you know that." The abused pet cowering in the corner disappeared. Once again, a spark burned within. "I had to make a choice. I didn't like making it. But I had to do it. I couldn't be in love with two men and be in two relationships. I had to choose one."

"I know. I was the expendable one."

"You were *never* expendable. You *aren't* expendable," he replied, rising from the chair. "You've no idea how much leaving you hurt me too."

"You're right," Dutch answered. His voice dripped with venom. "You left and stopped talking to me. No matter how many times I reached out to you. No matter how many times I extended my hand in friendship. You cut me out of your life without *once* thinking about how that would make me feel."

For a few moments, they stared at each other in silence. What could he say to Dutch's comment? He had severed all ties with Dutch, but not because he didn't care. It was just the opposite. Completely exiting his life was supposed to help Dutch move on.

"I thought it would be easier that way," he whispered.

"Are you *fucking* serious?"

"Yes," he said, nodding. "I figured if we stopped talking, you would eventually hate me and move on with your life a lot faster than I was able to."

Dutch grunted. "You're one of the stupidest men I've ever met."

"What the hell's that supposed to mean?"

"Not talking to you made me drink nonstop. Only alcohol numbed the pain."

Justin's eyes widened with the revelation. He'd truly had no idea how badly Dutch took their breakup. *How could something meant to spare pain have been the cause of so much?*

"How do you think the accident occurred?" Dutch asked. "I was drunk. I almost killed myself." Dutch raised his right arm and pointed at him. "Because of you."

Justin stepped back. The power of the accusation hit him hard. He fell into the chair, defeated and exhausted. The weight of the cosmos rested on his shoulders, and he felt as if his body was collapsing in upon itself.

His actions *were* unforgivable. Even though he'd never meant to be the cause of so much pain—to Dutch *or* Spencer—he was. *How had he turned into his father?*

"I want you to know something," he said, once the breath returned to his lungs. "Leaving you wasn't something I wanted to do. Finding you was like finding a part of myself I never knew existed. I fell for you so hard and so fast it was scary. One minute I wasn't in love with you; the next minute I was. It was like you turned on another switch inside my soul and inside my heart."

He stared at Dutch, hoping the emotions behind his words were soothing the pain he'd inflicted. "That love is still there," he said. "It still burns just as bright." He didn't want to admit what he still felt, but he needed to say it and Dutch needed to hear it. "Seeing you on that bed, hurting both physically and emotionally, is tearing me apart. Knowing that I caused it is so much more than I can bear, but I'm trying my best. I have no right to offer comfort. I've lost that, I know. But it still kills me to see you like this when all I want to do is crawl into that bed and stay here with you until you feel better."

"What's stopping you?" Dutch asked. The distrust in his eyes was apparent. Dutch didn't hear the truth in his words or in the emotion he'd hoped to express. To Dutch, nothing had changed. He had been cast aside and that was all that really mattered. His words were merely words.

"You," he replied.

"*Me?*" Dutch asked. "How am *I* stopping you from doing anything? Everyone knows no one stops you from doing *anything* you want to do."

"That's true," he admitted. Everyone knew being headstrong was his tragic flaw. He shot through life like a missile, making his way to his intended target. Little stopped him once he made a decision, but that wasn't the case this time. For the first time in a long time, he *really* was thinking about someone other than himself. "But going to you now would be a disservice to *you*. You've been hurt enough. You don't need any more pain. The best thing for you is to get me out of your system, to move on and find someone truly worthy of you. You don't deserve some asshole who fell in love with two men."

Dutch didn't respond. Justin knew that was Dutch's way of agreeing with him, especially when he didn't want to. Dutch deserved a love that was all his and no one else's.

The bitter freeze in Dutch's eyes melted as he acknowledged Justin's words. They looked renewed and filled with purpose, like they used to in the early bloom of their romance.

Even though he didn't want to, even though he wanted to deny it to himself and to Spencer, Justin still loved Dutch. Loving someone, though, meant doing what was best for *them,* not him. That was why his words no longer meant anything for Dutch. Only actions would be convincing.

"I need to go," he said, rising from the chair. "I have something I need to do."

Ice slowly crept back across Dutch's eyes. Justin suspected Dutch thought he was leaving, but he wasn't. At least not permanently.

"I'm coming back," he said. "I'm not leaving you like I did the last time. I'm going to see you through this. That's a promise. I know my promises don't mean shit, but I'll make you a believer again."

"What the hell do you expect in return?" Dutch asked, extremely skeptical.

"Nothing," he said.

"Liar."

"You're right," Justin admitted. "Maybe I'm hoping for forgiveness for all the wrong I've done. There're some things I can't fix, things you don't even know about. But there are things I *can* fix. I can help fix you. I can help undo the damage that I've done. If I'm truly responsible for starting you down this path, then I should be responsible for turning you around and getting you going in the right direction again."

"I'm not some community service project," Dutch told him.

"I know you're not. You're someone I love, someone I need to help get better, someone I need to help get back on his feet, so he can travel down whatever path he needs to get away from me. If I can do that for you, help you return to the person you were before me, it'll make me feel just a smidge better about myself. I'm not saying it'll undo the hurt or erase it in any way, but it might give me the strength *I* need to go on."

"I don't understand. Why do you care now?"

"The why isn't important. It just *is*," Justin said. "I'm not looking to get you back in my life. I'm not trying to win your heart. I'm not stupid. That ship has long since sailed. But I can do something about what I've done to you."

Without another word, he left Dutch's room with purpose, something he hadn't felt for far too long. It was time to make reparations, to fix what he had broken in his life and in others. Only then might he be able to once again live with himself.

CHAPTER 22

2009

FINDING a parking spot in downtown San Antonio on a weekend wasn't easy. Dutch considered using one of the parking garages or the valet at the restaurant, but both were pricy. He needed to conserve, not waste, money. Being unemployed didn't allow him to splurge. The dinner date alone might be more than he could afford, but the cost of the meal was justified if it meant getting to meet J-squared in person.

As he walked down N. St. Mary's, away from his free parking slot a couple of blocks from the restaurant, he reminded himself to call him Justin, not J-squared. He found it difficult to shift from Justin's screen name to his real name. For so long, he had known him as J-squared. When he thought about him, he thought of him as J-squared.

Now, he was Justin.

They had crossed the gulf from anonymity to a more familiar relationship. After tonight, their familiarity with each other might evolve into intimacy.

He lit a cigarette to ease his nerves. Even though he'd made numerous vows to quit smoking this year, he had yet to follow through. His life was too chaotic, too uncertain to give up the one vice that made the world not as harsh. The inhalation of smoke felt good and always calmed him down, no matter how anxious he got. Still, he really didn't want to go on the date smelling of smoke, especially since he was unsure of Justin's stand on smoking. Even so, his anxiety got the better of him.

The dinner was unnerving. The potential for more than just a chocolate mousse for dessert was terrifying.

He was uncertain how he felt about sex. While the idea excited him, it also filled him with apprehension. Justin was in a committed relationship with a man he still loved. S held Justin's heart.

He couldn't compete with that, and he felt like he shouldn't have to.

He was a good man and a great catch. Even though he was currently unemployed, he was educated, professional, intelligent, and pleasing to the eye. He might not be a waifish twink, which was currently all the rave, but he wasn't old, wrinkled, or saggy. He took good care of himself. His body wasn't perfect, but it wasn't grotesque either. If he set his mind to it, he would have no problem finding a man with less baggage and willing to commit to him, and only him.

Getting further involved with, for all intents and purposes, a "married" man wasn't like him. He knew better than that. A relationship between two people was sacred, not something to be trifled with.

Yet, despite that knowledge, Dutch's feet turned right on Crockett Street and ever closer to the restaurant where he would have his date with Justin.

The silver signage of the Watermark Hotel appeared as he turned the corner. The sign was sleek and modern in design, a standard for such a high-end four-star spa and hotel.

A doorman stood outside greeting passersby and opening the door for guests trying to escape South Texas's attempt at winter.

He was accustomed to the harsh winters of New England. It was almost February and only in the high forties today. In Boston, there was snow and blizzards in late January. This was more autumn than winter, but he found it amusing how the native Texans shivered and ran for warmth whenever the slightest cold snap blew into town.

A group of well-dressed women exited a limousine and walked through the door held open for them by the doorman. They ignored the doorman's greeting and disappeared inside the Watermark.

In just a few moments, Dutch would be one of those people—not a rude socialite, but a guest, and not a guest of the hotel but of the hotel's restaurant that sat on the River Walk, Pesca.

Dutch had never dined at Pesca before, even though many people he knew raved about the food. He felt the Watermark was too pretentious for his tastes; this feeling carried over to its restaurant.

He liked simpler fare. While he did enjoy good food and wine, he preferred more casual environments than those typically filled with society types who looked down their noses at those not of the elite.

He took one final drag on his cigarette and then flicked the still burning butt down a drainage ditch.

"Good evening, sir," the doorman greeted him. The man's smile was huge, and his mouth was filled with horse teeth. "Welcome to the Watermark Hotel and Spa."

"Thank you," Dutch responded. "How do I get to the restaurant?"

"To Pesca?" the doorman asked, as if the answer weren't obvious. Dutch nodded. "Go down the hallway to the elevator. Take the elevator down to the River Walk level. When you exit the elevator, take a right and you'll see Pesca."

"Thanks," he said as the doorman told him to enjoy his meal.

He walked across the cream marble tile of the Watermark's foyer and toward the elevators. He passed expansive floral arrangements sitting on oversized tables. Staff dressed in black uniforms busily went to and fro, performing tasks of upkeep or customer service. Guests relaxed on oversized chaise lounges or on overstuffed chairs with their feet propped upon ottomans.

He stuck out like a sore thumb.

Dressed in jeans and a long-sleeve black button-down shirt, he didn't resemble the other men in the hotel, who wore suits or blazers and dress pants. His leather jacket marked him a commoner, far below their social rank. Occasionally, he spotted a casually dressed tourist, but the suits and party dresses outnumbered them.

As he hit the elevator's down button, he stared at his reflection in the hard polished metal of the elevator door.

He might not be in a suit or coat and tie, but he looked damn good. His hair was perfectly combed and his mustache and goatee were neatly trimmed. The black leather of his jacket brought out the spattering of gray in his hair; he looked distinguished, not old-mannish. His jeans were snug in all the right places, and his black Cole Haan shoes were polished.

The elevator doors opened, and he stepped inside.

He was ready to meet Justin.

When the doors opened once again, he exited the elevator. Pesca was to his right, and the River Walk and the bustle of tourists were to his left. The hostess stand rested on the other side of two massive wooden doors with glass insets, allowing the tourists a view into the restaurant.

From what he could tell, Pesca was just as luxurious as the Watermark. A bar surrounded by four stone columns. Glassware hung from the ceiling, suspended by metal bars. Cherry wood ceiling fans comprised the outer perimeter of the bar, and oil lanterns were mounted throughout the restaurant. On the tables sat cobalt-blue goblets, which matched the fabric that covered the booth seat backs and the napkins sitting on the snow-white plates.

He wished he'd dressed up a bit more. If Justin showed up in a suit, he would die.

"Thinking about cutting out?"

He turned toward the voice behind him.

When he saw Justin, he held his breath. Justin's Cyber picture didn't do him justice. He was even more amazingly attractive in person.

His hair looked a bit longer than on his profile. The dark wavy strands blew back in the wind, and he brushed a pesky wisp from his eye. Even though Dutch didn't typically fancy men with longer hair, the look worked for Justin.

The primitive mane and the dark tuft of facial hair underneath his lower lip made him look rugged.

The long hair, the soul patch, the almond eyes, and the tan skin transformed Justin into a tropical fantasy usually found only in a loincloth on a deserted beach.

Justin crossed over to him, and the smile emblazoned on his face glowed brighter and friendlier in person. The smile exuded sincerity, and it didn't end at his mouth. His dark-brown eyes sparkled with a radiance more comforting than chocolate to a chocoholic.

Thankfully, Justin had dressed in blue jeans. He sported a black collared shirt with a tight-fitting mustard-colored cashmere sweater on top. The sweater and shirt looked to cover a nicely shaped chest.

"You okay?" Justin asked, staring at him in concern.

Dutch realized he hadn't responded to Justin's initial question.

"No, not backing out," he replied. He had no intention of telling Justin he felt out of place. "Just wondering where we'd meet up."

"Wonder no more," Justin said. His smile still lit up the area more brightly than all the oil lanterns combined. "Shall we go in?"

Dutch couldn't respond.

His body was having a reaction it had never had before. He felt like a moth drawn to the flame of Justin's smile. Everything and everyone around them simply ceased to be. All he could see was Justin, and all he could feel was the rapid beating of his own heart to the primal beat of a phantom tribal drum.

Before, he'd felt nervous and out of place. He felt uncertain about the evening and his actions, and he questioned his integrity. He was, after all, on a date with a "married" man.

Those concerns vanished like insects before the light of Justin's smile.

Still, he couldn't move. The light enthralled him. It beckoned him, and he had to answer the call. His will was no longer his own. What he was before this moment had become null and void. What happened next couldn't be avoided.

He took one step toward Justin, who stared at him in silence. Justin, too, looked transfixed, as if bound by unseen forces.

Justin advanced toward him as well.

The two matched each other's steps, as if partners in tune to some cosmic choreography.

While they were only a few feet apart, he felt as if miles separated them. He wanted nothing more than to close the gap as quickly as possible, but such things shouldn't be rushed.

The slow dance beat played in measured time. They needed to trust their bodies, which were on autopilot. They simply had to trust and let go.

Now only a few inches apart, he stared down into Justin's eyes. The brown chocolate pools invited him in for a swim. Justin's tanned flesh begged to be touched, and he wanted nothing more than to take Justin in his arms and hold his body against his own.

His arm stretched toward Justin. It found the back of Justin's neck, and his hand ran through the hair at the back of his head. His other hand encircled Justin's waist and pulled Justin the rest of the way into him.

He now held Justin in his arms outside a restaurant on the banks of San Antonio's famous River Walk, for all to see. He didn't care who was looking or what people were saying. All he knew was what was right now wrapped in his embrace.

He placed his thumb under Justin's chin and lifted his head upward. Looking down, he gazed into Justin's already parted lips and bent downward to meet them.

When their lips joined, mariachi music blared in the background as a band passed by on a riverboat. Some whistled while others cried in protest.

Those sounds became background noise. He could only hear the rhythm of their hearts beating in tune with the mariachi song, their souls soaring with the roar of the trumpets.

CHAPTER 23

2010

FROM behind the men's room door, which he held ajar, Spencer watched as Justin left Dutch's room and entered the elevator. If Justin hadn't announced he was leaving, he would have caught Spencer eavesdropping in the hall. Embarrassing questions would have been asked, and he wasn't in the mood to answer them, especially not after what he heard.

Justin had already admitted he fell in love with Dutch while they were together, but he had no idea Justin *still* loved Dutch. Did loving Dutch mean Justin was still *in* love with Dutch?

Justin's confession almost made him fall apart in the hallway. His knees buckled, and all breath was knocked out of his body. He had to grab onto the wall for support.

Coming back here was a mistake, he thought. He scanned the hallway to his left to make sure Justin had not returned.

I thought so too, his father's voice said. *But I was wrong. You needed to hear that. You needed to hear that spic say he loved someone else. Now you can move on, find yourself someone else, someone better. Maybe even someone with tits. Real tits. Not fake tranny tits, either!*

The reemergence of his father's voice irritated him. He thought his father had finally left for good earlier this morning, when he refused to hurt Dutch despite his father's urging.

I still think you should've done it. Would've made your life a lot simpler.

He knew differently. Hurting Dutch wouldn't have changed anything. Justin loved Dutch, and harming him wouldn't alter those feelings. Besides, he hadn't come here because of Justin. He'd come here to face his own demons, the ones he had yet to own up to. This was the *only* place to finally put that to rest.

No, goddamnit! his father screamed. *You need to leave well enough alone! Why open up* that *can of worms? Don't you have enough on your fucking plate?*

I'm not afraid of worms. He pushed open the men's room door and started down the hall to Dutch's room. *You taught me not to be afraid of anything.*

I also taught you to be smarter than this, his father yelled. *You fight one war at a time. You don't start a second war when you haven't even won the first!*

I'm not you, Dad, he replied. Dutch's door was open. *I'm stronger than you or I even think.*

Standing at the threshold, he looked at Dutch but said nothing. Dutch's attention was drawn to the window, looking outside but not seeing the sky or the clouds inching across its canvas. His eyes were far away, piercing this world and its concerns. His vision perhaps rested on a different world, where he and Justin lived happily ever after, and Spencer was nothing more than a passing thought.

It was time for him to become much more than that.

"Penny for your thoughts?" he asked and leaned nonchalantly against the door.

When Dutch turned to face him, his jaw went slack. All color drained from his cheeks until he looked as pale as the sterile hospital walls around him.

Spencer was pleased. He felt powerful, as if he held all the cards to some game the three of them were playing. If this was a game, he intended to win.

I love the attitude, his father said, filled with pride.

"Spencer," Dutch said, completely shocked. "Wh-what are you doing here?"

"As if you don't know," he said while strolling into the room. He crossed over to the small table in front of the window, where two vases filled with flowers sat. One vase held four sunflowers, the other contained bright pink roses and white daisies. He sniffed each bloom. "Such pretty flowers," he finally said. "I hear colorful arrangements are uplifting for injured bodies *and* troubled souls."

He emphasized the last two words while gauging Dutch's reaction. Dutch did his best to hide his emotions behind his poker face. Spencer had come to know him a bit better than that.

As always, his crystal blue eyes betrayed him. They swirled with a tempest of conflicting emotions. Worry and fear collided with genuine joy at seeing Spencer here in his hospital room.

After all, they *were* colleagues and, perhaps, a little bit more.

"They're from my sister," Dutch said. "The one with the roses and daisies. The sunflowers are from my niece and nephew."

"How sweet," he replied, still casually strolling about the room as if there was nothing wrong, as if he didn't know that Dutch had been fucking his partner. "I'm sure they're worried about you."

"They were, but I talked to them this morning," Dutch told him. His eyes followed Spencer about the room. The joy Spencer saw in his eyes fled. Worry and fear now completely dominated his gaze.

Dutch knew why he was there, but he wasn't willing to lay his cards on the table just yet.

Make him suffer, his father prodded. *Make him fire the first shot. The closing salvo will then be yours.*

"I'm glad you reassured them," he told Dutch. He sat down in the chair across from the bed; the same one Justin occupied a few minutes before. Justin's warmth still spread across the fabric. "How's the prognosis?"

"Improving," Dutch replied warily. "Paralyzed from the waist down, though, but I'm alive."

"Yes, you are," he replied, adding a touch of contempt to his tone. He hadn't meant to be such an asshole to Dutch. Dutch was paralyzed, after all, and that somehow seemed punishment enough for fucking around with his man. Still, he seemed incapable of stopping the cruelty when he also said, "We're all so thrilled." His father might approve of the bastard Spencer was being, but it made Spencer uncomfortable, as if the person he once was had vanished and been replaced by the son his father always wanted.

Apparently Dutch didn't know what to make of this new Spencer either. Dutch stared at him. His eyes darted back and forth, observing each movement and scanning the emotions on his face.

He gave Dutch nothing. He sat perfectly still, his right ankle resting calmly on his left knee. His fingers were laced together, lying on his lap, and he concentrated on draining all emotion from his face. He transformed into an unreadable statue.

Damn, you're good, his father praised him. Spencer had always wanted his father's approval, but he didn't want it to be for this.

"What's going on here?" Dutch finally asked.

He blinked twice before answering. "What do you mean?" His posture didn't change. His face betrayed nothing. "I'm just visiting a sick friend."

"I'm not sick," Dutch corrected. "I've been in an accident."

"I know. A *DWI*," he added.

Dutch flinched, not because of his catty comment, but because his response revealed all Dutch needed to know. "You know, don't you? That's why you're here."

He said nothing. His gaze met Dutch's, never flinching and refusing to look away. He locked onto him like a sniper looking through a scope at his target. If he blinked, he might lose his shot, so he stayed still. Dead still.

With each passing second, he became even more like his father.

"You know about me and Justin."

The words shot through Spencer's heart like arrows. Still, he kept the pain secretly folded up inside his chest, away from Dutch's prying eyes.

"I'm sorry," Dutch said. "I wish there was something else to say, but there isn't." His eyes reflected how miserable he felt. They drooped; the luster of the crystal blue lost.

Start the return fire, his father ordered. *Take him down. Now!*

For a few moments, he said nothing. He simply took in the gloom, absorbing the dark clouds of pain that filled the open air between them. The clouds, heavy with hurt, flooded his spirit with their deluge.

What the fuck are you waiting for? Tear that son of a bitch a new asshole!

"I'm sorry too," Spencer finally replied.

What? his father bellowed. *You're sorry? What the hell do you have to be sorry for? They fucked around on* you!

"Why aren't you yelling at me?" Dutch asked. "Or trying to knock the shit out of me?"

That's a fucking good question, his father added.

"I don't have the answer to that," he told Dutch. And he didn't. He'd intended to walk in here and do as his father instructed, fire shot after shot into Dutch until his body was riddled with pain. The fight, however, left him upon seeing the genuine torment in Dutch's eyes.

It mirrored his own. In Dutch's eyes, he saw the same hurt twisting within him. The pain born from the betrayal of a trusting lover. What right did he have to say his pain was worse?

What right? his father asked. *He's the other* fucking *woman! He's been sharing body fluids with the same person you've lived with for ten years!* That's *your fucking right to be pissed off!*

"You're the innocent victim here," Dutch said at last, breaking the uneasy silence. "You've every right to be pissed off. I betrayed you. And our friendship."

Spencer laughed. *Innocent victim?* He'd tossed that phrase aside when he struck his brother with that rock all those years ago. According to his father, there were no innocent victims, only those who allowed themselves to be continually victimized.

As he looked at some of the events from his life, he realized he was *far* from an innocent victim.

"What's so funny?" Dutch asked.

Clouds of concern hung over Dutch's eyes. No doubt he wondered whether Spencer was losing his grip on reality, unbalanced by the knowledge of the affair.

That was far from the truth. Up until this point, he had been trudging along as if he were an innocent victim. His attitude had fueled his contempt for Justin and Dutch and embittered his soul. After all, his father's voice had returned, when it had been silenced years ago. That alone was proof of how far he had fallen.

He had no desire to be like his father. The man he wanted to be, no, the man he had been, was much better than that.

He had to get that man back.

If things were to change, he had to man up and take responsibility for his contributions to this mess. Only then could they all heal and move on. After all, that was what he wanted, to be free to choose the next path of his life without the pain of the past darkening his choices, as it had done since Mike Lane.

This time, when he started again, it would be with a clean slate, free of the past. There would be no more armor and no more conversations with his father. He had the power to make those changes. He simply needed to use it.

"Spencer? Are you okay?"

Dutch's voice brought him out of his thoughts. "Yeah, just thinking."

"About?"

"About being an innocent victim," he told Dutch. "I'm not an innocent victim. You know that as well as I do."

Dutch nodded. "Maybe 'innocent victim' was the wrong choice of words. You're just not as guilty as me and Justin."

"Not as guilty," he agreed. "But I came pretty close."

"He doesn't know, does he?" Dutch asked. "About...."

He shook his head. He didn't want Dutch to finish the thought. Voicing it made it harder to ignore. He thought he was ready to face up to this. It was one of the reasons he came here. Now, with the words hanging unspoken in the air, he knew he wasn't ready.

His father was right. He had to finish one battle before starting another.

"I didn't think so," Dutch said. He slouched back in his bed from the weight of another burden thrown upon his chest. "I figured Justin would've said something."

"And I don't want him to know," he said. "Not yet."

"Why not?" Dutch asked. "Everything else is out in the open. Why not *this*?"

"I'm not ready."

"Why not? It doesn't make sense."

"I don't need to give you a reason, *damn it*," he yelled. The anger he'd kept bottled within exploded outward. "You of all people know why learning about Justin's affair with you was so devastating. I'm not ready to pile more pain on top of the heap. Are you?"

"I guess not," Dutch said. His eyes told Spencer he didn't agree with him.

"And I don't need you to agree with me," he told Dutch. He rose from the chair and crossed over to stand at Dutch's right. "This is *my* decision to make. You've taken enough from me already. The least you could do is offer me this *one* courtesy."

He glared into Dutch's defiant eyes. Within, he saw Dutch's resentment at being emotionally blackmailed. He didn't care. Dutch would give him what he wanted, and he wouldn't leave until he got it. "Promise me you'll keep the secret and you won't tell Justin I was here."

"That's two secrets you want me to keep," replied Dutch.

"And how many did you keep from me *all* those months?" he asked.

"Fine," Dutch replied. He averted his eyes and returned to gazing out the window. "I don't like it, but I'll do it."

"Thank you," he said, pleased with Dutch's acquiescence. For now, the secret would remain hidden.

"I hope you'll thank me when this blows up in our faces," Dutch said. "He loves you, you know? He always has. Even when we were together, he loved you and never stopped." His gaze returned to Spencer. "He'd forgive you anything. Especially now."

"The problem is he loves you too," he added. "I know it and you know it."

Dutch nodded reluctantly.

What he didn't admit, what they *both* didn't admit, was that they still loved Justin too.

The three of them danced to two different songs mashed together by some insane DJ, spinning the soundtracks of their lives. On one table the original song played, the one devoted to him and Justin, but their steps lost the beat as Dutch's song with Justin skidded into their tempo.

Their steps were off, and no one knew which dance to follow. They were trapped in an endless loop, destined to be forever out of synch unless one of the records was put on permanent pause.

It was up to Spencer to find the song that would remain on the playlist.

CHAPTER 24

2009

DUTCH and Justin's first kiss lasted far longer than the mariachi song. They lounged upon each other's lips like vacationers on a Mediterranean beach. Their flesh, warm from the exposure, burned with blistering passion, and the sweat drenching their bodies turned their kisses salty, like taffy.

When they finally parted, seafood was no longer on the menu. Their bodies hungered for more than what a dinner at Pesca could provide. Neither had to speak his desires; words were unnecessary.

Dutch simply took Justin by the hand and led him back up the elevator to the main floor of the Watermark Hotel. They proceeded to the front desk and booked a room for the evening. The hotel clerk who checked them in smiled knowingly. She saw the look in their eyes and knew what was up, especially since neither of them had luggage.

They proceeded back to the elevator and hit the numbered button corresponding to their floor. When the doors closed, Dutch once again enveloped Justin in his arms, pulling his smaller, tight frame against his own. Nuzzling his neck, he detected a faint whiff of worn leather and sandalwood. The manly smell sent his passion into overdrive, causing him to once again dive into Justin's lips, which still tasted minty from the lip balm applied prior to their date. The mint added a kick Dutch liked—fresh yet masculine, like aftershave.

The elevator chimed as the doors opened onto their floor, and they stumbled out, still kissing, still embracing. It took all of his willpower not to rip Justin out of his clothes right there in the hall.

With just one kiss, he was hooked. Justin had plucked him from the ocean, where he was once free to swim in whatever direction he pleased, and reeled him into his boat. There would be no returning to the ocean; that life simply no longer existed.

Slowly, they made their way down the hall to their room, stopping every few feet to enjoy the forceful kisses that caused their facial hair to scrape against their cheeks and their tongues. When they finally reached their room, Dutch slid the key card into the slot and the door unlocked.

He backed into the room, his arms around Justin's waist, and he nibbled at Justin's neck. The odor of leather and sandalwood mixed with the musky scent of sex. Justin moaned and squirmed as Dutch licked a trail from Justin's throat to the sensitive flesh behind his ear.

When the door finally shut behind them, Justin pulled Dutch's shirt out of his jeans and fumbled the buttons open. Justin then spread his strong, soft fingers through the generous layer of fur on his chest and bent down to lick his nipples.

Dutch caught his breath at the warm, wet sensation of Justin's mouth upon his sensitive skin. While Justin gently bit at his right nipple, sending dual waves of pleasure and pain crashing through his body, he stretched over Justin's back and pulled his sweater and shirt up and over his head.

They embraced each other, bare-chested. Justin's smooth, tanned skin felt like melted butter against his flesh. For a few moments, they stayed in that embrace, staring into each other's eyes and marveling at what they had inexplicably found.

In Justin, he found something more precious than diamonds. They had been friends online for weeks, but it had quickly grown into something so much more. They were there for each other when no one else was or when no one else could be. They'd offered a nonjudgmental ear and unconditional support. They'd bared their souls and opened their hearts.

What they had unknowingly done over the past few weeks was prepare the soil for the garden of their relationship to grow. It took root in their communication, it grew from their frankness and candor, and it bloomed because of their sincerity.

Now the garden they'd tilled together was ready to be harvested.

His lips once again found Justin's. The passion he inhaled from Justin invigorated him and breathed new life into his spirit. He felt freer than he had his whole life; unseen possibilities unfolded and stretched out before him. His road no longer extended into darkness, and he was no longer the only passenger in the car.

He'd found a copilot, his navigator, and the person who would keep him from getting lost whenever darkness descended or storms crossed their path.

He undid the button and zipper of Justin's jeans. He pushed them along with Justin's black papi underwear to the floor of the room. He looked in amazement at Justin's almost hairless, naked body. Though smaller in frame and stature, Justin's body was compact, lean, and taut. Dutch wanted nothing more than to partake in the bounty so eagerly presented before him.

Reaching out with his right hand, he brought Justin's naked body against his. Justin's hardness pressed against his own, still separated by Dutch's jeans. Having Justin naked in his arms while he was still half dressed made him feel powerful, in control. At his command and in his power was a man he would somehow do anything for, and to have that man completely under his spell made Dutch want him even more. More than anything, he longed to be out of his jeans, to press Justin's naked skin against his bare flesh. It was agonizing to be so close but so far, yet he lacked the strength to pull away. Now that Justin was in his arms, releasing him was no longer an option.

Justin once again ran his hands through his chest hair; each hair he stimulated with his fingers sent charges of electricity straight down to his ever-hardening cock. Justin then pinched the nipples, grinding them between his powerful fingers before traveling southward, undoing his jeans. Justin ran his fingertips along the bulge of his underwear, eliciting a shiver that traveled down the length of his spine. When Justin put his hands underneath the waistband, Dutch quivered at his touch.

After what seemed like an eternity of Justin jacking his hardness, Justin finally shucked Dutch's pants and underwear from his body. Now they were both naked, still standing just inside the front door, their bodies still touching. Occasionally, their lips brushed against one another, but their eyes were too busy staring and their hands were too busy exploring.

"You're so beautiful," Dutch whispered into Justin's ear as his left hand traveled from Justin's arms to his head. It came to rest on the back of Justin's head. As he pushed Justin into another fiery kiss, Justin's right hand journeyed from Dutch's shoulders to his ass.

"No. You are," Justin replied before they were locked in another long kiss. As their tongues outlined each other's lips, Justin squeezed Dutch's ass, kneading it with passion while Dutch ran his thick fingers through his hair and massaged the back of his scalp. Their bodies pressed together, their erections trapped in between. Their cocks, slick with sweat, slid over and beside one another as their hips instinctively drove upward.

The nerve receptors across their bodies sizzled on overload.

Dutch stepped toward the bed, and Justin matched his movement. The time had come for them to fully experience each other's bodies.

When they reached the bed, they got on it, kneeling and facing each other. Justin reached down and grabbed Dutch's cock in his sweaty, hot grasp. He stroked it with one hand and then with two. Dutch's eyes rolled back in his head; Justin's hands on his stiff prick drove him beyond passion and toward unbridled lust.

Dutch returned the favor. He took Justin's cock in his left hand while his right hand delved into the soft, furry crevice of Justin's ass. Their mutual masturbation was in synch, and every time Justin pulled down on his cock, Dutch pressed his finger a bit farther inside Justin.

Justin then broke their embrace by pushing him backward onto the bed. Justin fell on top of his crotch and quickly inhaled his swollen member. "Oh my God, that feels great," Dutch gasped. Justin's slick tongue and the wet slurp of his cock worship brought him too close to orgasm.

He reached over and grabbed Justin by his shoulders and flipped him onto his back. He licked his way from Justin's chest to his cock before swallowing him as Justin had eagerly sampled him. Quickly, he lost himself in the sweet tang of Justin's meat. The full head rested at the back of his throat, leaking sweet nectar inside him. He pulled back, swirling his tongue around Justin's fat knob in order to savor each drop. In response, Justin thrust himself forward, driving further into his mouth. Dutch pinched his nipples as he continued his mouth massage, causing Justin to moan and squirm.

"You're driving me crazy," Justin panted, his brown eyes aflame and his long hair matted to his face in sweat.

"Let's see what happens when I do this," Dutch responded before turning Justin over on his stomach. He now had access to Justin's twitching center. He parted the sculpted cheeks and dove in, lapping at the hairy middle and getting drunk on the musky taste. With every swirl or undulation of his tongue, Justin moaned and pushed backward, trying to drive his tongue farther inside.

"I need you inside me," Justin said breathlessly. He looked over his tanned shoulder, feeling his cheeks flush red, and pleaded for Dutch to fuck him.

Dutch didn't need to be asked twice. He knelt behind Justin, who presented himself on all fours before him. Dutch grabbed his cock and aimed it straight at the awaiting hole. He rubbed his erection along Justin's crack, eliciting whimpers of anticipation.

He spit into his hand and rubbed the natural lubrication all across his rigid tool, until it was slick enough to allow easy entry into a place he wanted to visit and never leave.

Pressing harder against Justin, he slowly eased himself within the soft, tight folds of Justin's body, clearing a place just for him. Justin's ass muscles clenched around his hardness as Dutch pushed farther, trying to penetrate the first ring of resistance. When Justin's body finally opened up to take all of Dutch inside, his prick popped into place and Justin's body gripped around his cock, holding him firm.

Justin rose up to his knees, making certain Dutch's rod stayed securely within him, and rested his back against Dutch's chest. He turned his head to the right and kissed Dutch as he dominated him from behind. Dutch kept his right hand on Justin's waist, using the hand to guide their movements and time their rhythm. He moved his left hand to Justin's neck in order to keep their lips locked while they were joined.

As he pistoned in and out of Justin's quivering hole, it felt like a thousand tiny hands were massaging him from deep within Justin. It caused him to slam into Justin harder and faster, until sweat dripped down his face and onto Justin's back.

"Give it to me," Justin demanded. "Shoot your spunk in my hole. Make me your bitch."

"You want my load?" he asked while pounding harder into Justin. "You want me to blow inside your ass?"

"Yes!" Justin screamed as he jacked his cock while being pummeled from behind.

Completely lost in their sexual frenzy, Dutch looked down and watched his hard meat slide in and out of Justin. His cock was fiery red and ready to explode, but he tried not to think about it. He wanted to make it last.

He focused on the sheen of sweat coating Justin's body, journeying down to rest on the small of his back. Dutch surfed his hands over the slick flesh until they came to rest on Justin's shoulders. He gripped them tightly, using them to ram himself harder and faster inside Justin's hole.

Justin bucked backward, hard. Their bodies crashed together in moist thumps as Dutch pierced further inside Justin, slipping past the second ring that increased the tightness of the grip on his manhood.

Justin's moans grew more intense, and the fervor with which he pulled on himself told Dutch how close he was to climax. Dutch also felt his own impending release. His left hand moved from Justin's shoulder to his cock. He timed his stroking of Justin's dick with his own thrusts within Justin's ass. With a few more strokes, Justin's body shook as he rubbed out Justin's seed, which generously coated his fingers and palm in its stickiness. Justin's hole clenched around his cock even harder, causing him to pump his sperm deep inside Justin's shuddering hole.

They crumpled into a heap on the bed, Dutch still on top of and inside Justin. He rested his head on Justin's back. Justin breathed heavily underneath him. They lay together in silence; words weren't only unnecessary, they weren't enough.

Words could never capture the fullness of heart and soul Dutch now felt. They couldn't communicate how connected he felt to Justin. Connected wasn't even a good enough word. They were intertwined, meshed, merged. They began the day as two and ended up as one.

It was kismet, destiny, providence, or fate.

The word didn't matter. The definition was useless.

It simply felt as if it was always meant to be.

CHAPTER 25

2010

DUTCH felt trapped, not just in his half-paralyzed body but by the secrets he'd agreed to keep from Justin. The truth needed to come out, no matter how difficult it might be to hear. But he'd promised Spencer he would keep quiet, and while he may be an adulterer and alcoholic, his word was his bond. Another important life lesson taught to him by his father.

Thinking about him, especially now, made Dutch miserable. The man was his hero, the ideal Dutch always wanted to live up to. So far, he was nowhere close to the man Fredrick Keller was. He'd failed at love and life. All the lessons his father had taught him, about how to live and how to grow into a good man, obviously never took root.

If they had, he never would have fallen in love with a "married" man, turned into a drunk, or practically ruined his body and his life.

Resting his head against the hospital pillow, he closed his eyes. The image of his father riding on the back of the phoenix sprang into view. Soaring through the night sky, his father cut a fiery swath through the darkness, lighting up his world. His hands held tightly onto the phoenix's flaming feathers as he steered the bird toward him, his guiding light in times of dark distress.

What are you trying to tell me? he wondered. *Am I making a mistake? Should I tell the truth even though I gave my word that I wouldn't?*

His father circled overhead, leaving trails of fire behind him. The phoenix looped into the circle over and over again until a bright ring of fire blazed high above him. Bursts of flame shot outward creating a halo like the sparklers he used to spin in circles on the Fourth of July.

I don't understand, he said, calling to his father. *What does that circle mean?*

Then, without a word, his father flew off into the darkness, leaving behind the circle of fire, which still blazed brightly above him.

He had no idea what it meant, but even from down below, he could feel the warmth of the fire. It reached out to him in a thousand warm embraces, encircling his body and filling him with love.

Love is the only worthwhile legacy we leave behind, his father's voice said.

Those were the words his father had said to him before he finally succumbed to cancer. Although he begged his father not to speak, imploring him to save his energy, his father refused. He wanted his son to know what was important about life, about how love made death not so final. Though they would no longer see each other, their love continued on in the sky above and in their hearts below.

In the end, all that really mattered was love.

"I'm back."

Justin's voice brought him out of his trance.

"Sorry," Justin said, carrying a Pizza Hut box and two Cokes into the room. "Did I wake you?"

"No," he replied. "Just thinking." His eyes immediately zeroed in on the food and drink in Justin's hands. Pizza and Coke were Dutch's favorite comfort food. In times of distress, nothing could beat greasy pepperoni and high fructose corn syrup, something Justin obviously remembered.

"Well, you can think *and* eat," added Justin.

He placed the box onto the rolling side table and opened the container. The intoxicating aroma of melted cheese and garlic filled the room. Justin took a folded napkin out of the pocket of his jeans and placed the biggest slice of pizza upon it. He handed the slice to Dutch as if they were best friends preparing to watch a movie instead of ex-lovers who had just gone a couple of rounds.

He held the napkin and pizza in his hand as Justin went to work on the Cokes. Justin unscrewed the cap on one then the other. From the tan water container, a standard in all hospitals, Justin undid the cap, which doubled as a cup, and filled it with Coke. The hearty fizzle of the carbonation made his mouth water as Justin placed the cup within his reach.

"Come on," Justin told him. "I know how much you love your pizza and Coke."

Dutch made no attempt to eat the pizza or drink the soda. He simply held the slice in his hand and stared at Justin. This simple act of kindness reminded him why he fell in love with Justin in the first place. It also made him feel even worse about the secret he kept in his pocket.

Justin had no clue what lay before him. Dutch wanted to tell him. It was the right thing to do. But staring into those big eyes, filled with concern and perhaps even love, he realized for the first time Spencer was right.

The truth would do more harm than good right now.

"What's wrong?" Justin asked.

"Nothing," he replied before he took a bite of the pizza. Justin's narrowed eyes revealed that Justin didn't believe him. But he was no longer focused on the secret he kept. The pizza tasted too damn good. The cheese and grease bomb momentarily trumped all his other concerns.

The meal transported him back to happier times, when this food was shared with family and friends. He'd inherited his love of pizza from his father. They'd often shared a whole pie and Coke to work through the problems of childhood. When he became an adult, eating a slice or two together was how they stayed in touch, no matter how busy Dutch's life got.

Halfway through the slice, he also recalled nights in college when he and his friends would lay about his dorm, eating pizza, drinking beer, and imagining the lives they would lead after graduation. Back then, life was an open ocean, not the edge of a cliff.

Eating pizza brought all the good memories up from the deep waters of his subconscious. The simple act of consuming cheese, pepperoni, garlic, and tomato sauce simplified his perspective. It reminded Dutch of the important times and people of his life, when his life was guided by only love.

He tentatively stared back at Justin, whose eyes still begged him to discuss what was troubling him. Instead, he grabbed the cup of Coke and took a long swig. The carbonation burned his throat on the way down and took his breath away. The combination left him incapable of speaking and thereby confessing the secret.

Justin shrugged, his sign that he was moving past the need to know. He fished another napkin out of his pocket and grabbed a slice of pizza from the open box. "The pizza will wreak havoc on my lactose-intolerant system, but it smells too good to pass up."

As Justin ate, Dutch feared he would somehow see what he tried to hide. If pressed, he also worried he might speak the truth and break the promise he'd reluctantly made to Spencer.

"I know something's wrong," said Justin. "But I won't pester you about it."

Dutch continued to eat the pizza, feigning indifference.

He finished the first slice and reached for another. Justin told him to remain still and retrieved another piece of pizza from the box for him.

"Thanks," he said when Justin placed the second serving in his hand. For the briefest moments, their fingers touched. The old flame that used to burn sparked to life. Its warmth traveled from his index finger and quickly circulated through his body, like a ring of fire.

From the slight blush to Justin's cheeks, it was obvious he felt it too.

Despite everything they had been through, there was something still there. No matter how hard he tried to deny it, no matter how much he wished it away, it blazed within their souls.

CHAPTER 26

2009

EVEN though he was spent, after having three intense orgasms, Dutch still burned with passion that wouldn't abate. He wanted more. No, he needed more; he needed to feel Justin's cock buried in his throat, unleashing another torrent of hot spunk down his gullet. He longed to once again mount Justin, watching his face contort in a mixture of pain and pleasure while begging him to pound away inside his ass harder.

More than the pleasure of the physical, he wanted to feel the connection that linked not just their bodies but their hearts and their souls. Never before had he felt such a strong connection with another person. It was eerie yet comforting.

"I can't believe how right that felt," Dutch said between ragged breaths.

Justin panted beside him, drenched in sweat. Instead of responding in words, Justin scooted closer to him and laid his head on Dutch's untrimmed chest; sandalwood and leather still clung to the air about him, except now it was coupled with the unmistakable heaviness of sweat and cum. Sighing deeply, he snuggled into the fold of Dutch's neck. His actions spoke louder than if Justin yelled it from the top of the Tower of the Americas in downtown San Antonio.

Justin obviously felt the distinctiveness of their union as well.

To experience such passion or such a connection with a man he had only just met boggled Dutch's mind. Past dalliances had certainly scorched the bed sheets, but once the climax arrived, the passion fizzled.

Not even most of the sex he had with past loves compared to the marathon lovemaking he and Justin completed. He'd dated men for years that never once came close to the intimate bond he felt forming between the two of them. Once he entered Justin, he left a part of himself behind. When Justin returned the favor, making love to him on his back without ever once looking away while they were joined, Justin too left a part of himself, which was more than just his DNA, inside Dutch as well.

He kissed the top of Justin's head and wrapped him in his arms. He ran his index finger up and down Justin's still moist back, all the way down to the cleft of his firm rear. Justin nuzzled against his pecs while his left hand journeyed down Dutch's treasure trail. He paused at the crown jewels, touched them with the tenderness of a feather, and then traveled back up the trail.

"I could stay like this forever," Dutch told Justin.

"That's what scares me."

The unforeseen response took Dutch by surprise. He was expecting agreement or a more romantic response than the one he got.

Immediately, he felt like a fool. This obviously meant more to Dutch than to Justin. For Justin, this was a one-night stand, a diversion from his problems at home. He never meant for their meeting to become anything more.

Once again, like Yosemite Sam, Dutch had leaped into a situation without thinking.

How many idiotic romantic blunders will I make in my lifetime?

"I'm sorry," he said, sitting up in bed. Justin's head slid off his chest. "I didn't mean to imply anything."

"What do you mean?"

Justin's confused expression perplexed him.

Hadn't Justin just implied he was reading more into this than was there? Didn't the tone of his response suggest regret for what they had done? Wasn't Justin now berating himself for cheating on S and regretting he'd ever met him?

"What do you mean 'what do you mean'?" Dutch asked.

"I'm really confused now," replied Justin with a laugh. He once again moved closer to Dutch. With his back against the headboard, Justin rested his head on Dutch's shoulder and let out a long exhale. He took Dutch's left hand within his right and held it firmly. "What's going on?" he finally asked. "Your mood has changed."

"Are you regretting what we just did?"

Justin didn't reply. He leaned against Dutch in silence, their hands still in each other's grasp, their bare legs entwined.

The silence became deafening. To Dutch, it validated his concerns. Justin was sorry for what they had done, and now he was most likely concocting scenarios on how to extract himself from the hotel and the situation. If he were a betting man, he would bet that after tonight, he would never see or hear from Justin again.

"I never imagined a bearish man to be *such* a drama queen," Justin said. He looked up at Dutch from where he rested on his shoulder and smiled. "I don't regret what we did."

He didn't believe Justin. "You don't?"

"No," Justin said emphatically. He shoved a tangled lock of hair out of his face. "The whole experience was almost...." He stopped before he finished the thought.

"Almost what?"

"Magical," answered Justin a bit apprehensively.

He watched as a different emotion washed over Justin. It definitely wasn't regret. It looked more akin to surprise with a hint of sorrow. "Why the look?"

"It's just that I haven't experienced something like that in a long time."

"What do you mean?"

Justin told him about the first time he saw S at the Bonham eight years ago.

"Confetti and noisemakers on a first kiss?" he asked. "That's a tough act to follow."

"I thought it was *impossible* to follow," Justin admitted. "But the blaring horns of mariachi music isn't too shabby."

Justin was right. But Dutch wondered what that meant. How was it possible for Justin to have two such momentous first kisses with *two* different men? Did it mean that his time with S was done? S had left him for Europe, after all. Maybe this was the universe's way of telling them he and Justin were now meant to be together.

Was that a possibility?

"What's wrong now?" Justin asked. He moved his head from Dutch's shoulder and positioned himself on the bed so that his head was now lying on Dutch's stomach; his full head of hair spread out onto Dutch's body. Justin looked squarely into Dutch's eyes.

"Nothing. I'm just wondering what it means."

"When you figure it out, let me know."

He smiled at Justin. The vision of Justin lying on his stomach filled him with warmth that was more than simple desire. Although his body was definitely gearing up for another round of lovemaking, the warmth that fueled him from within wasn't entirely fed by passion. It felt more like an old familiar blanket, one that you wrap around yourself when you're sick or in need of comfort.

As the warmth spread, Dutch felt as if he had come home.

"How much do you really value honesty?" Justin asked him.

The question came at Dutch like a curveball. "Are you asking me if it's okay for you to lie to me?"

Justin grinned. "Not at all. I'm just wondering how much of what I'm feeling do you really want to know."

"I want to know all of it," he said. "The good and the bad."

Justin looked away. While regret hadn't previously reflected in his eyes, it now emblazoned itself upon them. Dutch was determined to be a man of his word; he wanted only the truth. "Tell me," he told Justin.

"I don't regret what we did," he said. He looked at Dutch but then quickly looked away. "But I do regret what *I've* done to my relationship. I've betrayed the magic that brought us together. I broke a promise that I wouldn't cheat." He sighed heavily. "I've become my father."

He and Justin had yet to share the skeletons hidden in their family closets, but the comment told him a great deal about the kind of person Justin's father was and the kind of man Justin wanted to be.

For a few moments, they sat in silence. He fought the urge to immediately make Justin feel better; his paternal instinct to protect those he cared for was strong. Still, reassurance wasn't what Justin needed. The simple truth was, Justin had cheated. For all intents and purposes, he was now an adulterer, which made Dutch the mistress.

Words couldn't sugarcoat their actions.

"We *have* done an awful thing to your partner," he admitted. He found the words hard to say, and they seemed to be even harder for Justin to hear. Honesty, however, was the only way to navigate through the turbulent waters of an affair. "There's nothing we can do or say that will make this go away."

"I know," Justin said. His eyes still looked away from Dutch. They gazed somewhere beyond this moment, perhaps to Justin and S's first kiss, or to the first time they uttered the words "I love you" to each other.

"Your life at home is important to you, and I know that. I don't want to come between the two of you any more than I already have." Dutch swallowed hard. Although he meant what he said, he secretly wished he didn't. He had no desire to simply let Justin go after what they had shared, but the decision to stay or go wasn't Dutch's to make. "I know my saying this won't absolve either of us of the guilt. That's something we have to carry with us, but what we've done doesn't have to be the end of your relationship."

"So, you're okay with us never seeing each other again? Never doing *this* again?"

Justin's slightly almond-shaped eyes locked firmly onto Dutch's. Sadness now lingered in the corners of his vision.

"How much do *you* really value honesty?" Dutch asked.

"It means the world to me," replied Justin. "If the words of an adulterer mean anything."

"They do to me," Dutch told him. He wiped a stray strand of hair out of Justin's face and continued. "Yes, I would be okay with never seeing you again and never feeling your body against mine."

The sadness that crept at the edges of Justin's eyes sprang from the shadows. It was now in full view.

"Do I *want* to never see you again? Do I *want* to never feel your body against mine again? My answer would have to be no."

"Really?" Justin asked. A new emotion that could only be hope leaped from the back of Justin's eyes. It batted the sadness aside and beat it back into the darkness. "You still would want to see me even though it makes us awful people?"

"I don't think it makes us awful people," he said. "I think it makes us human. Humans are imperfect creatures who rarely live up to the ideals we hold ourselves up to. I never dreamed I would get involved with a man who is as good as married. I never imagined my life would consist of sharing a bed with someone who wasn't free to share his life with me. In the movies, those people are the villains. They're who we boo at. In real life, villainy is a lot less black and white."

"Do you really think so?"

He thought about it. In the movies, the cheaters were usually caricatures, one-dimensional people who lacked depth. They cracked wise and tossed around one-liners like a stand-up comedian, but the movies had it all wrong. All cheaters weren't callously abandoning a commitment for carnal pleasure. That was a logical fallacy, a broad generalization that had been accepted as fact.

If he and Justin were any indication of real-life cheaters, then there were many others out there who felt just as badly as they did.

Having an affair wasn't something sought, planned, or plotted. For the two of them, it felt scripted, as if some divine writer composed a manuscript that broke Justin and Spencer apart and then added Dutch to the mix. Their affair represented cosmic irony rather than malicious intent.

The universe had brought them together; what they did with it was up to them.

"Yes, I do," Dutch finally said.

Justin's furrowed brow told Dutch that Justin was in deep thought.

"What about you?" he asked Justin. "Do you want this to end now?"

Justin opened his mouth to answer, but Dutch placed his sizeable hand over Justin's mouth. "Be honest," he said. "I'm a big boy. I can take the truth."

When he removed his hand, Justin didn't immediately reply. He thought carefully about his answer, something Dutch appreciated. If Justin wanted their affair to end, then he would accept the decision and move on. He would harbor no animosity, and he would no longer pursue Justin. But if Justin was willing to see how this might play out, if he was willing to put his relationship on the line, then Dutch was equally as willing to place his heart on the chopping block.

"Before I answer that question, there's something you should know."

"What's that?"

"My partner is HIV positive."

The admission floored Dutch. He had no idea what to do with this new piece of information; his brain seemed incapable of processing the revelation and played it on a never ending loop.

"I'm not positive," Justin told him. "He was infected before I met him, and I get myself tested every six months, even though we always use a condom when we have anal sex. My last HIV test was two months ago."

"And we had unprotected sex?" Dutch asked no one in particular.

"I know," Justin said. "That was hugely irresponsible of me. I was so caught up in the moment. Even so, it's unforgiveable. I completely understand if you want me to leave."

"I don't," Dutch replied. He was surprised he meant those words. If someone else had kept such vital information from him, he would have been out the door. Dutch, like most gay guys, typically shied away from positive men to avoid even the slightest risk of HIV infection. Justin, however, wasn't positive; his partner was.

Even more amazing was that Justin had known S's status prior to falling in love with him. Yet, Justin still willingly gave his heart away to S. That dedication not only made Justin's affection for S more apparent, but in a strange way, it also redoubled Dutch's feelings for Justin.

For him, it demonstrated that Justin was definitely the kind of man he could spend the rest of his life with, the kind of man who risked anything for love, even his life.

In the face of such gallantry, could he risk any less?

"Really?" Justin asked, surprised. "It's okay?"

"I won't lie," Dutch said. "I would've preferred knowing before we jumped into bed, but neither of us were thinking about *any* consequences. If we were, we wouldn't have gotten naked to begin with."

"True."

"I need to ask you something, though."

"Okay."

"You've never had unprotected sex in the nine years you've been together. Why did you and I bareback the very first time?"

"I can't explain it," Justin said. "It just felt right, like it was supposed to be that way. As if you and I were meant to share each other's bodies without anything, even a condom, coming between us. Does that make sense?"

It did make sense, because Dutch felt exactly the same way. He'd always used condoms in the past. He'd even used them in past long-term relationships. But when the thought entered his mind to slap one on before entering Justin, he had quickly dismissed it. Their bodies were meant to be joined, free of all encumbrances.

"It makes perfect sense," Dutch told Justin.

"Do you still want me to answer your question?"

"What question?" Dutch didn't remember asking one.

"You asked me if I wanted this to end."

Dutch nodded. He remembered the question now. "Yes, please do."

"I love him," he told Dutch. Hearing those words caused his heart to sink. Justin's connection to S was simply too important for Justin to risk.

"Say no more," he said. Dutch sat up in bed, forcing Justin to move his head off his stomach. "I respect your decision."

"I'm sure you will," Justin said. "Once you hear what I have to say."

"There's really no need. You love your man. That tells me all I need to know."

Dutch stood up from the bed, his back to Justin.

"Can I please finish what I was going to say?"

"Like I said, no need."

"Will you listen to me, please?"

Dutch turned around to face Justin. Justin lay on his side, his head resting on his right arm. His still naked body managed to once again stir Dutch's passions even though his insides felt empty.

"I *do* love him," Justin repeated. "I'm not going to deny that. That would be a lie and would be unfair to you *and* him."

"There you go," he said. He turned his back once again to Justin.

Justin grasped his wrist. He gently tugged Dutch backward onto the bed. He sat on the edge of the bed while Justin moved behind him. Justin wrapped his arms around Dutch from behind and laid his head on Dutch's back, pressing his bare flesh against him.

"Even though I love him, I don't want *this* to end," Justin said. "Maybe I'm a selfish bastard who wants to have his cake and eat it too, but even before I met you, you were special to me. I confided in you my worst fears and opened myself up to you in a way I hadn't opened myself to anyone in a long time."

Dutch turned around in Justin's arms. They sat facing each other, naked and cross-legged. Their foreheads rested together while Justin spoke.

"On Cyber, you became my lifeline. Now that we've met and shared such a magical evening, you've become someone I don't think I could live without."

"Where do we go from here?" Dutch asked.

"I don't know," replied Justin. "But I'm willing to go wherever *whatever* this is takes us."

Relieved and terrified at the same time, Dutch sighed deeply. This was a risky venture for both of them. The road ahead twisted and turned, making it impossible to see what lay just beyond the bend. Far too many times had he placed his heart on the line only to have it mistreated and abused. Even so, he couldn't hold back the rising swell of hope that this time might be different, that this time, he might have found the one.

For such a prize, no other option existed.

"Me too," he said and kissed Justin on the lips.

With their souls laid as bare as their flesh, their kiss turned into an embrace that ended in one final joining of their bodies for the night.

CHAPTER 27

2010

"BE HONEST," Dutch said.

Justin felt the lightheartedness of their previous conversation die. Distracting Dutch from his medical and legal woes made him feel better, more like himself. At first, he pretended to be interested in their debate on the pros and cons of Dick Grayson, formerly Batman's partner Robin, taking up the cowl since Bruce Wayne's death. Discussing comic book characters, a favorite topic of theirs, over pizza and Coke made it easy to forget his pain over losing Spencer.

After a while, though, he was no longer pretending. He fell into their old routine quite easily, which comforted him and eased his troubled soul. Losing himself in comics had always been a defense mechanism since he was a child. When his father missed a birthday, he pulled out the latest *Justice League of America* comic and fought alongside his heroes as they battled the android Amazo or Starro the Conqueror. When a bully ruined his day or he battled his longings for other boys in class, Superman and Batman were there to whisk him away to a place where good always won and the endings were always happy.

That was why he gave himself so completely to their debate. He didn't agree with Dutch that Dick's Batman destroyed the Batman mythos. Dutch found Dick's humorous flair conflicted with the idea of striking fear in the hearts of criminals. Batman needed an edge to deal with the villains of Gotham, according to Dutch.

Justin disagreed completely. Bruce's Batman became too dark and too distant. Dick added a refreshing spark to the cape and cowl Bruce Wayne never captured. Dick kicked ass as Batman while Bruce's Batman floundered in gloom and grit.

Their debate, while often heated, felt as warm and soothing as chicken noodle soup on a cold day. This was what they were about, or at least what they used to be about. They could talk about comics, politics, education, even the weather, and their discussions were always easy, even if they disagreed.

For a few moments, he forgot the pain of the past few hours and the complete mess he'd made of his life. Worries about whether or not Spencer would forgive him, or even call, disappeared.

Their debate rekindled their connection, reminding him how they used to argue about events or popular issues while naked in bed on Sunday morning. They ate their breakfast and drank their coffee while trying to convince the other he was wrong, which never happened.

They saw things from different perspectives; that would never change, no matter how much they loved each other. They were destined to disagree on most every topic. While most couples might have found that a negative, he tallied it a positive. Not just because the relationship was so different from him and Spencer, since they usually agreed on everything, but because their differences never led to resentment. They grew together because of them.

Respect for each other's opinions brought them closer together instead of creating a yawning chasm. They never tried to change the other; their debates weren't about that. It never mattered if the other didn't share the same beliefs. It only counted that they were both secure enough in their relationship that the beliefs could be voiced without fear of drawing blood.

But as he launched into how Damian Wayne, Bruce Wayne's son and the new Robin, destroyed the balance of the dynamic duo, Dutch's question forced the pain of the real world back into view.

It made him realize their discussion, no matter how good it felt, was merely a distraction. Now, pain once again flooded his soul, washing away the ease and comfort that previously protected him.

"Why are you in so much pain?" Dutch asked him again.

He decided to lie and force the conversation back to comics. The pain threatened to drown him again, and he longed for the more soothing waters of distraction and denial.

"Be honest," reminded Dutch.

Justin held the lie back and looked away. He couldn't lie to Dutch, not now. Honesty was something they held dear, but on the shores of honesty rolled the heavy fog of hurt.

"Don't worry about it," he said at last. The pain gobbled him up on the inside. "It's just another mess I have to clean up."

"What kind of mess?" Dutch asked.

He didn't answer. He rose from Dutch's bedside, where during the course of their debate, he had come to rest. He couldn't sit next to Dutch any longer. Not only was the pain back, but he was annoyed with Dutch for refusing to let the subject drop. He crumpled up their dirty napkins and tossed them into the empty pizza box. He carried the box and the two empty Coke bottles to the trash can by the hospital room door.

Suddenly, waves of exhaustion and loss crashed over him. His insides writhed in misery he didn't want to share. He felt more forlorn than Karen Carpenter's hauntingly lonesome voice.

"I think I'm gonna go get some air," he said. "I'll be right back."

"Don't do that," Dutch told him. "Tell me what's going on."

"I can't," he replied. His attempt at a smile failed. It felt thin and forced.

"How about I guess?"

He laughed. "I don't think even you're that good."

"Spencer found out about us and left you."

His eyes widened in surprise, caught completely off guard by the accuracy of Dutch's guess. He found it impossible for Dutch to be able to know that. While they shared a strong connection, it had been months since their link was at its strongest. For Dutch to be able to sense what troubled him was too far-fetched.

He tried to respond, but the only word he could mutter was "How…?"

"I'm just *that* good," Dutch said.

For reasons he couldn't explain, Justin pegged his response as a lie. Dutch knew more than he was letting on. His eyes betrayed him. They glanced away and grew dark whenever he withheld information. It was one of Dutch's personality quirks. "I don't buy it," he told Dutch and moved closer to him to better gauge his facial expressions.

"I'm not asking you to," Dutch said. "You're obviously in pain. I think I know you well enough to be able to spot that at ten paces."

He nodded. They did know each other better than almost anyone else, but he still knew there was more to the story. "But to know with such precision tells me you know more than you're letting on." He leaned closer to Dutch, staring straight into his crystal blue eyes. "Spill."

Dutch's eyes darted back and forth nervously. They both knew he had been found out. Justin had no idea *how* Dutch knew but he intended to learn how the information made its way to Dutch's hospital bed.

Then, as suddenly as his crystal blue eyes darkened with deception, they turned ice cold in anger. "Listen, *I'm* not the one hiding things," he said, his tone short and curt. "I was just trying to help. If you don't want it, that's fine. You've lived without me for almost a year. You don't need me for jack shit. I get that."

Justin stepped back. No trace of deceit lingered in Dutch's eyes. Either it had never been there or Dutch's ability to lie had improved since they were last together. He felt foolish now for doubting him. "I'm sorry. I didn't mean to imply…." His voice trailed off, unable to complete the thought.

Misreading Dutch worried him. Had their link been severed *that* much?

"Don't worry about it," Dutch said. "Am I right, though?"

He nodded. Acknowledging the truth turned his stomach.

"So tell me."

He sat down at the edge of Dutch's bed and told his story.

"And where is Spencer now?"

"I don't know," he replied. His stomach flopped and twisted, threatening to bring up the pizza he'd just consumed. "I haven't been able to find him. He turned off his cell. Hasn't been back to my mom's or our house."

He stared into Dutch's eyes, once again the comforting crystal blue he always wanted to dive into. More than anything else, he longed for Dutch to wrap his arms around him and tell him everything would be okay. But that wasn't going to happen.

While concern drifted across Dutch's eyes, Justin mostly saw loss. Dutch understood the pain he felt was for Spencer, not him. Although he still loved Dutch, Spencer was the only concern he had. True, he felt guilty and responsible for Dutch's condition, and he had every intention of remaining by Dutch's side until he recuperated, but getting Spencer back was his ultimate goal. Nothing else mattered to him more than that.

Whatever the two of them had, no matter how exceptional, had to be over.

Dutch's crystal blue eyes turned translucent as he came to the same conclusion.

CHAPTER 28

2009

A CONCLUSION to the vast uncertainties in their lives was what they needed; Dutch knew that. For too long, he had allowed Justin to wallow in indecision, to flounder like a fish at the ocean's edge unable to fling his body back into the ocean.

They couldn't live that way anymore. *He* couldn't live that way anymore.

Since their first night together almost five months ago, their relationship had grown by leaps and bounds, and in directions he never expected. They'd spent countless days and nights together, getting to know each other in that special way two individuals do when they were building something lasting between each other.

Though they were different in many ways, those differences somehow magically tethered them together like the kiss they'd shared outside Pesca on the River Walk. There was something between them that words lacked the power to explain. All he knew was that in Justin he had found something beyond rare, something that likely only happened once in a lifetime.

Whenever he doubted that, which he did more frequently in the past month, since Spencer's return from England, he simply remembered how Justin comforted him when his mother died in March. Not once did Justin leave his side. In fact, he accompanied him to Boston for her funeral and stood as his rock amidst the emotional tempest his mother's death created in his world.

Without Justin, he never would have survived the loss, and though it had happened during such a dark time in his life, it was during his grief that Justin first told him he loved him. Of course, he returned the declaration as soon as the words left Justin's lips. For Dutch, saying, "I love you" to each other caused the fears he had of Justin leaving him for Spencer to flee from his heart. Justin's love had occupied the space where the fears and the doubts once resided.

Now, those same fears and doubts had resurfaced like a submarine, breaking through the calm waters of his life with torpedoes armed and ready to fire.

Since Spencer's return, he and Justin met once or twice a week. A strong connection still existed between them. They felt it whenever they were together, whether in bed or just cuddling on the couch. The connection was as much a part of their bodies as their limbs or their organs.

But the connection was changing.

Justin withdrew, spending less time with him *or* Spencer. He stayed later at work, throwing himself into one school crisis after another.

At first, Dutch thought it was in response to how busy his own life had gotten recently with work. Even in the midst of their affair, he'd finished his graduate degree in photography. His photographs had even caught the eye of local art patron Sharon Davis, when he displayed at a downtown art gallery.

Justin attended the event to show his support, but stayed in the corners, away from Dutch's art admirers. He knew Justin was hiding from anyone who might know Spencer, but his presence meant the world to him.

Justin had become his personal muse. Since he gave his heart to Justin, his art had never been more promising. He took greater risks with camera angles and shutter speeds. He played with light and shadows in ways that hadn't been done before.

He was on an artistic high, and he expected Justin to share in that happiness. Justin, however, became increasingly miserable and retreated to work. Dutch wanted to help, but Justin said he couldn't talk about it. At least not yet.

So he gave him space. While Justin brooded, Dutch moved forward professionally.

He managed to sell enough of his work to make a modest living, but it wasn't enough to keep him financially afloat forever. He needed work that would supplement his income without intruding on his pursuits in art.

Luckily, Sharon told him about an adjunct professor position at St. Mary's University. The private Catholic school was looking to expand its offerings in fine art, and with Sharon as a frequent benefactor to the school, she pushed for a brand new photography program. Sharon knew the dean of Arts, Humanities, and Social Sciences and put in a good word for him.

After snagging an interview and meeting with the hiring committee, he got the position.

Justin didn't know about the new job at St. Mary's. It was one of the many things they would discuss tonight. Being gainfully employed and able to stand on his own financially gave him the strength he needed for this evening—to finally address the pink elephant that continued to take over every aspect of their relationship. Justin needed to quit floundering and choose either him or Spencer.

Tonight, it was time for the conversation.

It was Wednesday evening, when Spencer had weekly nighttime meetings that lasted until 9:00 p.m. Although Dutch had finally learned that S stood for Spencer, he still didn't know what type of work Spencer did because Justin preferred to keep Spencer as anonymous as possible. Since Spencer knew nothing about him, Justin thought it only fair that Dutch know nothing about Spencer.

He understood, but only because he didn't want to know much about the man whose heart would break when Justin hopefully chose him. Not knowing Spencer assuaged a portion of the guilt he felt for the continued affair.

Keys rattled at his front door. Justin was here.

He exhaled, hoping his nerves would flee with his breath. He really needed a cigarette right now, but he gave those up a month ago.

The door swung inward, and Justin entered, his eyes aflame with anger.

"Tell me it's not true," Justin bellowed. "Tell me you're not working at St. Mary's!"

Surprised by the anger, he took a step back. Not only did he have no idea why Justin was angry but he couldn't fathom how Justin knew about the job.

Justin's eyes were as wild as his hair, which looked uncombed and tangled. Since they met, it had grown another three inches and now rested on his shoulders. Tonight, though, Justin's hair, like a threatened animal's fur, was raised.

"What's the matter with you?" he asked.

"Just answer the question," replied Justin. He slammed the door behind him to punctuate his desire for an answer.

"I was going to tell you tonight, but, yes, I'm working at St. Mary's. I was offered a position as an adjunct instructor in photography. I start teaching this coming fall."

Justin paced back and forth, his fists clenching at his sides, his posture when facing unbridled anger. Dutch had only seen it once before, when his father called him out of the blue a few months ago, wanting to reconnect with the son he abandoned.

"I thought you'd be happy for me," he said, aggravated with Justin's ridiculous behavior.

"You have no idea what you've done," Justin said in a strained whisper.

"What exactly have I done?" He crossed his arms and stood his ground. He had no intention of entertaining Justin's temper tantrum. If Justin had something on his mind, he needed to man up and express it.

"You met Spencer at the interview."

He couldn't believe his ears. There was no way he met Spencer at St. Mary's. Spencer wasn't in higher education. "What are you talking about? Isn't Spencer a businessman?"

Justin laughed. No pleasure came from the sound; it resonated only fury and desperation. "I let you think that because I didn't want your paths to ever cross. A lot of good that did me."

Dutch walked over to Justin, who seethed in front of the couch, and placed his hand on Justin's shoulder. Even though he failed to comprehend Justin's irrational anger, he wanted to calm Justin down enough so that he could at least be made to understand. But when his fingers gently stroked the nape of his neck, Justin jumped at his touch and walked away.

That had never happened before.

"Spencer was Dr. Harrison at your interview."

His jaw dropped. Of course he remembered Dr. Harrison. Emerald colored eyes, pale white skin, and sandy-blond hair. His features looked delicate and hard at the same time, like the gem his eyes resembled.

During the interview, he found out how hard Dr. Harrison was. At first, he seemed disinterested in Dutch as a candidate, not really paying attention to the questions asked by the dean or the department chair. It made him incredibly nervous and even a bit pissed off. He didn't feel as if he was being given a chance.

But after a few minutes, the tough questions began. Evidently, Dr. Harrison didn't think an untested instructor should be given a brand new art program. His questions probed every weakness imaginable—his unproven record in education, his relatively newness in the discipline, and his lack of sustainable roots in San Antonio.

Luckily, Dutch won him and the committee over with his answers. Dr. Harrison even took him out to lunch a couple of days ago. After lunch, Dutch couldn't decide if he should tell Justin about the shared meal. Now that he knew Dr. Harrison and Spencer were the same person, he had no plans to reveal what had happened, especially in light of how incensed Justin currently was.

"Well, say something," Justin said.

"I don't know what to say," he replied. He felt as if Justin expected him to fix this situation, as if he were the one who'd made some unforgiveable mistake. He resented being made to feel that way. "It's a random confluence of events," he finally said, trying to remain calm and ease his rising anger. They couldn't afford to both fly off the handle right now. "I didn't set out to meet Spencer; I had no idea he even worked at St. Mary's."

"Well, he does," Justin fumed. "What are you going to do about it?"

The accusing tone greatly irked him. Apparently, he *was* being expected to fix this. "What do you mean by that?" he asked, meeting Justin's steely gaze with his own.

"You can't still be thinking of taking the job? Of working on the same campus as Spencer?"

Dutch exhaled, trying to blow out his lit fuse. He couldn't believe Justin was so selfish as to think that he should sacrifice needed income just to stay out of Spencer's path. "I *need* the job," he finally said, when he felt calm enough to speak. "You know I do."

"Apply elsewhere," Justin ordered. "If you got this job, you could get another." Justin walked over to where he stood. His eyes filled with hope because he expected Dutch to seriously consider an alternative.

He wanted to tell Justin to quit acting like a child, to grow up and deal with the consequences of actions he'd set into motion. Instead, he simply shook his head. "I can't take that chance. I got this job because of Sharon. She knows the dean. I might not get so lucky on another campus."

He figured the logic of the argument would be enough to end the discussion, so they could deal with the true heart of the matter. Instead, the hope in Justin's eyes turned to desperation. "You can't do this to us," Justin told him. "To me."

"You did this to *yourself*," Dutch replied. He could hold back his anger no longer. "You were the one who needed the secrecy. If you told me, *from the very beginning*, where Spencer worked, I might not have ever considered applying for the job. But you didn't and I did."

He knew his eyes were more than likely ice cold at the moment. From past boyfriends he had learned that when he got angry, all warmth drained from his eyes. He'd never intended to look upon Justin that way, but he had been provoked. Besides, it was past time for him to stand his ground. Justin needed to realize the world didn't revolve around him or his wants. Other people mattered too. "I'm not going back on the offer," he said sternly, to prove that there would be no further debate on the subject.

"I can't have you both working so closely together," Justin said. "Not while I'm seeing both of you. Not while I'm still trying to decide."

At last, Dutch realized the root of Justin's anger. He wasn't angry that Dutch and Spencer were working at the same university. He was ticked off because he felt as if he was being forced into a decision, and Justin *hated* to be forced into anything.

"I know how much you hate being forced to do something," he said. "But it's time to make a choice. You *have* to decide. I can't go on living like this and neither can you."

Justin grew tense as he walked over and slowly lowered himself onto the couch.

"You've changed over the past few weeks. You've become more isolated, spending more time at work than with either Spencer or me. This indecision is eating you alive, and it has to stop."

Justin fidgeted on the edge of the couch. "You're right."

He expected to be relieved when he heard Justin say those words, but the timbre of Justin's voice told him the decision had been made before he even got here.

"I haven't known what to do," Justin began. He rubbed his nose, something he did whenever he was about to say something unpleasant. "I truly love *both* of you, and you're right, it's been tearing me up inside. I've committed myself to two wonderful men, and I can't find a solution that would be easy for everyone."

"This was never going to be easy for *anyone*," he said, while putting on his poker face. He knew exactly where this was headed. This was Justin's good-bye speech.

"I know," Justin said. He looked up at Dutch, his eyes reflecting the shattered pieces of his soul. "I finally realized that. I knew I had to make a decision. I just didn't know which one to make. But tonight, when Spencer told me about the new photography adjunct he helped hire, I just knew it was you. I knew it before he told me your name; it was like magic. And the only thought that crossed my mind was how *Spencer* could never find out."

Dutch made sure his face showed no emotion. He imagined himself made of steel; it was what he needed to survive being dumped by a man he loved more than anyone else.

"If my first thought was Spencer, then that means I've made my choice," Justin said. "I have to stay with him. And only him."

Dutch forced a smile. Even though he knew it might always end this way, he'd always secretly hoped Justin would choose him. He didn't want Justin to see that, though.

When Justin entered his life, they were both vulnerable and weak. He wanted to be strong and self-assured when Justin exited, to prove that he had grown, that he would be fine, even though he only felt dead on the inside.

Justin stood from the couch and walked over to stand in front of him.

His arms were still crossed, and he lacked the strength to move them. If he did, he might lose all of his resolve.

Justin stared at him, his eyes asking for some kind of response.

He *wanted* to yell and throw things. He *wanted* to curse Justin for breaking his heart. He *wanted* to make Justin hurt.

But that would give Justin too much power. Justin had taken too much from him already. He wasn't going to hand over his self-respect or his dignity the same way he'd foolishly offered his heart.

"I understand your choice, and I love you for it," he finally said. It was a lie, but it was a response that spoke volumes. It told Justin that he would be fine, that he didn't need to have Justin to be happy. It told Justin that he was the better person. Not only did he understand and accept the decision, but he was still man enough, strong enough, to admit that he still loved Justin regardless.

His words told Justin he would be fine, but his words were a lie.

Justin didn't reply. Instead, he hugged him, but Dutch's body remained rigid.

He had no intention of returning the embrace. All he wanted was for Justin to go.

Justin sensed his desire; they were still in tune to each other to some degree. Once again, like on the night they first met, words were no longer necessary and couldn't express the depths of their emotions.

Justin turned around. He placed the key to Dutch's house on the coffee table and walked out the front door without another word or a final glance back.

When the door finally closed shut, Dutch continued staring at the wooden door. He was incapable of moving, incapable of emotion.

His body was frozen, his heart a block of ice.

The man he was before this moment simply ceased to be, lost to the coldness of space, where emotion couldn't survive in the engulfing darkness or lifeless void.

CHAPTER 29

2010

AFTER Justin entered the elevator, Spencer once again made his way to Dutch's room. His last visit hadn't been as productive as he would have liked. He'd intended to settle the unfinished business between him and Dutch, but when Dutch brought up the subject, he couldn't do it. All he managed was to get Dutch to promise to keep the secret.

Their secret wouldn't remain hidden forever. He accepted that. But there were things that needed to be done before it surfaced. They were trapped, unable to gain any ground as their wheels spun in the mud pit they'd made of their lives. In order for progress to be made, they needed traction; they needed something to force them free before all three of them were destroyed.

While he drove around town after his last visit to the hospital, he came up with a plan that would hopefully do just that. What he needed from Dutch was his consent to go along with it.

It was a tricky proposition, one Dutch might not willingly agree to. But it had to be done. If successful, the three of them could be truly free of the lies they had all woven. The mud would be cleared from their path, allowing them to drive in whatever directions they needed to go.

It's the worst fucking idea I've ever heard, his father said. *You can't really think this is a good plan? Your armor won't protect you from this, not if you're the one that sets all this in motion. If it goes wrong, you'll hate yourself forever. You'll never forgive yourself. You know that.*

He knew the risks. His plan was the equivalent of walking into a battlefield without a gun or body armor. Serious injury was likely, but he saw no other option. Sometimes sacrifices had to be made in war.

Sure, sacrifices have to be made, his father agreed. *But this is just plain stupid. There's no need for this. You're throwing yourself into the line of fire for no good reason. Don't worry about the spic or his whore. Worry about you.*

That's not being a very good soldier, he told his father. *Never leave a man behind on the battlefield. Those are your words. Not mine.*

This isn't a fucking war, damn it, his father ranted. *This is your* life. *This is your heart, the one damn thing you've always been so protective of. Hasn't it been burned enough? Why do you feel the need to toss it back into the battle before it's recovered?*

You know why, he replied.

For Christ's sake, his father said, disgusted. *Not this again! You need to let it* go.

I can't, he said. *Now for the final time,* shut the fuck up!

His father's voice continued to rail inside his head, until it slowly decreased to a barely audible whisper.

Logically, he knew his father was right. There was no need to put himself through this. The best thing for him, and his heart, was simply to beat a hasty retreat. Sometimes living to fight another day was a victory in itself. His armor was back on, and it would keep him safe for the rest of his life.

But he'd come to realize, after his talk with Dutch, that being safe wasn't living. For too long, he'd lived without fear of being hurt because he never let anyone get close enough to hurt him. Family, friends, lovers were kept at a distance, on the other side of his armor, and while they lived and loved and suffered and rejoiced, he was safe. But he was also alone and miserable.

He'd never realized how miserable he was until Justin. When he let the armor go and embraced Justin, it was similar to being reborn into a world of experience he had previously denied himself. Nothing protected him. Everything affected him. And it was all good, even the pain, even the hurt. Feeling meant he was alive, not the emotionless, unfeeling zombie he had become.

Returning to that lifeless creature no longer appealed to him, despite the pain that still racked his body. The pain he felt told him he loved Justin, despite the affair. If he didn't, he would feel nothing, only indifference. Something he hadn't realized until his previous talk with Dutch.

Reuniting with Justin, rebuilding what they once had was impossible, though, unless he knew for certain that Justin wanted to be with him. The only way for that to happen was for there to be closure.

And the only way for there to be closure was to put all three of them through this test. When it was over, they would all know exactly what path their lives would take.

It might end differently than he expected, but he had to take the chance. He had to expose himself to hurt. Being vulnerable wasn't something he enjoyed, but it was the only way to find the magic again.

With purpose, he walked into Dutch's room and revealed his plan, hoping that their secret past would remain hidden long enough for his plan to bear fruit.

CHAPTER 30

2009

DUTCH ascended the wooden stairway of Reinbolt Hall. The air, heavy with a woodsy fragrance, reminded him of the Cathedral of the Holy Cross in Boston, where his parents used to worship every Sunday. The mixture of wood, oil, and must took him back to happier times, when he sat in the pew as a child.

Sitting there, his parents on both sides, made him feel safe and loved. This was his holy place, not for the reasons his parents taught him, but for his own. For his parents, the church was a place where they communed with God and received his blessings. It was sacred, holy. For him, his family was all he knew of holiness. Their love was unconditional and everywhere. It was like God to him. Not that he didn't believe in God as a child. He did. But he never saw God. He *always* saw his parents, and their love worked the miracles in his life.

Now his parents were gone. Their love lost, returned to the heavens with their spirits. Its absence left him hollow and dead. For the briefest of moments, he believed he'd found something just as special, just as sacred—a love that would see him through this dark and turbulent world until he inevitably met his end.

He'd embraced it, given himself to it like a child trusting his parents to never do harm. And he had been hurt. Abandoned. Cast off. The love had been a lie, and he was alone and lost, drifting through the world without a compass, without a beacon.

Looking out the second-floor window of Reinbolt Hall and watching the underclassmen in the quad below filled him with no joy. Their smiles and exuberance couldn't alter his outlook, not when he knew that despair and apathy waited in the shadows for the opportunity to ground such high spirits with harsh reality.

True happiness was an unachievable dream, something everyone searched for but few, if any, ever found. Whatever love they experienced proved fleeting or false. No longevity could be found in love, not when human nature was a part of the mix. As with everything God given, humans had corrupted love and tainted it with personal agendas.

He arrived at that conclusion a few weeks after Justin left him.

At first, he accepted Justin's decision to return to Spencer, but he stupidly believed they could at least remain friends. After all, they began as friends on Cyber. They'd helped each other through tough times they could never have endured alone. Why couldn't they simply return to where they began?

So he tried to remain in contact. He sent Justin numerous messages on Cyber. He never sent texts for fear of Spencer discovering them. Justin replied at first, politely asking how he was doing. Dutch even inquired if any progress had been made with patching up his relationship with Spencer.

Soon, days would pass before Justin replied to a Cyber message. When he did, his messages were distant. A few weeks later, Justin's profile disappeared.

When he discovered the profile was missing from his favorites list, he scrolled through pages and pages of profiles in San Antonio. He held onto hope that perhaps Justin had purchased a new phone and therefore created a new account. He even toyed with the idea that he had accidentally removed J-squared as a favorite the last time he sent Justin a message.

Eventually, he accepted the truth: Justin had deleted the account.

He thought about calling Justin or texting him, but he never did. He got the hint. Justin no longer wanted to communicate with him.

He threw himself into his work instead of wallowing in his grief.

Creating the new photography classes for St. Mary's got him through the summer but now that fall was here, now that he was working, he found it difficult to remain focused, especially since the source of his pain resided in the adjacent building.

Standing on the landing, he looked up at his objective—the third floor, where the majority of language faculty offices were located. On that floor, he would find the office of Dr. Spencer Harrison.

At Fall Convocation, which was St. Mary's yearly faculty meeting, he spotted Spencer sitting with the dean and the department chair, who had hired him. They made many attempts to get his attention, probably hoping he would join them at their table, but he pretended not to see them, choosing instead to sit at a table filled with math faculty.

Avoiding Spencer after that proved easy enough. Though they were in the same academic school, they were in different departments and housed in different buildings. Spencer sent a few e-mails welcoming him to St. Mary's, and he responded politely, but he always refused the lunch offers.

He had no intention of spending any time alone with Spencer, not when he might catch a whiff of Justin's sandalwood and leather scent on Spencer's clothes.

Last night, after he picked up a dark-haired twink at one of the local gay clubs called The Heat, he had an epiphany. His trick enjoyed it rough. He begged for it. Dutch smacked his ass hard until red handprints sprang across his flesh. He even wrapped his big hands around the lithe neck and squeezed tightly while he slammed in and out of the guy's ass, which he failed to lubricate.

Still, he wanted more abuse, and Dutch was happy to oblige. He pinched his nipples and bit them. He tugged on his balls. He called him a filthy-no-good-faggot-cum-pig and then dumped his load in his hole. Afterward, he smacked the twink's ass with a belt until he finally shot his load.

When he left, he felt powerful, as if he had regained some of the dignity and respect Justin stole. Degrading someone else, making that twink submissive to him, restored his power and his manhood. He no longer felt lost. He felt anchored by the abject brutality.

He had no intention of losing that control again. And the only way to maintain it, the only way to assure that the power would forever remain his, was to go to the source of his pain and take from it what was taken from him.

Then, all would be right in his world. Balance would be restored.

He found Spencer's office door open, but the office empty. He figured Spencer couldn't be far, so he walked in and made himself at home.

Bookshelves lined with textbooks made up a majority of the left wall. A filing cabinet sat to the left with an assortment of colored folders stacked neatly on top. Above the desk hung a painting. It depicted a ship crashing onto rocks and a lone woman, in the painting's foreground, looking at the disaster. Her eyes showed both horror and heartbreak.

Obviously, someone she loved was about to perish.

He thought the painting both appropriate and portentous. Not that he was planning on hurting anyone, at least not physically. The wounds he intended to inflict would cut much deeper than the flesh.

His gaze drifted from the painting to a side table, where photographs were prominently displayed. His heart caught in his throat.

Pictures of Justin or Justin and Spencer filled the desk. Their smiles glowed brightly within the frames, as if the glass barrier couldn't contain their love. They held hands in one picture. In another, they kissed.

He wanted to smash those pictures into a million pieces.

"Well, well, look who's finally come to see me."

He turned around. Spencer's warm smile greeted him. At first, he was taken aback. The memory of the photographs still stoked his fury, but he had to maintain his composure. Showing his hand now would accomplish nothing.

"Sorry about that," he lied. He extended his hand to Spencer, trying his best to act as nonchalant as possible. "It's been a crazy few weeks."

"I completely understand," Spencer replied, taking Dutch's offered hand. They shook hands, and the feel of Spencer's delicate white flesh caused his determination to waver.

In Spencer's eyes and in his touch rested absolute trust and camaraderie. Absent of all guile, he represented the epitome of decency. He truly was an innocent, someone who didn't deserve to be the object of his contempt.

"I'm just glad you finally stopped by," said Spencer. He rounded his desk and sat in the executive chair positioned behind it. "Please sit." His gaze moved to one of two leather tub chairs positioned in front of his desk.

Dutch took a seat. Guilt washed over him. Spencer's jade eyes sparkled with clear joy at his unannounced visit. He obviously felt some sense of familiarity existed between them, most likely born from being on Dutch's interview committee.

However, Dutch knew how far their familiarity truly ran. They shared more than just an interview. They shared a lover.

That knowledge triggered his more nurturing side, the person he was before Justin. The man who took care of others before taking care of himself. That man begged him to reconsider, to abandon his vindictiveness before it was too late.

As far as he was concerned, it was already too late.

"Well, just because I haven't been to visit doesn't mean I haven't thought about you." He sat back in the chair, allowing his words to bathe in the allure he dipped them in prior to speaking.

A cloud of suspicion momentarily floated across Spencer's vision. "What do you mean?"

"Your lunch offers," he replied. "Haven't been able to forget about them. Especially since I've been brown-bagging it."

"Ah," Spencer said. The winds of trust blew away the previous suspicion. "Name the day and time, and I'll be a man of my word."

"How about today?" he asked. "Just being here makes me ravenous." Suspicion wafted back into view. He enjoyed keeping Spencer off balance. "I could eat an entire side of beef."

"You have quite an appetite," replied Spencer.

He winked. "You have no idea."

Spencer said nothing. He simply stared at Dutch, trying to gauge his intentions. Dutch was obviously being flirtatious, but most gay men were horrible flirts. Usually, the sexually charged dialogue was harmless, even meaningless. Spencer's confused face told Dutch he was trying to determine whether meaning existed in them or not.

"I have to ask," Spencer at last said. "Are you gay?"

He wasn't expecting that question. Still, he nodded. "Guilty."

"And since you were in my office before I got here, I naturally assume you saw pictures of me with my *partner*?" Spencer asked, emphasizing the word "partner" for him.

"I did," he admitted.

"Well, then, you know I'm gay as well," Spencer said. "Is that why you think it's acceptable to flirt with me in *my* office in our place of *work*?"

Spencer appeared irritated. His previously friendly jade eyes darkened considerably, and he constantly clicked on the pen he picked up from his desk.

"I apologize," Dutch said, needing to salvage the situation. Losing Spencer's trust now would only complicate his plans. "I'm a huge flirt, and I don't know when to turn it off, especially when I find another man attractive."

"Well, you need to learn," Spencer warned. "I'm a married man and completely unavailable." His eyes locked onto Dutch's. "No matter how attractive I may be."

The tone in Spencer's last comment confused him. It sounded more playful than angry, as if the boundary previously drawn never existed. That's when he remembered something Justin told him about Spencer.

Spencer loved to tease. In fact, the harder he tried, the more difficult it was for Spencer to maintain the act.

"You're teasing me," he finally said. "I can see it."

Spencer's resolve faded into a hearty laugh. "Damn, I hate that I can't keep a straight face," he said. "Justin, that's my partner, tells me I have the worst poker face in the world."

"You had me going for a few seconds there," he admitted, pleased to see the return of the friendly twinkle. "I thought I had really pissed you off."

Spencer waved the comment away. "Not at all. I'm a big boy and quite capable of handling harmless flirtation." He stared intently at Dutch. "It *was* harmless, right?"

Dutch said nothing at first, letting the question linger between them until it consumed all the air in the room. "We'll have to wait and see," he finally said with a laugh.

Spencer laughed as well, but his laughter represented uncertainty rather than true amusement. Spencer didn't know what to make of him, and Dutch liked it that way. He wanted to keep Spencer guessing.

"You most definitely are a flirt, Mr. Keller," Spencer finally said. "Just like Justin. The two of you should meet. Perhaps you can come for dinner one night."

"I don't think so," he said much too quickly to be casual. Spencer's face clearly expressed bewilderment at his hasty response. "Not that I don't want to meet your partner," he added quickly. "I'm just really busy after work these days. Right now, I'm barely two class days ahead of my students. My evenings are reserved for quick meals, research, and planning. I'm sure you understand."

Spencer nodded. "I remember those days, but it does get better. Next semester, you'll be able to relax a bit on planning. But then you'll see all the areas that need to be fixed and the process starts all over again."

"Thanks," he replied. "I feel so much better."

Spencer laughed. "It takes a few years to get comfortable with your curriculum and teaching styles. You'll always make adjustments. I know I still do, but it's nowhere near as hectic as your first year. I promise."

Spencer's friendly reassurance made him feel awful again. This game was mean and spiteful, and Spencer deserved better. He truly was a good man. Dutch could feel it. His eyes and his demeanor revealed a good heart and a good soul. He could even see why Justin fell in love with this man.

The best thing for him to do was to abandon this plan, to not let the darkness, which angrily swirled within him, take him away and turn him into somebody he wouldn't even recognize.

"Now, let's do lunch," Spencer said, rising from his desk. "Have you been to Henry's Puffy Tacos?"

He shook his head.

"Do you like Mexican food?"

"I love Mexican food," he answered. "And I'm partial to dark-skinned men too."

Spencer chuckled. "Me too," he said. "I gravitate toward them like it's my job or something."

Now it was his turn to laugh. "But I never turn down a good piece of white meat." He winked suggestively at Spencer once again, unable to stop himself.

"Who can?" Spencer asked. "White meat is much better for you." Spencer winked back. His eyes sparkled not only with playfulness but also with a hint of coquettishness. "Now let's go," he said. Spencer grabbed his keys and walked toward the office door. "I'm famished, and the waiters there are cute. I shamelessly flirt with them whenever I go."

"I bet," Dutch replied while walking out of Spencer's office and into the hall.

"And I get great service."

Spencer locked his office door, and they walked toward the stairway. As they descended, doubts once again surfaced. This wasn't the type of man Dutch wanted to be, yet he felt powerless to stop the train that was already barreling down the track.

CHAPTER 31

2010

AS JUSTIN parked his car and walked toward the hospital, his routine for the past week, he was pleased that things, at least with Dutch, appeared to be on the right track. He'd promised Dutch he wouldn't abandon him as he did the last time, and he intended to keep his word. Every day after school, he brought Dutch a treat. Yesterday it was a chocolate milkshake from McDonald's. Today, it was an Ocean Water slushie from Sonic. It wasn't much, but Dutch appreciated the break from the hospital food, which was getting increasingly harder for him to stomach.

Dutch's recuperation steadily progressed. Though still paralyzed from the waist down, his internal injuries had all but healed. Tomorrow was his scheduled discharge from the hospital, with daily rehabilitation at the hospital's outpatient clinic. With luck and with patience, Dutch would reach full mobility again by Christmas.

Tomorrow was a big day for Dutch. And for him. Tomorrow was also the day he had to move out of the house he'd shared with Spencer for the past nine years. He had no desire to leave Spencer or their house, but Spencer refused to listen to argument. He wouldn't even speak with Justin on the phone or in person.

Communication between them had been reduced to voice mails and e-mails. Spencer denied all his requests to talk in person, whether he begged to be let in at the office or home door. Spencer's response was always the same: *I have nothing else to say.* According to Spencer's last e-mail, their relationship was over. He had to start over, and the only way for him to do that was for Justin to move out.

Spencer had made it clear there were no other options.

So tomorrow, while Dutch left the hospital, Justin would be leaving his house and moving in with his mother, who was distraught. She hated the idea of her boys separating. She attempted to contact Spencer to intervene, but Spencer had cut all ties with not only Justin but his family and their friends.

Spencer lived in isolation now, safe behind the walls Justin had once broken down. He hated himself for doing that to Spencer, for causing him to revert to his previous introverted personality. The man he knew was the social butterfly, the one who planned all the get-togethers and dinner parties.

The man who now inhabited Spencer's body was a stranger, someone neither he nor his friends knew. Although the majority of their friends were angry with Justin for cheating, they were equally upset with Spencer for turning his back on them. They didn't understand why he'd cut them out of his life.

Frankly, Justin didn't understand it either.

He knew Spencer better than anyone. Spencer never acted foolishly, and his behavior, whether it was brought on by the affair or not, was foolish. It made him wonder if something else was going on, but when he tried to figure out what it could possibly be, he came up empty.

All he was left with was that the pain he inflicted had been too much for Spencer to handle, so he'd shut down completely.

The chime of the elevator doors snapped him out of his troublesome thoughts. When the doors opened, he exited and walked down the hall to Dutch's room.

While his relationship with Spencer spiraled toward disaster, his friendship with Dutch remained unchanged. He still loved Dutch immensely. He wanted nothing more than for Dutch to fully recover from his injuries. But he wasn't deluding himself. His relationship with Dutch had to end in order for there to be a future for him and Spencer.

A future his friends and his family didn't believe would happen as long as he visited Dutch. No one understood why he continued to come to the hospital.

You're not showing him you're sorry, his mother fretted.

This is just fucked up, Tyler yelled at him. *If I were Spencer, I'd think you'd chosen Dutch too! Cut him out of your life. Don't talk to him. Don't visit him. Just be done with him.*

You know, you're ruining your chances to reconcile, don't you? both Jill and Chris asked him over dinner.

I'm gonna kick your ass if you don't stop being such a dipshit, Patrick told him while Heather begged her husband to calm down.

He's not talking to us because of you, Teresa told him. *He's embarrassed. You're embarrassing him* and *yourself.*

He'd given up trying to explain his actions. There was no way they could understand. The affair had hurt Spencer *and* Dutch. Justin broke both of their hearts and was responsible for setting both of them right once again. He refused to be any more like his father than he already was.

How could they understand that he had to rectify what he had done and the only way to do that was to see both Spencer *and* Dutch through their pain?

He wanted to rebuild his life with Spencer, but his efforts were blocked on all fronts. After tomorrow, though, his energies would once again focus on only Spencer, even if he was moving out of their house. Dutch's discharge from the hospital meant his work was complete. He'd seen Dutch through his recuperation and would feel no guilt when he returned his attention to Spencer.

Spencer might have said they were over, but Justin refused to accept it. If it took him the rest of his life, he planned on once again channeling the magic that brought them together in the first place.

"I'm back," he told Dutch, who sat up in his hospital bed watching *Jeopardy*. Over the past week, Dutch had started to look like his old self. The majority of his cuts and bruises had healed. His lips were no longer cracked and bloodied. The angry red cut on his cheek had lost its fury, but a scar remained as a reminder of the tragedy. "Still watching television, I see."

"I fucking hate Alex Trebek," Dutch said, turning off the television set with the bedside remote. "He thinks he's so smart when he has all the damn answers on his monitor screen."

"You just hate that you don't get most of the harder questions," he told Dutch while handing him the slushie from Sonic.

"I do not," Dutch lied. He took a sip of the slushie and grinned. "I choose *not* to answer those."

Justin only smirked in response. He wasn't getting drawn into another *Jeopardy* debate about how the questions were given to the contestants in order to make the average American feel stupid. It was wiser, and easier, to switch subjects. "So, big day tomorrow?" he asked. "You excited about being sprung from this joint?"

Dutch nodded while sucking down more of the slushie. "I can't wait to be home. Sleep in my own bed. And no Nurse Ratched to come skulking around at night."

He laughed. Everyone hated Nurse Ratched, whose bedside manner was rude at best. "You never know, she might just pay you nightly visits at your house."

"Shut your mouth," Dutch said. "That would scare the crap out of me!" He put the half-finished drink on the rollaway table. "Besides, she was almost pleasant last night. I considered asking her if she'd run over a small child or something."

It had been so long since someone quoted *Steel Magnolias* to him that Justin couldn't help but laugh uncontrollably. The laughter felt good, transporting him back to happier times.

"Sorry about getting all Clairee Belcher on you," Dutch said. "But I *love* that movie even though you don't. It's got some great one-liners."

"I know," he told Dutch, who had no idea that *Steel Magnolias* was his and Spencer's favorite movie. While he'd shared many things about his life with Spencer, he'd neglected to share that part with Dutch. He knew the movie was a favorite of Dutch's, but months ago, when Dutch asked him if he wanted to watch it with him, he told him no. He'd lied and said he hated the movie.

He never understood why he did that. Dutch already knew so much about his life with Spencer, and the two of them had already slept together. Still, he didn't want to watch the movie with Dutch. It was something that was just for him and Spencer.

"So, what happens after tomorrow?" Dutch asked.

"What do you mean?"

"Where are you going to go? I know tomorrow's the day you move out."

"I'll move in with my mom," he said. "I'm not looking forward to that. Not that I hate my mom or anything, but it's a step backwards. Going back home means failure to me. And I don't do failure very well."

"Maybe you don't have to," Dutch told him. "Move in with me."

The suggestion took him off guard. While he wasn't excited about moving in with his mother, he had no intention of moving in with Dutch. The idea was ridiculous. "What the hell are you talking about?"

"You heard me. Move in with me."

He eyed Dutch suspiciously. Dutch knew he intended to get back with Spencer. Moving in together would only hurt those chances. "I'm not moving in with you," he finally said. "And you know why."

"Stop staring at me as if I'm crazy or trying to ruin your chances of reuniting with Spencer," Dutch said. His eyes were clear and focused. "I'm not on the make to keep you in my life forever."

"Then *why* do you want me to move in with you?"

"Move in together?" Heidi exclaimed. Dutch's sister rushed into the hospital room, completely oblivious to the fact that she was intruding. "That would be a load off my mind."

"What?" he asked her absently. He was still reeling from the absurdity of Dutch's suggestion and trying to gauge the true intentions behind the request. "Why would you say that?"

"I have to get home to the kids soon," she said. Heidi plopped herself down into the chair next to Dutch's bed. She propped her feet onto the mattress and sat back in the chair. "Naturally, I wanted Lukas to come with me, but his attorney told me there was no way my dumbass brother would be allowed to leave the city, much less the state, after his DWI."

"What?" Dutch asked. "How long am I stuck here?"

Heidi shrugged her shoulders in response. "That's up to the judge, but you'll likely be doing serious community service for a few years, and with your injuries, you probably won't do jail time. You may face house arrest for six days, though. It's your first offense, so you'll get some leniency, especially since no one else but you was hurt, but you won't get enough leeway to leave the state. You'll have to pay some hefty fines and attend DWI school."

Justin watched the magnitude of Heidi's words weigh down upon Dutch. He had been so focused on his recuperation he'd completely forgotten about the consequences of his drunk driving.

"That's why I'm happy to hear Justin will be moving in with you," Heidi said.

"I haven't said I was," he added. "That was Dutch's harebrained idea."

Heidi's expression changed swiftly. Her wide, friendly hazel eyes grew cloudy with anger. The lively green drained from the irises, leaving only a harsh brown that threatened to go black. Her wide smile, the one that always joyously greeted him, tightened. She rose slowly from her reclined position and took measured steps toward him.

He had no idea what caused the change. According to Dutch, his sister was the most even-tempered person in the world. He told stories of Heidi staying calm when everyone else around her had lost their senses. She was described as a peacemaker, the one who smoothed over disagreements, the voice of reason.

That woman was nowhere to be seen.

"Harebrained?" she asked, her voice low and tense. "My brother is paralyzed from driving while drunk because he was so upset that you left him, that you suddenly grew a conscience and realized cheating on your man was wrong."

"Heidi, listen…."

"My brother needs the support and care of his family," she continued, as if he hadn't spoken. "Support that can't be given, no matter how much I want to give it, because he can't come home with me. He's stuck here because he fucked up, but he's stuck here because you fucked him up while fucking him. I can't stay here forever. I have children who need me. He can't come home with me. And you have the gall to say that moving in with him is a harebrained idea."

"It's just that I have to focus on Spencer and me right now."

"That's right," Heidi said. She was now standing toe to toe with him. "It's always about you, isn't it? It's never about anyone else. It's always what Justin wants."

"That's not fair," he said while putting some distance between them, but the truth of her words stung him harder than if she had slapped him. Justin *was* selfish and self-centered. The mess he was currently in was because he not only cheated but fell in love with another man. This whole situation centered on *his* wants, *his* needs, *his* desires. When was he going to think about someone else beside himself?

"Who said it was fair?" Heidi asked, drawing him out of his self-loathing. Her voice was still low, but the anger within it was all-consuming. "Nothing about this situation is fair. But you owe it to my brother to help him now. You weren't there before, and you say you're sorry. Well, now it's time to prove it. Be a man and do something or do what you're best at and leave."

"I don't need any favors," Dutch said. "I can make it on my own."

Heidi spun around. The hell storm was now headed for him.

"You need to stop being so bullheaded," she told her brother. "You need help, and you'll have it before I leave."

"I'm perfectly capable of taking care of myself," Dutch announced.

"Yes," she said. "You've done a fabulous job of that so far."

Justin stood in front of them, quietly contemplating his options. Was this why Dutch had asked him to move in? Did he know Heidi was leaving? Was the request Dutch's way of asking for more help? Was he once again being self-centered and not recognizing that?

He had promised to help Dutch through his recuperation, and if he said no now, he would once again be abandoning Dutch in his time of need. But if he agreed, he also gambled with losing Spencer for good.

For the second time, he faced making a choice between Dutch and Spencer. He wanted to choose Spencer, but that was a selfish choice. It was about what he wanted, not about what he *should* do. Besides, Spencer's last words were about how the two of them were *never* supposed to be a choice. They just were.

He still didn't fully understand what that meant, but he knew enough that if he were ever to get Spencer back, choice wouldn't be a part of the equation. It would just be.

"I'll do it," Justin finally agreed.

Heidi turned back toward him. The winds of her storm abated.

"You're right," he told Heidi. He approached her cautiously and took her hand. "I have to make amends to more than just Spencer. I need to set things right with Dutch too. I made a promise to him, and I intend to keep it."

As swiftly as the storm came on, it disappeared. Her smile and her wide eyes once again lit Heidi's face. She took Justin in her arms and hugged him tightly. "Thank you, Justin. I knew you wouldn't let me down."

She embraced him. While they hugged, a strange expression flashed across Dutch's face. It was a combination of satisfaction and worry. He wondered why those emotions floated so closely to Dutch's surface.

For some inexplicable reason, his world felt out of his control, as if some unseen hand was directing his actions.

CHAPTER 32

2009

APPROPRIATE self-control tumbled from Spencer's grasp as he stood outside Treadaway Hall, which housed single-room student dorms and the faculty offices for the Speech Communications and Fine Arts Department.

Dutch's office was located on the second floor, and even though he knew he shouldn't climb the steps to the office, he *wanted* to see Dutch, to rekindle a friendship that had grown despite their awkward lunch about a month ago. Since that lunch, not being alone with Dutch had proved a more prudent course of action, but today he felt compelled to abandon caution in order to find the truth behind the recent changes in Dutch and their friendship.

He genuinely liked Dutch, and they frequently had lunch together, up until a couple of weeks ago, when Dutch stopped returning his calls and e-mails. He had withdrawn, not only from him but from the rest of the world. When he was on campus, which wasn't very frequently these days, he stayed in his office, behind a closed door. He only opened it when the occasional student came by to see him, although most of his students now ran in the other direction when they saw him coming.

According to Dr. Peggy Cutting, his dear friend and department chair, Dutch's attitude and attendance had sharply declined. Several students complained about him every other week, citing gruff behavior and unclear assignments as their chief grievances. Dr. Cutting and the dean were beginning to regret their decision to hire Dutch. Plans were already in motion to either put him on notice or terminate him outright.

He couldn't help but wonder if Dutch's new attitude had anything to do with what had happened at lunch. He thought they had gotten past it, but no matter how hard Spencer tried to act indifferently about it, Dutch appeared to know better, as if he could peer through Spencer's layers and see the truth.

Do you even know what the truth is? his father's voice asked.

The return of his father's voice startled him. For almost ten years, his father hadn't spoken to him from the depths of his subconscious, not since Justin's love quieted his rants. When it disappeared, he thought his father's stint as his super ego had finally concluded. Apparently, that was no longer the case.

Oh, don't be so surprised to hear from me, his father said. *Especially now. I always resurface in times of real distress. And, boy, you're in over your queer little head.*

I have no idea what you're referring to, he thought. *I'm just here to help a friend who's in distress. I'm not the one in trouble.*

His father laughed. As always, no joy emanated from his father. His laughter was the equivalent of mocking. *You will be soon enough.*

Silence followed the last comment. In the past, his father's voice would taunt him, sometimes for hours. Never before had his father grown quiet so quickly. That worried Spencer immensely.

Was he right? he wondered. Was he walking into a situation he should instead be running from?

Unable to move, still battling for self-control, Spencer leaned against the brown brick wall opposite the big wooden doors that led up to the office complex on the second floor. His mind drifted back to the lunch he and Dutch had shared several weeks ago.

The waiter, who was exceptionally cute and no more than twenty, sat them at a table for two along the far west wall of the restaurant. Even though Henry's was quite busy, as it always was during lunchtime, the hostess quickly saw that a table was prepared for Spencer. As a regular of more than five years, he enjoyed some special treatment.

"I enjoy lunching with a man who has pull," Dutch said while nodding toward other customers who were still waiting to be seated.

"What can I say?" he asked. "I'm quite popular."

"I see that," Dutch added. "Our waiter couldn't keep his eyes off you."

Spencer laughed. He'd also noticed the way their waiter stared at him with a spark of attraction lighting up his eyes. "Are you surprised that you're not the only one who finds me attractive?"

His comment unsettled Dutch. He averted his eyes and squirmed in his seat. "What do you mean?"

"You told me you thought I was attractive in my office, remember? How quickly they forget!" he joked.

Dutch sighed, while appearing visibly relieved. "Of course," he finally said. "Then you scared me by insinuating sexual harassment."

"I insinuated nothing," he responded. "It was indeed sexual harassment. You were just lucky I enjoy being sexually harassed." He winked at Dutch, signaling to him that the joke was still in play. Yet he wondered why his previous comment unsettled Dutch so much. He looked like someone who had been found out instead of someone who had already been let in on the joke.

"This place is nice," Dutch said, looking around the restaurant.

Spencer nodded in agreement. He followed Dutch's gaze around the room. Although he practically had the décor memorized from all the lunches he'd eaten here over the years, the interior always made him feel at home.

"I enjoy it," he added as he followed the multicolored lights that ran diagonally from one corner of the restaurant to the other. "That's why I come here like two or three times a week."

"Damn." Dutch whistled. "How do you manage to stay in such good shape?"

"I have a high metabolism. Plus, I work out three to four times a week."

"Very nice," replied Dutch, eying him up and down.

"I see you're flirting again, Mr. Keller."

"Not at all," Dutch said. "I'm merely checking out the goods. I'm a gay man. It's what we do."

Spencer laughed. He was enjoying the sexually charged banter. It took his mind off his trouble at home. Since he had returned from England, he and Justin had worked hard to put their relationship back together. Progress had been made, even though he'd thought they were headed for an official parting of the ways at first.

When he returned, Justin was extremely glad to have him home. He was happy to see Justin too. After all, they had been separated for four months. He had expected their first night home together to be filled with passion, a veritable fuck fest to end all fuck fests.

Instead, they talked. They talked about what they wanted and where the relationship was going, and even if it was ending. When they both decided to continue to work things out, they went to bed, without having sex.

When they finally had sex the following morning, their rhythm felt off. The intimacy was still good, but it wasn't the same. It was like Justin still held a part of himself back, fearful that Spencer would once again leave. He tried to assure Justin he wasn't going anywhere, that he had learned his lesson. What they needed was to be together, not apart.

For the next few weeks, Justin remained distant, spending more time at work than at home. But one day, the distance ended. He came home to a Justin who reminded him of the man he first met at the Bonham. His brown eyes were wild with desire, and in his eyes he saw only his reflection, as if Spencer was the only person who existed in Justin's world.

That night, they had the best sex of their lives, multiple times.

He had no idea what had happened to cause the change. He was simply grateful that it had.

Recently, though, a subtle change came over Justin. He looked depressed, as if he had lost something dear to him and had no idea how to find it. Whenever Spencer asked him what was wrong, Justin replied that there was nothing wrong. That everything was A-OK.

He wanted to call him a liar, but he saw the truth in Justin's eyes. Justin truly believed that nothing was wrong. He had no idea he sighed heavily or that his shoulders constantly slumped, when his posture used to be straight and confident.

Try as he might, Spencer couldn't figure out the cause of Justin's unhappiness, and he spent many sleepless nights trying to arrive at an answer. The only one he consistently found was that Justin no longer wanted to be with him and regretted trying to patch their relationship back together.

But he had no idea why he might feel that way now, when they had practically returned to the way things once were.

"Where did you just go?"

Dutch's question brought him out of his thoughts. "What?"

"You zoned out there for awhile. I kept calling your name, but you wouldn't respond."

"Sorry about that," he said. "Just lost in thought, I guess."

"Looked like some pretty heavy thoughts," Dutch added. "Feel like sharing?"

Spencer had many friends he could have opened up to if he wanted, but he never felt like he could. All his friends were Justin's friends. If he told them his fears, they would overreact and confront Justin. He didn't want that.

Dutch wouldn't do that. He didn't know him and Justin as a couple. Dutch only knew him and could provide his perspective, either telling him he was crazy or confirming his fears.

Before he could say anything though, the waiter returned to take their orders. He ordered a Henry's Puffy Taco Plate with two carne guisada tacos. Dutch said he would have the same. They both ordered tea.

"So, you going to tell me or not?" Dutch asked once the waiter left their table.

For reasons he couldn't explain, his desire to confess all to Dutch disappeared. Perhaps it was the relative newness of their friendship or his preference to keep his private life private, but Spencer no longer wished to divulge his relationship concerns.

"Nothing interesting, really," he lied. "Just a project Dr. Cutting has me working on." Before Dutch could ask, he added, "And I don't want to talk business on my lunch hour."

Dutch nodded his understanding. From the shadows, which lurked in the corners of his eyes, Spencer could tell Dutch didn't believe him. He was simply letting the matter drop. Spencer appreciated the gesture.

"No business," Dutch agreed. "I preferred our previous topic anyway."

"What topic was that?" he asked.

"You liking sexual harassment," Dutch reminded him. "It bodes well for our continued friendship."

Spencer chuckled. "Does it now?"

Dutch nodded. "I'm guessing you and your partner have an open relationship?"

The question took Spencer by surprise. "Why would you say that?"

"Just an assumption," responded Dutch. "Based purely on your fondness of sexual harassment from other men."

Spencer couldn't help but feel there was more to his new friend's comment. There was something just behind the curiosity that told him Dutch had a secret of some kind just itching to be told. "So," he said, adding emphasis to the vowel to punctuate his response, "you think I'm some insatiable man whore who isn't satisfied by just one man?"

"Not at all," Dutch answered. Spencer found his backpedaling amusing. "I was simply curious as to the nature of your relationship. I apologize if I've crossed a line."

"You have, but to set the record straight, we don't have an open relationship. I just enjoy flirting. It's harmless and fun."

"I see," Dutch said. "And the two of you have never had a threesome?"

Spencer was floored. He had never been asked such personal questions by someone he didn't know very well, much less someone he worked with. He found the questions rude and inappropriate. He really wanted to tell Dutch to mind his own business, but when he stared into his crystal blue eyes, the words refused to form on his lips.

Those eyes were dangerous, something he'd noticed when they first met at Dutch's interview. They had struck him dumb and made him virtually useless. Had he not recovered in time, he would have made a complete fool of himself in front of his boss and his boss's boss.

"Yes, we have," he finally admitted, surprising himself by answering. "But we don't do that anymore. It caused problems."

"I can understand that," replied Dutch. "If I had someone like you in my bed, I wouldn't dare let anyone else touch you."

Dutch ran his big index finger along the back of Spencer's hand and up his wrist. The touch was delicate and sensual, a long feathery stroke that sent thousands of vibrations rippling through his body. Spencer found the contact arousing and troublesome.

He couldn't deny his sexual attraction to Dutch. He had been instantly drawn to him upon first meeting, but he was in love with Justin. He was committed to him and had been for almost a decade.

Now, though, he envisioned Dutch naked in bed, his hairy body rubbing against his smooth white skin. His big hands rubbing across his flesh, pinching his nipples. The feel of his rock-hard erection pushing against his stomach. Hot, wet kisses covering his chest and his face. The scraping of Dutch's scruffy face against his inner thighs and his ass. The smell of sex and sweat stifling the room.

His cheeks sizzled. He knew they were flushed. The images were hot but unsettling. He felt dirty, his soul and heart polluted.

He felt like an adulterer.

Instantly, he withdrew his hand from Dutch's touch. "Although I appreciate flirtation, I think physical contact blurs lines that need to remain in focus." He placed his hands in his lap, covering the rock-hard bulge in his trousers.

"I apologize," Dutch said, a smile hanging on his lips. He looked like a kid who got caught eating candy but still wanted more. "I just felt this connection between us and thought that maybe...,well, it doesn't matter. I was wrong."

"Yes," he told Dutch, "you were."

The waiter brought their glasses of tea. Spencer grabbed his glass and swallowed at least half of its contents.

"I apologize again," Dutch said while taking a sip of his tea.

"I want us to be friends," Spencer replied, once he finally caught his breath. "Nothing more."

Dutch nodded his understanding and changed the subject to the recent revision of the attendance policy on campus. Spencer found the shift jarring but went with the conversation flow. They discussed the nuances of the revised policy, and he helped Dutch understand some parts he claimed to be confused about.

But while they talked, and throughout the rest of lunch, Spencer felt the weight of their sexual tension pressing against him. It urged him closer to Dutch, and the look in Dutch's eyes told him that Dutch was merely biding his time, as if he knew they would end up naked in bed eventually.

"Have a good afternoon, Dr. Harrison," one of his students from Intermediate Spanish told him while walking by. Spencer returned the greeting, and then continued staring at the wooden doors.

He had a decision to make. Either he was going to go through the doors, go up the stairs, and confront his friend about the startling shift in his professional and personal attitude, or he was going to walk back to his building, ignoring a friend in potential trouble but remaining true to his decision not to be alone with Dutch.

"He's a friend," he whispered. "And he's in trouble."

Spencer pushed away from the wall and made his way toward the wooden doors. He'd never walked away from a friend in need before. He didn't intend on starting now.

I hope you're prepared for the consequences, his father said as he journeyed up the steps.

CHAPTER 33

2010

IT WAS a daring journey, one Dutch wasn't comfortable with. It reminded him more of a train speeding toward a bend in the tracks, risking derailment, than a trip designed to bring about closure. Still, it was one he'd promised to undertake.

Whether he liked it or not, and he didn't, he was along for the ride.

Justin carried in his suitcase, filled with clothes that had once hung in the closet he shared with Spencer. Those clothes would now hang in the spare bedroom in Dutch's house, where they would live together until Dutch was physically rehabilitated and freed from house arrest, probation, and DWI school.

Dutch sat in his wheelchair, watching Justin silently transport his belongings from his car to the guest bedroom, down the hall from Dutch's room. It was difficult for him to see Justin once again in his house, where they had shared their bodies and their lives.

In the guest bedroom, while they'd both hung a new ceiling fan, they had discussed their families and how much they loved them. They revealed family secrets most people in their lives didn't know. Justin's Aunt Olga once had an affair with a car salesman that almost ended her marriage; his brother-in-law Chase currently resided in a Massachusetts Correctional Facility in Cedar Junction for identity fraud.

While they shaved in the bathroom, they'd told stories of their childhoods. Dutch once convinced his sister to get in the dryer to see what happened when he turned it on. He told her it would be like a carnival ride. Luckily, his mother stopped him before he permanently pressed his sister. Justin once dared his cousin Henry, his Uncle Ricky's son, to lie in front of his bike while Justin attempted to hop over him. The experiment failed, and Henry suffered a few cracked ribs, which was nothing compared to the spanking Justin received from both his Uncle Ricky and his mother.

During meal preparation in the kitchen and then at the dining room table, they had talked about past relationships. Before Spencer, Justin had the hots for his current best friend Tyler. But his feelings for Tyler were a rebound emotion. He had still been getting over the failure of his two-year relationship with Kyle. It had ended because Justin refused to come out of the closet; at that time, he wasn't ready for the world to know. Dutch told Justin about Todd, his last long-term relationship. He had been drawn to Todd's adventurous spirit, but after moving in together, he realized adventurous also meant rudderless. Todd lacked ambition and drive; he stayed home all day playing computer games while Dutch worked. Eventually, the strain killed the relationship.

His house and all its rooms had similar stories. They had discussed politics in the living room; Dutch was fiscally conservative but socially liberal. Justin was a full-fledged Democrat. In the master bedroom, they talked about religion and its effect on the nation's laws. Both wanted more separation between church and state, but their views on religion greatly differed. They were both Roman Catholic, but that was where their similarities ended. A devout Catholic, Dutch had difficulty with Justin's animosity toward the church. The church's stance against homosexuality and their leniency on pedophilia in the priesthood enraged him. Justin thought the Catholic Church to be overrun with hypocrites and dangerous extremists, including Pope Benedict. They'd debated the church in almost every room of the house.

Everywhere Dutch looked, memories of happier times haunted him. They shimmered in and out of existence like echoes of the past. To reside here together, with those memories around them, was going to be difficult.

Justin realized it as well.

He was ominously silent, the gravity of this move weighing heavily upon him. As Justin carried his belongings through the house, his gaze darted around the rooms; he was apparently haunted by the same memories. But more than the memories of his time with Dutch probably preoccupied Justin.

Dutch knew Justin was worried that moving in with him signaled the final nail in the coffin of his relationship with Spencer. He wanted to tell Spencer in person that he was moving in with Dutch, and he wanted to explain why. Justin feared Spencer would infer that he was choosing Dutch.

Justin wasn't choosing him. Even he knew that.

Making amends was Justin's only motivation. He was doing what he could to help him literally get back on his feet. Justin couldn't tell Spencer that if he couldn't contact him, and Spencer refused to take his calls or see him in person. He didn't want to leave a voice mail or a message with anyone else. Spencer deserved to hear the news in person, not secondhand.

For the past few days, Dutch had witnessed all of Justin's frantic attempts to find Spencer. He was manic and obsessed. But Justin never thought to ask the one person who knew where Spencer was.

Justin never asked him.

Justin had been fretting over whether Spencer would understand his decision to help him through his rehabilitation. He had no clue that the only reason Dutch suggested it was because it was Spencer's idea. While it was information Dutch wanted to share, remaining quiet was part of Spencer's grand plan.

"I'm sure you'll find him soon enough," he told Justin while he carted the last suitcase and hanging clothes bag through the front door.

"Thanks," Justin said, but his tone and his slumped posture revealed his misery. He placed the suitcase on the living room floor and draped the garment bag over the couch. "I'm starting to think I won't. Spencer obviously wants nothing more to do with me."

"Are you sure about that?" he asked. It was a question he already knew the answer to. He wheeled his chair closer to Justin, close enough for his gesture to offer comfort without crossing an intimacy line neither of them was willing to cross.

Justin replied quickly. "I am."

Dutch didn't believe him. Justin's answer was spoken too hastily, which wasn't like him. Justin thought carefully about serious subjects. He wasn't the kind of man to make rash decisions. With the exception of their affair, Justin proceeded through life very methodically, with his heart and his intellect as his compass.

"Spencer's done with me." Defeated, he sat on the couch, where they used to cuddle in front of the television. It was obvious that memory wasn't playing for Justin; instead, he lamented the loss of Spencer.

Dutch had thought Spencer was crazy for insisting on this living arrangement when he visited him in the hospital. Spencer claimed if their lives were ever going to be set right again, they needed closure. Whether Dutch liked it or not, the three of them were in an unhealthy, dysfunctional relationship.

He couldn't argue with the logic.

They both loved Justin, despite everything.

But even more problematic, Justin still loved *both* of them. He just didn't see it. He believed he loved *only* Spencer, that Spencer was his only motivation. Justin was lying to himself. Dutch knew it, and Spencer knew it.

Justin could have refused his request. He could have left Dutch alone and gone straight for Spencer. He didn't.

He'd agreed to move in while still searching for Spencer, meaning his heart remained at odds.

CHAPTER 34

2009

BEING ignored made Spencer angry, especially considering he had previously been at odds with himself on whether or not to come up to Dutch's office. According to the secretary, Dutch was in his office, but he refused to answer the door, no matter how many times he knocked. He even announced it was him, expecting Dutch to immediately open the door. Five minutes later, no response came.

He didn't understand why he was being ignored. As far as he was concerned, he had done nothing wrong. Dutch was the one who'd suddenly withdrawn, severing all communication.

If anyone deserved to be angry, it was him. And if he had done something wrong, he deserved to at least know what that was.

Once again, he knocked on the door. No answer. He knocked again, louder. Nothing. Finally, he pounded on the door continuously, making such a racket that other professors poked their heads out into the hall to see what was going on.

"Is there a problem, Dr. Harrison?" Dr. Carlos Aguayo inquired. Dr. Aguayo was a professor of speech and one of the biggest assholes in the department.

"No problem at all," he responded. "Just trying to get a response."

Dr. Aguayo looked around at the other professors standing in the hall. "It looks like you got one," he said. His eyes narrowed, displaying his distaste for the interruption. "Perhaps you should return when Mr. Keller is actually *in* his office."

"Oh, he's in," Spencer told him. "I'm just refusing to be ignored."

"If only you could be ignored," Dr. Aguayo said. "This is a place of work. You may have forgotten that in whatever blind desperation drives you to knock so loudly and rudely upon a colleague's door."

"Dutch is more than a colleague," he announced. Not once did he stop pounding on the door. "He's a friend. And a friend that I intend to speak with."

"Perhaps Mr. Keller doesn't want to speak to *you*. Has that thought ever once crossed your mind?"

Suddenly the door opened. Spencer stepped back as Dutch entered the hallway. Everyone stared at him with disdain. "I apologize for the ruckus," he announced. He held up the white earphones that dangled from his neck. "I had my iPod on while I was working and only just realized someone was banging on my door."

Dr. Aguayo harrumphed. "Might I advise that you lower the volume? It will save us all a lot of trouble the next time Dr. Harrison comes to visit."

Spencer wanted to tell the man off, but Dutch agreed to Dr. Aguayo's request and pulled Spencer into his office. He immediately closed the door behind them.

"What the hell?" Dutch asked. He was visibly upset. "Why are you banging on my door like some lunatic?"

"I don't appreciate being ignored," he replied.

Dutch waved the earphones in front of his face. "I was listening to my iPod, remember?" He crossed his office and walked over to his desk. "Are you trying to get me fired or something?"

"I think you're doing a good enough job of that on your own."

Dutch sat back in his chair. "Excuse me?"

"You've changed lately," he told Dutch. "A lot." Even though Dutch didn't invite him to take a seat, Spencer sat down across from him anyway. "Your professionalism on this campus has turned piss-poor, and it's been noticed."

"*My* professionalism?" Dutch asked. "I wasn't the one pounding on someone else's door and disturbing the entire office complex."

"Forget the damn door," he retorted. "You've been absent. A lot. You've received numerous student complaints. Almost weekly." He leaned forward in the chair, hoping his body language would drive his point home. "You're not the person we hired."

For a few moments, Dutch said nothing. He only glared at Spencer. A storm brewed in his eyes. "I didn't realize you were promoted to department chair," he said at last. "I must've missed that e-mail."

"This is exactly the type of attitude I'm talking about," he said, trying to keep his voice under control. The last thing he needed was to get into a shouting match that would further enflame Dr. Aguayo and prompt him to call their boss, if he hadn't already done so.

"My attitude here isn't the problem," Dutch announced. "It's yours."

Spencer was stunned. "*My* attitude?"

Dutch nodded. "You come to my office, spouting off about my employment issues. What authority do *you* have to come here and chastise *me*?"

"I'm your friend," Spencer told him. "I'm here because I'm worried about you. I don't want you to lose your job."

"And who says I'm in danger of losing my job?" Dutch asked. "And before you answer that, consider *your* reply carefully. If someone, let's say our esteemed department chair, who *everyone* knows is your best friend, has been gossiping to you about sensitive personnel information, then admitting such will get *her* fired. Not me."

He said nothing, not just because Dutch was right. Peggy shouldn't have shared such information with him. It was a perk he enjoyed as her best friend on campus and one of her closest confidants. He always knew private information before anyone else in the School of Arts, Humanities, and Social Sciences. She confided in no one else, primarily because she couldn't. Her job prohibited voicing such private information, but as a gossip lover, she needed someone to share the inside track with, someone she could trust. That person was Spencer.

Even so, protecting Peggy wasn't the only reason Spencer went mute. Dutch's comment was an overt threat against a woman he cared very deeply for, a fact Dutch was completely aware of.

The warning proved to him how much Dutch had changed.

"I don't need to be told by anyone about your lack of professionalism these days," he lied. Even though he knew Dutch didn't buy it, he continued. "I've heard the students complain about you in *my* class before I start. I've come by to see you several times in the past couple of weeks, and you haven't been in."

"Nice recovery," Dutch smirked.

Spencer ignored the comment. "You're right, though, I'm *not* your boss, and my broaching of this subject may have been bungled, but the sentiment is real." He looked deeply into Dutch's eyes, trying to tell him with more than his words how worried he was. "I'm your friend. And I'm worried."

"Why is that?" Dutch asked.

He saw a glint in Dutch's eyes that chased the anger away. For a moment, he wondered if the anger had ever truly been there in the first place.

"You mean beyond everything I've just said?"

Dutch nodded. "You're only telling me half-truths," he said. "There's more to this than *just* my continued employment here."

"Like what?"

"You tell me," Dutch said. He rose from his chair and came around the desk. He sat at the edge, looking down at Spencer.

Spencer felt like he was on the witness stand, staring into the eyes of a prosecuting attorney who was hell-bent on getting him to confess to some fictional crime. He had nothing else to offer. Dutch was his friend, and Spencer was concerned about how his attitude change on campus was affecting his employment.

"Other than the neglecting of your duties, there's nothing else."

"Nothing else I've been neglecting?" Dutch asked.

"I think that would be quite enough," he said. "Not being available to students. Being rude to them. Being unclear in assignments. Not answering their calls or e-mails. Not even answering *my* calls or e-mails."

"And *there* it is," Dutch said. A huge smile stretched across his lips.

"There *what* is?" he asked, completely confused.

In response, Dutch reached down and took Spencer by his wrists, jerking Spencer upward and into his arms. He smelled like salt and sex, a mixture Spencer found almost too tantalizing. But since he had been pulled into an embrace he hadn't asked for, he pushed back against Dutch's chest, trying to extract himself from the huge arms that encircled his body and rested comfortably against his hips.

"This is what you want," Dutch whispered into his ear. Dutch's hot breath against his skin made him tremble. His heart raced in his chest. The air in his lungs burned, filling with the salty goodness that permeated every pore of Dutch's body. "You're here because I've been neglecting *you*."

Suddenly, Dutch nibbled on his right ear and licked a trail from the ear lobe to Spencer's neck. Spencer clawed at the shirt covering Dutch's massive back, but he couldn't tell if he was trying to get away or pry the fabric from his body. That was how crazy Dutch was making him. Finally, he admitted that, more than anything else, he wanted to rip the shirt off Dutch and feel his hairy flesh scrape against his own.

Dutch's tongue traveled from Spencer's neck to his throat, which Dutch proceeded to passionately kiss. The stubble from the unshaven face scratched against Spencer's delicate flesh, scraping angry red marks upon his pale skin. The rugged, forced contact caused his hips to instinctively thrust forward. When he did, he rubbed against Dutch's enormous erection, which added more fuel to his fire.

Spencer surfed his hands down Dutch's back until they found his ass. He squeezed the muscled globes, pressing Dutch farther into him, while Dutch continued to lick and kiss his neck. Dutch moved his hands from Spencer's waist to his chest, where he began fumbling open the buttons of his shirt.

With the task accomplished, he parted the fabric with his big hands. One hand tweaked Spencer's right nipple while Dutch moved his mouth downward to the left nipple, where he proceeded to feast. Dutch bit so hard, Spencer expected to see blood trailing down his flesh.

Spencer moaned from the sensation of Dutch's hot mouth causing him such delicious pain. He encircled Dutch's neck, using his hands to force his face harder against his chest. Dutch growled in response and lifted Spencer off his feet, forcing him to wrap his legs around Dutch's waist.

From this position, Spencer could feel Dutch's hardness rubbing against his still clothed ass. He wished Dutch's cock was freed from its trousers and was working its way inside him, parting his hole until the entire length rested snugly within him.

He feverishly ground his pelvis into Dutch's erection while Dutch moved to rest Spencer upon the surface of the desk. Once he'd been placed on the smooth desktop, Dutch pulled Spencer's shirt from his body and began undoing his belt. Spencer followed his lead. He went to work immediately on Dutch's shirt, opening it to reveal the dark chest hair that covered Dutch's pecs and abdomen.

He buried his face in the abundant chest hair, licking it and the rugged flesh it covered. While he got drunk on the salty taste of Dutch's skin and the musky smell emanating from armpits not coated in deodorant, he quickly undid Dutch's belt and unzipped the trousers, which Dutch helped push to the floor, along with his blue Andrew Christian briefs.

Dutch stood before him; his hardness looked to be at least eight impressive inches, and the thick, veiny shaft, which pulsed as if it were alive, jutted from a thick brush of dark pubic hair.

They were moments away from turning their friendship into something more. The only barrier that remained to their new relationship was the pair of boxer briefs that still covered Spencer. His black trousers already rested in a heap, along with the shirt Dutch had cast aside and the dress shoes he'd kicked off just moments before.

Once again, Dutch pulled him into an embrace. His hard cock pressed against Spencer's erection, still confined behind fabric but desperately wanting to be freed. Dutch surfed his fingertips along his back, riding the curve of his body to the waistband of his underwear. There, he paused and rested.

Spencer looked into his eyes, and he saw an intense passion aflame within. Dutch wanted this as much as he did, but there was something else. Beyond the desire, he saw conflict, as if Dutch was trying to convince himself to go the last bit of distance that remained—removing his underwear and penetrating his flesh.

Then, for the briefest of seconds, Spencer saw Justin, not Dutch. He saw the man who crossed the Bonham and cut through the crowd with only one objective in mind—him. He saw the dark-brown eyes set inside their almond-shaped frame.

In that moment, the years of their relationship rippled through him like a raindrop falling onto a calm pond. Each memory triggered a surge of emotions that rushed toward the shore, where he and Dutch stood. The love tugged on his heart like a riptide, pulling him back to Justin and away from the hot, massive beast who wanted to carry him out of the water of his previous relationship and onto a shore he didn't recognize.

Dutch crossed what little distance remained between them, his lips headed straight for Spencer's. As he closed the gap, Dutch slowly pushed down the waistband of his briefs.

Since that night, almost a decade ago, he had never kissed another man without Justin being present in the room. All that was about to end. Once he kissed Dutch, once he crossed that boundary and left the warm waters of his relationship, there would be no returning to the gentle, rolling ocean of their life.

He refused to allow that to happen. He wouldn't betray Justin the way Mike Lane had betrayed him. He had no intention of sinking to those depths, now or in this lifetime.

"Stop," Spencer ordered, turning to the left, which caused Dutch to brush his cheek instead of his lips. He pushed Dutch backward, away from him.

He couldn't do this. He couldn't cheat on Justin, no matter how badly he wanted to. It would be a betrayal of the magic that had brought them together. The magic might have waned. It might not be as strong as it once was, but Spencer had faith it was still there.

"What's wrong?" Dutch asked, trying to pull Spencer into another embrace.

"I said stop," Spencer repeated with more force this time. He bent down to retrieve his clothes and began to put them back on. "I'm sorry," he said. "I can't do this."

"No one has to know," Dutch told him.

Spencer pulled his pants back on and stared into Dutch's eyes. "*I* will know," he responded. "That's all that matters."

Without another word, he put the rest of his clothes back on and watched Dutch as he did the same. When they were both dressed, he walked toward the closed office door. "I feel as if I've been awful to you," he told Dutch, unable to look at him. "I apologize for that. I should never have let it get this far. I should've been stronger." His hand rested on the cold surface of the doorknob. "I only ask that you consider not allowing this to ruin our friendship."

Dutch made no reply.

Spencer then opened the door and exited the office. After closing the door quietly behind him, he walked through the office complex and down the stairs of Treadaway Hall. His father's laughter echoed within him.

I told you there would be consequences, his father taunted. *Now, you have to live with what you've done. And tonight, when you crawl into bed with Justin and you look into those eyes that you claim to love so much, you'll start to die inside. You've just ruined everything you've worked to rebuild. And this time, you can't blame Justin or Cyber or three-ways. This time, it's all* your *fault.*

Spencer couldn't stop the tears when he realized his father was right.

CHAPTER 35

2010

SPENCER sat in his car, observing Dutch's house and wondering if he was doing the right thing. A few minutes ago, Justin had left for work and waved good-bye to Dutch, who watched him pull out of the driveway. The smiles on both of their faces made Spencer uneasy. They looked like a couple following a morning routine instead of ex-lovers he had forced to live together.

I told you there would be consequences, his father scolded. *But you don't listen to me anymore. And now you may have just shoved the man you claim to love into the arms of another.*

He didn't want to accept that. It was far too soon for Justin to have chosen Dutch, to have completely forgotten about him and the love they once shared. Forcing Justin and Dutch together while making himself disappear was supposed to compel Justin to him. He meant for the move to jumpstart the magic that had brought them together at the Bonham. Justin was supposed to be lost without him, unable to carry on until they were reunited.

Based on the smile Justin wore as he drove away, that wasn't happening. Justin appeared to be content with the arrangement, perhaps even thriving. Maybe it *was* over between them. Perhaps their relationship had come to its end, and he had yet to accept it. Their relationship might have ended for Justin long before Spencer's return. After all, how else could he explain the melancholy Justin floundered in for a good part of the past year?

Even though he'd had no knowledge of Justin's affair, he'd seen that Justin seemed lost, unable to find direction or purpose. Had that been because he secretly longed for Dutch? Had Dutch replaced Spencer in Justin's heart?

God, I hope so, his father said. *Then maybe you can find where you misplaced your balls and move the fuck on.*

Would you please just leave me alone? he asked his father's irritating voice.

I wish I could, the voice responded. *But you keep fucking up your life, which keeps dragging me up to talk to you. I hope you don't think I enjoy these little talks, because I don't. I wish to Christ that you would just be a normal man and know when to shit or get off the pot. But I apparently failed at teaching you that. I thought you finally learned how to survive when you knocked your brother on his ass, but you've turned back into that little pussy crying in front of our house because someone has hurt you.*

I'm not *a pussy,* he told his father.

If it smells like pussy and looks like pussy, then it's pussy, his father replied. *And we both know that I'm an expert on pussy.*

Could you be any more disgusting? he asked. Spencer's stomach twisted and jumped. *If you're supposed to be my subconscious, why can't you be a little more like me?*

His father's voice gave way to hysterics for several moments. *Damn, that was funny! If I were like you, you'd never learn, you'd never grow. You need someone like me to push you, to get you moving in a direction other than neutral. That's where you've been stuck for so long. You don't even realize that you've been spinning your wheels like some dumbass redneck too stupid to realize he's not making progress.*

Then how do you explain your silence for the last ten years? Spencer asked. *I've done just fine without you for a long time.*

Not from where I'm sitting, his father said, spitting out the words as if they were poison. *You may have believed you were happy, but when you realized your life wasn't the perfect little picture you always imagined it to be, you ran to London. When you came home and realized Justin was still unhappy, you dug yourself underneath tons of denial. You couldn't even hear my voice even though I was screaming at you. I was only able to get through once you were faced with just how much of a shit pile your life truly was. And now, now you're piling even more shit upon the heap.*

This is going to work, he told his father. *Justin loves me. I know it. He'll come back to me. He'll return to me as the man he once was. I have faith in that.*

But will you *be the same man he knew?* his father asked. *You fail to see the obvious, boy. You're walking a path with blinders on, and what you don't see is going to knock you on your ass. I guarantee it.*

Spencer got out of his car and slammed the door, hard. He knew what he was doing. Once the romantic fantasy Justin created around Dutch was removed, Justin would see the world as clearly as he did. The only way for that to happen was to force that fantasy into the real world, reveal it as being nothing more substantial than a dream. Once exposed to the harsh light of reality, the wrinkles and the warts would be visible, sending Justin back into his arms. This time for good, he thought as he walked up to the front door and knocked.

"Coming," Dutch announced, responding to Spencer's knock upon the door. As he waited for Dutch to wheel himself to the door, he looked around the small stucco porch.

Not much had changed since his last visit several months ago, when he'd stopped by to make sure Dutch was coming in to work after a long weekend. Of course, at that time, he had no idea Dutch had been sleeping with Justin or that their friendship had been built upon a lie.

As his eyes followed the brown stucco to the forest-green trim, he realized his relationship with Dutch was never real. For the past few weeks, he had been so consumed with Justin's betrayal that he'd completely ignored Dutch's. Their friendship had been important to him. He'd counted on it since it was the only part of his life separate from Justin and their friends, a part of his life that gave him the individual identity he had lost to couplehood.

It had all been a lie. The entire time they built a friendship, Dutch had kept the truth of his affair with Justin a secret. Yet, Dutch pursued the relationship. He invited Spencer to coffee. They ate lunch together at least twice a week. They exchanged e-mails, recipes, and news about their day's events.

They even flirted shamelessly with each other. Sometimes, the flirtations got out of hand, but once he'd brought perspective back to their situation, they were fine.

Until Dutch changed. Until he spiraled so out of control that his job was on the line. As his friend, Spencer had done whatever he could to help Dutch.

Maybe his father was right. Maybe this was a mistake.

Dutch wasn't the person Spencer thought he was. He was a lying adulterer who got his jollies by striking up a friendship with the partner of the man he had an affair with. Those weren't the actions of a kind, generous soul, the type of man he'd always believed Dutch to be.

Those were the actions of someone vile, and he had willingly allowed Justin back into this man's clutches.

"I was wondering when you'd get here," Dutch said after opening the front door. On his lap rested his blue backpack containing everything he needed for the physical therapy Spencer had agreed to take him to. "I thought we were gonna be late."

"Fuck you," Spencer shouted. He punched Dutch square in the nose. Blood poured from Dutch's nostrils, and his hands went immediately to his face. "You're a goddamned bastard," he said, wanting to take another swing and make Dutch bleed even more.

Now, that's what I'm *talking about,* his father cheered.

Spencer had never before felt so overcome by anger or hatred so intense. His body burned hotter than a star about to go supernova. As he stood there contemplating another assault and looking down at Dutch, who complained loudly about his nose, realization of what he had done slowly dawned upon him.

No matter how Dutch had betrayed and hurt him, Dutch was in a wheelchair. Not only was this not a fair fight, but Spencer had crossed a line. He was turning into a man he never intended to be, a man too much like his father.

Come on! his father said, hooting and hollering as if he were ringside at a boxing match. *Hit him again! Beat that fucker senseless and make him bleed. Infect that bastard with your blood!*

Infect? he thought while looking down at his hand. It too was bloody, and not just from Dutch. His knuckles had split open from the punch. Blood ran down his fingers and dripped to the cement porch below.

"Oh my God," he whispered. He pushed Dutch's wheelchair backward, causing him to roll a few inches to the right. Frantically, he dashed into the kitchen, opening cabinet after cabinet. He found a spare plastic bag and wrapped it around his bleeding hand. "Where do you keep the hydrogen peroxide or alcohol? I need to wash out your wound."

"Bathroom cabinet," Dutch responded, his voice muffled with blood.

Spencer remembered the bathroom was down the hall to the right of the living room. He sprinted into the bathroom, flung open the cabinet, and plucked everything he needed from within. In seconds, he was once again at Dutch's side.

He tore open some gauze and doused it with hydrogen peroxide and alcohol, which he applied to the wound. Dutch winced in pain, but made no reply or move to retaliate. He simply sat and allowed Spencer to attempt to clean up the horrible thing he had just done.

"I think I'll live," Dutch said after ten minutes of gauze applications generously doused with alcohol and hydrogen peroxide. "You can stop now."

"I can't," he said, tearing open another gauze bandage. "The wound *has* to be cleaned. It *has* to!"

Dutch reached out and took Spencer's plastic-bag covered hand in his. "I'll be fine," he told Spencer. "The chances of my being infected with HIV because of this are relatively low."

He backed away from Dutch. He couldn't believe Dutch knew about his HIV status. He couldn't believe Justin would have divulged such personal information to anyone, much less the man he had been cheating with.

"Your viral count is undetectable and has been for years," Dutch reminded him.

"He told you," Spencer muttered. "I can't believe he told you."

"We had a sexual relationship," Dutch said. "It *was* the right thing to do."

Logically, he knew it was, but the fact still enraged him, almost back to the point of wanting to resume punching. But he couldn't. The fight had drained out of him with the blood he already spilled.

Before he could stop it, he started to cry. He could hear his father yelling at him to stop crying like a sissy, to stand up and be a man. He lacked the willpower. All his defenses fell; his armor tumbled off his body, leaving him naked and vulnerable.

Spencer felt defeated. And horribly alone.

"Please, don't," pleaded Dutch. He wheeled himself closer. "I've been waiting for you to lose your cool for awhile now. I'm glad you finally did." He placed his right hand on Spencer's shoulder. "I deserved that. I deserve much worse."

"You're damned right you do," he yelled at Dutch through his tears. He knocked Dutch's hand off his shoulder and stood up. His anger once again burned hot, forcing the tears to cease. "You were my friend," he said. "You made me…."

He stopped before finishing his thought.

"I know," Dutch said. "I know." He looked away. Deep sorrow and regret filled his eyes. "I'm an awful person," he admitted. "I deserve everything that's happened to me. Your hatred. The paralysis. The DWI. The potential loss of my job. HIV."

"HIV?" he asked. "I thought…."

"It won't be because of you," Dutch said. "It's because of *me*. The way I've lived since Justin and I…." He stopped, unable to say the words. "Well, I would be surprised if I *wasn't* HIV positive."

"But you don't know for sure?" Spencer asked. Dutch shook his head in response. "Then don't be wishing for something that might not even be true. You need to get tested. I'll take you after physical therapy."

Dutch stared at him, confused. "You're still taking me to physical therapy?"

He nodded. "I'm still angry at you. For a lot of things. Things that we'll need to discuss. But right now, we need to get cleaned up and get you to your appointment."

He was halfway through the living room before Dutch's voice stopped him. "Why are you really doing this?" Dutch asked. "*All* of this. Not just the physical therapy. But Justin and me living together. *Why?*"

Spencer thought about it for a few moments before answering. "Things have to be set right," he responded. "Things Justin has done. Things you've done." He paused for a minute, recalling how close *he* had come to cheating on Justin with Dutch. "Things *I've* done."

Dutch nodded in understanding. They both had mistakes to atone for, but so far the only person who truly seemed to be performing penance was Justin. That staggering realization made Spencer recognize that perhaps he was being unfair to the man he professed to love so much.

If that was true, he not only needed to stop being unfair to Justin, he needed to find out just *why* he was acting like someone who had done no wrong.

CHAPTER 36

2009

DUTCH tried his best to act as if he wasn't drunk, but as he staggered up the stairwell to his office and nearly tripped on the third step, several students smiled nervously at him as they made their way past. Evidently, he wasn't succeeding in portraying the picture of sobriety. He fought the desire to tell them to fuck off and to stop staring at him. Fortunately, they bounded down the last few steps and out the doors before he could muster the energy.

He didn't have time to yell at them anyway. He'd already missed his first two classes, Digital Photography and Design I, and if he didn't concentrate harder on making it up the last flight of steps, he would miss his Black and White class, which started in thirty minutes.

No doubt his nosy secretary, Janice Mitchell, had already alerted the department chair, perhaps even the dean, about the two missed classes. He was already on Dr. Cutting's shit list, and this latest stunt wouldn't ingratiate him to her. Most likely, there was an e-mail or voice message on his office phone from Dr. Cutting requesting to see him the moment he arrived on campus.

He *so* wanted to tell Dr. Cutting to take a flying suck to his ass.

Besides, it wasn't his fault his alarm didn't go off. True, he forgot to set it last night when he finally stumbled into bed at 4:00 a.m., but it had been set to go off at the appropriate time. He just forgot to turn it on.

All he had to do was make up some lie about a power outage or something along those lines. Those things happened all the time, so the excuse would be believable enough. Dr. Cutting didn't need to know he was up all night drinking and fucking. That was none of her damned business, even though she seemed to think every move he made on campus these days fell under her scrutiny.

Dutch finally made it to the second-floor landing and walked through the glass doors and into the office complex, where Janice eyed him warily from behind her desk. Her phone was glued to her ear, and if he had to guess, Dr. Cutting was likely on the other end.

By the time he reached her desk, she'd hung up the phone.

"Hey, Janice," he said, pretending to be cordial, even though he hated her. While Janice was a competent enough secretary, she was far too conservative for his taste. She also had her nose shoved so far up Dr. Cutting's ass it was amazing she could breathe without smelling what Dr. Cutting had for breakfast.

"Good morning," she muttered politely. "You do realize you missed your first two classes?" she asked while staring at the office clock mounted on the wall to the left of her desk.

"I do," he said through gritted teeth. "Power outage in the neighborhood," he told her. "I just woke up a few minutes ago."

"I see," she responded. Her tone indicated she didn't believe a word of his story. "Dr. Cutting requests that you stop by her office after your last class."

"I'll see if I can make it," he told her as he walked past her desk.

"I'll let her know," Janice replied, once again picking up her phone.

"I'm sure you will," he said. Before she could respond, he turned the corner and proceeded down the small hallway toward his office.

He fumbled his keys out of his khaki pants and tried three times to unlock his office. The knob kept moving to the left and right, so he constantly missed his mark. "Damn key," he muttered to himself.

"Don't blame the key for operator error," a voice behind him said.

Dutch turned to see Spencer standing behind him with a smug look on his face. He let out a long exhale to let Spencer know he had neither the time nor the energy to deal with him. "Don't have time to socialize," he told Spencer while turning once again to face his door. "I've got class in thirty minutes." He tried once again, unsuccessfully, to get the key into the keyhole.

"It's more like twenty minutes, now," Spencer announced.

"Do you also have the week's forecast?" he asked after finally opening the door.

"Not for the week," Spencer said. He then pushed Dutch inside the office and slammed the door behind them. "But the forecast for the next hour is mostly cloudy with a 100 percent chance of an ass-chewing."

Dutch leered at Spencer. "Kinky," he said. "But I don't have time right now. Come back later this afternoon if you still want to eat out my ass."

"What the *hell* is wrong with you?" Spencer yelled. "Are you trying to get fired?"

"Why are you so interested in my employment status? I thought we covered that the last time we were here in my office together." He walked up to Spencer and stared right into his jade-green eyes. The green hue darkened, indicating Spencer was extremely upset. "Or have you forgotten?"

Spencer pushed him backward. Dutch stumbled into his desk and almost fell over. "Oh, I remember," Spencer told him. "I remember we screwed up that day and since then you've completely ignored me. I tried to apologize. I tried to make things better, but you never once reciprocated any of my offers."

Dutch stood up straight and walked around his desk. "Maybe you should've gotten the hint," he told Spencer. "I'm done playing your little cat-and-mouse games."

"My *what*?"

"Stop the innocent routine," Dutch fumed. "I've had enough of it. You pretend as if you're sweet and kind, the perfect employee, the perfect friend, the perfect partner. But you're not *so* perfect. You're just as flawed and damaged as the rest of us. Everyone just doesn't see it because you put on a good show. But I've gotten to know the real Spencer Harrison. The one your students don't see. The one Dr. Cutting or your admirers in upper administration can't see. The one your loving partner, who adores you more than *anyone* else doesn't even know exists."

"I have no idea what the fuck you're talking about," Spencer answered. He was still angry, but his voice turned calm, his way of trying to defuse the situation. "I never said I was perfect, and I have no *idea* where all that came from. All I ever wanted was to be your friend."

He couldn't help but snicker at Spencer's naïveté. "Friends?" he asked incredulously. "You've wanted to be more than that since the interview. You know it. I know it."

Spencer's face drooped in surprise. He looked like a child caught in his own web of lies.

"You've had the hots for me from the very beginning," Dutch declared, finally giving voice to a truth he knew Spencer had yet to fully acknowledge. "Don't think I didn't notice at the interview. You could barely keep your mouth closed or the spit from dripping onto your chin. Then after I was hired, you invited me to lunch. And flirted. When I got to campus, you sent e-mail after e-mail. You called and left messages inviting me to lunch or coffee. Didn't you realize how desperate that made you look?"

Spencer tried to speak, but Dutch held his hand up for him to stop. He wasn't finished, and he wasn't about to be interrupted. "So I finally gave in. Took you up on lunch. And I flirted with you to test the waters, to see if it was just friendship you wanted. When you flirted right back, it told me all I needed to know. But when I touched you, you hesitated. Probably thinking about poor little Justin and how you just *couldn't* wrong him. So I pulled back. But you wouldn't let up. You kept pursuing me and pursuing me. I tried to get away. I tried to put some distance between us, but you wouldn't let up. So I thought, fine, let's get this over with. And when I finally made my move, finally got you naked and ready to go, you backpedaled again and ran away." He sat down behind his desk and folded his hands on top. "And then you started all over again. Phone calls. E-mails. And now here you are in my office. Again." He leaned forward in his chair. "What are you looking for *this* time?"

"I was here trying to look out for my friend," Spencer told him. "I thought that's what we had become over all those lunches we shared. *Before* we almost had sex. I screwed up that day. I own up to that. But our friendship was never about trying to get into your pants. We got to know each other over those few weeks. I thought we developed a bond. I guess I was wrong."

"You were dead wrong," Dutch replied. He looked into Spencer's eyes. The anger inside dimmed, replaced with a deep loss and an even deeper sadness. He had no desire to hurt Spencer. He did, in fact, think of him as a friend. And as his friend, he wanted nothing more than for Spencer to get as far away from him as possible.

He was damaged goods. No, worse than that. He was poison.

If Spencer got much closer, he would infect him with the bile that ran deep in his heart and in his soul. Spencer didn't deserve that. He might have initially set out to ruin Spencer, to get him into bed and destroy his relationship with Justin. But he'd abandoned that plan once he got to know Spencer. Once he realized how much of a good guy he was.

Seeking revenge had brought him to Spencer. Now the only way to spare Spencer was to send him running in the other direction.

"We never had a friendship," he continued. "We had lunches that masqueraded as cruising sessions, each one of us trying to see how far we could push before the other gave in. If you thought that was friendship, then you have a seriously warped view of what that word really means."

"Why are you being so hateful?" Spencer asked. His eyes looked wet. "I hear your words, but I know you don't mean them. I can see it in your eyes." He crossed the room and leaned over the desk at Dutch. "You claim we aren't friends, but as you say these awful things to me, your eyes betray you. Like they always do."

Dutch hated that Spencer had come to know him so well. In the weeks they spent together, Spencer had been able to interpret his eyes and his body language as if he was someone who had known him for years. Only two people had ever been able to read him so well: Justin and his father.

He had no other choice. If he was determined to save Spencer, things were going to have to get uglier.

"Don't pretend as if you know me so well," Dutch said. "You don't. What you think you know are only things I allow you to see." He stood up quickly, toppling his desk chair over. He turned to face out the small office window, so Spencer couldn't read his eyes. "What you see in my eyes is regret for letting this *charade* go as far as it did." He knew his voice would be convincing because he spoke the truth. He regretted venturing down this path at all with Spencer. He never regretted the friendship. "And you also see the pity I feel for how desperately clingy you are. It's amazing Justin has been able to stand you all these years."

"I still don't buy it," Spencer said. "I'm not an idiot. There's something else going on here." Spencer stood behind him and gently rested his hand on Dutch's shoulder. "Be honest with me," he pleaded. "I know you're in trouble. Otherwise, you wouldn't be missing work or coming *into* work still drunk."

Dutch spun around. "I'm *not* drunk!"

"I can smell the alcohol on your breath," Spencer stated. "Your body reeks of it."

"Maybe what you smell is the sweat from a night of hardcore fucking."

"I've no doubt that's there too," Spencer replied, unaffected by his coarse admission. "But the alcohol overpowers everything else."

"So what?" Dutch asked. "Who the fuck cares?"

"I care," Spencer replied. He turned Dutch around, so he could look into his eyes. "And Dr. Cutting will care. Showing up to work drunk is an offense worthy of termination."

"So let her fire me," Dutch replied. He felt his eyes turn cold. He'd had enough of this conversation. He didn't want to hurt Spencer's feelings more than was necessary, but Spencer had crossed the line by calling him a drunk.

"I know you don't want that," Spencer told him. "You've told me countless times how much you need this job to fund your own art. When you were hired, your exuberance, not your experience, got you this job. Those things don't just go away."

"Oh my *fucking* God!" Dutch yelled. "I'm so sick of you right now, it's not even funny. Let me worry about *my* job. About *my* expenses. About *my fucking life*!" He walked behind Spencer and toward his office door. "You're not my *fucking* partner. You're not even really my friend. Why don't you go home to your man and worry about him and mind your own *fucking business*?"

Dutch opened the door to his office.

"Is that really what you want?" Spencer asked.

"Are you kidding me?" he asked. "What more do I have to do or say to get you to leave me alone?"

"Nothing more," Spencer replied and walked out the door, which Dutch slammed behind him.

Behind the closed door, Dutch collapsed to the floor of his office. Guilt overpowered him. He felt sick and nauseous. His life had spiraled even further out of control, and he felt even more powerless than before.

CHAPTER 37

2010

"YOU know I'm right," Justin told Dutch as they lay on the floor together. Justin had Dutch's right leg on his chest and was pressing onto him with his full body weight to stretch out the quadriceps. This was a nightly routine they had to follow to help Dutch get strong enough to walk on his own once again.

"Bullshit," he replied, staring up into Justin's mischievous eyes. "You're only saying Hal Jordan is a hotter Green Lantern than Kyle Rayner because you know it isn't true."

"Do *not*," Justin teased as they switched to stretching out the left quad muscle.

Dutch refused to reply and simply rolled his eyes. Justin chuckled and applied his full weight onto Dutch's leg once again.

Justin cited all the reasons why Hal Jordan was hotter, but Dutch no longer listened. His mind drifted to the sensation of Justin's body against his. Even through Justin's gym shorts, he could feel the weight of Justin's cock against his leg. He started to become aroused.

He couldn't allow that to happen. Instead, he shifted his thoughts to the progress he'd made with physical therapy over the past six weeks. Although sensation in his legs had returned, his nerve endings weren't registering 100 percent of what they should be. His muscles were stronger but couldn't support his full weight. He could walk on crutches for a few steps but beyond that his legs were useless.

He tried not to be disheartened by his lack of full mobility, but some days it was difficult *not* to be depressed. He fancied himself a strong man, completely independent and capable of doing anything on his own. These days, though, he relied on other people for *everything*, from transportation to physical therapy to getting into his own damned bed.

He was simply beyond frustrated with being an invalid, of being stuck in a wheelchair and at the mercy of others. That wasn't the man he was. It certainly wasn't the man his father *ever* was.

"Don't get lazy on me now," Justin told him. "Turn your ass over!"

"I'm not that easy," he said, while twisting his top half, grateful that Justin's order prevented him from feeling even sorrier for himself, something he had been doing too much of lately.

Justin helped him lie on his stomach by turning over his bottom half. It was time for Justin to massage his feet and calves.

"You're even easier than *that*." Justin laughed and began massaging.

He laughed too. Not just now, but when his moods turned dark, as they had recently, Justin did what he could to lift his spirits. They played games or watched movies whenever Justin noticed his gloomy disposition. Sometimes, they read comic books or just chatted.

Dutch cherished those times *and* Justin's efforts. It reminded him of when they first met on Cyber, and the friendship they'd developed online. Their conversations and interactions were easy and unforced. They truly connected on almost every level, even though sex was no longer a part of their relationship.

In fact, without the sex clouding their relationship, he found that his friendship with Justin grew stronger than before.

That was why it was so hard for him to watch the sadness that sometimes descended on Justin like a fog bank rolling onto the coastline. It enveloped him body and soul, and Dutch knew the reason: Justin missed Spencer.

Although Spencer was recently working on his unfair treatment of Justin, he still refused to talk to or see him. Spencer felt doing so prematurely might cloud his judgment. In the meantime, Justin still remained clueless that they were living together at Spencer's request or that Spencer took Dutch to each of his physical therapy appointments while Justin was at work.

He told Justin that a friend was taking him because he wanted to give Justin a break during the day from having to cater to him. Justin accepted the reasoning, not knowing that the friend who was taking him was Spencer.

And the weird part of that was Spencer *had* become his friend. Again.

They had started working through their issues after Spencer decked him on his first day of physical therapy. Although it was difficult to admit, he'd revealed his initial motives for pursuing a friendship with Spencer and why, after they had become friends and after they almost had sex in his office, he had to turn his back on Spencer.

He did it for both of them. Reluctantly, Spencer agreed it was the right decision.

Since then, Spencer became an indispensable source of support during grueling physical therapy sessions. He acted as cheerleader for the successes and a counselor for the setbacks.

Spencer helped him see the good in his life, despite the mess he had made. Even though he was no longer under house arrest, he still was on probation and had been fired from his position at St. Mary's. Spencer reminded him there were other colleges in San Antonio that would hire him, and he still had the unconditional support of his art patron, Sharon.

As a recovering alcoholic herself, Sharon championed Dutch in the art community. She sold his work at art shows, and her support, along with encouragement from both Justin and Spencer, allowed him to once again focus on *making* art instead of teaching it.

Even paralyzed, he had a lot of good things happening in his life.

What he was having increasing difficulty with was the lies.

Dutch no longer believed Spencer was right. Keeping their many secrets and living with Justin wasn't providing the closure Spencer anticipated.

Instead, it seemed to further muddy an already murky situation.

His relationships with both Justin and Spencer had improved. He was definitely on the mend. What remained broken was the relationship between Justin and Spencer. The piece that needed the most attention was being ignored.

Justin was ready, but Spencer wasn't. Dutch wondered if Spencer would ever be ready. All he knew was that it was past time for Justin to learn the truth about their living arrangement and about his past and present with Spencer.

If Spencer was unwilling to do it, then it was up to him. His father had told him to never go back on a promise, but he had learned that there were some promises that *must* be broken.

"Okay, massage done," Justin told him. "Let's turn you over and get you back in your chair."

Dutch lifted himself off the carpet by doing a push-up, and he felt Justin's hands on his waist and legs, ready to help him turn over. Justin and he pushed at the same time, and he rolled over onto his back.

"Let me get the chair."

"Not yet," Dutch said.

Justin sat on his knees to Dutch's left. "You okay? Does something hurt?"

"No, I'm good. I just want to talk. Can you help prop me up on the side of the couch?"

Justin nodded. Within a few minutes, Dutch's back was resting comfortably against the couch. Justin sat cross-legged in front of him, his elbows resting on his knees and his chin upon his hands. He looked like a child about to be spoken to by his parent.

"So, what's up?" Justin asked.

"I want to talk about Spencer," he said.

Justin averted his eyes. For some reason, he looked guilty, as if Dutch had discovered top-secret information. His hands also moved to the carpet, where he began playing with the fabric threads. Whenever Justin was nervous, his hands found the nearest object and manipulated it until the nervousness passed.

"How'd you find out?" Justin asked him.

Dutch was extremely confused. He was the one who was supposed to deliver surprise information, not Justin. "Find out what?"

Justin's eyebrows arched in surprise, and he released the carpet fabric from his anxious fingers. "You mean you don't know?"

"Apparently not," he said. "Tell me what I don't know."

Justin's fingers returned to the fabric. He poked and prodded at it until a strand stood up big enough for him to twine around his finger. "I didn't want to upset you."

"Not telling me is upsetting me more," Dutch announced.

"I'm having lunch with Spencer tomorrow," Justin finally said.

Dutch was shocked. Apparently, Spencer *was* ready, and that realization made him happier than it should. He'd known the day would come, but he'd figured when it did, it would depress him, threaten his newly created resolve and sobriety. He felt none of those emotions. "I'm glad," he told Justin. And he truly meant it.

Justin released the carpet fabric and leaned forward. "Really? You're not just saying that?"

Dutch shook his head. "Not at all. I know you've been dying to talk to him since the last time you saw each other at your mother's house."

"I have," Justin admitted. "I called him this morning, and he actually answered." The joy in Justin's voice was unmistakable. He was almost giddy. "We didn't talk for long, but he agreed to meet me for lunch tomorrow. I suggested Henry's Puffy Tacos, since I know that's his favorite place to eat, but he said no."

Dutch nodded. He understood why Spencer had declined to meet at Henry's. That was where they'd lunched together. "Where are you two meeting?"

"Pico De Gallo," Justin answered. Dutch knew the restaurant. The food was good, but since it was close to downtown, it had recently become quite the tourist trap. "It's halfway between both our campuses."

Dutch's continued delight in Justin's news lifted a major weight from his shoulders, the guilt he carried for coming between them. In Justin and Spencer's potentially revitalized romance, he felt renewed himself, as if the man he had become for those few, dark months had finally been shed.

For too long, he'd concerned himself with only his pain, never once seeing the truth of the situation. Justin had been the villain, the scoundrel who stole Dutch's heart and self-esteem, causing him to drown his pain in alcohol and anonymous sexual encounters.

Now, it was all too clear. This situation didn't have villains. It wasn't black and white like he once thought. Justin wasn't the vile, unrepentant criminal any more than he was the completely guiltless victim who was set upon by someone too crafty to be denied.

Justin couldn't be faulted for decisions Dutch had made. He'd entered into their relationship knowing his heart had a good chance of being ripped to shreds. He'd had many opportunities to opt out of the potential heartache. He never took that option.

Besides, Justin's love for him wasn't a lie. He knew that now. Especially now. Not only had Justin moved in with him, but he'd never once acted resentful of being asked to help Dutch recuperate. Only someone with true love in his heart did that.

Still, he realized, perhaps for the first time, Justin's love for him *wasn't* the only pan on the fire. Justin truly loved him as much as he loved Spencer. He just hadn't known what to do with those feelings. Dutch truly understood that now.

His refusal to do so had been his undoing. His descent began there, clinging to a small pinprick of hope that Justin would choose *only* him, when that was a choice completely beyond Justin's abilities. That baseless hope was responsible for the damage he'd ultimately inflicted onto his body and professional career.

Dutch was responsible for the shithole his life had become, and he was the one who had begun to turn it around. But he hadn't done it alone.

Justin and Spencer were both there for him, and he loved them *both* for that.

Perhaps in that love the three of them somehow shared, there was a potential for something greater than even *they* realized. Maybe they weren't seeing the forest for the trees, as his father often said. They were too busy trying to find answers to questions asked of traditional relationships, when their relationship was anything *but* traditional.

Dutch felt as if he was onto something, a track of thinking that could truly bring all the pain and misery to an end, but he couldn't go there. Yet. Problems still existed between Justin and Spencer. They needed to be fixed first, and he would do whatever it took to help that along.

"Why so quiet?" Justin asked. "Are you angry?"

"Nope," he answered. In fact, he couldn't have felt better. There was something great for them out there. He *felt* it. The three of them just had to find it. Together. "I'm just really excited for you. I want the lunch to go well. For both your sakes."

Justin exhaled. "I can't believe how well you're taking this. I thought you might be…."

"Jealous?" he asked, completing Justin's thought.

Justin laughed. "Well, yeah."

"Well, I'm not," he replied, and he wasn't lying. In order for them to find true happiness, Justin and Spencer had to find their way back to each other again. Once that happened, *anything* was possible.

"Thanks, Dutch," Justin said. "I can't tell you how much that means to me."

"It means a lot to me too," he admitted. "Happiness is all I've ever wanted for you. And for me."

He smiled at Justin, and it felt good. For too long, his smile had hid his true emotions—pain, anger, and resentment. This smile possessed none of those old emotions. The darkness was simply gone. He wasn't sure when the murky shadows of discontent had dissipated, and he didn't care. He liked how being happy made him feel.

He never wanted to be the awful man he'd turned into before his accident. *That* man was vile and self-destructive. *That* man had nothing to live for. The man he was now didn't live in darkness. He now embraced the light and promised never to stand in the darkness again.

CHAPTER 38

2009

DUTCH stood in line behind a seventy-year-old polar bear, who kept turning around and winking at him. Being hit on by an old geezer wasn't helping his mood.

It was Thanksgiving, and he was alone. A plane ticket home was too expensive for him, and he couldn't ask his sister to fork over the money for it. As the sole breadwinner in her family while her husband completed his prison sentence, she lacked the funds as well.

He had to face the family holiday alone.

At first, it didn't bother him. But as the holiday grew closer and thoughts of Justin and Spencer spending the holiday together in marital bliss filled his mind, the darkness within him grew to immense proportions.

Had Justin been true to the love he professed to have for Dutch a few months ago, they would be spending the holiday together. Dutch would be preparing a turkey in the house they shared together, stealing kisses while chopping vegetables and drinking wine. In the background, music would play on the computer, maybe some soothing guitar instrumental.

Instead, he stood behind an old man at The Club, one of San Antonio's gay bath houses, waiting his turn to pay the entrance fee in order to get to fuck the holiday away. It was pathetic, and he knew it. But there was nowhere else for him to go, nothing else for him to do.

Drinking half a bottle of vodka had done nothing to dull his pain or quiet the angry voices that told him to drive over to Justin and Spencer's house and reveal all. To both of them. When he grabbed his keys and left his driveway, that was where he'd intended to go.

He ended up here instead.

"Welcome to The Club, gorgeous," the fat, effeminate man behind the glassed-in counter told him. The man held his hand up and waved. When he did so, his short-sleeve button-down shirt lifted and revealed the enormous white belly the fabric struggled to contain. Dutch wanted to vomit. "You want a locker or a room?"

"Locker," Dutch replied while shoving his money and driver's license underneath the glass partition. He hoped his gruff attitude would be interpreted as he meant it. He had no intention to engage in idle chatter.

The fat man's right hand, which had gaudy rings on each finger, picked up the driver's license and looked at his picture. "Aren't you a big one, Lukas?" he asked, while biting on his plump left pinky finger. The move was meant to be seductive. It was more horrifying than anything else. "You're going to be quite popular in there."

Dutch made no reply. Instead, he looked past the fat man into the hallway beyond. Numerous men, dressed only in white towels cinched at the waist, walked to and fro, searching for someone to fuck or someone to fuck them.

A buzzer sounded as the door to his left opened. Fatty McFatass must have finally gotten the point and simply proceeded in processing the transaction. Dutch walked through the open door and turned left, where Fatty waited at a small, barred window. He pushed a white towel and a key attached to an armband underneath the five-inch space between the bars and the wooden counter. "You're in locker thirty-two," the man said and then turned to greet the next guest.

Dutch took the towel and the key. He eyed a box to his left, generously filled with an assortment of condoms, and walked past it in search of his locker.

Locker thirty-two was a few rows from the front door. He opened his locker and quickly disrobed. Naked, he felt free, less encumbered by the gloom, which previously swirled within and about him. Now his body felt alive and fully charged, causing his cock to grow semi-hard in anticipation of the evening's festivities.

By the time he closed the locker and draped the towel around his naked body, he turned to find the hallway filled with men leering at him. Their desperate eyes told him they each wanted to be his first for the night and would let him do *whatever* he wanted to them.

He strutted toward the gathered crowd, avoiding eye contact with all of them and trying not think about how the sticky floor pulled on the soles of his feet as he walked. He imagined he was walking over spilled Coke, but his mind knew better. It begged for him to leave this place, to go home and sleep off the buzz, which still distorted his vision.

He had no intention of leaving until he filled at least half a dozen holes with his spunk. Once that was accomplished, then he would contemplate departing. But until then, he was a man on a mission.

As Dutch made his way through the gathered admirers, who had watched him undress, a few pinched his ass or made a grab for his cock, trying to entice him into a fuck right there in the hall, but none of them made the cut. His blank stare told them to back off, and they did.

Beyond the crowd and down the shadowed hallway, Dutch entered a dark room filled with bunk beds. Several of the beds were occupied. Men moaned while others loudly slurped a cock down their eager throats. All were hidden in the shadows. Only their darkened outlines were visible against the light from the television room next door, which played porn nonstop.

Dutch walked through the television room, where the polar bear who stood in front of him in line busily feasted on the cock of an obese man who resembled Jabba the Hutt. Jabba sat back and watched the porno while his cock was being serviced. Dutch exited the porno room through the far right door just as Jabba exploded inside the thirsty old man's mouth.

The porno room led to a maze. This room was better lit than the bunk room but not as bright as the television room. In here, he could actually see the faces of the men who passed him.

Some of the men in here had potential. There was a Latino in a jockstrap, which accentuated his perfect ass and attempted to restrain a raging boner. Jockstrap even licked his lips as Dutch walked by. There was also a thin white boy who massaged his crotch for Dutch before turning a corner. Both of them appealed to him a great deal, and he contemplated following one, or both of them, but he wasn't ready to settle on one yet. He had to do a lap around the building, see what this place had to offer before he picked the one who would ultimately receive his first load of the night.

So far, the maze looked to be the best of the rooms he had seen. Glory holes were everywhere, and there were many benches and corners where good fucks could be had. If he didn't find a better room than this, he would return to the maze and make his choice.

Once out of the maze, he headed down another hallway, which was lined with rooms. Many of the doors were closed. Behind them, he could hear men begging to be fucked harder or grunting as they fucked themselves to orgasm. Bodies thumped against walls almost in tune to the music, which was pumped through the speakers mounted in the corners.

He found it amusing that Britney Spears sang about three-ways as he progressed down the hallway. No doubt some of the closed doors held more than just two men pounding away at each other.

Before he exited the hallway, he passed a section of rooms where the doors stood open. Some of the men stroked their dicks while staring at passersby, waving their cocks in invitation to a private party. Others lay on their stomachs, waiting for the next customer to come in, close the door, and make a deposit in their ass.

He turned left and proceeded down another dimly lit passageway with even more rooms lining the hall. At the end of the corridor was a dark room, where many men entered and exited. Curious, he crossed the pitch-black threshold of the room, where not a centimeter of space was illuminated.

The room smelled like Clorox and ass. Obviously, the attendants doused the room with copious amounts of Clorox in vain attempts at sanitizing the area and eliminating the odors of excessive butt-fucking.

Undeterred by the stench, Dutch walked farther into the room. His feet sloshed through body fluids spilled upon the floor. Normally, he would find the sensation disgusting. For some reason, the squish of spooge between his toes made him hard.

It felt taboo, vile. His soul and flesh were soiled by simply standing in this room, where men fucked other men they couldn't see.

The darkness within the room called to him, beckoning him farther inside. It encircled him, and in its embrace, he felt a kinship, as if they were long-lost brothers separated at birth and kept apart by a cruel and sadistic world.

With arms open wide, he inhaled the darkness, filling his lungs full with the polluted air. The foulness coursed through his body, setting free the inhibitions that wrestled within the constraints of his conscious mind.

Now freed, they sought release.

He reached out into the darkness and found a hand. He grasped onto it, pulling it to him. A body, small yet sturdy, rested against him. Dutch released his towel, which fell into the darkness below, and he quickly removed the towel of the body next to him.

Within minutes, his tongue was exploring the mouth of the man in the dark. The kisses were bitter and dry, as if the stranger had been feasting on cock for hours. Turned on by the filthiness of the stranger, Dutch ran his hands over the man's flesh, delighting in the feel of sinew.

Further still his hand descended, until it found a rigid cock. He grasped it tightly, jerking it rudely up and down.

The man in his arms whimpered, thrusting his tongue farther inside Dutch's mouth. His hands kneaded Dutch's back muscles, traveling southward to clench his ass. The man's hand moved to his front and found his dick. He turned around in Dutch's arms, resting his bare ass against Dutch's cock. He bucked backward, and in one steady motion, Dutch's cock filled the man's already well-lubricated hole.

He pummeled the man's ass, eliciting screams of pain mixed with pleasure that echoed off the walls. As he slid in and out, Dutch closed his eyes, concentrating on the pleasure extending from the tip to the base of his cock.

As he fucked away, he opened his eyes to find that the darkness had parted. The man he fucked became Justin. Justin looked over his shoulder, begging him to fuck harder. He did. As he worked on the ass like a piston, Justin told him he loved him, how much he missed him. How he was a fool for ever leaving him.

"Damn straight," Dutch muttered, driving his tool deeper within Justin's folds, carving out a place inside that belonged *only* to him. Justin screamed for more, telling him to make it hurt, to make it last forever.

Justin reached toward the floor, giving Dutch better access to his ass. He needed no further invitation and slammed away even harder. His cock turned to steel as his hairy balls slammed against Justin's smooth ass. Justin's hole clenched down upon his erection like a vise. He was in danger of cumming much too soon.

He wanted to grant Justin's request. He wanted their union to last forever, so he slowed down his thrusts, barely inching in and out of Justin, who yelled for more and whose appetite was more insatiable than ever.

"Fill me up," Justin pleaded over and over again. "Fill my ass with your baby batter."

Justin slammed his ass backward, fucking himself on Dutch's cock. Dutch released his grip on Justin's waist and let Justin continue to rear backward. As he righted himself, a new pair of hands caressed his chest, pinching his nipples and sliding through his thick coat of hair.

A hard cock rested against his ass. It slipped between Dutch's cheeks, inching ever closer to his hole.

Dutch turned sideways and saw Spencer. He grabbed Spencer by the neck and pulled him into a passionate kiss. While they kissed, Spencer's cock rubbed against his manhole, threatening to push the folds aside and enter him while Justin continued to ram his ass onto Dutch's cock.

He spat on his hand and reached for Spencer's thick cock. Grabbing it by the base, he coated Spencer's rod with his spit and then rubbed the remainder onto his asshole. He guided Spencer to his hungry center and held him there. He took a deep breath, loosening his ass muscles, and allowed Spencer through the portal.

Spencer felt so good inside him that he imagined he was flying instead of fucking. Being with Justin had always made him feel loved and special, but now having Spencer plugged into him while he was inside Justin made him feel complete.

Justin whimpered in front of him as Dutch resumed his previous speed. Spencer moaned behind him as he drove his cock in and out of Dutch. Caught in-between, Dutch grunted. His body more alive now than it had been in too many months. Never before had he been happier than he was at this moment.

Sweat dripped off his body in rivulets. It fell onto Justin's back while Spencer drenched Dutch from behind with his own. The three of them were working themselves into a fuck frenzy that was nearing release. Spencer's cock grew rock hard inside him. His cock throbbed angrily inside Justin, and Justin's hole spasmed uncontrollably around his dick.

With one final thrust, their bodies exploded. As he shot his load up Justin's chute, Dutch felt Spencer's cock pulsate within him, filling him with seed. Justin shouted as he pumped out his own jizz onto the floor.

"Man, that was hot," panted the voice behind him.

Dutch looked around but could see nothing. Sometime during his mind-blowing orgasm, the darkness had returned. Spencer and Justin were no longer there, replaced by shadows moving about the inky void.

"You fuck good," said an exhausted voice from the darkness in front of him.

Dutch didn't reply. He simply stood there in shock while his hands inspected his body. His cock felt raw and slick. His asshole was wet and sloppy.

He couldn't believe he just bottomed in a dark room for a stranger, someone who he would never be able to pick out of a lineup. He had topped many asses, bareback, in the past few months, most of whom he didn't remember either.

This was different, though. Unsafe sex as a top was risky enough. Fucking bareback as the bottom and having someone's spunk in your ass made it even deadlier.

Is this what I've been reduced to? he wondered. *Fucking raw in a bathhouse in a dark room? Is this what I've become?*

The answer was a resounding yes. His life was now worse that shit. It had become so bad that he longed for the days when it was simply *just* shit. Not only was he still in love with Justin, but now there was Spencer.

The man he'd sought revenge against. The man who'd become his friend. The man who stirred something frighteningly familiar within him.

I can't do this, he thought. *Not again. I'm not making things better. I'm making them worse. I don't deserve anyone, and I don't deserve to live.*

Dutch reached out again into the darkness, searching for a new hand. He stumbled around until he found one that was attached to another hard cock. He pulled the arm to him and placed the hard cock against his already moist ass. As the new cock slid inside him, Dutch hoped he had found what he was looking for, the cock that would ultimately be the death of him and put an end to his miserable life.

CHAPTER 39

2010

SPENCER felt exposed and powerless, which only added to his misery. The task before him was daunting enough; he didn't need to add helplessness to the emotions that spun inside him like a tornado. Regardless of his desires, vulnerability swept across him as he sat in the restaurant booth, waiting for Justin to join him for lunch.

In a few minutes, he would once again look into the face he fell so madly in love with. The face that belonged to the man who betrayed him by sleeping with Dutch and falling in love with him. A face he hadn't seen for two months. A face that had the power to bypass his defenses, despite the pain already inflicted.

He'd spent the past few weeks working through his anger, and still the thought of Justin and Dutch together caused his blood to rapidly boil. To think that he could have been so trusting to not once entertain the idea that Justin fooled around while he was in England made him feel stupid. Spencer assumed since he had been faithful, Justin had been too.

Still, he didn't know what right he had to continue to be angry. He had been faithful in the strictest definition of the word. But in its loose interpretation, he landed just shy of true fidelity.

The anger he believed to be righteous turned out to be far from it. Over the course of the past few weeks, he'd come to the realization that his anger wasn't entirely based on Justin's betrayal. That was certainly a good part of it. What also disturbed him was that he felt betrayed by Justin *and* Dutch.

For reasons he couldn't yet comprehend, he felt Dutch belonged to him. Dutch was *his* secret friend, *his* personal connection. The two of them had created a special bond, and Justin infringed upon that. Even worse, Dutch let it happen.

Justin shared a part of Dutch that Spencer hadn't experienced. Not because he didn't want to but because he was trying to remain faithful to his relationship with Justin. To learn that his sacrifice hadn't been equally met made him bitter with resentment.

Yet he realized Dutch was right; it was time to let that go. He could no longer hold Justin solely responsible for the problems in their relationship or for mistakes that were not only his. Justin could no longer be expected to shoulder the brunt of the burden. It was time to clean up the mess he'd contributed to.

That was why he agreed to meet Justin for lunch today.

"I thought I would be the first to arrive," Justin said sliding in the booth opposite of him. "Sorry if you've been waiting long."

The suddenness of Justin's appearance threw him. One minute he was staring at the wooden back of the booth opposite him and the next Justin's face had magically appeared. Typically, he became angry at any intrusion upon his thoughts, but staring into Justin's eyes, he found himself lost on the sandy beach of Justin's brown eyes.

"I haven't been here long," he replied, averting his eyes from Justin's. Even though he wanted to hammer out some of their problems, he had no intention of looking like a lovesick schoolgirl.

"You look great," Justin told him. "It's been too long. Far too long."

Spencer wanted to agree, but his mouth refused to give voice to his heart. He felt vulnerable enough without admitting that he too had longed to see Justin. "Thank you," was what he replied. "You seem no worse for the wear yourself."

"It's all smoke and mirrors."

"Well, it seems to be working for you."

"I don't know about that, but I'm glad you think so."

For a few moments, they sat in silence and drank each other in. Their gazes crawled over each other's bodies. They skimmed the curves of the jaw line and surfed the downward plunge of the throat to the chest. Gliding along the swell of rounded pectorals straining against fabric, they slid down the chest wall, which descended past the wooden table at which they sat.

The connection that once so tightly bound them to each other reformed. It was a pale version of the previous tether, but he was pleased to see it still existed between them.

"Have you ordered?" Justin asked, picking up the menu. His face flushed red. "The migas here are great!"

"I've never eaten here," Spencer told him, as a warmth also spread across his cheeks. "But I know how much you love your migas."

"You can't go wrong with fried corn tortillas, scrambled eggs, and cheese," Justin said while setting the menu back down. His cheeks had returned to their normal tanned hue.

"Migas it is, then," Spencer replied as the waitress came to take their order. When she left, an uncomfortable quiet descended upon them. Suddenly, the weight of too many unspoken words pressed upon their chests, making speech almost impossible.

"Why did you want to meet?" Spencer asked, forcing himself to break the silence. "You must obviously have something you want to say to me that we haven't already said." His last comment sounded snarkier than he intended, and Justin's surprised expression strummed a pang of guilt. He fought the urge to apologize as he waited for Justin's answer.

"I've been trying to see you since you left my mother's house," Justin finally answered.

"I know," Spencer admitted. "You've left numerous messages for me everywhere. My phone. At work. With *everyone* we know."

"Why haven't you called me back?"

"I didn't see the point."

Justin gulped in reply. Spencer knew what that meant. Justin was attempting to suppress a rising sob. He had only seen him cry maybe three times in the ten years they were together. He hated himself for deriving small pleasure from Justin's pain, as if his hurt somehow paid a debt of misery owed to Spencer.

"I wanted to tell you something that you probably already know," Justin said.

"Which is?" He knew what Justin wanted to tell him. After all, moving in with Dutch was his idea. The revelation wouldn't be a surprise, but it was one Justin had to make. He had to see his decision for what it was. That was partly why Spencer had agreed to lunch in the first place. Sure, he had his own confessions to make, but Justin needed to finally understand his actions and what they revealed about his true emotions.

"I've moved in with Dutch."

Spencer stared at him blankly. He didn't want to give anything away prematurely. "And you're telling me this why?"

Justin reached across the table to hold Spencer's hand, but Spencer moved his hands to his lap. It was too soon for physical contact. "Because I wanted you to hear it from me. To understand that I *only* moved in with him because I feel responsible for his injuries. I'm just trying to help him recuperate. Get him back on his feet. It's nothing more than that."

He sighed. Justin still refused to see the truth. "You really still believe that?"

"What do you mean?" Justin asked. He looked hurt. "I'm telling you the truth. I *only* want to be with you. I would move back in with you now if you'd let me."

"I can't decide if you're lying to me or to yourself."

"I'm not lying to anyone. Honest to God."

"But you are, Justin. For some reason, you can't see that."

Justin exhaled deeply. He ran his fingers through his short hair. It was Justin's way of dealing with irritation, as if the simple act of fingers combing through hair had any connection to his mood. "I see everything just fine," he finally said.

"That's where you're wrong," pointed out Spencer. "You're in denial."

"You know I hate it when someone tells *me* how I'm feeling," Justin said. It was true. Justin hated when anyone presumed to know him better than he knew himself. Even when they did. "Tell me what *you* think I'm denying."

"The truth."

"You want the truth?" Justin asked, more than slightly irritated. "Well, here it is. I love you, Spence. I always have. I always will. You don't believe me. You don't trust me. I get that. And I understand why. But don't tell me that I don't love you. Not when every cell in my body cries out for you every night that we don't sleep together. Not when the only thing I want to do *this very moment* is to take you in my arms."

Spencer's upper lip trembled. The sincerity in Justin's words told him he was being truthful, but he also knew that Justin still remained blind to reality, a reality he had to see if there was any hope to resurrect their love from the flames of betrayal. "I hear what you're saying," he finally said. "But you're not hearing what *I'm* saying."

"Okay," Justin said. His irritation slowly slipped away. "Tell me what I'm not hearing. I *want* to hear you. I *want* to make this better."

"And I *want* to tell you. I really do, but I can't help but feel as if telling you defeats the purpose. This is something you've got to arrive at on your own."

"That's a cop-out," Justin replied. "You're passing the buck, not willing to share in the responsibility of working this out, of fixing us."

"You have *no* idea how wrong you are," he told Justin. "You're completely clueless as to what I've done to try to fix this."

"What have you done?" Justin asked. "Because from where I sit, it looks like all you've done is run." Anger quickly overcame his irritation. Justin apparently harbored secret resentment of his own. "You let your hurt force you to turn tail instead of facing up to your problem."

Spencer reeled. All he did was face their problems, but Justin didn't know that. He wanted Justin to see the truth, but he had failed to see the truth through Justin's eyes. How could Justin not think he had been running? Justin had no knowledge of the plan he set into motion.

"I haven't been running," he finally told Justin. "I've been fighting for us."

"I don't see how."

"I realize that now, and I'm truly sorry for that. That's part of what this lunch is for. To clear the air. To see things from *both* our perspectives. But you're going to have to open your eyes too, Justin. You need to see what you're not seeing."

"You keep saying that," Justin responded. "What am I not seeing? Please tell me."

"You won't like what I'm going to say, but I'm going to say it anyway."

"Okay, then. I'm ready."

"You got irritated at me just awhile ago for thinking I know what you feel." Justin nodded, waiting for him to continue. "But I know you better than most anyone else. Sometimes even better than you know yourself."

"I can accept that," Justin responded.

"Then consider this," Spencer said. "Consider that *this* might be one of those instances. Maybe *this* is like the time you were hurt about your father spending time with your cousins and not you. You *pretended* as if it didn't bother you. *I* knew better. You were angry at me then too, remember?"

"I was furious with you," Justin corrected. "But, yes, you were right. I was hurt."

"It's my opinion, as someone who has spent the last ten years of his life living with you, that you're *not* seeing this situation any more clearly than you see your father. There's something you're not admitting to yourself out of fear. *That* is keeping you from moving on. From *us* moving on."

"Okay," Justin said. "Then why not tell me what it is?"

"That would be like asking either one of us to explain the magic that brought us together," he responded. "It's something that lives beyond explanation. It's just something that *is*."

"Do you think I don't really love you anymore?"

"Is that true?" Spencer asked.

"No," Justin replied, confidently. "I do."

"Then maybe it's not your love for *me* that's the problem."

"Oh my God!" Justin exclaimed, sitting bolt upright in the booth. "You think I'm still in love with Dutch!"

"Are you?"

Justin opened his mouth to answer but then stopped himself, suddenly incapable of speech. For the first time, he was seeing the situation for what it was, but he refused to accept it. "I love you," Justin replied, forcing the truth beyond his grasp. "*Only* you."

"Don't lie now," Spencer said. "Now's the time for truth."

"I did fall in love with him while you were gone," Justin admitted. "I told you that already."

Spencer nodded. "But did you ever fall *out* of love with Dutch?"

Justin sighed miserably; the truth declined to be swept away. "No," he responded. "I never did."

Spencer smiled, not because the man he loved was still in love with another man, but that he had *finally* admitted it to himself. Loving and being in love were two very different emotions. Justin had embraced his love for Dutch, but always refused to see that he was still *in love* with Dutch.

Now that he saw that, now that he accepted the fact that his heart remained divided between him *and* Dutch, progress was possible.

Without acknowledging his love for Dutch, Justin could never rediscover the magic that once brought them together. His feelings for Dutch had prevented that from happening. But now that he knew, now that he faced his feelings head-on, he could deal with them.

The road ahead was still rife with danger. They were traveling along unfamiliar terrain, after all, and their car carried an additional passenger neither of them had expected. Still, Spencer was willing to gamble on their magic being strong enough to reform and reconnect them, perhaps in ways they'd never even expected.

The hardest part, though, was done. Justin had a lot to process, so he couldn't reveal his past with Dutch or the fact that he and Dutch had become friends. Getting Justin to admit his feelings was enough. For now.

Dutch wouldn't like the decision, but he felt confident he could get him to agree to keep the secret for just a bit longer.

Once he told Dutch about their conversation, he would see the merits in keeping their secret awhile longer. Justin needed a few days, maybe a week, to deal with what he just now realized. Once that was done, once he was stronger, they could reveal everything.

After all, there was no sense churning up an already tense situation; that would accomplish nothing. Not when things were changing, not when progress was being made. The three of them had lived under the oppressive fog of hurt and betrayal, and a refreshing breeze had started to blow.

Change was in the air; the atmosphere of wretchedness that enveloped the three of them for too long was on the verge of being blown away.

CHAPTER 40

2009

JUSTIN scanned the crowd, soaking up the atmosphere. Everywhere, people danced as the DJ spun the current remix of Lady Gaga's "Just Dance." Numerous revelers jumped up and down, their hands, curled like paws, pumping in the air. Putting your paws up was a signature Gaga move, something she asked at her concerts. Now, her gay followers mimicked the move at the clubs in honor of their new icon.

Besides those getting down with Gaga on the dance floor, others were ogling the strippers, stuffing one-dollar bills down their padded G-strings. Most didn't care that the strippers were obviously straight, doling out the majority of their stripper affection to the many fag hags and straight women currently packed into The Bonham for the 2009 New Year's Eve bash.

It had been too long since he had been here, the place where his journey with Spencer had started. When Spencer came up with the idea to ring in 2010 here, to celebrate the beginning of the next ten years of their lives together, he thought the idea brilliant. And romantic.

Spencer called all their friends, begging them to cancel whatever plans made in order to celebrate with them here. It didn't take much convincing. They all agreed. Even Xavier and Alex, who were there when it all started. Xavier and Alex were currently huddled together, catching up. Apparently, they hadn't seen each other since their one-night stand over ten years ago.

From the looks of their body language, another casual dalliance was in the works.

Justin couldn't remember the last time they were all together. Over the years, their nights and weekends spent together had gradually decreased as work and children dominated the lives of the group. Sam and Teresa were up to three children. Chris and Jill and Patrick and Heather had two each. Chuck and Don adopted a baby last year.

Tyler and Jerry, who had been dating for a few years now, were the only other childless couple in the group. Still, they rarely hung out these days. Work for everyone had been crazy, and their lives were filled with adult responsibilities that unfortunately no longer included the carefree lives of before, when the future seemed distant.

As Justin looked around at the faces of his dear friends, who all stood around one of the circular tables to the right of the main bar, he was reminded of how much they all truly loved each other, no matter the time and distance that now separated them. They were true friends, and they would be so until the end of time.

"Think less. Drink more," Patrick told him, handing him another vodka and Sprite. "You look too damn serious, buddy. We're supposed to be celebrating."

He smiled and took the offered drink. "I *am* celebrating," he said. "I'm just enjoying all of us being together again. It's been too damn long."

"Amen!" Heather said, knocking back a shot of tequila. "We need to do this more. I was just telling Pat the other day how much I've missed you guys."

"Me too," Chuck said. A Miller Lite rested in his right hand, while his left arm dangled around Don's neck. "We need to cut loose more. I'm tired of being an adult all the time. We need to get stupid drunk together at least once a month."

"I can plan that," Spencer interjected. His voice quivered with excitement. "I'll get everyone's schedules and come up with a good day and time."

Everyone laughed, causing Spencer to frown. Spencer's type A personality and obsessive-compulsive nature in regards to planning had always been an inside joke among them. He was the Martha Stewart of their previous social life, arranging the dates, setting up the meals, assigning the dishes everyone would bring, and even picking out the entertainment for the night.

"I love you, my Spencey," Teresa said while giving Spencer a peck on the cheek. "I've missed your phone calls making sure I was bringing the salad or the texts counting down the hours till the get-together."

Spencer stuck his tongue out at her.

"Don't tease my man," Justin said, puffing out his chest. "I must come to his defense." He wrapped his arm protectively around Spencer's waist.

"And the three of us will take you down!" Jill said, putting her arms around Teresa and Heather. "You know you can't withstand the power of our breasts!"

"Good Lord, no!" Justin said, waving his hands in surrender. "Those mammaries of yours are dangerous!"

"Yes, they are," Chris said while plunging his face in Jill's ample bosom. She hollered in response and smacked him on the head.

"Y'all need to get a room," Tyler said. "This is a gay club. We don't tolerate public displays of hetero affection in here."

"We're here, we're *not* queer, get used to it!" Chris said before diving in Jill's cleavage again.

As they laughed, Justin's eyes wandered around the room. A shiver traveled up and down his spine. That only happened to him when he was being watched. Somewhere in this room, a pair of unseen eyes was staring at him.

He surveyed the crowd, looking to see if he could find the eyes that had triggered his spine tingling reaction. All he saw were numerous twinks drinking heavily, fag hags spinning on the dance floor, and pristinely dressed gay guys cruising each other.

Nothing unusual at all.

Suddenly, an arm draped around his neck. It was Xavier. He had finally extracted himself from Alex long enough to come and speak to him. Xavier smirked at Justin and held his usual bottle of Dos Equis in his right hand. "It's been a long time," he said between sips.

"Too long," he replied, giving Xavier a kiss. "I've missed you."

"Of course you have," Xavier said with a grin.

Xavier wasn't one for sentimentality. Whenever emotions became real, he laughed them off. It kept him safe, but it also left him alone. After all these years, Xavier still hadn't found a lasting relationship. Although Justin rarely pitied people he considered true friends, his heart broke at Xavier's looks of longing whenever he saw Spencer and him together.

"As humble as ever, I see," he told Xavier.

"And twice as hot," Xavier replied, flexing his biceps, which had definitely become more chiseled over the years. Instead of devoting himself to another person, Xavier poured his focus into his body.

"You do look good."

"Thanks," Xavier said. "You've got to fine-tune the product in order to get anyone to buy."

"I take it you have some pending orders?"

"A few," Xavier replied, looking sideways at Alex. "But that's old and tired. I try not to repeat myself."

"You're awful," he told Xavier. "Alex seems to be a nice guy."

"I suppose," Xavier said with a shrug. "But the bitch needs to dump that puka shell necklace."

They laughed. It had been too long since he and Xavier spent time together. They used to be best friends, deeply entangled in every aspect of each other's daily lives. Now, they rarely texted and mostly communicated through Facebook.

"I have to ask," Xavier said, a familiar twinkle in his eyes. It was the same look Xavier used to give him before they started their weekly pickup game. "You and Spencer still into three-ways?"

The question startled him. He wasn't sure if Xavier was propositioning him to be their third in bed for the evening or if he was trying to restart their old game. "Keep your voice down," he told Xavier. "Only you and Tyler know that Spencer and I used to play with a third. I don't think the straights would be able to handle that."

Xavier laughed. "They can't hear us," he said. "The music is much too loud. Besides, they're passing around cell phone pics of each other's children. They aren't paying attention to us."

Justin looked toward the table. Everyone had a cell phone in hand, cooing about how cute everyone else's children were. Their attentions were diverted, and Ke$ha was currently belting out her latest track over the speakers.

"So?" Xavier asked. His eyebrows arched upward, his way of signaling Justin to answer his question.

"No," he replied. "We don't do that anymore."

"Too bad."

"Why?"

"Because there's a big bear of a man standing on the other side of the room who can't seem to take his eyes off you."

"I thought I felt someone staring at me," Justin admitted. He once again inspected the room, searching for his secret admirer. "Where is he?" he asked.

"God, man," Xavier complained. He tightened his grip around Justin's neck, preventing him from looking around. "Have you lost all the moves I taught you? You need to be a bit more discreet than that!"

"Why do I need to be discreet?" he asked. "It's not like anything's going to come of it. I *have* a man." He regretted his comment when he noticed the faint sting of pain reflected in Xavier's eyes. He hadn't meant to sound cruel. "I just want to see what he looks like. Maybe I can get him for you."

Xavier laughed. "Like I need your help." The pain in his eyes flitted away as quickly as it descended. "I was the undisputed pickup king, as you no doubt remember."

"Yes, you were," Justin told him. "Now, where is he?"

Xavier sighed. "To the left of the cowboy go-go dancer, standing against the wall of televisions."

Justin turned his head slightly. On the wall of televisions, Ke$ha's "Tik Tok" video played. Underneath the pop star's smirking face stood Dutch. He held an empty glass, and his eyes simmered with rage.

The breath caught in Justin's throat. He hadn't seen Dutch since he'd broken up with him. He didn't know what to do or how to act. He felt as if everyone instinctively knew that the two of them had once been an item, had shared a bed in Spencer's absence.

"He is one hot hunk of man flesh, isn't he?" Xavier asked. "He seems quite into you. Too bad you don't play around anymore."

Justin nodded and swallowed, hard. He couldn't speak. Seeing Dutch brought all the old feelings to the surface. He fought the urge to go to him, to see how he was doing, to once again surrender within his arms.

When Dutch saw him staring back, he lifted his empty glass in a mock toast. A devious smile lit across his face. For a few seconds, Justin worried Dutch would come over to him, make his presence and their affair known to all.

Instead, Dutch turned to the twink at his side and enveloped him in his arms. He shoved his tongue inside the young man's mouth and made a grab for his ass. Even from across the crowded bar, Justin could tell Dutch was putting on a show for him.

"I guess he wasn't that in to you after all," Xavier said with a laugh.

"Who are you guys talking about?" Spencer asked, suddenly at their side. The familiar emerald fire of love burned in his eyes. Spencer appeared truly happy, despite the months of misery they'd recently worked through.

Justin opened his mouth to respond, but no words came out. He found himself constantly looking over Spencer's shoulder at Dutch, who was leading his twink to the bar for another drink.

Xavier noticed Justin's reaction and came to the rescue. "I was trying to get Justin to play our pickup game again, but he's not having it."

"Good!" Spencer declared. His hand rested on Justin's shoulder, staking his claim. "Besides, he's got a sure thing right here."

Justin nodded, still unable to speak. He took a long drink of his vodka and Sprite. The liquid burned his throat, sending fiery flames shooting through his body. The blaze of alcohol spurred his voice back to life. "That's right, love," he replied at last. "No need to play that game anymore when I've already won."

Spencer kissed him on the lips. The physical contact made him feel even worse. Spencer's kiss imparted absolute trust and unwavering love. It told him how devoted Spencer was to their renewed commitment. Their lives hadn't been easy, but they'd worked diligently to get back to where they once were.

Justin thought they were there and had been for some time. But seeing Dutch raised his doubts. The connection he felt to Dutch remained. He still felt tethered to a man he hadn't seen in more than six months, and from the look on Dutch's face and despite his actions, Dutch still felt it too.

"You know I love you more than my luggage," Tyler told Patrick, who moaned. The sound of one of his friends quoting *Steel Magnolias* got his attention. He turned back to the group, who were all hissing at Tyler.

"Let's not start that again!" Patrick said. "I was just finally able to watch that movie again!"

"Don't be a *Steel Magnolias* hater," Spencer scolded. "It's a great movie."

As his friends launched into yet another *Steel Magnolias* debate, Justin followed Dutch's movements. He'd abandoned the twink he kissed earlier in favor of a different one. This one had dark skin and looked no more than nineteen. Dutch bought the boy a drink and practically molested him at the bar.

Justin finished his beverage. The sight of Dutch shamelessly throwing himself around like a common piece of bar trash unnerved him. Dutch was better than that.

"Another round?" Chris asked, to which everyone agreed.

"I'll get this one," Justin offered. Everyone thanked him but being generous wasn't his motive. Buying the next round of drinks would take him to the bar and put him in closer proximity to Dutch.

"Want some help, sweetie?" Spencer asked, rising from the table.

Before Justin could reply, Xavier responded. "I'll help him." He downed the rest of his Dos Equis in one gulp. "You stay here and help decide who'd win in a fight between Ouiser and Clairee," he told Spencer.

Spencer nodded and sat back down, completely unaware of Justin's distracted state.

Within moments, Justin stood in line at the bar, a few feet away from Dutch, who was now hitting on the nineteen-year-old twink's friend. He leaned over the even younger boy, stroking his cheek. The twink, obviously new to such aggressive flirtation, blushed and laughed nervously.

"All right," Xavier said, standing at Justin's side. "Tell me what the hell's going on."

Justin looked at Xavier as if he hadn't seen him in years. "What are you talking about?"

"Spencer may be blind to what's going on, but I'm a pro at this," Xavier reminded him. "There's something going on between you and that muscle bear. Now what is it?"

"I don't know what you're talking about," Justin replied, looking straight ahead instead of at Dutch. He hated that Xavier knew all about cheating glances since Xavier was a consummate cheater.

"Lies don't work on me, honey," Xavier said. "Besides, you know me better than that. Truth is the truth. I don't judge."

"There's nothing going on," Justin lied. There was no way he was admitting to his affair with Dutch tonight or any other night. That secret was going with him to his grave. "I just got distracted, is all. He's pretty hot, and I wanted to get a better look."

Xavier stared at him, unable to decide if Justin spoke the truth or not. Finally, the suspicion in his eyes vanished when Xavier took note of the guy standing beside him. Always distracted by the chance to hook up, Xavier discarded his previous concerns for the sake of the hunt.

Justin walked up to the bar and placed his drink order. While he waited, he watched as Dutch made out with both twinks just a few feet away from him. Their tongues rolled around in each other's mouths for all to see. He found the sight distasteful and unworthy of Dutch.

Dutch opened his eyes and stared at him. He switched from one young hungry mouth to the next as if he were a father bird feeding his young hatchlings. As he swapped spit with his two twinks, he never once looked away from Justin.

His eyes beamed with satisfaction, as if he were the winner at some game Justin didn't realize they had been playing.

The bartender placed his ordered drinks in front of him, and Justin paid the amount due. He coerced Xavier away from his potential trick so the two of them could carry their drinks back to the table.

When they returned with the drinks, they were greeted as heroes. Each grabbed their drink and set to the task of draining their glasses dry. In their absence, the debate had been decided: Ouiser was declared the winner by a landslide.

"I'll be right back," Justin whispered in Spencer's ear. "Must pee."

"You know how small your bladder is," Spencer reminded him. "Once you start, you won't be able to stop."

"I know, but I gotta go."

"Hurry back," Spencer urged before giving Justin a kiss.

As Justin departed the table, only Xavier eyed him suspiciously. Justin didn't care. He would deal with Xavier's questions later. Right now, he had to talk to Dutch. He had to make him see how stupidly he was acting. He wasn't some college kid on the prowl. He was a forty-year-old man, who needed to possess more decorum than he was currently displaying. After all, he worked at St. Mary's. What if one of his students was here?

He followed Dutch and his new twink out of the main bar and into the hallway entrance. The two of them stumbled down the hall together, groping each other's crotches. They turned down the small hallway to the left that led to the men's restrooms.

Justin was relieved. It made him feel like less of a liar.

When he entered the restroom, he saw Dutch close the door behind him in the stall. From underneath, he could see two pairs of feet and the unmistakable sound of a cock being slurped.

He couldn't believe Dutch was getting a blowjob in a public restroom. What had happened to the man he once knew?

Before he could think, Justin pounded on the stall door.

"Occupied," Dutch said, his voice overfull with pleasure. He remembered how much Dutch enjoyed the feel of a wet mouth around his hard cock.

Justin continued to knock on the door, more determined than ever to get one of them to open it. Finally, the twink opened the door, pissed off. "What the fuck, man?" he asked. "We're a little busy in here."

Without a word, he grabbed the twink by his gray skintight shirt and yanked him out of the stall. The boy shrieked in protest. Justin entered the stall and locked the door behind him.

"What do *you* want?" Dutch asked, tucking his still hard cock into his underwear. He leaned against the wall, looking down at Justin in complete disdain.

"I'm trying to save you from yourself," Justin responded. "Do you realize what a complete fool you're making of yourself out there?"

Dutch snickered. "What the hell makes you think *I* care what you or any of these queens think?" He zipped up his fly and adjusted himself. "I'm single, and I'm here to party."

He tried to walk around Justin, but Justin blocked his path. "Is that why you're making a complete ass of yourself? Have you even considered the fact that one or more of your students might be here?"

Dutch crossed his arms, his typical angry stance. His biceps bulged underneath his tight black Armani shirt. "Look, I don't want to have to move you out of my way, so don't force me," he warned. "You know exactly how strong I am."

"I'm not afraid of you," Justin replied. His eyes never wavered. Dutch would never hurt him. Of that, he was certain. "I'm trying to help."

"I don't want your help," Dutch announced. "I don't want *anything* from you."

Dutch's words stung. This wasn't the man he fell in love with. This was a completely different man. The Dutch he knew possessed a heart much bigger and stronger than the body that housed it. This Dutch looked cruel and spoke harshly. He didn't care about the love they'd once shared. In fact, he seemed perfectly content with destroying all traces of that previous bond.

"Why are you acting this way?" he asked Dutch.

"Are you kidding me?" Dutch asked. "You left me for Spencer. Did you expect me to give you a fucking *hug* when we saw each other again?"

"No," Justin replied. "But I don't think I deserve *this*."

"Well, here's a newsflash. *I* don't give a flying fuck what you think you deserve. When you walked out my door, you left the Dutch who loved you behind. Now, you've got the new Dutch. The one who doesn't care about anything. Least of all you."

"This new Dutch is an asshole," Justin stated.

"That would bother the old Dutch," he said, inching closer to Justin until their faces were only a few centimeters apart. In the air between them, he caught a whiff of Dutch's natural body odor that always hung about him and that still turned him on. "The new Dutch couldn't care less."

Justin stared into his cold blue eyes. Their crystal blue hue had always been inviting, like the warm, tropical waters of the Caribbean. The warmth was now gone, replaced by the frigid waters of the Arctic.

But as he looked deeply into the numbing cold stare, Justin could see the old Dutch, clinging onto an ice floe and hanging on for dear life. He struggled to pull himself from the frozen waters, but the angry current prevented any progress from being made.

"I'm sorry," Justin said. "I never meant to hurt you. To turn you into this."

Dutch's eyes widened in surprise. The old Dutch gained a foothold. He strained to lift himself from the icy grip of indifference. The coolness within faltered slightly before the chilly tentacles once again strangled him from within.

"Save your pity," Dutch told him. Venom dripped from his mouth. "I don't need it and I don't want it." He placed his index finger on Justin's chest and pushed him backward. "I like who I am now. I enjoy myself more than I have in years. I've had more sex recently than you've probably had in the past few months." A devilish grin stretched across his lips. "You'd be surprised who I've been naked with recently."

"What's *that* supposed to mean?"

Dutch laughed. "Nothing. Don't worry about it." He unlocked the stall door and opened it. "Now why don't you march yourself back to Spencer? The loving and faithful man you've decided to spend the rest of your life with. I've got better things to do."

He pushed open the door. On the other side, the twink Justin expelled from the stall stood at the sink, his hands on his hips.

"Fine," Justin said. He walked toward the door.

"And Justin," Dutch called out. Justin paused in front of the door and turned around. Dutch walked over to the twink, wrapping his arms around the boy. "The next time we run into each other, here or anywhere else, be a pal and pretend like you don't know me."

Justin exited the bathroom and shut the door behind him. He had leaned against the wall, hoping to regain his composure, when he heard the bathroom door lock behind him. The click of the lock infuriated him.

Dutch and his twink were likely already naked and resuming their previous position before he disturbed them. The thought of Dutch with someone else hit him harder than he expected. When he first saw Dutch making out with all those guys, he told himself that he had to stop Dutch before he ruined his professional reputation.

He realized that was a lie. He wanted to stop Dutch not out of concern but out of jealousy.

Seeing Dutch with someone else hurt him, deeply. The only person Dutch should be with was him, but he had left Dutch and returned to Spencer. He had no reason to feel this way, and the fact that he did bothered him a great deal.

After all, he was here with Spencer. Tonight, they were celebrating New Year's Eve at the place where their romance began. When they kissed at midnight, they would be inaugurating the next ten years of their lives together.

How could he do that when his feelings for Dutch had resurfaced like a buried treasure? He'd never hated himself more than at this moment.

To make things better, to be able to go on, he had to force his feelings for Dutch back down, bury them even further inside himself before they destroyed his life entirely. Dutch had moved on, and he made it quite clear he wanted nothing more to do with Justin.

Justin had to focus on Spencer. And only Spencer. Their love was real and lasting, more powerful than whatever he might still feel for Dutch. He couldn't allow those emotions to distract him any longer.

As he closed his eyes, he sealed the lid on his love for Dutch and buried it beneath the sands of his subconscious, where it would forever remain.

Justin made his way back to the bar, to ring in the New Year with Spencer. His mind felt clearer, his heart no longer in turmoil.

CHAPTER 41

2010

JUSTIN sat on the couch in Dutch's living room, staring at the dark television screen while his soul writhed in turmoil. The remote lay in his hand, which was numb and useless. Since lunch with Spencer a few hours ago, he had been unable to feel anything.

The food he ate, mostly in silence, lacked taste. The tea he drank possessed no flavor. He couldn't recall their conversation while they ate or what they said in the parking lot before going their separate ways.

When Spencer forced him to realize he was still in love with Dutch, his body went into shock, incapable of processing anything further until he dealt with the revelation. He couldn't even remember driving home. He recalled getting into his car but not much more after that.

What he needed to do was head into work, but he found himself walking into Dutch's house and plopping onto the couch, where he sat in silence for at least an hour.

Justin refused to accept he was still *in love* with Dutch even though he'd admitted those feelings to Spencer a few hours ago. In rebuttal, he rationalized everything: he'd agreed to help Dutch recuperate not because he was still in love with him but because he felt liable for Dutch's self-destructive behavior. It was ridiculous for feelings he'd long since abandoned to resurface, especially considering he had rededicated himself to Spencer for the past year.

Spencer had been his one and only focus, until Heidi shattered it with her phone call. That was when things blurred, but not because he was still in love with Dutch. He lost focus because the secret he tried to keep had been exposed. There was nothing else to it.

His heart thudded in his chest. Its rapid beat signaled its disagreement as the buried love for Dutch shot to the surface. Recent images flashed in his mind, and Justin felt the true emotions attached to each mental picture.

Seeing Dutch at the Bonham last New Year's Eve. Heidi telling him Dutch had been in accident. Visiting Dutch for the first time in the hospital. Sharing pizza and Coke while debating Batman. Preparing dinner together for the past few months, exercising and stretching every night, and living together in peaceful harmony.

Each image contained love, untainted by bile and unweathered by time. It felt as if it was simply meant to be like the magic that first drew him to Spencer. Choice wasn't involved. Although he'd debated the wisdom of moving in together, when asked, it hadn't taken much convincing for him to agree. He did it knowing full well that doing so might mean the end of his relationship with Spencer. Forever.

Why did I do that? he wondered. *Why would I readily agree to move in with Dutch if I knew it might cost me Spencer?*

His heart skipped a beat in response. It already knew what his mind refused to accept.

"Because I'm still in love with him," he whispered.

Justin rose from the couch. His body trembled as his previously anesthetized soul filled with self-loathing. He saw everything clearly now. His love for both men *never* went away. He buried his love for Dutch in an act of self-preservation, not because he had fallen out of love with him.

When Spencer left and he fell in love with Dutch, he truly believed his time with Spencer was over, that Spencer's departure for London signaled their end even though neither he nor Spencer admitted it. After all, Spencer abandoned him like his father had done to both him and his mother so many years ago. He believed, based on previous experience, that a relationship never endured desertion.

Besides, Dutch lived in his heart, almost from the moment of their first kiss on the Riverwalk. Their kiss and their first time in bed together were magical, as if the force that once brought him and Spencer together had reconstituted itself, willing itself back into existence to right the wrong committed by Spencer. It brought Justin his new soul mate, the man who he would now love until the end of time.

That was why he gave himself so completely to Dutch, as he had once done with Spencer. Doing so felt predetermined, as if their being together was something bigger than themselves, a power they couldn't fight, even if they wanted to.

When Spencer ultimately returned, Justin fully expected to end things with him for good. To his surprise, his love for Spencer still existed. It never went away. Seeing Spencer brought their love back into the open.

It left him confused. He had no idea what to do, which was why he waffled on making a decision. His heart had been divided, and he saw no way to make a choice without hurting himself and someone he loved.

Eventually, he chose Spencer, not because he loved Dutch any less but because Spencer held prior claim to his heart.

At first, all was well. He and Spencer reconnected, and the magic that brought them together sparked to life once again. However, something ate away inside him, gnawing at his heart and his soul and making him feel lost and empty.

He had no idea what it was at the time. He believed he had somehow stumbled into the doldrums and figured eventually he would find his way back out. What was actually happening, though, was his undying love for Dutch was fighting back against his callous mistreatment of the bond they'd forged.

It refused to be ignored. His heart missed a vital piece it needed to survive and begged for him to find that piece to once again make it whole.

It seemed so clear to Justin now. Their love burned within him like a fire left unwatched. It spread like a wildfire, incinerating everything in its path and turning his insides into ash.

Not until he saw Dutch again in the hospital did that burned out, empty feeling dissipate. The missing piece had been found, and his heart sighed in relief.

But in finding Dutch again, he lost Spencer, the other piece vital to his well-being.

Living with Dutch would never make him happy. Being with Spencer didn't make him happy. He seemed destined to be miserable forever unless he could find some way to bring it all together.

He had no clue what that meant. It sounded impractical and selfish, as if he wanted to have his cake and eat it too. But that wasn't what this was about. His self-centered desires had dictated his life for too long already.

In pursuit of his own needs, he had fallen in love with two men and was now incapable of being happy without *both* of them in his life.

"You're home," Dutch said, wheeling himself into the living room. "I had to take a nap after physical therapy," he admitted while rubbing his still red eyes. "I thought you were going back to work after lunch with Spencer."

"I took the rest of the day off," he said, suddenly remembering calling his secretary on his drive home. "I need to think."

Dutch positioned himself in front of the couch. Curiosity washed over his face. He was apparently dying to learn how lunch went. "So, how'd it go?" he asked. "Did the two of you work things out?"

The genuineness of Dutch's question hit him in the gut. Dutch's eyes reflected endless pools of hope. He sincerely wanted Justin and Spencer to work things out, to find their way back together. Justin had no idea what he'd ever done to deserve such deep-seated love from two great men.

"Not quite," Justin announced. He turned around, facing the wall opposite Dutch. He couldn't stare into those beautiful blue eyes, gazing at him with both adoration and heartbreak.

"What happened?"

"I don't want to talk about it," replied Justin. He walked away from Dutch, headed for his bedroom.

"Where are you going?" Dutch asked. "Was it *that* bad?"

"Yes."

"Justin, stop," Dutch said. His voice was firm but still saturated with worry. "Talk to me." His wheelchair scraped against the floor as he drew nearer. "Don't shut me out. I want to help."

"There's nothing you can do to help," Justin said, his back still to Dutch. "I need to work through this on my own. Without you. Without Spencer."

"Work through what?" Dutch wheeled himself around Justin, so he could stare into his eyes. "I can tell something happened. What was it?"

"As if you don't know," he replied. He figured since Spencer knew he was still in love with both of them, Dutch must have figured it out too.

Dutch cast his eyes downward. Guilt flowed readily to the surface, turning his crystal blue eyes a murky gray. Justin was right. *He* was the only one who was ignorant of his true feelings. In his mind, that made him both an idiot and an embarrassment.

"I'm sorry," Dutch finally said. "I wanted to tell you from the beginning but Spencer made me promise to keep it a secret. He figured this was the only way to give all three of us closure."

Justin stared at Dutch, dumbfounded. *Did I hear Dutch correctly? Did Dutch just admit to making a promise to Spencer? How was that possible?*

"Keep what a secret?" he asked, still unable to believe his ears. *What secrets are Spencer and Dutch keeping from me? When did the two of them meet to discuss their situation, and why am I just finding out about it now?*

Dutch stared at him quizzically. The look in his eyes told Justin they were talking about two different subjects. "What do you mean?" Dutch asked. "Didn't Spencer finally tell you about his plan?"

Justin had no idea what was happening. He had felt confused and done in before, when all he had to deal with was being in love with two men. This turn of events, this secret plan that Spencer concocted and Dutch apparently went along with, sent him spinning. "What are you talking about?" he finally asked Dutch. "What plan?"

Dutch looked alarmed. He finally realized he had prematurely spilled the beans. "It's nothing," he told Justin, trying to get his wheelchair moving down the hall.

Justin grabbed the handles of the chair and stopped him. "You're not going anywhere until you tell me what the hell is going on here."

"I can't," replied Dutch. "I made a promise."

Justin knelt in front of the chair, determined to get an answer to his question. "I don't care about any promise you made to Spencer," he pointed out. "You're keeping something from me. Both of you are. I deserve to know what it is." He stared directly into Dutch's eyes, locking onto them in order to discern truth from deception. "I was under the assumption that the lies had stopped, that all our cards were on the table. If they're not, I deserve to know. Everything."

Dutch sighed in defeat. "I know," he said. When he opened his mouth the second time, a slew of hidden truths rushed forward.

Justin leaned against the wall for support as the world was suddenly yanked from beneath his feet. He couldn't believe Spencer had planned their current living arrangements. He also found it difficult to accept that Spencer was the friend who had been taking Dutch to his physical therapy appointments for the past four months or that the two of them had actually become friends.

"So when I was looking for Spencer, you knew where he was the whole time?" he finally asked, once again finding his voice.

Dutch nodded. "I wanted to tell you, especially when I saw how crazy you were getting. I even went to Spencer and begged him to reconsider, but he said this was the only way to get our lives back on track."

"How was living with *you* supposed to accomplish that impossible task?" he asked. "And why did the two of you think making decisions for *me* would in any way help?"

"It was supposed to help you see the situation for what it was," Dutch replied. "We did it for you. To get you to see that you were in love with *both* of us."

"Well, I see that," Justin spat out. "A lot of good that does *me* now." He walked away from Dutch, worried he wouldn't be able to control the anger that raged within. He hated being made to look a fool. "Instead of engaging in this mad charade, all anyone had to do was sit down and talk with me about it, the way Spencer did today."

"But you were in such denial," Dutch responded. "You didn't realize the true depth of your feelings for Spencer while we were together any more than you realized how you felt about me when you left me *for* Spencer."

"That still doesn't give either of you the right," Justin replied through gritted teeth. "The two of you were playing God, manipulating me and my emotions. And I still have to ask myself why."

"I just told you why," Dutch answered. Once again, he looked away. Justin could see there were still truths to be told.

"But you haven't told me everything," he said. "I can see it as plain as the stubble on your cheeks."

"There's nothing more."

"That's a lie, and you know it!"

Dutch's stare turned blank. "I've nothing more to say."

Justin went cold.

For too long, he had placed all blame squarely upon his shoulders, trying to figure out a way to undo the damage he'd caused, but this whole time, he had been ignorant to the secrets Spencer and Dutch guarded. That had come to an end. He would no longer play the part of the whipping boy, who crawled on his belly begging for forgiveness from two men who needed to seek their own absolution from him.

It was past time for him to wrest control of his life from *both* of them. They would no longer be his puppet masters, and he would no longer dance to the strings they joyously plucked.

Justin was done.

"Keep your secrets," he told Dutch. "I no longer care, and I no longer want to know. Both of you condemned me for my actions, for being in love with the both of you. For hurting you. I never wanted *any* of that to happen, but it did. And I can't tell you how sorry I am for that." He crossed the living room and headed for the front door. "But I'm tired of being the only one who's sorry. The two of you apparently aren't sorry for your lies." He picked up his keys, struggling to free the key to Dutch's house from the ring for the second and final time. "The truth is, I don't need your truths anymore. I've found my own." Dutch's key finally came free. He threw it at Dutch, who deflected it. It clanged and bounced under the sofa table to his right.

Dutch opened his mouth, but Justin cut him off. "Save it. I don't want to hear it." He opened the front door and stepped across the threshold. "Your plan worked. I've got my *closure*. The both of you can go to hell."

Justin slammed the door shut and within seconds screeched out of Dutch's driveway. He drove without direction, but for the first time in months, the darkened road beyond his headlights didn't fill him with fear.

He released his burdens and cast away his conflict. The road he traveled was his own.

CHAPTER 42

2010

SPENCER'S inner turmoil rolled within him like a turbulent sea. He felt helpless and lost, tossed about by the furious waves as they flung him from one angry arm to the next. He never expected his lunch with Justin to make him feel this way.

While he knew discussing Justin's love for Dutch was something they had to bring out into the open, since Justin seemed intent on suppressing the truth, he foolishly believed the revelation would somehow make everything better. Since he'd returned to his office from lunch, he hadn't felt that way at all.

He'd felt that magical connection restart at first, but it petered out halfway through the lunch, as if Justin's acceptance of his love for Dutch had thrown a bucket of water upon a struggling spark.

When they parted ways in the parking lot, Justin detached, as he often did when faced with too much emotional stress. Spencer tried to draw him back in by making him feel better and telling him that he saw a light at the end of the tunnel, but Justin didn't seem to hear any of that. He only nodded and gazed far away, too preoccupied with his rediscovered love for Dutch.

How I created such a stupid son is beyond me, his father spat in disgust. *You're so fucking blind that I could just knock you on that dumb ass of yours!*

Oh, for crying out loud! Spencer told his father. *What the* hell *are you talking about now?* He rose from his seat behind his desk and stood to look out the window to the quad below.

Some students dashed to afternoon classes while others lounged along the bricked pathways, chatting with friends. Spencer envied their ignorance to the true pains of the world. For them, life was still all about endless opportunities. For Spencer, life seemed more finite, filled with labyrinthian paths that led nowhere except dead ends.

Don't be envying them for your stupidity, his father announced. *The shithole your life has become is nobody's fault but your own.*

And what have I done exactly? he asked. *Thrill me with your poetic insights into my psyche.*

His father laughed, but it was a sound full of pity and scorn. *You may talk pretty, princess. And you may wish upon whatever fucking star you see for your handsome prince to come and rescue you, but no prince can rescue you from yourself!*

I'm not a helpless victim, he said. *I can take care of myself.*

You're doing a bang-up job so far, his father replied. *Sure, you got Justin to admit his feelings for Dutch, but what about yours?*

What about mine? I know exactly how I feel.

Sweetheart, you don't know a damn thing!

Spencer was about to retort when a loud bang shook his office. Startled, he jumped. His eyes darted around, unsure where the noise emanated from. It sounded like a mini-explosion, its blast still echoing in his ears.

Another explosion shook his office, followed by another. He spun around to face his closed office door. Someone was ruthlessly banging against it, hell-bent on gaining entrance or bashing it down.

"Who's there?" he called out, ashamed of the fear that gripped his voice.

"Open the fucking door," the voice commanded, filled with rage. "Now!"

Spencer stared at the door, confused. It sounded like Justin, but never before had he heard him so angry. "Justin?" he asked, still unsure if the crazed person banging on his door was the man he lived with for the past decade.

"Who else would it be?" he asked, still pounding ceaselessly against his door. "Now open up!"

He approached the door cautiously, uncertain why Justin sounded so angry or so uncharacteristically violent. While Justin did have a quick temper, he rarely expressed so much hostility.

What about when he punched a hole in the wall at Christmas? his father asked.

That was different, he told his father. *It was one single outburst.*

Looks like this time will be different, his father commented, almost too pleased with the current turn in events. *I told you that you fucked things up. I'm pretty sure it's all coming back to bite you in the ass now.*

Spencer ignored his father's last words, for there was nothing he had done for Justin to be this insanely furious about. Even so, Justin was a man possessed, still hammering upon the door with his fists, insisting that Spencer open the door.

He knew Justin would never physically hurt him, but he couldn't find the strength to unlock and open the door. His father's words haunted him, hanging over him like an unseen wraith intending to inflict harm.

"Sir, step away from the door," a voice from the hall commanded. "Now!"

He knew whom the voice belonged to. It was one of the campus security guards.

"I will not," Justin called back. "Not until I see Spencer Harrison."

"I won't ask you a second time," the voice told him. "Step away from the door."

Spencer swung the door open and walked out into the hall. Justin had backed away from the door and stood directly across from the security guard, whose hand hovered over his mace, in a showdown reminiscent of old spaghetti westerns.

"Officer, I apologize for this scene," he said, trying to defuse the situation. "This is my partner, and we obviously have things to discuss. There's no problem here," he commented while turning to stare into Justin's eyes. "And there won't be any further outbursts."

"This is a place of work, Dr. Harrison," the guard told him. "Not the place for domestic disputes."

"I understand." He nodded. "It won't happen again."

"I'll have to submit an incident report to Dr. Cutting. She'll likely need to speak with you about this."

He nodded again. "I'll make an appointment with her first thing tomorrow morning."

The security guard nodded, still eying Justin warily. He then turned around and proceeded to the stairwell, where Spencer was certain he would wait in case a further disturbance occurred.

"Come on in," he told Justin while stepping out of the doorway.

Justin entered his office without making eye contact. He still seemed to be fuming over whatever brought him here in the first place. When they were both inside his office, Spencer closed the door and locked it. He didn't want anyone to barge in and interrupt them if further argument ensued.

"Would you mind telling me what *that* was all about?" he asked. He waited for a response, but none was offered.

Instead, Justin stared at the pictures of them adorning the table along the far wall. When Justin helped him set up his office a few years ago, he joked that the numerous photographs resembled an altar of their relationship. It was more of an ode than an altar. For Spencer, their love was a piece of art, something carefully sculpted by the both of them and worthy of being admired by those individuals who appreciated such beauty.

Justin glared at this ode to their relationship as if it were now a parody. His eyes burned in anger, and his body language was rigid and unforgiving.

"Justin?" Spencer asked, trying to get an answer to his question. "What's wrong? Why are you so angry?"

"Why do you think I'm angry?" he asked, still refusing to look at him, still staring at the pictures of their past selves.

"I really have no clue," Spencer responded. "Should I assume you're angry that I think you're still in love with Dutch?"

Justin laughed, and his laughter caught Spencer off guard. It sounded more like his father than Justin.

"What's so funny?" he asked. "I'd love to be let in on the joke."

"You're funny," Justin commented, turning to face him. His eyes were filled with animosity, but another emotion floated near the surface. If Spencer didn't know better, he would have pegged it as the look of betrayal.

"Why are you looking at me like that? What have I done to deserve those looks?"

"How about playing God with my life?" Justin asked. "How's that for starters?"

Spencer's heart skipped a beat. Somehow, Justin had learned the truth about the living arrangements.

It sucks when your house of cards comes crashing down around you, doesn't it? his father asked smugly.

"Don't deny it," Justin told him. "Dutch let the cat out of the bag. The two of you have been conspiring behind my back, moving me about like some chess piece."

"You're being a tad melodramatic," Spencer said. "No one has been treating you like a pawn." Justin crossed his arms and stood his ground, his standard defiant pose. "I did what I thought I had to do. You cheated, and you were still in love with the man you cheated on me with. I knew that. Dutch knew that. But you didn't know it."

Justin opened his mouth to speak, but Spencer gestured for him to stop. He wanted to be allowed to speak his piece first, to hopefully release some of Justin's anger with the logic of his words. When Justin nodded, he continued. "I was there at the hospital when you first saw Dutch. You didn't know it, but I was in the hall. I heard your entire conversation. I heard how you spoke to him. How much you cared for him. How much he cared for you." His voice cracked, but he suppressed the rising sob. "I wanted to hate you. I wanted to hurt you. But I *couldn't*. Because I still loved you like some damn fool!"

"So *why* do this?" Justin asked. "Why play these games? Why couldn't we just try to patch things together?"

"How could I patch things up with you when you were still in love with someone else?" Spencer asked. Justin couldn't reply to that, for they both knew what the answer was. "You pursued me after I learned of the affair. And I *wanted* to let you come to me. I *wanted* to work things out, but I wasn't about to give you my heart again, let you inside the walls you broke down all those years ago, just for you to destroy me again. I might love you, Justin, but I love myself too."

Justin sighed. The exhalation released the pressure of his anger. "I can understand that. I guess," he conceded. "But why did you think moving in with Dutch would make things better? How could that make *anything* better between *us*?"

"I foolishly thought once Dutch became a real person, not some fantasy you could run to in order to escape our problems, that you would realize *I* was the only man you wanted." It was Spencer's turn to sigh, but his was filled with failure not a release of anger. "I was wrong," he finally told Justin. "Your bond with Dutch has only gotten stronger."

"Maybe," Justin admitted. "But my feelings for you have never changed." He crossed the void toward him and took his hands in his own. "I yearned for you every day we were apart. I wanted to be with you, to work things out. You can ask Dutch if you don't believe me."

"He told me that too, but I couldn't believe it."

"Why not?"

"Because how could you choose me when you had already chosen Dutch?"

"I don't understand," Justin said. "What are you talking about?"

"That morning, when I found out about your affair, I went to see Dutch in the hospital. I was only there for a bit, and he didn't know I was there. But when I got back to my car, I saw you running through the parking lot, frantically trying to get to Dutch's room to be at his side. I learned a lot that night. I learned that your feelings for Dutch overpowered whatever you felt for me."

"You dumbass," Justin said, laughing. "I went to Dutch's hospital room looking for you! I put myself in your shoes, and I tried to think where *I* would go if the situation was reversed. The first place I would go would be to confront the other man." He gripped tightly onto Spencer's hands, trying to use the power of his touch to force Spencer to see the truth. "I went there looking for *you,* not to see Dutch."

Could that be the truth? he wondered. *Did I misinterpret Justin's actions that morning? Did Justin really go to Dutch's room for me?*

You're not seriously buying this load of crap? his father asked. *He's a Mexican! They fucking lie about everything!*

"I believe you," Spencer finally told Justin.

"Thank God," Justin said. His face broadened into a smile filled with pure joy. More than anything else, Spencer wanted to get lost in Justin's beaming expression. For years, Justin's smile had lit up his world. He longed for it to lead them out of the darkness that enveloped them for too long.

Just when he was about to give himself over to it, to use the light to cross the distance that separated them, Justin's smile drifted away.

"There's just one more thing," he said.

"What is it?"

"What is your *true* relationship with Dutch?"

The question unbalanced him. Spencer's world tumbled before him, and he was uncertain how to once again set it right.

You've been caught in your own web of lies, his father announced. *Good luck with that!*

"What do you mean?" Spencer asked.

"Dutch told me you've become friends, that you've been taking him to his physical therapy appointments all this time."

"So," he asked, dragging out the vowel, not in an effort to punctuate a point, like he typically did, but in an effort to delay a response. "Is that a crime? To help out someone who needs it?"

Justin shook his head. "Not a crime at all," he said. "But I'm not stupid. I know you *much* too well. You would never *ever* become friends with the man who I cheated with, and that's exactly what the two of you have become. That wouldn't happen *unless* there was something more, some other part of this story that I don't yet know about." He stared into Spencer's eyes, scanning for a hidden truth. "I deserve to know what it is."

Spencer opened his mouth to answer, but this time it was Justin who asked him to wait until he was finished. "We operated on truth before all this, Spence. I know I lied and I cheated, and I feel we're working through that, but I need to know whatever truth you're keeping from me. The truth Dutch is keeping from me. I know it's there. I saw it in Dutch's eyes, and I can see it in yours." He took a deep breath. "Tell me what it is."

This is it! his father said, clapping like a child watching a circus. *This is the moment I've been waiting for. Do it, son! Drop the bomb on him. Let him see what it feels like!*

His father was right and so was Justin. Now was the time for the complete and absolute truth. There could be no going back. All the cards needed to be on the table if reconciliation or closure were ever to occur. Justin had fought hard to close the gap that existed. Spencer could see that clearly more than ever.

Now, it was his turn.

When he spoke, the truth was finally revealed. He told Justin everything, about their friendship *prior* to learning of the affair, their many flirtations, and the moment in Dutch's office when they were both naked and almost had sex.

Justin took two steps backward. His face contorted in pain as if he had been sucker punched. Spencer reached out to take Justin's hands, to reestablish the connection that had once again began to form between the two of them.

Justin batted his hands away.

"Don't touch me!"

"Justin, please…."

"You've made me feel like *shit* for the affair, for what happened with Dutch when you walked out on me for London. But the whole time you've been back, the whole time we were rebuilding our relationship, you were carrying on with Dutch, you were *cheating* on me!"

"I *never* cheated," Spencer rebutted. "We never crossed *that* line."

"That's splitting hairs, and you fucking know it," Justin muttered angrily. "I may have cheated. I may have kept that from you, but only because I thought you and I were over. I didn't continue the affair once we were really trying to put our life back together again. I turned my back on Dutch. I choose you over him. You *never* gave me the same courtesy!"

He turned around and knocked all the pictures of them on the table onto the floor with one wave of his hand. "This has all been some sick joke you and Dutch have been playing on me! I've been beating myself up, hating myself for hurting you, for hurting Dutch. And the entire *fucking* time, the two of you have been carrying on behind my back!"

"No, we haven't," replied Spencer. He rushed over to Justin, but Justin crossed to the other side of the office. "Dutch was my friend. That was all. Yes, things got out of hand. Once. But I drew the line, and it was never crossed again."

Justin laughed. It was filled with anger and ridicule. "I don't buy it, Spencer! Any more than you do." He paced around the room like a prisoner looking for escape. "You know deep down in your soul that what you did, what you allowed to continue between the two of you, was wrong. The whole time it was happening. I know you well enough to know that with absolute certainty. But you did it anyway."

"Maybe," Spencer admitted. "But unlike you, I never had sex with him."

"Oh no," Justin replied, shaking his finger at him. "Don't try to turn this around on me. I've owned up to what I did. I've been man enough to accept that. You've been the chickenshit coward who's been too afraid to admit what *he's* done wrong. And you still refuse to see it. And you say that I've been blind to my feelings."

"Then tell me," he told Justin. "Tell me what I'm not seeing."

"That's not gonna happen. *You* need to think about it. Just like you forced me to. You need to figure out *why* you developed a friendship with Dutch *after* you learned I slept with him. Most people would've cut that person out of their lives. They *never* would've taken him to his physical therapy appointments or conspired with him, much less *continue* to be his friend. Anyone else on this planet would've been glad to see him suffer in pain. You didn't. You allowed your relationship with him to persist, *despite* what you knew."

Justin headed for the door. To Spencer, it seemed that Justin finally mustered the strength to exit this situation.

"Justin, wait," Spencer called out. "Where are you going?"

Justin gave him his profile, so he wouldn't have to look him in the eyes. "I don't know. Even if I did, I wouldn't tell you," he said, repeating the words Spencer spoke to him prior to leaving him and their house all those months ago. "You, and Dutch, no longer have the right to know where I go or what I do."

He then walked out the door without slamming it behind him. Justin simply left it floating open as if it didn't matter, as if he no longer mattered.

Spencer fell to his knees as Justin's parting words opened a hole in his heart.

CHAPTER 43

2010

FOR the past few weeks, Spencer had tried not to think about the truth of Justin's last words to him that day in his office. The truth of the accusations weighed heavily upon him for the first few days, but he had to push them aside because those words threatened to drive him crazy.

He still had difficulty understanding Justin's anger. After all, *he* wasn't the adulterer. Justin was. Still, lingering paranoia about some hidden, unseen truth gnawed away at him from time to time, especially whenever he sat idle for too long, as he was doing now, waiting in his usual chair a few feet away from Dutch and his physical therapist, George.

Focusing on something else or someone else's problems proved easier than dealing with the mess he made of his life. So instead of falling into that well-known pit of despair, he focused on Dutch and his physical therapy regimen. Right now, George pushed Dutch's limits, ordering him to take more steps between the parallel bars that had become Dutch's enemy.

Sweat poured off Dutch, staining the front of his yellow muscle shirt. The tendons in his neck fanned outward as he struggled to shuffle forward on unsteady legs while cursing both his lower extremities and George.

"My fucking legs can't do this! They're useless, you motherfucking cunt!"

As always, George took the abuse. He'd told Spencer a couple of months ago that being cussed out was a part of his job, and he didn't take offense, even though some of the things Dutch called him were horrible.

"Can't you see I'm done, you worthless bitch? Or do you get your rocks off watching someone else in pain? I bet you go home and beat off to the torture you inflict on your patients."

Dutch progressed halfway between the parallel bars but then begged for his wheelchair. George refused the request, which elicited another string of profanity in response.

While they argued, again, Spencer's thoughts returned to Justin. It had been almost a month since their confrontation, and no one had seen him since.

Spencer had stopped by the high school, but Gladys, Justin's secretary, had no idea where Justin was, only that he'd called in sick for the rest of the semester. Apparently, Justin had used all his accrued sick days to take an extended leave from work. The school district wasn't happy, according to Gladys, but Justin's assistant principal kept them at bay. She reminded the superintendent of his excellent record of the past several years, which had spared his job for the time being. Spencer hoped Justin would return to work before the goodwill of upper administration wore out.

Their friends were even less help in finding Justin, and they were all furious with Spencer for what he had done. Forcing Justin to move in with Dutch was an idiotic move in their eyes, and they agreed that Justin had every right to be angry, especially considering what they now knew about Spencer's relationship with Dutch. Though they promised to let him know if they heard from Justin, Spencer doubted they would. After all, they'd kept Spencer's whereabouts from Justin for months, so he figured turnabout was going to be fair play.

Elena's anger, though, was the hardest for Spencer to take. Through tear-stained eyes, she accused him of making her baby run away, not only from him but from her. She was lost without her son, whom she usually communicated with daily. Since his departure, she hadn't heard from him, and the indisputable fear in her eyes for her son's safety told Spencer she spoke the truth.

Christmas came and went without a single word from Justin. Everyone now feared the worst. Next to New Year's, Christmas was his favorite holiday. Spending time with his family and getting the house decorated for the special day always lit up Justin's face, turning him into the little boy who anxiously awaited Santa Claus.

When he missed Christmas, Elena went to the police. Unfortunately, a grown man who had a fight with his lover and took off didn't rate high on their priority list. The officer handling the case promised to keep his eyes open but didn't make any assurances beyond that.

Spencer wanted to go down to the police station and throttle the officer, but Elena ordered him not to. He had done enough damage, according to her.

Since then four days had passed and all Spencer could do was fret. He felt awful about what he had done. He wanted to make amends, to tell

Justin he was sorry and try to once again explain the situation. He left numerous messages on Justin's voice mail, begging him to call or come home. Justin never did, and since the mailbox on Justin's cell phone was now full, Spencer could no longer leave messages for Justin.

Dutch took Justin's absence just as hard as he did. Over the past few weeks, his mood had worsened. A storm constantly raged inside his eyes as he berated himself for going along with Spencer's plan. Dutch had always feared what Justin would do when he learned the whole truth about the two of them. He'd never expected for Justin to leave without a word to anyone, though.

"Spencer, I need you to do me a favor," George called from across the room.

He stood up and walked over to them, grateful to be pulled away from his inner unrest. Dutch sat in his wheelchair behind the parallel bars, his body completely covered in perspiration. An angry scowl took up residence on his lips.

"What can I do?" he asked.

"I want you to stand at the opposite end of the bars," George instructed.

Spencer nodded and proceeded to his assigned place. "What now?" he asked. "You want me to show this big baby how it's done?"

George laughed while Dutch flipped Spencer off. "No, I want you to stand there and be Dutch's inspiration."

"His what?"

"Inspiration," George repeated. He helped Dutch get to his feet even though he loudly protested being forced to stand again. "I want you to be the prize at the end of the road. What better incentive is there than to walk, on your own, into the arms of the man you love?"

Spencer stood there quietly, unable to speak for a few moments. Dutch, too, stared at George with mouth agape. He looked just as stunned as Spencer. When the shock passed, he said, "Dutch and I aren't an item."

"Oh, please," said George. "Don't be embarrassed. It's almost 2011 and not everyone is freaked out by two men in love." He steadied Dutch on his feet. "I think it's sweet how you bring him to all his appointments and wait here until he's done. Some couples don't do that for each other. Believe me, I know. I've seen husbands drop off wives and not return for them until two hours after our sessions have ended. Stupid punkass bastards."

"We aren't a couple," Dutch grunted as his full weight once again rested upon his arms. "Spencer's just my ride."

"Really?" George asked, astonished. He glanced at Spencer and then back at Dutch. "The two of you talk and act like a couple. Hell, you remind me of me and my girlfriend, the way you like the same things and finish each other's thoughts."

"We what?" Spencer asked. "What are you talking about?"

"Just the other day," George began while getting Dutch moving forward. "The two of you were quoting that movie to each other. You know, the one with Sally Field and Julia Roberts."

"*Steel Magnolias*?"

"That's the one," George told Spencer. "My girlfriend loves that movie. I think it's okay, but the two of you obviously love it. You even did the whole scene where Julia Roberts and Sally Field tell all them women that Julia Roberts has been on dialysis."

Spencer remembered that. It had happened two weeks ago, when George noticed some nasty cuts on Dutch's arm. He had fallen off the bed and sliced himself on the corner of the bed stand. Almost on cue, he and Dutch started talking about nails being driven up his arm, the famous scene where the characters make light of a serious condition.

Afterward, they'd started talking about the movie, quoting their favorite lines. They had been simply sharing a movie they loved, nothing more.

"We just both happen to like the movie," Spencer said. "Yeah, there's...."

"Nothing more to it," Dutch said, completing his thought.

George laughed. "Whatever you boys say." He completely let go of Dutch and stepped back. "You're on your own now, Dutch. No wheelchair. No nothing from me. You gotta walk your lazy ass to Spencer."

Spencer watched the strain in Dutch's eyes. His legs lifted and fell in short, somewhat steady movements. His hands shuffled forward on the parallel bars as he gripped them, white-knuckle tight, to keep him upright and moving forward.

As Dutch approached, he thought about George's words. He and Dutch had become friends. Certainly that was all there was to their relationship. There couldn't be anything more, could there?

Like I told you before, his father's voice said, drifting upward once again. *What you don't see will knock you on your ass.*

His father's statement startled him. Was there more to his feelings for Dutch? Did they go beyond merely friendship? Was there substance to Justin's allegations?

Do you almost sleep with all *your friends?* his father asked.

Of course not, he replied. *That was a mistake. A once- in-a-lifetime lapse in judgment.*

Once in a lifetime, huh? his father snorted. *Then explain to yourself* why *you constantly pursued this man after the interview? You knew you were attracted to him from the start, but instead of going in the other direction, you went for it. You went for* him *despite the time you and Justin were investing in rebuilding a relationship you claimed to cherish. You sent numerous lunch invitations, just trying to get him alone. And when you finally did, when you were finally going to get him to fuck you, you backed out, supposedly because of Justin.*

There's no supposedly *about it. I was being faithful*, Spencer refuted. *To my partner.*

Physically, yes, his father agreed. *Emotionally, no. Just like Justin said, not every spouse becomes friends with their husband's mistress. Your mother never chummed up with any of mine. But you did. Despite what you knew.*

This is insane! I love Justin. Hell, even Dutch still loves Justin.

You think? his father asked. *If you two love Justin so much, why have the two of* you *been spending all these months together, getting to know each other?*

Spencer had no answer.

I told you your plan was a mistake. I told you not to do this. You've created an even bigger mess than you had before. All the armor in the world won't protect you from yourself.

The last person Spencer needed protection from was from himself. His self-preservation safeguarded him from many of life's problems *before* Justin. He was good at keeping himself safe.

Besides, there was nothing more to his relationship with Dutch. True, they had a special connection, a bond he inexplicably felt, but that connection was based on friendship and mutual affinity.

He wouldn't deny his attraction to Dutch. He was an extremely attractive man. But his heart belonged to Justin. It had *always* belonged to Justin. Dutch posed no true threat to their union, no matter what his friends, his father, or even Justin thought.

He knew his own mind and his own heart better than anyone else, and he resented anyone thinking their perceptions were more accurate than his own.

Now you sound like Justin, his father's voice accused before going quiet.

"Fuck," Dutch cursed. "I can't do this!"

Though confused by his father's statement, Spencer put aside his internal monologue and focused on Dutch, who needed his help now more than ever. "You can do it," he told Dutch. "I have faith in you."

As he stared into Dutch's eyes, the bond that had previously existed between them grew taut and strengthened. A renewed determination descended quickly upon Dutch, almost as if someone turned on an internal switch.

Dutch inched forward, drawing ever closer to him, the unseen tether pulling Dutch to him as if a force greater than the two of them were at work. After a few steps, sweat once again poured down Dutch's body, and his muscles strained against the bars. But Spencer could see unflagging resolve inside Dutch. A new spark, never ignited before this moment, grew and consumed the entirety of his body, making him stronger than he ever was before.

To Spencer's surprise, Dutch released the bars and stood straight, on his own and without support. George cried out and rushed to Dutch's side, fearful that Dutch would fall and injure himself.

Spencer didn't move. His faith in Dutch was complete. Dutch was going to do this. He was going to walk.

With that faith, something unexpected happened. George's cheers and the encouraging words from surrounding patients and therapists disappeared. Only the two of them remained in the room. The rest of the world simply ceased to be.

Spencer felt strange. Charged with electricity, his body turned into a living lightning rod that had just been struck three times in rapid succession. He was caught, not in the middle of a natural storm, but within the path of an emotional hurricane that bore down upon him.

The approaching storm front didn't frighten him. No pressing need to scramble for safety elicited his feet to turn and run in the opposite direction. Instead, he stood his ground. What headed his way intended him no harm. In fact, in its center, in the eye of the hurricane, peace and serenity waited.

As Hurricane Dutch drew ever closer, Spencer was incapable of movement, frozen in place, not out of fear but in anxious anticipation of what would come next. He hadn't felt this way in years, not since the first time he saw Justin at The Bonham.

Hauntingly familiar, the sensation brought back emotions and memories he hadn't recalled with such clarity for far too long. The churning waters of the hurricane dredged up from the murky recesses of his memory the love and security that Justin had once buoyed within the sea of his heart. Those feelings, unfettered by pain and betrayal, once again drifted freely across the watery expanse. The icy freeze of the Arctic that had held dominion over his emotions in recent months gave way to the warmer, more tropical waters of the Caribbean.

Within those waters, Dutch took one small step and then another. His feet and his body pointed toward Spencer, as if there were no other direction for him to go. His path, like a storm, had been charted. The air currents and the jet stream pushed him toward landfall, toward Spencer, standing on the other side, waiting to be overcome by the tempest that madly swirled around the two of them.

From Dutch's eyes, Spencer knew Dutch didn't fear the storm he carried toward him either. No shadows troubled the crystal blue waters of his eyes. They stared straight at him, focused and clear. Though the winds of the storm howled and bellowed, the tranquility to be found within its heart sang sweetly to the both of them.

Dutch now stood before him, resting on legs that were no longer shaky and no longer wobbled. Sweat dripped in vast quantities down his face and chest, matting his shirt to his skin. Still, a victorious smile rested on his lips like a beacon of light amidst the storm that continued to rage, that even now held them in its thrall.

Buffeted on winds far stronger than the two of them, Spencer crossed the distance still separating him from Dutch. Dutch's right hand greeted his cheek and hooked his chin, turning his head slightly to the right.

They were now in the center of the storm, at the heart of the phenomenon that started at Dutch's interview and then continued to grow over the course of their friendship. Everything they had shared, every experience and every event, was simply a precursor to this one event in their lives.

The eventual colliding of the storm upon the land.

In a moment that lasted a lifetime, their lips met, and the waves of Dutch's storm engulfed the calm harbor where Spencer had previously resided and brought forth a rainstorm as refreshing as it was renewing to their troubled hearts and souls. As Dutch's tongue rolled inside his mouth and as he breathed life into the storm, their bodies and their souls crashed together at last.

And while they kissed and held onto each other, the winds of the storm abated. The howling roar dulled to a serene breeze. When the winds died down completely, cheers and applause exploded within the room as the storm dissipated and returned them to the world they'd briefly left behind.

They looked around as George applauded, congratulating Dutch on his progress. Tears flowed down the faces of several nurses and patients who were not only moved by Dutch finally being able to walk again but by the tender affection they'd just witnessed between the two of them.

Spencer stood invigorated in the refreshing breeze, but in the back of his mind, he saw Justin, set adrift on the opposite side of the harbor from where he and Dutch now stood, a victim of their storm.

What he and Dutch had just done defied explanation and proved to him that everyone else but him was right.

A few moments before, he'd longed to reconnect with Justin. He'd wanted to explain his actions, to hopefully get Justin to understand the reasoning behind his covert manipulations and his continued relationship with Dutch. Those words would be meaningless now.

Now he was uncertain about everything. The force that compelled him toward Justin a decade ago had just returned. But instead of pulling him to Justin, it brought him to Dutch.

CHAPTER 44

2010

DUTCH hoped preparing dinner might allow his mind to find the answers to the questions that invaded his thoughts, but as he added the tablespoon of salt and half a teaspoon of oregano to the breadcrumbs he'd mixed previously, all he could focus on was kissing Spencer at the rehabilitation clinic earlier in the week.

As he mercilessly beat an egg in his Pyrex bowl, he replayed the event over and over in his mind. His body had been exhausted from George pushing him that day, and he'd lacked any strength to continue the exercises. Despite his tired and aching muscles, despite the complete fatigue that weighed him down like a bag of stones, he released the bars and walked. His steps were slow and measured, but he knew he could do it, as if Spencer's faith and encouragement somehow flipped on a switch in his brain that healed the remaining damage to his spinal cord.

Their celebratory kiss afterward had blown his mind more than his ability to walk again. He'd never planned on kissing Spencer, but when he finally reached him, the kiss seemed preordained, as if there could be no other conclusion to such a phenomenon as the return of his mobility.

The kiss itself was a force all its own, strikingly similar to his first kiss with Justin on the Riverwalk as the passing mariachi music heralded the occasion. Like his kiss with Justin, it held a promise of more to come. It wasn't merely a kiss of celebration. It marked the beginning of something neither of them could identify.

When he and Spencer left the clinic, they didn't discuss the kiss, not because they were embarrassed, but because words failed to express their feelings. In fact, they were silent for much of the ride back to Dutch's house. They only spoke after Dutch asked Spencer to come for dinner tonight, to thank him for his help.

Spencer agreed to the invitation quickly, probably more out of his need to leave and contemplate what occurred than actual excitement about dining together.

When they agreed to Friday night for dinner, they planned it without realizing the day's significance. It was New Year's Eve, Justin's favorite holiday and a special night for Justin and Spencer's relationship.

But Justin wasn't here. And no one knew where he was. Since learning of the lies he and Spencer kept, he had taken off for parts unknown and hadn't been seen or heard from since.

Dutch had suspected something like this might happen. Justin wasn't the type of man who appreciated secrets, although he was good at keeping his own. Even though Justin had a selfish streak a mile wide, Dutch understood Justin's anger.

The lies he and Spencer hid were monumental. They covered up their past and present relationship, not only out of fear for how Justin might react but because *they* truly didn't understand the depths of their relationship either.

But now that he had time to think about it, he saw everything clearly, as if the repaired damage to his spine had somehow removed the blinders from his vision.

Somewhere along his deluded path of revenge against Spencer, he had fallen in love with him.

The evidence was so obvious he was amazed that he hadn't seen it before. Why else would he have continued a relationship with the man Justin had left him for? He'd abandoned his quest for revenge because he didn't want to hurt Spencer. What else but love would have prompted that? He had been too caught up in his pain to realize that he ached because his heart wanted two men he couldn't have. That was why he fell to alcohol and sex. He was lost without them in his life, and he now realized that he had to find some way to forge a life with *both* of them in it.

How could he live without Justin, the man he was inexplicably drawn to on the banks of the Riverwalk? How could he live without Spencer, the man he magically walked to on the other end of the parallel bars?

Those rare moments in a person's life *meant* something. They shouldn't be overlooked because they were unusual. A relationship between three men was uncommon but not unheard of. Perhaps there was a way the three of them could live together.

It was a subject he wanted to bring up to Spencer tonight, and the origin of all the questions that rattled within his head. He was clueless how to broach such a bizarre topic. He couldn't just casually mention it after asking Spencer if he wanted another glass of wine.

Instead, he hoped conversation would somehow turn to the subject. Stranger things had happened, after all. The universe had brought them all together, so he felt confident the fates wouldn't let him down now.

SPENCER was tired of being tossed about by the whims of fate; the universe would no longer knock him around like some cosmic Hacky Sack. It was time for him to take charge of his life again, to settle matters with Dutch and then find Justin and make things better.

It was past time for him to quit sitting on the sidelines of his life as if he were a spectator instead of a participant. Instead of taking action, of telling Justin or Dutch what he felt or what he wanted, he'd sat quietly by as people acted on the stage he had set instead of directing the actions as he should have been the entire time.

He never should have waited for Justin to choose him. It was idiotic to push away the man he wanted, no matter how hurt he was. If he loved Justin as much as he claimed he did, he should have been fighting tooth and nail for him all along.

Beyond a shadow of a doubt, he knew that the bond he and Justin had forged still existed. He felt it in every corner of his soul. It was how he knew Justin was okay even though no one had heard from him in far too long. Justin was staying away by choice, not because he was wounded. Or worse. He simply needed time to think, to assess, and, hopefully, to recover from the lies he and Dutch had squirreled away. When his pain eased enough for him to get past that, Justin would return to him.

In that, he had absolute faith.

Oh God, his father said. *I'm gonna fucking barf!*

If you don't like it, then leave, Spencer replied. *I won't stop you.*

You're pretty stupid for someone with as much schooling as you've had! Is that how you think this works? That I can just leave? I'm not really your father, you know?

I don't have time for this, Spencer replied. *I'm already late as it is.*

I know, his father commented with a chuckle. *Late for a date with Dutch.*

Spencer turned on the radio in his car, hoping the racket would drown out, if not drive away completely, his father's irritating discourse.

Katy Perry's song "Firework" blared from the speakers. Hearing the melody made him miss Justin even more, especially since the pop hit was the ringtone Justin had assigned to his phone for Spencer.

Talk about a kick in the pants, his father's voice screamed in his ear, refusing to be covered up by Katy's contralto voice. *Justin's song for* you *plays while you drive to Dutch's house for a dinner date. On the very same night commemorating your eleventh year of meeting Justin.*

Spencer turned off the radio quickly. While he hated to admit it, his father was right. Even though he had things to settle with Dutch, he shouldn't be spending the evening, *this* evening with Dutch. New Year's Eve was his and Justin's special night. The only person he should be spending tonight with was Justin.

But he had no other choice.

He had to go through with the dinner. He and Dutch needed to work through what happened at rehab. They needed to sort through their emotions and come to some understanding of what their relationship actually was. Those conversations had to occur *before* Justin returned.

Once he knew where he and Dutch stood with each other, he would be better prepared to mend his relationship with Justin.

Right now, that was priority number one, whether the dinner fell on an important anniversary for him and Justin or not. This evening with Dutch had to happen. For all their sakes.

After all, Justin had been gone for over a month. What was the likelihood that Justin would return to him *tonight*?

AS HE drove down I-35, Justin knew tonight was the night. He had been gone too long already. His mother and his family had no doubt worked themselves into a state of panic for which they might never forgive him.

He'd hated being out of contact with them for this long. Too many times, he'd picked up the phone to call them and let them know he was okay, but he stopped himself. He simply hadn't been ready yet. There were too many problems he had to work through before he could reestablish contact with any of them.

If he called before he was ready, his family's pleas for him to return home would have weakened his resolve. He would have returned to them solely to make them feel better, which would have done nothing for *his* state of mind.

The only option he had to guarantee a return to some semblance of sanity was to remain disconnected. In order to center himself, to calm the raging waters of pain and turmoil that stirred within, he had to keep his distance and find the elusive answers that had constantly evaded him the past few months.

So he stayed with Pat and Heather at their house in New Braunfels, and like the good friends they are, they kept his whereabouts a secret from Spencer and his family, despite the never-ending inquiries everyone made about him.

Heather hated lying to everyone, especially his mother. Elena's tears almost caused her to break her promise on more than one occasion. Every time she hung up the phone after speaking to his mother, Heather told Justin how much she hated him for doing this to her and to everyone who loved him.

Pat came to his defense. He told Heather that Justin needed space. It was a "man thing" that was difficult for women to understand. Naturally, Heather told him that was bullshit, but she kept to her word.

Justin had never loved them both more than he had in the past few weeks.

They let him recuperate in their spare bedroom, where he stayed the majority of the time. Rarely did he come out to join them to watch television or even eat a meal. Only after they were in bed would he venture into the rest of the house or walk around outside. He had too much to think about, too much to try to put back together, and he couldn't afford to be distracted by anything or anyone.

His heart lay in so many pieces that it was an arduous task to sift through the mess and find the parts to once again make it whole.

This morning, on New Year's Eve, no less, he believed he'd finally accomplished such an impossible feat.

He loved Spencer with all his heart, and he loved Dutch just as much, if that was at all possible. While Spencer and Dutch had lied to him, while they had kept their past and present relationship a secret, it was no different from the secrets he'd kept from them or the awful way he treated them both.

His pride had simply gotten the better of him when he learned the truth. Not only was that wrong, but it was entirely selfish, a trait he'd had trouble combating for most of his life.

Now, though, it was time to work past the pain, past the selfishness, and focus on what could actually be when they worked in concert instead of crossed swords in conflict.

If Dutch and Spencer had somehow forged such a strong bond on their own, how could that bond be wrong, especially when he felt just as strongly connected to them both? Maybe there was a way for the three of them to fashion a connection even stronger than the ones that currently existed.

It was that realization that reached inside his soul and tugged him back home. Whenever such an event occurred, like when he first met Spencer or first kissed Dutch, he released all inhibitions and gave himself over entirely to the feeling.

He had always let the magic be his guiding light, and it had never steered him wrong before. Today, he hoped for no less than the miracles it had previously brought to his existence.

CHAPTER 45

2010/2011

AS IF by some miracle, Dutch and Spencer made it through the entire meal of chicken scaloppini with al dente angel hair pasta drizzled in a lemon butter sauce, steamed broccoli, freshly made bread, and a tossed Caesar salad without once delving into serious conversation.

Dutch had some serious topics to bring up with Spencer, and from the determined look in Spencer's eyes when he arrived, significant thoughts weighed heavily on his mind as well.

Instead of diving headfirst into such weighty discussion, they engaged in small talk about nothing in particular throughout dinner, which eased any lingering anxiety. Dutch shared his search for full-time employment and his continued improvement at rehabilitation to further strengthen his lower extremities. They chatted about Spencer's progress on several committees on campus and his possible chance at being named department chair once his dear friend, Dr. Peggy Cutting, retired.

"Would you like some more wine?" Dutch asked, lifting the bottle of Sangiovese in Spencer's direction. When he first offered Spencer a glass of the 2003 Antinori Santa Cristina, Spencer had refused, not wishing to upset Dutch's progress along the twelve-step path. He assured Spencer he would be fine.

Ever since he woke up from the coma half paralyzed, his desire to drink had never once returned. Although he knew substance addiction was a monkey that never truly jumped off your back, he now felt strong enough to resist the temptation.

He was even strong enough to stand on his own two feet. Again. That was all the motivation he needed to never take a drink again.

"I'd love some," Spencer responded. He held out his glass while Dutch poured another generous portion. "This wine is excellent, and the color is so vibrant." He once again stuck his nose in the glass and inhaled deeply. "Very fruity too!"

Dutch laughed. "Just like you."

Spencer's eyebrows knitted in pretend anger. If he were really angry, the fury line, as Dutch called it, would crease down from between Spencer's eyebrows almost to his nose. Over the past few months, he had become an expert on most things Spencer. No fury line meant no anger. "How dare you make such an accusation?" Spencer replied in mock resentment. "I'm not a fruit. I'm gay. There *is* a difference, you know?"

"Okay, Dr. Harrison, esteemed professor, former colleague, and future department chair, just *what* is the difference?"

Spencer harrumphed, still pretending to be upset, and rose from the table. He placed his left hand behind his back while the right hand gently cupped the bowl of the wine glass. He then proceeded to lecture like a professor. "A fruit, Mr. Keller, is a derogatory and inflammatory term used to express derision and prejudice at someone of the homosexual persuasion. The term itself connotes a man who falls far short of the masculine stereotype of the hairy oversized brute and therefore someone to be shunned and ostracized."

"Hey!" Dutch exclaimed. "Are you calling me a hairy oversized brute?"

"Please do *not* interrupt, Mr. Keller," Spencer playfully chided as he strolled through the dining room as if it were a classroom. "The term 'gay' no longer carries such negative stereotypes as it once did. In today's society, gay simply means someone who is attracted to others of the same gender. The word *gay* doesn't imply someone is less of a man for sleeping with other men. It doesn't indicate that a person is somehow inferior to another based on something as slight as sexual attraction."

He paused at Dutch's right. His left hand lingered on Dutch's shoulder for a moment before he quickly withdrew it. "I may not be a hairy brute like *some* people," he said as he resumed pacing, "and I may enjoy having sex with men. But I'm *not* nor will I ever be a *fruit*."

"I don't know," Dutch said, apparently unconvinced. "The way you're talking right now sounds pretty fruity to me."

Spencer gasped in pretend horror, and Dutch laughed. Spencer tried to carry on the charade, but the laughter proved infectious and made any continued attempts at being serious ineffectual. Before they knew it, they were both laughing hysterically with tears streaming down their faces.

Out of breath, Spencer was leaning against the wall opposite Dutch when something miraculous happened. The green sparkle in his eyes that Dutch hadn't seen for months suddenly returned. It started with a slight flicker of light, like when a star suddenly blinks in and out of existence in the night sky. At first, Dutch wondered if it had really happened or if it was a result of the dining room lights reflecting off his corneas.

When the small flash quickly grew to a radiant burst of joy, Dutch saw the original Spencer, the one who had existed prior to the lies and betrayals, return in full force. He stood there, his green eyes as bright as jade, their former pastel hue gone, and when Dutch looked into those deep green eyes, the force that had pulled him out of his wheelchair and onto his own two feet once again tugged at him, drawing him up from his seat and toward Spencer.

As he crossed the room, forgetting all about the conversation he planned on having, Spencer stood straight, no fear in his eyes, no hint of regret hiding in the rich pools of pure green. He simply waited for the return of the inevitable, the moment when Dutch's lips would once again meet his.

This time, though, a kiss wouldn't be enough.

JUSTIN couldn't believe Spencer wasn't home; he'd had enough of being apart, and it was time to bring that to an end. Yes, they had serious conversations ahead of them and a lot of things to set right, but he knew they could overcome anything as long as they were together.

Even though "together" now included Dutch in its definition, he somehow felt secure that the idea would be welcome. And the more he examined the prospect, the more familiar it became and the more it felt right.

Dutch was brought into their lives for a reason. He was sent to add something special to what he and Spencer created. For too long, Dutch had been a perceived threat when they should have been considering what he brought to their lives instead of what he subtracted from their relationship.

But before he could work on fixing anything, he had to find Spencer first. Veering onto I-35 once again, he ran down the possible places Spencer might be spending New Year's Eve.

Naturally, Tyler and the rest of their shared friends came to mind first, but when he thought carefully about Spencer's whereabouts, the answer arrived like a fortune teller's premonition: he was with Dutch.

Justin pointed his car toward Dutch's house, and as mile after mile brought him ever closer, he realized what a good sign this was.

New Year's Eve was his and Spencer's special day. The magic that drew them together first had manifested itself at midnight, which was only a few minutes away, and it was entirely possible that the same power that first joined him and Spencer might reform tonight and help forge the three of them into something two people alone could never create.

As he approached Dutch's house, he saw Spencer's car sitting in the driveway. A broad smile stretched across his face. The fact that he knew Spencer was with Dutch revealed the strength of the bond that still connected them to each other. If the magic that brought them together had truly fizzled, he never would have wound up here.

Justin parked his car in front of Dutch's house and exited the vehicle. As he proceeded up the sidewalk toward the house, the unmistakable sounds of laughter resounded from within. Dutch's hearty chuckle accompanied Spencer's breathless giggles in a symphony of merriment.

They were evidently having a good time. For Justin, this meant his plan to merge their three lives into one definitely had potential. If Spencer and Dutch could overcome their differences, *anything* was truly possible.

Instead of walking to the front door, he cut a path across the front yard toward the window to the left of the entrance. He just had to see for himself what they were doing. He wanted to experience the purity of the scene before he broke it with his unannounced presence. After all anything that could bring about such amusement was worth admiring for a moment or two.

When he finally drew close enough to peer through the dining room window, he saw Spencer pacing about, pretending to be mad. Spencer's overexaggerated facial expressions made him smile. He loved it when Spencer creased his brow in feigned anger, sometimes with hands on his hips and a curl to his lip. When Spencer couldn't keep up the pretend pissiness, he and Dutch broke into laughter that Justin hadn't seen from the two of them in far too many months.

Even Dutch looked like a new man. The darkness that had hovered around him no longer existed. His strong face looked radiant, and he beamed when he smiled. Obviously, since his departure, Dutch had rediscovered himself, finally wrenching himself free from the pain that pulled him downward like quicksand.

Exhausted from the endless laughter, Spencer propped himself up against the wall, and when he looked at Dutch, his eyes changed. When Spencer had learned of his affair with Dutch, Spencer's emerald-colored eyes had turned pastel green. That lifeless color no longer reflected in his eyes. Their green brilliance sparkled like a thousand gems. The light he had snuffed out once again reignited.

At first, Justin was elated. He wanted to charge into the dining room, sweep Spencer off his feet like in some bad romance movie, but his elation quickly subsided. The light in Spencer's eyes had returned because of Dutch. Not because of him.

He felt confused, as if he had just awoken from a long nap, when the mind was still fuzzy and vision remained blurred.

Dutch then rose from the table, and Justin almost fell backward in surprise. He hadn't even noticed Dutch wasn't sitting in his wheelchair. Sometime during his stay in New Braunfels, Dutch's spinal injury had healed, and now Justin watched as Dutch crossed the room toward Spencer.

His mind pleaded with him to turn away, but he stood transfixed as he watched in horror as the two men who held dominion over his heart languished in each other's arms and kissed so passionately and so beautifully that it felt as if he was an intruder.

Around him, the neighborhood went crazy. People screamed, "Happy New Year!" to friends across the street. Fireworks were launched into the air to commemorate 2011. The explosions and the cheers became ever more distant when Justin realized that New Year's Eve wasn't going to bring the three of them together. In fact, New Year's no longer belonged to him and Spencer.

It now belonged to them.

By the time Spencer and Dutch started to remove their clothes, Justin's vision turned fluid. The tears he'd kept bottled within since he first received Heidi's phone call came flooding out of his body.

In a watery torrent he'd never experienced before in his life, his soul poured out endless waves of agony when he realized that a future as a trio was no longer possible. Spencer and Dutch had found something new, together. And without him. Once he was out of the picture, no, once he had removed himself from the picture, they were able to find the happiness that had evaded them both while they were with him.

In response, his spirit writhed in unimaginable anguish, twisting and contorting inside him like a whirlpool intent on turning him inside out. The love that had once again buoyed in his heart capsized and slipped beneath the tortured waters of his soul, and as it sank to the shadowy depths below, his lungs searched for breath in between his endless sobs.

He sank to the ground, his knees submerging beneath the wet grass just outside the window. The cold, damp mud, a result of a recent winter downpour, stung his flesh, but the frigid hand that now clenched onto his heart and his soul hurt him the most.

In order to survive the pain, he latched onto the chilly grasp and allowed it to consume him. The anesthetizing sensation crept slowly through his body, inside and out, until his soul was as cold as the winter air around him. In that moment, he stopped feeling anything at all.

His tears ceased flowing, for no heart remained to mourn. It had died just as suddenly as it had been reborn. As he watched Spencer and Dutch naked in each other's arms, a chilly indifference not only completely embraced him but plumed outward from his lungs.

He walked back to his car in unhurried footsteps. There was no need to rush. He thankfully no longer felt pain. When he started his car and peeled down the street, Justin accepted that he would never care about anything again.

SPENCER once again stood naked in Dutch's arms. His body trembled to life as Dutch's rough hands traveled up and down his bare flesh, inciting not only goose bumps but also sparking flames of desire that raged across his flesh.

The last time they were both in this position, they were in Dutch's office, about to take their friendship to a level Spencer wanted to pursue but couldn't out of fear of hurting Justin and their relationship. The consequences at that time were so dangerous, so insurmountable that he was able to gather his wits and stop them before they went too far.

Tonight, no such apprehension existed, which took his usually reserved nature by surprise. Spencer felt only reborn and safe, two emotions he hadn't experienced in far too long. He welcomed the sensations Dutch jumpstarted as they traveled throughout his body, filling him with the warmth of the blistering Texas summer sun.

"You're so beautiful," Dutch whispered softly in his ear as he stroked Spencer's cock with his right hand and he pressed their bodies together with his left. In response, Spencer greedily explored Dutch's open mouth, which tasted sweet and syrupy from the iced tea during dinner. He took Dutch's bottom lip between his teeth and gently bit down on it, causing Dutch to growl and pin him against the dining room wall.

Dutch grabbed his arms and held them above his head, pushing him against the wall. Once Spencer was restrained, Dutch licked a scorching trail down his neck to his nipples, which he then proceeded to bite. Spencer whined and squirmed against Dutch's insistent nibbles, and his body begged for Dutch to do more.

"Oh God, yes," Spencer whimpered while every nerve ending on his flesh crackled to life. Outside, fireworks popped in the distance and neighbors cheered in the street.

It was now officially 2011, and for the briefest of moments, he thought of Justin, of how this night had always been their special night. It was the night the universe brought them together. But as he looked down at Dutch, thoughts of Justin flew from his mind as quickly as they entered.

All he wanted at this moment was the man he'd secretly desired for far too long.

Almost on cue, Dutch looked up, and his eyes reflected the same hunger Spencer felt completely consuming him. Spencer smiled broadly in silent agreement to their matching lusts and then Dutch turned Spencer around, trapping him against the cold plaster wall and his hot, hard body.

He kissed and gnawed at Spencer's neck while his furry chest scratched against his back. Spencer cocked his head to the right, desperately trying to capture as many kisses from Dutch as he could. When their lips connected again, Dutch gripped onto Spencer's hips and teased his ass with the head of his cock, rubbing the leaking precum along the length of his crack.

They both panted heavily as Spencer bucked backward, trying to force Dutch's hardness inside him, but before he had a chance to will his body open enough to take the engorged member inside, Dutch swept him off his feet and carried him to the dining room table.

"I'm finally going to have you," Dutch told him as he cradled Spencer in his strong arms. "There's no way I can stop now."

"Good," Spencer replied as Dutch gently placed him down on the wooden top. "I don't want you to stop."

A seductive grin stretched lazily across Dutch's face in response. Then he sank to his knees and began eating at the very center of Spencer's being. Spencer spread his legs wide for Dutch, wanting to give him access to the deepest parts of his body.

Dutch panted heavily against his back door while his tongue alternated between circling the outer rim of his hole and probing at the opening until the tip of his tongue slipped inside. Spencer gasped for air as Dutch's urging, wet tongue undulated deeper and deeper inside him.

From between his legs, Dutch moaned as he continued his feverish dance around Spencer's trembling opening. Spencer's chute finally gave away to Dutch's insistent nudges, opening more and more with each slippery prodding. Excess spit slid down his hole and ran down his taint until it dripped onto the floor below.

After what seemed like an eternity of agonizing pleasure, Dutch stood up between his legs. "I think I've opened you up enough," he said while revealing his cock, which was already sheathed in a condom no doubt retrieved from Dutch's discarded pants.

"Yes," Spencer panted. "Give it to me. Give me all you got."

"Oh, you'll get it all," Dutch answered. He leaned over Spencer's body and stroked his face gently before once again engulfing his mouth with his own. The tangy taste of Spencer's own body was still ripe on Dutch's tongue. The musky kiss further enflamed his passion.

Dutch wrapped his left hand around his waist while his right hand aimed his engorged cock toward its prize, ready to claim all it had to offer. As Dutch cleared a path inside his body, Spencer cried out. He clutched Dutch's back, relaxing his muscles to accommodate Dutch's size. Pain seized his body, but after a few tense moments, when he was finally able to relax, the pain turned into pleasure, and he returned Dutch's fiery kisses with his own.

Their lips never lost contact as Dutch began to slowly piston himself in and out of his body. Spencer's eyes rolled in the back of his head as he succumbed to the force of Dutch's hard cock pushing inside him. Clawing at Dutch's shoulders and back, he bucked upward, trying to force more and more of Dutch's body inside. He needed more of Dutch within him if he was to be truly satisfied.

As Dutch drove harder and faster inside him, a car peeled away outside. The momentary distraction couldn't deter the passion swelling inside him. He held Dutch close, burying his face between Dutch's quivering pecs and inhaling the natural body odor that Dutch never masked with deodorant or cologne. The heady scent spurred him on to match Dutch's fevered movements.

Dutch increased the speed of his pounding thrusts, massaging his internal pleasure button dangerously close to the point of no return. Spencer's rigid cock throbbed violently between them, threatening to spill his seed onto his stomach. When Dutch began to moan and growl like an animal, indicating how close he was to his own orgasm, Spencer closed his eyes and let his body go.

He wanted them both to climax at the same time.

Dutch's thrusts became frenzied and primal. His face dripped with sweat, splattering onto Spencer's chest and his face. Spencer, wild for a drink, licked the salty drops from his chin and from Dutch's jaw. Dutch responded by kissing then biting Spencer's lips. Spencer moaned and gyrated back against him, bearing down around Dutch's hardness to increase the friction, and felt the beginning of his own impending release.

"I'm gonna fucking shoot!" Dutch cried out while gripping Spencer's shoulders, which were slick with sweat, and pulled him closer. Dutch was on the verge of climax and intent on propelling them both over the edge.

Holding Dutch even closer to his body, nuzzling his face into the crook of his neck, Spencer moaned, "Me too!"

Together, like animals locked in primal contact, their bodies exploded. Spencer felt Dutch's hardness pulsate within him, growing perhaps two inches wider in girth as he flooded the condom with his spunk. At the same time, Spencer's cock shuddered violently, ejecting his seed between them and cementing their bodies together.

Dutch collapsed on top of him, exhausted and spent. Spencer kissed his forehead and held him tight. As he basked in the warm light of their lovemaking, he felt his heart beating in rhythm with Dutch's, and for the first time in months, he felt truly joined to another human being.

CHAPTER 46

2011

NAKED and wrapped in each other's arms, as if they defied anyone to sever their union, Dutch looked into Spencer's bright green eyes and found that he couldn't turn away. They held some magical power over him, as if they possessed a missing piece to the puzzle of his soul, a piece he never knew he'd lost. Now that he'd found it, however, he reasoned he would never be able to part with it again.

Spencer had changed him from a lost soul set adrift in a sea of chaos and uncertainty and brought him direction and purpose. Like a homing beacon, Spencer became the candle in the window that ultimately led him home.

The sensation was surreal yet familiar. The last time he felt this way, it was Justin who was in his arms. But now, amidst the tangled mess they'd made of his sheets during their latest sexual frenzy, it was Spencer who now brought forth these powerful emotions.

Dutch pulled Spencer into a tight embrace, wanting, no *needing* to feel his delicate white flesh against his own. Spencer didn't resist. He completely gave himself over to Dutch's request, and when they snuggled even closer, unseen cogs within their souls clicked seamlessly together, further proving that being together was not only natural but destined to be.

Spencer's head rested against his chin, and he caught a scent of pomegranate shampoo mixed with the sweat and musk of their sexual encounter. It was an intoxicating blend that stirred not only further passion but stoked the fires of deep adoration that blazed brightly within him.

Holding Spencer so close, feeling every part of his body against his own, felt completely right, not some unmentionable sin or unspeakable violation that they'd both feared it might be.

"Is it wrong that this feels so right?" he finally asked, giving voice to the emotions that wafted up inside.

Spencer looked up from his place at his shoulder. Wide and filled with boundless hope, his eyes burned more brightly than any star of his childhood, than even Pegasus, his childhood protector. "I was just about to ask you the same thing," Spencer replied. His lips then brushed against Dutch's chin, and like a live wire, sent sparks of desire through him as Spencer traveled up to his cheek and then his mouth. When they kissed once again, electrical currents traveled between them.

"Why did we wait this long?"

The fire in Spencer's eyes dimmed for the briefest of moments, and Dutch noted the change. He knew instinctively the diffusion of joy wasn't caused by regret or any other emotion that negated what they meant to each other. Dutch understood the look for what it was.

Spencer was thinking of Justin. It was hard not to. Dutch's love for Spencer couldn't negate the love he felt for Justin. Spencer most likely felt the same way.

"Because of Justin," Dutch replied, answering his own question.

"Yeah," Spencer agreed, pulling Dutch even closer to him, refusing to let the mention of Justin's name drive them apart. "I couldn't hurt him that time in your office. I wasn't ready. *You* weren't ready."

"Are we ready now?"

Spencer sighed deeply. For a few moments, only silence followed. Dutch didn't interpret the pause as a bad omen. He knew Spencer well enough to understand that silence only meant thought. Nothing more.

"I don't think I'll ever be ready to hurt Justin."

"Me either," he replied. "I love him, Spencer. I still do."

Spencer nodded. "I know. I do too."

"But I love you too," he said. He shifted Spencer in his arms, so they were looking into each other's eyes, so they could read the emotions that lay on the surface. There was nothing to hide. There was *nowhere* to hide the truth as their souls lay as bare between them as their exposed flesh. All they could do was accept the truth for what it was. "I *really* do love you," he repeated.

Spencer smiled and ran his lithe fingers through Dutch's short-cropped hair. "I know you do," he said. "And I love you too. I think I have for quite awhile now."

"Yeah," he said with a laugh. "Me too."

"So what do we do now?" Spencer asked. "Where do we go from here? This situation is *beyond* fucked up."

"It doesn't have to be," he replied. Although he'd feared Spencer's response to the idea of living as a trio before, he found no such hesitation with Spencer in his arms. He knew it was time, so he finally gave voice to his thoughts.

"What do you think?" he asked Spencer when he was done.

"I think you're crazy."

"Really?"

"Yes, really!" Spencer replied emphatically. "So," he began, drawing out the word as he did whenever he was on the edge of pissiness. "What's going to happen when you or Justin gets another wild hair up his ass and cheats? Are we then going to be, what? A quartet?" He sat up in bed and pushed away. The previous intimacy and connection vanished almost completely. "A relationship isn't a team sport, Dutch. You don't just keep recruiting new members."

Dutch was floored by Spencer's irritation. The three of them loved each other a great deal. Why did he refuse to see the solution to their problem? "I'm not implying that," he replied defensively. "I'm only pointing out that the three of us love each other. If we love each other that much, why not simply embrace that love? Together."

"You call that simple," Spencer replied, looking at Dutch as if he were stupid. "There's nothing simple about what you're proposing."

"Why not?"

"Are you serious? You can't really be seriously asking me that question?"

He stared into Spencer's eyes, which no longer blazed with passion. Anger now threatened to spark. "I am," he replied. Even though he knew his answer would fan the burning embers, he added, "I don't think you're seeing this logically."

Spencer snorted. "I'm the *only* one here who is. Your solution to live together in some homo commune is ridiculous. That's *not* how relationships work!"

"They can work that way," he stated. "I've known several trios. I agree that they're uncommon, but they're not impossible."

"They're not common because they're insulting." Spencer rose from the bed and proceeded to put his clothes back on. "They're insulting to the millions of other couples who are capable of fidelity, who *can* commit themselves to *only* one other person for the rest of their lives. And I'm not about to prove all those Christian fundamentalists out there right."

"That's what you're worried about? The religious crackpots?"

"Don't be ridiculous. You know what I'm talking about. I'm not going to be one of those stereotypical gay men who makes decisions solely on his dick getting hard."

"Is that all I am?" Dutch asked. "Someone who gets your dick hard? You just said you loved me. That you still love Justin. That certainly sounds like a trio to me already. I think you're having difficulty with this because it shatters your fantasy about what a relationship looks like. You don't have to be like everyone else, Spencer. *We* don't have to be like everyone else."

Spencer didn't respond. Instead, he finished putting on the rest of his clothes.

"I know you, Spencer. You're very resistant to change, to things that are unfamiliar to you. You avoided relationships out of fear of getting hurt. You told me that, remember? But Justin changed that. And look how happy he made you."

"Until he cheated," Spencer replied, zipping up his jeans. "With you."

"Are we really going there?" he asked. "When you're busy getting dressed after fucking around in my bed?"

"You're right," Spencer responded. "I'm not better than the two of you. I used to be. Until you dragged me into your insane world."

"Dragged you?"

"Yes, dragged me. I was perfectly happy with Justin. My life was coasting along just fine. Until *he* cheated. Until *you* set about seducing me. I wasn't confused about what I wanted. I wanted my life with Justin back, but apparently that's impossible. I see that now."

"Whoa!" Dutch replied, getting out of the bed. "When did you become the innocent victim here? *You* left Justin. Isn't that what got this whole thing started? Plus, *you* flirted with me when you were *supposedly* working things out with him *and* almost had sex with me in my office. And now, well, now *you've* just finished cumming at least three times." He crossed over to Spencer, still naked. "You need to take a good hard look at *yourself.*"

"And you need to back up," Spencer warned. "Don't think you can intimidate me." Spencer crossed the remaining distance between them, standing toe to toe with Dutch. "I'm not scared of you. Not. One. Bit."

"How the hell did we get here?" Dutch asked, backing away. He wasn't trying to intimidate Spencer. He simply wanted him to calm down, to see how irrational he was being. They both needed to calm down, quickly. "We just had a beautiful evening together."

"Well, that's over now," commented Spencer. "Thanks for ruining it."

"I still don't understand," he said. "I don't know what went wrong."

"What went wrong is that I realized what a fool I've been. This has *never* been about you and me or me and Justin. This has been about you and Justin the whole time."

"What are you talking about?"

"This is what you've both wanted the whole time, isn't it? A way to assuage your guilt. To clear your consciences. Get *me* to agree to a trio so that you two get to have your cake and eat it too. You both get each other while I get whatever scraps the two of you are willing to dole out to me. I deserve better than that."

"That's not it at all," Dutch said. "I would never do that to you. I love you. That's not how you treat someone you love."

"No," he said. "It's not. I realize that now more than ever."

"What does that mean?" he asked Spencer. He tried to pull Spencer into an embrace, but Spencer refused, crossing over to the bedroom door instead.

"Loving someone means you don't hurt them. What the three of us have been doing *isn't* love. It's some warped version of the real thing. Justin betrayed me. You betrayed me. We both betrayed Justin by lying to him and by fucking each other tonight. This isn't love, Dutch. It's three grown men acting like spoiled brats."

"You can't believe that," he argued. "Not after everything we've shared these past few months."

"I can and I do," Spencer replied. "I've been deluding myself. Thinking that these feelings, *whatever* they are, are real. But they can't be. I thought that Justin and I had something special. I thought you and I had something special. But when you brought up the idea of the three of us living together as a trio, I realized there's nothing special about a fuck frenzy."

"The three of us aren't a fuck frenzy," Dutch pointed out, perturbed that Spencer was reducing their relationships to something so crude. "I'm in love with you." Even though Spencer fought him, he wrapped his arms around him and held him close, refusing to let him view their shared love in any negative light. "This relationship the three of us have stopped being about any two of us a long time ago. And deep down inside you know that."

"Don't tell me what I know," Spencer argued while straining against his embrace.

"We fell in love with each other," he continued, ignoring Spencer's curses and struggles. "While it might be scary and while it might be nontraditional, it doesn't make it wrong. It doesn't make *us* wrong."

Spencer wiggled in his arms, trying to force his way free. Dutch wouldn't let him go. He was strong enough, both physically and emotionally, to keep Spencer from erecting those barriers that protected him. Even though Spencer didn't know that was what he was doing, Dutch had finally put it together.

Spencer's reaction stemmed from fear, of how vulnerable he would be in a relationship with two men. He was almost destroyed by just one man. Two men had the potential to obliterate him completely. For all his bravado, there lived within Spencer a scared little boy searching desperately for the love and security his family never gave him.

"You're safe," he told Spencer. "With the both of us. I promise you."

"You can't promise me that. No one can," Spencer replied. While his tone remained rigid, much of the fight left his body, almost as if he had given himself up to the hope that Dutch might be speaking the truth.

"I can," Dutch assured him. "And tomorrow, when we find Justin, he'll make the same promise."

Spencer squeezed him tightly. The fight was gone. His need to fortify himself had passed. While his trembling body still told Dutch he was afraid of the possibility, his green eyes now mirrored hope, not fear. "We need to find him. We need to make him come home."

"We will," he told Spencer. "In the morning, we'll turn this city upside down. We'll go to all your friends' houses and make them tell us the truth if they know it. Together, we will *make* it happen. We can make *anything* happen."

JUSTIN sped down I-35, swerving between cars that traveled much too slowly for his agitated state. He had neither the patience nor the time to deal with their leisurely speeds. He had to get out of San Antonio as quickly as possible. There was nothing left for him here anymore.

His future now existed somewhere out there in the darkness, beyond the reach of the arcing headlights of his car. The road he had believed to be paved before him, the one that included Spencer and Dutch, cracked and crumbled, turning into an endless stretch of gravelly country road that led to no place in particular and certainly no place special.

The lack of a clear path used to frighten him. He always needed a focus, a direction, to give him purpose, or he feared he might somehow drive off the road into the open air that waited to claim him just beyond the painted yellow lines.

That need for control had sprung to life the moment his father walked away from him for no reason. He'd felt abandoned on the side of the road, left to find his way in a world that never heard the pleas or the tears of a frightened young boy who only wanted someone to rescue him and bring him home.

That scared little boy no longer waited on the shoulder of life's road. He now drove on the asphalt, passing by car after car, putting as much distance as he could between him and the people who'd hurt him far worse than his father ever had.

Spencer and Dutch had cured him of his need for control. They'd reminded him that control was an illusion, that permanence was fleeting, and that eventually everyone rejoined the traffic of lost souls, searching for a new home once the previous life kicked all to the curb without warning.

That would never happen to him again. From now until the day he died, he would operate his life, like his car, as a single passenger. There would be neither need nor room for anyone else to occupy the second seat.

The carpool lane in his life was closed down permanently, and that suited him fine.

His days would forever be his own. Free from the ties of a relationship and the pain of heartbreak, he could sail through his remaining years on the open road without any baggage cluttering up the trunk of his existence.

Life would now be one endless, carefree road trip.

Unexpectedly, the Toyota Tundra to his right swerved into his lane. Justin steered his vehicle onto the far left side of the highway while at the same time pounding away on his horn. "Motherfucker!" he screamed at the driver. "Watch where the *fuck* you're going!"

In response, a hand suddenly appeared out of the driver's side window and flipped him off.

"Fuck that shit!" Justin yelled. He slammed his foot against the accelerator to match the now speeding truck. Once he drew parallel with the truck, he lowered the passenger side window and returned the hand gesture with his own. "Learn how to drive, cocksucker!" he bellowed as the two vehicles shot down the interstate.

The driver of the truck shouted something back at him, but the high speeds and whipping wind made it impossible to comprehend. Now angry beyond reason that someone could drive so recklessly, without any regard for the safety of others on the road, Justin yanked his wheel to the right to prove a point. He wanted the other driver to experience what it felt like to have someone cross into his lane of traffic.

The truck's horn blared in response to Justin's move, and the driver swerved right to avoid Justin, but in doing so, the driver overcorrected and lost control of his vehicle, smacking into the side rail.

Sparks flew around the Toyota as metal scraped against the side rail before the truck came to a complete stop.

Justin laughed and looked in the rearview mirror as the driver got out of his truck and ran after him, as if he had any hope of catching up to Justin as he sped away into the night.

When Justin returned his eyes to the road, he had just enough time to register that he had come to a bend in the highway. The road directly in front of him no longer existed as the interstate snaked left. All that waited in front of him was the emptiness of the night sky.

He slammed on the brakes, spinning the steering wheel to his left in an attempt to change his course, but his speed prevented such hasty correction. His car crashed through the guardrail and hung suspended for a few seconds in midair before plummeting to the ground below.

SPENCER chased Justin down a winding road; the rocky ground below his feet made it difficult for him to close the gap, to get any closer to Justin, who sprinted ahead of him and refused to stop despite his many pleas.

He had to reach Justin, who wasn't looking where he was going. He didn't seem to notice the sharp twists and turns of the path, or the fact that the road gave way to open air, which dropped down a very steep and dangerous hill.

One misstep or one inopportune stumble might send him off the path and into the darkness beyond, where Spencer couldn't reach him. No matter how hard he tried.

"Justin!" he screamed again. His voice was course and strained. He had been yelling at Justin for what seemed like hours, trying to get him to listen, to understand what happened between him and Dutch.

Still, Justin's mad dash never slowed. He tripped and teetered close to the cliff's edge, but then he found his footing and once again darted down the road, away from Spencer, who only wanted to keep him safe.

Spencer pumped his legs faster, pouring every last bit of energy he had into his limbs and forcing them to reach speeds never before achieved in his life. But his legs grew increasingly heavier until they seemed made of stone instead of flesh and bone.

His full-out run slowed to a trot and then to a jog before he finally collapsed onto the dusty ground, unable to move or get up.

"Justin!" he screamed. "Please stop!"

If he heard, Justin made no attempt to slow down. He ran wildly ahead, oblivious to the dangers around him until his feet carried him over the edge of the cliff and he dropped out of sight and into the darkness below.

"Justin!" Spencer cried out as he sat up in bed, drenched in sweat. His heart thudded in his chest, and fear reached inside his gut and violently pulled on his stomach.

"Justin, no!" Dutch shouted, sitting straight up and scrambling out of the bed they'd both crawled back into together. His eyes were wide in fear as he looked around the room, searching for Justin in the darkness of the night and wanting to pull him within his ever-protective embrace.

"He's hurt," Spencer announced.

"I know," replied Dutch. "Something's wrong."

Spencer's cell phone suddenly started blaring "Stop in the Name of Love" by Diana Ross and the Supremes, the ringtone he and Justin used for Justin's mother Elena. He eyed the phone suspiciously, not wanting to answer it and knowing deep within his breaking heart that something was seriously wrong. Diana Ross's crooning voice didn't fool him. Nothing but bad news awaited him on the other end of the phone.

Ignorant to the sense of dread, or perhaps choosing to ignore it, Dutch clambered naked over the bed to retrieve the phone. He answered it in one swipe while at the same time handing the phone over to Spencer.

Shaking his head, Spencer refused the phone. He didn't want to hear the news Elena wanted to share. If he didn't hear what she had to say, it wouldn't be real. Justin would still be okay. He wouldn't be hurt. Or worse.

No, it was better *not* to know. *Anything* was better than that.

"Spencer?" He heard Elena's voice come from the phone. She sounded awful, as if someone ripped her heart out of her chest and kicked it around like a soccer ball. "Spencer, are you there?"

He backed away from the phone, putting more distance between the phone, Dutch's outstretched hand, and himself, as if by increasing the gap he could further separate himself from the foreboding words waiting to spill from his mother-in-law's lips.

"Take it," whispered Dutch, trying to keep his presence with Spencer this late at night from Justin's mother. "We *need* to know."

Tentatively, Spencer reached for the phone. When he finally held it in his palm, the cool rubber casing sent icy chills shooting down his hand into his arm until they found his heart and mercilessly stabbed at it with careless abandon.

He took a deep breath and hit the speaker button. He couldn't handle hearing the news alone. Dutch needed to hear it too.

"I'm here, Elena," he finally replied.

At the sound of his voice, she broke into heart-wrenching sobs. The agony in those tears ripped his already punctured heart to shreds, causing him to almost fall over. Dutch luckily reached his side in time to steady him. When he wrapped his arms around Spencer, his body quakes slowly became still and calm.

"What's wrong?" he asked. "What's happened?"

"It's Justin," she wailed. "He's hurt so bad."

Spencer's knees buckled, but Dutch caught him. The world around him spun out of control. He was in danger of blacking out, of shutting down so he wouldn't have to deal with the truth, so he wouldn't have to learn what had happened to the man he still loved so desperately.

"Is he...?" he said, trying to suppress the rising panic straining his voice, but he couldn't complete the question. His hand once again shook so violently he almost dropped the phone, but Dutch's massive quivering hand reached out to steady him, and together, they were able to steady their shared tremors of dread.

"The doctors…," she began, fighting back the sobs that made it impossible for her to communicate. "Th-they say… oh, Spencer, I can't say it. Just come. *Please* come," she begged. "He's at Methodist Hospital."

Spencer nodded. He couldn't reply. His vocal chords refused to cooperate.

"Come quickly," she said before hanging up the phone.

No longer able to hold it, the phone tumbled from Spencer's grasp. It landed on its glass face and shattered. Tiny slivers of glass exploded outward, littering the floor with the pieces that had once made it whole.

CHAPTER 47

2011

STARING at Justin's broken body nearly sent Spencer over the edge.

The blue plastic tubes inserted down his throat forced air into his lungs. Yards of medical bandages wrapped around his head, his chest, and his right leg. Justin's left arm rested at a forty-five degree angle, enclosed in a cast from his palm to just below his elbow.

His right eye had swollen shut, his once beautiful caramel nose transformed into a purple mess, and dozens of lacerations cut across his previously immaculate cheeks and forehead.

At his bedside, medical instruments hissed like angry snakes. Others beeped like an alarm clock, faithfully marking the beat of each breath or pump of Justin's heart. The discordance threatened to drive Spencer insane and send him running from the room, from the nightmare that followed him out of his dreams and into his reality.

But he was done with running. Whatever time he had left with Justin would be spent at his side. Too much of this past year had been wasted already with bitterness and bile. It was time to begin anew, to focus on rebuilding not just Justin but everything else they had broken in the madness they both created.

Spencer reached out and stroked Justin's cheek. When he made contact with Justin's warm skin, tears poured down his cheeks and unstoppable sobs of agony and regret unleashed from Spencer's soul.

He felt awful for what he had done, for how he had contributed to Justin's accident. While he knew nothing of the details, he felt confident in his guilt, and his self-hate was not only warranted but just.

Let's put things in perspective, shall we? his father's voice asked, once again rising from the depths of his sub-conscious. *What you feel bad about is fucking Dutch while Justin almost died.*

You're right, Spencer admitted. He wiped the tears from his eyes. Crying would do him no good right now. Justin needed him to be strong, to be his anchor, so he could find his way back to the land of the living. *I do feel bad about that.*

What? his father asked in disbelief. *You're actually agreeing with me? You're not going to say I'm crazy? Or that I'm wrong? Or tell me to shut up?*

Spencer shook his head. *You're right. I've been denying too many things for far too long. Doing so has only brought me here. No, not just me. Us. All* three *of us.*

Well, hallelujah! I think we're finally making some motherfucking progress!

I think so, he admitted while holding Justin's left hand in his own. *You've been right about so many things. My feelings for Dutch. The source of my real anger for Justin. I've wanted things that I've been too afraid to admit, like a stupid little boy. But I'm not a boy. I'm a man. I may not have had the balls to say this before, but I do now. I want Justin and Dutch. I love them both.*

Fuck me! his father's voice interjected. It was his father's way of agreeing with someone, when they finally understood something he had been trying to explain to them for far longer than was necessary. *Maybe you're not so stupid after all. Maybe you* are *the son I helped raise.*

His father's voice grew quiet. Spencer knew he wasn't gone. He could feel his presence lurking in the background, wanting to say something but apprehensive about giving voice to it.

Maybe you don't need me anymore, his father finally muttered.

Maybe I don't, Spencer replied.

"You okay?" Dutch asked from behind him.

His voice startled Spencer. He had almost forgotten Dutch was in the room with him. They had come together, and they intended to both be here for Justin. After all, they *both* loved him, and they hoped even in his present condition that Justin would sense the love in their hearts and come back to them both.

Dutch rested his big hand on Spencer's shoulder, trying to offer comfort. Spencer loved him for that. "You've been quiet for a long time," Dutch commented.

"I'm fine," Spencer replied. He covered Dutch's hand with his remaining free hand. The other still held Justin's firmly in its grasp. Holding onto both their hands at the same time felt right. It felt natural. It also gave him the strength he needed to move on.

I think you're right, his father said. His voice sounded distant in his head, almost as if he were walking into a dark, deep tunnel. *It's time for us* both *to move on.*

Dad! he called out. His voice sounded more like a child than a grown man.

What is it, son?

Thanks.

His father voiced no reply. All Spencer heard were his father's footsteps echoing in the distance until the sound disappeared altogether.

THOUGH Spencer's voice seemed distant, which caught Dutch off guard, an unusual confidence emanated from him, and he had no idea why. Justin's condition looked dire. For Spencer to seem this self-assured made him wonder if Spencer were perhaps suppressing his feelings instead of dealing with them, instead of accepting how they might have contributed to Justin's current state.

"Are you sure?" he asked again.

"I am," Spencer repeated. "I think everything's going to be okay. I really do."

"I truly hope so," a voice from behind them said. "I *truly* hope so."

They turned around and saw Justin's mother, Elena, a woman he heard a lot about but someone he had never previously met, standing behind them. She clutched her black purse as if it was the only lifeline to sanity she had, as if it was the one thing keeping her from falling apart.

When they got here, she had been consulting with the doctors, too busy to talk to them. But now she stood before them. Her stony face betrayed no emotion. She was terrified, and she was angry.

"Elena," Spencer said as he moved to greet her. She held out her arm, stopping him from embracing her. She stared at Spencer and him suspiciously. The weight of her gaze told him she blamed them both for what happened to her son.

"I assume you're Dutch," she said, staring only at him. She moved past Spencer as if he weren't there, as if he no longer mattered in her world. The look of pain in his eyes told Dutch that Elena's actions hurt him deeply.

"Yes, ma'am," he replied. Although he was almost twice her size, Elena towered over him. Her body was rigid, ready to strike out and seriously damage anyone who might further threaten her son. "I'm sorry for what's happened to Justin. I'm sorry for everything," he said in complete misery.

"You're sorry?" She laughed. "My son is standing at death's doorway, and *you're* sorry?"

Dutch made no reply. He simply cowered before her, his posture reflecting his wretchedness and his complete subservience to her authority.

"My son left me *weeks* ago, and *neither* of you did *one* thing to find him, to bring him back to me." She glared at them both and looked as if she wanted to slap them. Very hard. "My son might have hurt you. He might have made mistakes, but he *loved* you both. *Very* much."

She shooed Dutch away from Justin's bedside, forcing him to stand side by side with Spencer as if they were criminals lined up to face charges she was about to read to a courtroom. "What did you do for *him* while he was gone?" She asked while throwing her purse to the floor like the proverbial gauntlet. "From the looks of you both, the answer is quite obvious. Not a damn thing!"

Beside him, Spencer winced. Dutch understood what that meant. Elena Jimenez never cursed, and by doing so now, she was about to unleash a mother's fury upon them.

"It seems to me the *only* thing you boys, not men, *boys*, have done is screw around with each other. Did you think this would somehow even the score? Did Justin mean that little to you *both*?"

They said nothing. All they could do was accept her anger because they both knew she was right.

"*Answer me!*" she screamed at them.

"I don't know what to say," Spencer replied. "We messed up. We should have done more."

"We do love your son, Mrs. Jimenez," Dutch finally said. "We love him a lot. And if we could take back these past few weeks, if we could do it all over again, we would do things differently."

Elena seemed unconvinced. Her gaze remained steady and dangerous.

"But none of that matters at this point. We're here *now*. The *both* of us. And we'll do whatever we can to make Justin better. To make him come back to us. To *you*."

Slowly, her eyes wavered. Tears she held back rose quickly, and unable to stop them, they fell with such force they almost knocked her off her feet. She was in deep misery, facing a fear most parents in the world never wanted to confront—the possibility of outliving her child.

Dutch rushed to her side and took her in his arms. At first, she resisted. She fought back. She beat his chest and yelled at him. "This is all your fault," she screamed. "You should be the one fighting for your life on that bed. Not my son," she bawled. "*Not my son!*"

Her naked sorrow ripped through his soul like a blade, not only because of the power of her anguish but because her words were true. He *should* be the one fighting for his life. He was the one who had brought all this pain into their world. If he had been strong enough, if he hadn't self-destructed, he *never* would have had his accident, his sister *never* would have called Justin, and Justin and Spencer would still be living their happy lives without him.

"I would take his place in a heartbeat," he admitted to her as he stroked her hair. Dutch wanted her to feel his sincerity through his words but also through his touch.

Although she resisted his comfort at first, trying with all her might to wriggle herself free from his arms, the fight suddenly left her body as she sank deeply into his chest. Her tears rolled out of her body, covering his shirt until it was soaked worse than if he had been caught in a cloudburst. "I would die for him," he told her.

"I would too," Spencer said, embracing Elena from behind. "I know you're angry with me, and you have every right to be. But my love for your son hasn't changed. It will never change. It took me a long time to realize that, but I realize it now. I'll make this right," Spencer told her. "If it's the last thing I do on this earth."

Her body still convulsed in insurmountable torment, refusing to accept what she heard as fact. But after a few minutes wedged between two men who professed their undying love for her son, her heaving body slowly quieted. Her sobs gave way to heavy exhalations until at last she was calm.

She looked up into their eyes. First at Dutch. Then at Spencer. She gazed deeply, searching their souls for the truth and determined to ferret out any dishonesty. When she found none, when she realized what they told her to be undeniably true, her tense body relaxed.

"You *do* love him," she said. "Both of you."

They nodded simultaneously.

"But there's something you're not admitting to me," she told them. "I can see it."

"What do you mean?" Spencer asked.

Dutch was confused as well. "What do you think we're hiding?"

She wiped her tear-stained face and stood directly between them. "You love my son," she said. "I believe that. But I can see you also love each *other*."

They stared at Elena in disbelief. Dutch couldn't believe how incredibly perceptive Justin's mother was. Justin had always told him that it was difficult to keep anything from her, but he found the accuracy of her insight not only uncanny but almost magical.

"Am I right?"

Spencer nodded.

"You're right," he told her.

At that moment, the beeping monitors that kept time to Justin's beating heart sounded in alarm. All three of them turned and watched as the pulse monitor, which previously displayed a dark green line rising and falling, suddenly dropped into a straight flat line.

JUSTIN drifted flat on his back amidst a dark black sea. The waves slapped against his body mercilessly, threatening to drown him and drag him down to the gloomy depths below. Every so often, one of the unforgiving waves washed over his face, forcing water down his nose and throat.

He expelled the vile liquid, which tasted like swill, by violently coughing, but each time another wave forced him to inhale more water, it became more difficult to recover.

His body grew increasingly weary from trying to stay afloat while at the same time keeping even more water from swamping over him. Simply trying to hold his head above water seemed increasingly impossible, for it appeared to weigh fifty pounds instead of the average of nine pounds.

Even his legs found it difficult to stay at the water line. Anchored with what felt like stones, they kept slipping beneath the water. Forcing them back up to maintain his buoyancy proved more problematic with each passing second.

He knew it was only a matter of time before the dark sea claimed his body.

The thought didn't fill him with the abject terror he expected. He was, after all, deathly afraid of water, and being stranded in the middle of the ocean was one of his most frequently recurring nightmares. Right now, he should be panicking, kicking and flailing at the water while searching for some foothold, some lifeline that would keep him afloat.

Instead, he felt only calm. A dead calm.

There was simply no reason to be afraid. Death was part of life, after all. It was the end every living thing ultimately faced, and he found he was more than ready to embrace it.

A reason to live no longer existed. He had seen the love in Spencer and Dutch's eyes. It was a love that was all their own and didn't include him. They had found what they had been searching for, what had been missing in their lives. They had found each other.

While he was angry at first, he realized now that he had no right to be. He had hurt them both a great deal. In his quest to understand his emotions for the both of them, he'd nearly destroyed the two men he claimed to have loved. That wasn't what love was supposed to do. It was supposed to be a nurturing force, something that created only joy not heartache.

Perhaps he was never meant to live his life with Spencer. Or Dutch. Maybe his entire purpose was to bring Spencer and Dutch together so that when he died he left them with someone to fill the void he had uncaringly created.

When he thought about it, he hoped that was his final gift to them both. He wanted to believe that his life, that everything he had done the past few years, had some meaning, some divine purpose that he at first failed to comprehend.

His purpose might never have been to keep true love for himself but to grant it to two men far more deserving of each other than he was of either of them.

When he thought about it in those terms, it made his inevitable end much easier to accept. It filled him with a sense of satisfaction that made his heart less heavy and his spirit soar.

The internal exuberance did nothing to stop the increasing weight of his body, however. His legs now dangled well below the surface. He listed at an awkward forty-five degree angle, ready to plummet downward into the waiting arms of death below.

He fought to right himself, not quite ready to disappear beneath the water, to quietly slip into the fathoms below. Flapping his arms back and forth like a wounded fish, he attempted to force his legs back to the surface, and at first they started to rise, slowly.

But no sooner did they ascend a few inches then another wave rolled over him, filling his lungs with water and weighing down his already exhausted limbs.

His lungs contracted uncontrollably, attempting to squeeze all liquid from its airy sacs up and out his throat. In this endeavor, they failed.

There was simply too much water to combat in his lungs and in the churning ocean around him. Wave after wave assaulted his already fatigued body. It no longer possessed the strength it needed to fight or to keep him afloat.

Instead of fighting a losing battle, Justin surrendered. He gazed up into the darkness that loomed above him as his body resumed its unstoppable journey beneath the watery surface.

Hanging over him in the dark sky a single pinprick of light blinked into existence. Its presence filled him with warmth that only came from love. He wanted to reach for it, but his arms were too heavy. Already, they dangled helplessly underwater with the majority of his body.

As the water rose above his waist and abdomen, the light above sparked into a coil of flame. It stretched across the sky, igniting another spark and then another until an entire constellation of stars somehow blazed to life overhead.

The water reached his chest and then his neck, but still all he could focus on was the swirling mass of fire and light. It bulged outward, trying to take on a shape as if it battled the very darkness that surrounded him, as if it refused to be snuffed out and would only stop once light once again held dominion over all.

An expansive fiery wing erupted into view. Then another wing split the sky with tremendous fury that sent shockwaves of flame raining down around him and the water, which had now risen to his chin.

In the center of the blazing wings, a familiar form took shape. It was a horse, a flying horse made of fire.

He knew of the constellations called the Phoenix and the one named Pegasus, but never before had he heard of an amalgamation of the two in the stars. This, however, was what the flaming creature seemed to be—a union of two constellations that somehow merged into a third, more beautiful creation never imagined before.

The newly born creature whinnied above him and then darted through the sky, headed straight for him. On its back sat two forms. He couldn't make out who they were, but they seemed familiar, as if he had known them his entire life.

Before the fiery flying horse could reach him, before he could identify the people who rode on the magical creature's back, his head slipped below the water's surface. He fell deeper into the dark, watery folds until the light of the blazing horse was suddenly snuffed out of view.

When its light was gone, only darkness remained.

CHAPTER 48

2011

SPENCER looked around at the hollowed-out remains of the house he and Justin had shared for almost ten years. Once filled with the treasures of their past—pictures of numerous trips around the world, furniture purchased for the apartment they once shared, and scores of other objects with their own stories—the house now stood completely empty. The memories they'd spent years collecting were now safely packed away in boxes and loaded into the moving van waiting outside.

Even though he knew it was time to move on, to close this chapter in his life and live the next one just waiting to be written, Spencer still found it difficult to say good-bye. This house and the life he'd lived here with Justin had made up some of the happiest times of his life.

On their first Christmas in the house, Justin had invited every single family member over for dinner, as well as all their friends. More than fifty people had crammed into the house to share the holiday with them. The house was filled beyond capacity with more than just people. It was filled with love.

They'd celebrated Spencer's tenure at St. Mary's University with a bottle of Dom Pérignon at the dining room table, which was accompanied by a meal prepared by Justin's inexperienced culinary skills. The food was awful, bone-dry chicken and rock-hard white rice, but the love and care that went into the meal meant more to Spencer than a superbly prepared gourmet supper. On that night, Justin beamed with pride regarding Spencer's new role as a full professor, happier and prouder of him than any person had ever been in his life. Not even his parents rejoiced his accomplishments with such relish.

A cherished holiday memory, special occasion, or romantic anniversary existed in almost every square inch of the house. It was impossible for him to simply walk away from it without a special commemorative ceremony.

Spencer crossed over to the sole box that remained in the house. Chris and Jill had already removed the rest of the boxes and were at this moment securing everything in the van for the move. In a few minutes, they would return, and it would be time to leave this house and drive to his new house to begin his new life.

From the box he withdrew a single champagne flute and a bottle of Dom Pérignon. He unfastened the wire that held the foil secure and then worked the cork out of the bottle with a slight pop. Expertly removed, none of the precious liquid exploded outward or fell to the floor. He poured the glass half full and turned to face the house.

"Here's to our house and here's to us, Justin," he said while taking a long sip of the champagne. "The two of us had a remarkable life here, and I'll always treasure every *single* moment and memory."

"Who're you talking to?" Chris asked while staring at him suspiciously. "You hearing voices again? Did your dad come back to haunt you?"

Spencer rolled his eyes. Over the past few months, since Justin's accident, he'd told his friends and loved ones about his internal conversations with his father. Although he understood that his father's voice was simply a figment of his imagination, his moral conscience rising to the surface to help guide him to resolutions for his conflicts, he hoped by discussing the internal working of his minds with those he trusted they would make him feel better, less crazy.

That wasn't what he had gotten. Instead, they'd told him he was crazy and needed to see a psychologist. His father's voice was now just another thing they teased him about.

"No, you dumbass," Spencer said. "I was saying good-bye to the house."

"Yeah, that's not crazy at all," Chris muttered while grabbing the last box.

Spencer responded by sticking out his tongue, and Chris laughed. "Pat called me from Dutch's house," Chris told him. "They're almost packed up there too. Hopefully, we can finish the move before dinner. I'm starving!" He headed out the door, but before leaving, he said, "Tell the house good-bye for me too. I'm gonna miss it here."

Spencer smiled at Chris as he walked out the door.

Spencer took one final look around, devouring every single detail of the house one last time. Tomorrow, its new owners, a young newlywed couple, would take possession and begin filling it with the treasures of their life together. It would become for them what the house had been for him and Justin.

It would become their haven from the rest of the world.

Spencer crossed the threshold for the last time and closed the door shut behind him. It was time for him to drive across town, enter his new home, and embrace the new life that waited for him there with open, outstretched arms.

DUTCH stood at the open front door to his house, peering inside one final time. All of his belongings now sat neatly stacked according to Spencer's packing system in the moving van, which idled in the driveway.

"Let's move!" Pat called from the driver's side window. "We've got lots to do, and my belly's hungering for some food!"

"Be right there!" Dutch yelled back at Pat, who smiled broadly from the van. Thanks to Pat and his wife Heather, Dutch's house was now completely empty. Everything he owned now waited to take up space in their new house, the one that would contain the memories he would cherish for the rest of his life.

Still, he found it difficult to leave this part of his life behind. Even though bad memories and some hard times haunted the halls of this residence, the good memories still lingered. Their light far outshone the bad.

In the living room on one of the darkest days of his life, he'd first met Justin on Cyber. Their friendship and ultimately their love had carried him through some of his life's hardest crises, such as the death of his mother. Without Justin, he doubted he would have survived. The strength Dutch had been able to draw from him allowed him not only to grieve but to move on.

Justin's encouraging words had helped him recover his mobility far sooner than he would have been capable of doing alone. When his body told him no, when it refused to cooperate, Justin told him yes. He had given him the affirmation he needed to stop feeling sorry for himself and pull himself up into a better, more positive state of mind.

"Dude, you okay?" Pat asked from his left side.

His new friend's sudden presence startled him. Dutch hadn't heard Pat exit the vehicle or walk over to him.

"I'm fine," he said.

"Are you sure?" Heather asked. She took up residence on his right, the two of them preparing to be the bookends of support he might need.

"I'm sure," he replied. They put their arms around him, and the friendship they freely offered made saying good-bye a bit easier to bear.

Ever since Justin's accident, when he'd finally met the friends Justin and Spencer spoke so often about, they'd opened their arms and their hearts to him without any reservation. They looked past the problems he'd helped instigate between their two friends and saw only a man in pain, a man who needed someone to be there for him.

Since then, that was exactly what they had all done. For each other.

He attended dinners with Pat and Heather. He watched football games with Chris and Jill. Teresa shared his passion for scary movies, and they had weekly dates of bad horror movies and popcorn. Tyler and Jerry enjoyed home renovations as much as he did, and they often worked on household projects together. They all went to the bars, both straight and gay, and enjoyed drinks and each other's companionship.

For the first time in far too long, he'd found friends with whom he truly belonged. The only part that truly saddened him was that it took Justin's accident for all of them to come together.

Still, today wasn't about sadness. Even though he was saying good-bye to an important part of his life, a new beginning wafted on the spring breeze. He inhaled deeply, allowing the breath of the new season into his soul, refreshing his spirit and revitalizing his heavy heart.

"Let's do this," he told Pat and Heather. "Let's get me home."

Dutch followed his friends to the moving van. He stopped for a second, taking one final glance at his old house, the place where it all began, and he smiled.

He was ready, and though he was still a little nervous, he couldn't wait to live the new life the universe helped create for him.

EVERYWHERE he looked, his loved ones busied themselves with getting the house prepared for the rest of the vans that were already en route. Tyler and Jerry brought in the last of the boxes from the first moving truck. Sam worked on unloading the study while Teresa took charge of the kitchen boxes.

"Justin!" Xavier called out when he entered the front door. He held Alex's hand tightly in his own, and his friend's face beamed more brightly than the sun.

"Thanks for coming to help," Justin said. He crossed over to give both Xavier and Alex a hug. Since his accident, when everyone had feared the worst, Xavier had been living with a new lease on life. He was no longer scared of commitment, and he no longer wanted to bed every piece of man flesh he ran across. Now, he was actually in a relationship with Spencer's friend Alex, whom he would forever call Puka Shell Boy.

Justin immediately set Xavier and Alex to a task, unpacking the dining room boxes while he worked on opening the boxes in the living room. He hoped to have as many of the boxes unpacked as possible prior to Spencer and Dutch's arrival.

His stomach fluttered with excitement at the future that stretched before the three of them, a future he never expected to have when he died that morning in the hospital. Once he fell into the darkness, he was ready to let go, to leave the world behind. The only thing he hoped was that Spencer and Dutch would find happiness together.

Instead, the fiery horse dove into the water after him and brought him back to the light. When he opened his eyes, he didn't see the doctor standing over him with the defibrillator paddles in his hand or the nurses who stood around him monitoring his newly restarted vital signs, the only faces he saw were Spencer and Dutch, standing off to the side and smiling at him without anger or resentment. Only love.

It was their love that brought him back to life, and it was the two of them he'd seen riding on the back of the horse. He owed his continued breaths on this planet to them, and he planned to live the rest of his life proving he deserved not only a second chance but the both of them.

After all, they'd remained by his side during his recovery. They helped him get stronger physically, mentally, spiritually, and emotionally. And together, they also worked through the tangled mess they'd made of their lives.

Spencer and Dutch revealed their love for him and each other, and he freely embraced his love for the two of them. After that, it was simply a matter of working out the intricacies of a relationship between three men.

It was a new concept for them and the world. After all, love was a joining of two hearts, two pieces of the same soul that locked together seamlessly. That was how the world functioned. Two people, two hearts, one relationship. That was the paradigm the rest of the world followed.

But they didn't fit that model. Their hearts and their relationship were bigger than what society had preconceived notions about. After all, it was the universe's magic, some unseen force, that brought them together. That bond pulled Justin and Spencer initially to each other, but it was that same power that brought Dutch into their lives, that somehow called both of them to Dutch, separately, just as strongly as it tugged upon him.

How else could they explain their immediate attractions to Dutch? What other possible explanation was there to describe how drawn Dutch was to both of them?

They weren't meant to be a couple. They were destined to be a trio.

So they sold the houses they owned individually and purchased a house together, where the three of them would live for the rest of their lives. The road ahead was scary. A relationship with three people was far from common but not unheard of.

They would have to deal with the strange looks from people who didn't understand *three* men in a relationship with each other. The world was still trying to handle *two* men living together.

Already, they faced dissenters. Naturally, Spencer's parents were among that group. They refused to accept Dutch in their lives, much less as a part of their relationship. Since they hadn't embraced him over the past ten years, Justin knew their chances of willingly recognizing their trio would be next to nil for the Harrison clan. Justin's mother even had some problems accepting the arrangement at first, but as usual, she went with the flow. As long as her son was happy and healthy, not much else mattered.

Some people at their jobs looked down their noses at them, but after a few weeks, none of them cared what *anyone* thought. The people that mattered the most to them, their friends and the family members who were accepting, embraced their new relationship.

More importantly than that, they had each other.

"Spencer and Dutch are here," his mother announced. She had been unpacking the master bedroom for the past hour. Now that the rest of the family was here, she was as eager to greet them just as he was.

"Thanks, Mom," he said. Before rushing off to greet the loves of his life, he stopped to give his mother a great big hug and an even bigger kiss. "You're the best!"

"Yes, I know," she agreed. "Now go get those men of yours in here. There's lots of work to be done."

Justin nodded and rushed out the front door.

Dutch climbed out of the passenger seat of the van parked in the front of their house while Spencer crossed the lawn from the van parked in the driveway. Justin walked down the sidewalk, and the three of them met in the middle.

"You're home," Justin said while reaching for both Spencer and Dutch. The three of them formed a circle and placed their arms around the shoulders of the other two. It was the way they hugged each other once they were all home.

"It's good to be home," Dutch said. "Especially to such sexy men as the two of you."

"Mr. Keller, are you attempting to seduce us?" Spencer asked, pretending to be outraged by such obvious flattery.

"Every day of my life," Dutch replied, first kissing Spencer and then him.

"I'm glad to hear it," Spencer replied.

"Me too," said Justin. The three of them said nothing for a few moments. They simply gazed into each other's eyes, happier than they had any right to be. Dutch combed his hands through Justin's and Spencer's hair. Spencer rubbed his hands up and down both of their backs, and Justin brought each of them closer to him, needing to feel both of their bodies against his.

"How was it closing up the houses?" Justin asked.

"It was hard," Dutch admitted. "So many good memories there."

"Yeah," Spencer said. "It was almost too much. I just couldn't say good-bye."

"That's why I didn't do it," Justin said. "The two of you are much stronger than I am. I think I would've broken down."

"You?" Spencer and Dutch said in unison.

"I'm capable of emotion," Justin said, pouting.

"Once every ten years, perhaps," Spencer added, to which Dutch laughed heartily.

"Is this what I have to look forward to?" Justin asked. "The two of you ganging up on me for the rest of my life?"

"Yes," Spencer replied.

"Absolutely," said Dutch.

They all laughed, and then they held onto each other tightly, never wanting to let the other two go for even a second.

"Okay, break it up," Chris commented as he passed them. "You've got a bedroom for that."

"Spencer!" Elena called from inside the house. "Someone put your boxes marked study in the living room!"

"It was Tyler," Jill accused from inside the house.

"Liar!" Tyler replied. "It was Pat."

"How the hell did I get dragged into this?" Pat asked. "I think it was Teresa."

"Oh no you didn't!" Teresa exclaimed.

The voices of their friends erupted into a faux fight. Justin, Spencer, and Dutch looked at each other and then at their new house, quickly filling up with the items of their new life and the sounds of friends who loved them as much as the three of them loved each other.

"Shall we?" Spencer asked.

Dutch nodded. "If we don't get in there quickly, they're gonna kill each other."

"Let's do it," Justin said. "Together."

The three of them strolled up the sidewalk to the house. When they walked inside and closed the door, they were officially home.

JACOB Z. FLORES lives a double life. During the day, he is a respected college English professor and mid-level administrator. At night and during his summer vacation, he loosens the tie and tosses aside the trendy sports coat to write man on man fiction, where the hard-ass assessor of freshman-level composition turns his attention to the firm posteriors and other rigid appendages of the characters in his fictional world.

Summers in Provincetown, Massachusetts, provide Jacob with inspiration for his fiction. The abundance of barely clothed manflesh and daily debauchery stimulates his personal muse. When he isn't stroking the keyboard, Jacob spends time with his husband, Bruce, their three children, and two dogs, who represent a bright blue blip in an otherwise predominantly red swath in south Texas.

You can follow Jacob's musings on his blog at http://jacobzflores.com or become a part of his social media network by visiting http://www.facebook.com/jacob.flores2 or http://twitter.com/#!/JacobZFlores.

Romance from DREAMSPINNER PRESS

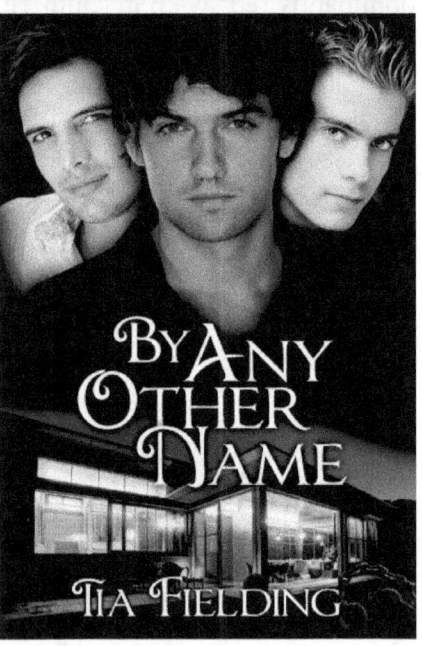

http://www.dreamspinnerpress.com

Romance from DREAMSPINNER PRESS

THE STRONGEST SHAPE

Tessa Cárdenas

http://www.dreamspinnerpress.com

www.ingramcontent.com/pod-product-compliance
Lightning Source LLC
Chambersburg PA
CBHW050036030726

47506CB00001B/300